The Great Orchid Heist

The Great Orchid Heist

Eleanor Vendrell

MLP

First published in 2025 by Mountain Leopard Press
An Imprint of HEADLINE PUBLISHING GROUP

2

Cataloguing in Publication Data is available from the British Library

ISBN 978 1 0354 2345 3 (Paperback)

Typeset in Sabon by CC Book Production

Printed and bound in Great Britain by Clays Ltd, Elcograf S.p.A.

Headline Publishing Group Limited
An Hachette UK Company
Carmelite House
50 Victoria Embankment
London EC4Y 0DZ

The authorised representative in the EEA is Hachette Ireland,
8 Castlecourt Centre, Dublin 15, D15 XTP3, Ireland
(email: info@hbgi.ie)

www.headline.co.uk
www.hachette.co.uk

For Marc – thank you for the idea

Chapter One

I lean against the bar, ignoring the din around me, and imagine – for probably the twelfth time today – winning the lottery. The familiar embrace of the fantasy is like slipping into a hot bath.

It would be an embarrassingly enormous win; one that makes headlines. *Local Woman Lifted from Mundanity. Ascends to heights of wealth so enormous that she'll definitely go a bit weird.*

There'd be a picture of me in my uniform at the cinema, looking vaguely unkempt and as though I'd just been smacked in the head by a solid brick of fifty-pound notes, which would essentially be what had happened.

'What will you do with the money?' a reporter would screech, waving one of those fluffy microphones.

'I'm just so shocked!' I'd say, unable to hear them over the roaring in my ears, probably crying or throwing up from sheer overwhelm. 'This is going to change my life!'

1

To be honest, I'd be happy with a fraction of that. A million. Half a million. Even a few hundred thousand. I could pay off our debts, move out of my dad's house. Breathe for the first time in years.

It's not that I don't want to work. It's that I'd like to not think about the exchange rate of my time for money every moment of the day.

Like now, for instance. I've been at the bar for at least three minutes, card in hand, and the bartender's been studiously looking in the other direction. I got served a lot more quickly back when I had long hair and wore skirts and stuff. Maybe I should have brought a male gaze disguise this evening. I'm clearly not this bartender's type any more, with my growing-out buzz cut, loose black T-shirt, no makeup.

That's OK. He's not mine either, given that he looks like a Disney prince from the days when all the Disney princes were identical. Remember Snow White's boyfriend? Of course you don't. He might as well be a piece of soft white bread dressed in primary colours.

A woman nudges past to lean against the bar on my right. Long blonde hair, cheekbones like a sculpture. A grim expression that does nothing to hide her glorious face. Well.

It's funny; looking at her, I'm distracted from my gloom. I feel as though we've met before. I don't recall her face, though, and I have a good memory for faces. Just a strange feeling of, Oh, there you are.

Maybe she's a celebrity or something. My friend once saw Paul Mescal in a pub and, assuming he was an acquaintance

2

he couldn't place, greeted him with an 'All right?' and a slap on the back before realising his mistake.

The bartender is there in a flash, but the woman jerks her head towards me, saying, 'She was first.'

To my own surprise, I say, 'After you.' This feels like a generous move on my part, given how much I'd like a beer, but also maybe it's not. I'm hoping it'll work to soften the set corners of her mouth. I'm willing to bet she'd be even prettier.

But the woman just scowls and orders a double G&T. The bartender, who's flung his tea towel over his shoulder in a notably casual way, looks disappointed as he reaches for the gin.

Fine. No smile for either of us, mate. I'm meant to be meeting my friend Chaz anyway, but I can't see him. I scan round the bar.

A single potted plant droops in its place next to the bottles of spirits. A smudge-covered mirror impassively reflects our faces back to us. My hair looks dark and extremely scruffy next to the blonde woman's glossy waves, as though we're at opposing ends on the spectrum of butch to femme. Our eyes meet for a moment in the reflection.

Then she looks away, tapping the bar with her card. Irritation emanates from her and I'm suddenly curious to know what she'll do next. She looks like she's gearing up for something as she watches the gin splashing into her glass, the bartender slotting the bottle back into place.

Then she blurts, 'You're over-watering that aspidistra.'

The bartender looks round. 'Pardon me?'

3

'The aspidistra?' She points at it. 'Or cast-iron plant.'

All three of us regard it. The leaves do look a bit yellowish.

The bartender shrugs. 'I thought that was fake.' He turns to select a slice of lemon.

The woman stares at him in disbelief. Maybe she's used to being listened to. Her mouth is slightly open, I see in the mirror, and her lips are full and painted a flattering reddish-brown that makes her pale skin luminous.

I turn to check the real person too before I say, in what I hope is a helpful tone, 'You've got a little,' I gesture at her mouth, 'tiny bit of lipstick on your teeth.'

She swipes at it furiously, then glares at me. 'Why are you staring at my teeth?'

Either I've forgotten how to interact with people or this is uncalled for. 'Um, I wasn't,' I say. 'I'm not a teeth guy.' I close my eyes briefly. 'Just trying to help you out.'

Don't people want to know when they have lipstick on their teeth? I would, if I ever wore lipstick any more.

She drags the back of her hand across her mouth once more, removing a layer of colour. 'Oh, who cares anyway?' she mutters.

Her glare is so intense and her chin so set in fury that I'm considering answering this obviously rhetorical question when someone tugs at my elbow.

'Evening, ladies.' My friend Chaz has popped up beside me, an impish expression on his face. 'Is my friend bothering you?' he asks the woman, pretend-earnestly, indicating at me. She looks momentarily startled.

'Chaz.' I yank my elbow away. 'No, I'm not bothering her,' I say, my sense of humour deserting me. 'Sorry,' I tell the woman, whose confusion is only growing. 'He always does this. Just a running joke. You're bothering *me* now,' I tell him.

'Don't worry, I'll take her away,' Chaz says reassuringly, still talking to the blonde. 'I've got our drinks already.'

'Oh my God.' I shake my head. 'OK, well, have a super fun night,' I say, raising a hand to the woman and, for some reason, doing a peace sign.

She doesn't respond as I breeze away as best I can. She just stares, and not in a complimentary way.

'Who was that?' Chaz asks as we sit at a small table where he's already set us up with drinks. I sling my leather jacket over the back of the chair.

'No idea,' I say, flopping down. 'Why must you always embarrass me as much as possible, is the real question.'

We could have had a nice, innocent moment of flirtation, if only she'd been at all interested and not almost certainly straight. Her glimmer of surprise when Chaz got there suggests she wasn't actually bothered by me, at least.

'I have to get my kicks somehow, Phil. And we've got big things to discuss. I had to get your attention. Here.' Chaz pushes a pint towards me. 'I have,' he leans forward importantly, 'a solution to all your problems.'

Chaz has never been one for small talk. It would freak people out at school: the way he would start talking as though you were in the middle of a conversation. It used to annoy me, but if I consciously remind myself to relax, it's fine. It actually takes the pressure off, having no idea what someone's on about.

'Great news,' I say. 'I'll drink to that.'

He frowns as I clink my glass against his. 'Seriously, Phil. All your problems.'

I sit back and rest a hand on my leg. The pub is chatty, the light from the wall sconces glowing against the vividly patterned carpet. It's surprisingly good vibes given it's a Wednesday night in this nowhere town. 'You don't know what my problems are, Chaz.'

We haven't seen each other for a few weeks, although we both still live in this town where we grew up. Chaz spends his time holed up in a dark room coding or attending virtual conferences with names I don't understand and using words like Artificial Intelligence, Analytics, Big Data. Meanwhile, I'm here.

'Don't I?' Chaz eyes me as he sips his Appletiser. 'How's your dad's financial situation these days?'

I frown. In a moment of tipsy weakness a few months ago, I told Chaz something I usually never talk about. I had hoped he'd forgotten.

'Are you going to be a dick this evening?' I ask, instead of answering him. 'Because if you are, I'll attend to my other social engagements.'

'Sure,' he scoffs. 'And no, but,' he leans closer, 'has anything changed?'

'Why are you even asking?' I snap. 'Obviously not. Don't you think I'd have quit my stupid shit jobs? Thrown a party?'

'OK, OK.' If it wasn't ridiculous, I'd say Chaz is . . . excited by this news. He's staring at me with a strange gleam in his eye. 'I have a proposition. I want you to meet someone.'

'Oh for—' I slap my hand down. 'No more blind dates! I've told you.' I couldn't be less in the mood. Before coming here, I popped home to check on Dad. He was on the couch holding an unopened envelope like he'd been there for a while. When he saw me, he shoved it down the couch arm as though that would stop me from noticing.

Hopefully I'm being paranoid, but I'll need to hunt it down later to check. If I leave the pub early, I'll be home before he's back from film club. It's a weekly community centre event we both look forward to: him because they show classic romcoms he complains about but secretly loves; me because it gives me an entire evening per week blissfully alone in the house, secure in the knowledge my dad is somewhere fine and normal and unproblematic.

'Not for a date!' Chaz's fingers, which have been tapping on the table as though he's typing, speed up. 'For a *heist*.'

Despite my mood and my urge to smack Chaz's fingers away from their tippety-tapping, which is making me want to scream, I snort. 'A heist.'

'Yes. I'm not joking,' he adds.

I stare at him for a minute. 'You're not, are you? Go on then.' I wave a hand. 'Tell me more.' This should at least pass the time. I stop myself from looking over my shoulder to see if the blonde woman is still there.

'His name is Miles,' Chaz starts, taking another sip of his drink, 'and he's got a plan.'

'Whose name is Miles?' I ask.

'This guy.'

'What guy?'

'The heist guy,' he says as though I'm the one being annoying.

'Chaz.' I rub the bridge of my nose. 'What are you on about?'

He looks pleased to have raised a reaction. 'This guy Miles has this idea and can't do it himself, but he saw me in the papers or something,' he shrugs disdainfully, 'and got in touch. Anyway, he'll be here any minute.'

'You invited—' I sit up. 'Chaz!'

'What?' The problem is Chaz genuinely believes this is a fine and normal thing to do. 'Actually, I think that's him now.'

I whip round. A young man has pushed open the door of the pub. He's wearing a greenish jacket with tartan on the turned-over cuffs and an open, friendly expression. His wavy chestnut hair is glossy, like a racehorse, and carefully styled. I don't watch the racing but my dad does.

Chaz waves. 'Miles!'

Miles nods in recognition, clocks me, smiles inscrutably, then makes the universal I'll-just-grab-a-drink gesture.

I grip Chaz's wrist as Miles goes to the bar. 'Why have you done this?'

'Because,' he frowns, 'I thought you'd be interested. Miles's plan is a three-person job. He asked if I knew anyone who could help and needs the money. So I thought of you.'

'Wow, thanks,' I say. Just because I've known Chaz for

years doesn't make it any less shitty to hear that. 'D'you think we're in a knock-off *Ocean's* film? Come on.'

'But you do, don't you? And you'd be good at it. We thought you should meet, so he can explain.' His tone is so reasonable it suddenly makes me furious.

'Listen, you're being scammed,' I say, taking a gulp of beer. I just want to get home, even if home is . . . what it's like. 'Miles is a scam artist. I can tell you that for free. And I'm not interested in being scammed too. I have enough to worry about.'

'Are you leaving?' Chaz exclaims as I scoop up my jacket.

'It's been a long day.' I take another slurp of beer, despite the bubbles from the last one still fizzing uncomfortably as they go down.

'I'm only trying to help.' He looks confused more than anything. A pang of guilt sprouts in my chest. Chaz can't help that he spends more time around computers than people. And I haven't seen any of my friends for weeks. And I guess I am a tiny bit interested in what this so-called Miles has to say about a heist.

A *heist*.

'Fine,' I relent. 'But no signing me up to anything.'

Chaz holds his hands up in surrender as Miles strolls over.

'You must be Phil,' Miles says as he folds his long frame gracefully into the chair.

'Yep.' I cross my arms.

'I'm Miles. Chaz told me about you.' His voice is smooth honey with cut-glass vowels.

'All good stuff, no doubt,' I say, the requisite response to this statement.

He looks me up and down, taking in my black T-shirt and tattooed arms.

'Oh yes,' he purrs. His expression is pleasant, polite.

'So,' I twist my pint on its coaster. 'Shall we talk about why we're here?'

'Absolutely.' He smiles. 'Thank you for agreeing to meet me.'

It seems useless to mention that this wasn't in my control, so I hold my tongue as he asks, 'You know Felborough, right?'

'Er,' I say. I can't tell if he's joking or this is an attempt to warm me up with the most tepid intro ever. Do I *know* the biggest and most famous botanic garden in the UK, if not the world, that's ten minutes down the road from here? Why yes, Miles.

'I've sure heard of it.' I shoot a glance at Chaz to ask, Is this guy for real?

Unfortunately, Chaz, who often misses my telepathic communications, just nods placidly and says, 'Great start.'

'We went on school trips there,' I point out. 'And you can look around this pub right now and point out at least three people who came to our town specifically to visit Felborough.'

Even here, in this clearly local pub stubbornly ignoring the gentrification that's already happened to the bars and restaurants closest to Felborough, it's obvious. The couple over there in the corner, for example, the Americans I can hear from here, have definitely visited the gardens today. Even if they didn't have a branded bag of gift shop loot with an excessively tall plant poking out the top, you'd know.

There's no other reason tourists come here. They're even easier to spot when Felborough holds events. Exhibitions, Christmas-lights walks; that kind of stuff. There was a thing a few years ago where they had a massive flower – Titan-something – and people started pouring into our town to see it in the flesh (so to speak). There were obvious academic botanical types, carrying tote bags printed with their research institutes, and common or garden gardeners, with dirt under the fingernails and weathered complexions. The rest were general tourists, here for a day out to visit a big old flower and maybe buy a difficult-to-transport plant of their own to remember the experience.

Miles nods once, then reaches into his jacket pocket. Before I can suppress a wild thought that he's reaching for a gun or a custard pie, and then the follow-up realisation of how little I'm reacting to either possibility, he pulls out a leaflet with Felborough's distinctive green and white logo and places it on the table.

Hmm. Felborough don't normally advertise much; they don't need to. So this must be a big event. Chaz and I lean in.

It's glossy, full colour. It proclaims in bold, curly letters, **Presenting the Splendid Paradise Orchid for the First Time.**

Below, in even curlier font, it reads, **Grand Reopening of Felborough Glasshouses.**

Other than the date – 1 June, just over a month away – and address, the flyer is taken up with a watercolour picture: an intricate building moulded from hundreds of panes that I recognise immediately as the Felborough glasshouses. In this image, they're open at the front to reveal a huge deep-blue flower. I raise an eyebrow. Either this rare orchid is the size of a car or the designer was given (or took) a lot of artistic licence.

Also, there's something very funny to me about a flower that literally has the word 'splendid' in the name. It's confident, it's assertive. It promises a lot.

'Um,' I say, when no one's said anything for almost a minute. 'Just how splendid *is* this orchid?'

'Very,' Miles murmurs. 'A magnificent specimen.' Then he looks up, into my eyes. His are dark blue, like the orchid petals. 'Chaz says you might be interested in helping me steal it.'

The lights in the pub flicker and his face blinks into shadow. Absolutely ridiculous timing.

'I never said that,' I counter, squinting as the lights steady again. 'Why do you want to steal a flower anyway?'

Miles holds my gaze. Then he smiles slightly and, instead of answering, asks, 'What do you know about Felborough, Phil?'

'Enough.' I say. Other than the obvious, I know it's a huge, fancy house that looks like a castle but which is now a science institute; it has gardens and glasshouses and a lake and probably thousands of botanical specimens. On a school trip, my class rampaged around some lawns and we were bundled into the coach early because someone tried to vandalise this weird fountain and we 'weren't being a credit to the school'. 'It's old, isn't it? Historical and stuff.'

Miles nods. 'The house and gardens have been a phenomenon since the time of Henry VIII.'

I've not visited for years. But it's coming back to me. Memories swim to the surface of an avenue of towering trees and bright flowers.

'The gardens have a huge collection,' Miles continues, 'but the rarest plants are kept in the glasshouses.' A strange expression flits across his face. It's gone before I can parse it. 'That's where the Splendid Paradise Orchid is.'

I look back down at the picture. Miles's air reminds me of someone standing in front of a crowd and declaiming the word of the Lord. It's unsettling, in a sexy way. His annoying posh voice is smooth like a secret and I want him to tell me things I already know in a manner I wouldn't even find annoying until reflecting on it later.

I drag my gaze up to find his eyes boring into mine, his stare so heavy my back prickles with warmth.

'I want this orchid, Phil,' he says, his voice low, treacly. 'And I think you can help me get it.'

The moment hangs in the air. No one moves; even Chaz doesn't fidget. Then Miles sits back, reaching for his pint. I release a breath and take a long drag of mine too, finishing it off. This is all a lot.

'Right, well.' I push my chair out. 'This has been interesting. But I should go. No, don't get up,' I add, as Miles half-rises.

I think he's about to protest but instead, after a pause, he holds out his hand. 'Meet me tomorrow?'

I focus on it. He's wearing a signet ring with a seal that

looks like a lion holding a snake in its mouth. All of this is a red flag for me personally, but when I look into his face, it's open, trustworthy.

'Where?' I ask, to my own surprise. I meant to say 'Why?'

'I'll text you the address.'

'You haven't got my number.'

'I'll get it from Chaz.' He tilts an eyebrow, asking my permission.

'Fine,' I give in. It would be stupid to meet him, obviously. But I've not come across anyone like Miles in a long time. At least he's interesting. Maybe he'd actually be the answer to all my problems.

Chapter Two

I tut at the very idea all the way home. I just allowed a posh, shiny man to *flirt* with me. I don't like posh, shiny men. I remember that, now I'm away from him. Miles can't just rock up and ask me to participate in a heist, at Felborough of all places. It must be the most highly guarded location for a hundred miles.

I don't need him. I'm going to win the lottery; that's my plan. Not a great plan, maybe, especially as I never buy lottery tickets. After what's happened to my dad, I'll never touch anything even resembling gambling. But it's fine; I have other options. Loads, in fact.

'Dad?' I call out of habit as I let myself in, giving the door the little kick it needs to encourage it to open.

To my surprise, my dad hurries out of the living room. 'Hi, love,' he says, too brightly, brushing off the ratty brown jumper he wears most days. 'I was just thinking of heading out.'

'Why aren't you at film club?' I ask, suspicions immediately firing at level one hundred. He shouldn't be here! They were watching *You've Got Mail*! That's got a run time of almost two hours, I checked. I should have another half-hour at least.

My dad is angling his body in the living-room doorway, trying to shield something from my view. But I'm quite tall, five-eight, and he's getting shorter every year, so it's not hard to peer over his shoulder to see ... something smouldering in the fireplace.

'What's that?' I demand.

'What?' he asks, guarded.

I point. 'Does the fireplace even work? I thought the chimney was blocked off.'

'Nothing,' he says, resting his hands together. The sight makes my own fingers clench in response. He's getting itchy fingers.

I take hold of him by the shoulder. 'Dad, are you OK?'

I'm desperate to rush to the fireplace, shake an answer out of him, force him to tell me what was on that paper, if he's burning old betting slips or bills or, or ... whatever it was he doesn't want me to know about. Why didn't he go to the film? What's happened?

But experience has hammered home that it doesn't work like that. I take a deep breath, staring at him as I do, squeezing his shoulder gently. Sometimes it works to make him take a deep breath too, as long as he doesn't realise he's doing it.

'Why don't I make us a tea?' I say. 'And I'll have some toast. Have you eaten?'

He looks past me, like a drowning man offered a lifeline made of gossamer. We stand there in a deadlock for a moment. I clench my jaw to prevent the shouting inside my head from spilling out: Don't go. Talk to me.

Then he nods. 'OK. I'll have a tea.'

I pat his shoulder. 'Great.'

In the kitchen, I take the fidget toy from the bowl on the shelf and pop it in the middle of the table by Dad's usual seat, as though it's been there all day. He uses it like a stress ball when I remind him so subtly that he thinks it's his idea.

He sits, absently picking it up. He starts to fiddle with it. I breathe the kind of sigh I imagine a bomb-disposal expert would give after a successful mission.

I make us tea and toast: his with marmalade, mine with Marmite. Back in the living room, Dad clicks the TV on. Moments later, women in frilly period dresses promenade across a field as he settles onto the couch, fidget toy spinning away in one hand. Could be *Downton* or an Austen film.

Dad got into watching this stuff after Mum left. Place a bet, have a beer, watch a period drama. I don't think anyone would have predicted it. But it does maintain the illusion that he's having a wholesome time, despite all evidence to the contrary.

And I admit it's soothing at times like this. The tension slowly notches down over the next hour or so as we both start to breathe normally again. At last, as the credits roll, he stretches and says, 'I'll be off to bed. Night, love.'

No mention of the weirdness or break in routine. But at

least he left his fidget toy down here, which means he's relaxed enough not to need it.

As soon as his bedroom door clicks shut, I rush to investigate the fireplace. All that's left in the grate is ash and a few scraps of paper that disintegrate when I try to sift through them.

I can just make out the word 'default' on one. 'Payment', clear in black and white, on another. I drop to a seat on the floor, heart thumping.

I sort the recycling every week. We don't talk about it but Dad knows I go through his letters. I need to know what's going on; one of us needs to have a handle on things. He lets me do it, usually.

Has he lost more money? Is he gambling again? The familiar spiral takes off, swirling through me. Oh God. Not after all my efforts, not when I've barely got a grip on our situation as it is. What is he hiding?

If he's going to these lengths to destroy the letter, it must be serious.

Panic thunders through my chest. This can't be happening, not when it finally seemed like things were getting better. I haven't had to intervene like that for months. He hasn't had a proper lapse in over a year. Something must've happened.

I go up to bed and lie there in the dark, fully dressed. I don't know how much longer we can live like this. Images flit past my closed eyelids: my dad's sad brown jumper, the words 'default' and 'payment'. A deep blue orchid, as big as a car. Chaz's innocent face, saying, 'You need the money.'

I grit my teeth and pull the pillow over my head. Then I sit up again. This is not what I do. I need more information. So, one step at a time.

Half an hour later, I drop my phone onto the duvet and rub my eyes. I don't know what Miles's game is and I definitely don't trust him – and yet. Several tabs are open on my phone and my head is spinning.

The Felborough website looks up at me from where my phone landed. The site's tasteful dark green and white scheme, all the nice pictures of plants, the way the awards are listed at the bottom of every page, are mocking me.

About us

Felborough Botanic Gardens, sometimes called the jewel of the European botanical scene, is a UNESCO World Heritage Site and centre for research excellence. Our mission, as an organisation with charitable status, is to sustain the biodiversity of our planet and undertake crucial work on conservation.

We house a vast, rich variety of plant life, with more than 30,000 specimens in our living collection and over a million preserved specimens.

Felborough itself encompasses what was once the estate belonging to the Mountjoy family. It comprises Felborough Hall, famously once occupied by Anne Boleyn for a brief period in 1530, the fishing lake, hundreds of acres of parkland and, of course, the glasshouses.

The glasshouses themselves are masterpieces of engineering, built in the late 1800s . . .

I tap away when I receive a message from Chaz. He's sent a LinkedIn profile in response to my earlier question of, Who the hell *is* this guy? A photo of Miles appears, wearing a dark suit and a smirk, when I click on it. *Miles DeLancy. Business Intelligence and Proactive Designs*, whatever that means.

He graduated from Oxford five years ago, almost exactly when I would have graduated if I'd stuck it out, rather than dropping out of university shortly before finishing my first year. Uni wasn't for me. That's what I tell people who ask. Not that many do, these days.

I scroll down Miles's profile. He did rowing and studied PPE. Google tells me this doesn't refer to personal protective equipment but is, in fact, Politics, Philosophy and Economics: the degree course that nearly every one of our 'old boy' prime ministers has done. So that doesn't bode well.

Is that meant to convince me? I text Chaz. **He still seems like a scammer, just a posh one.**

Clicking away from LinkedIn – worst site in the world – I return to the Felborough website and find the link to another page, which I keep reading and rereading.

20

The Great Orchid Heist

Upcoming Event:
Splendid Paradise Orchid Flowering

A new species of orchid was recently discovered by Richard Hook in the conflict-afflicted Darien Gap which spans the border between Colombia and Panama. This swathe of rainforest is one of the most dangerous in the world. It is roadless, wild and carries enormous risk for those who attempt to cross.

Its many natural dangers include snakes, poison dart frogs and jaguars, but far more deadly are the area's numerous drug traffickers, paramilitary forces and guerrilla fighters. Migrants must brave this deadly journey through swamps and mountains in the attempt to reach Central America; tourists are warned to stay away.

Our international reputation at Felborough for plant conservation and our focus on flowers allows us to make a strong case for the benefit of sharing specimens internationally. The Colombian and Panamanian governments have generously given their permission to bring back a single specimen: the *Calanthe Caerulissimus Hookiae* or the Splendid Paradise Orchid.

It will be nurtured and studied here at Felborough: the first time this magnificent orchid, whose properties are yet unknown, is grown in captivity.

21

I see why they call it the Splendid Paradise Orchid. Calanthe carry-whatnot doesn't exactly roll off the tongue.

Something about the story sends a tingle down my spine. I'm not sure if I'm nervous or excited or if the text just paints an effectively dramatic picture. They obviously have a good marketing team.

A message from Chaz in response to mine. **Babe, white collar crime doesn't count.**

YES IT DOES, I type back. Then I make a mental note to look up prison time for orchid offences.

My phone rings. 'Please, Phil,' Chaz whines when I answer. 'Everything's so boring. This town is desperate, but this is finally something interesting for once. And it won't be possible or, crucially, *fun* without you. And we never hang out any more.'

I rub my forehead. 'Why can't you just entertain yourself with your usual genre of criminal activity? Go and hack something or break into a building.'

'I've done everything already. Go on, just meet us tomorrow. You can always back out later, once you have all the lovely facts.' He's mocking me but also himself; Chaz loves facts as much as I do. 'Plus, you love historical shit. And you'll get to see inside Felborough Hall. They're renovating it, did you know? Once-in-a-lifetime stuff, mate.'

I sigh. Although not technically relevant, that's harder to argue with.

'And Miles likes you already,' Chaz presses his advantage. 'He's willing to split the proceeds. One hundred grand each.'

I roll my eyes to hide the lurch in my stomach at these words. 'Goodbye, Chaz.'

But after we've hung up, the number keeps flashing in my mind. One hundred thousand pounds.

Think what I could do with that money. It kind of *would* solve all my problems, just like Chaz said. All the problems I know about, anyway, and maybe the new ones too. It's almost exactly the amount Dad owed, last time I checked.

Well. By 'checked', I mean I forced him to talk about it after his last lapse when I realised if we didn't, I might actually explode. We both hated the conversation so much we could hardly look at each other for a week; him because he was humiliated and me because ... well. Because I was both furious and pitying. It was a heady mix of rage at someone who was meant to be a parent refusing their role and gambling away all our savings and pure tragic pity at the grip of this addiction. No wonder we couldn't face each other.

Recently, he seemed kind of OK. It's not easy with him not being able to work since his health stuff, but he's been mostly keeping to the careful routine we set up and he's seemed fairly calm. I thought I knew where he was at these days. But after this evening maybe I don't at all.

One hundred grand, though.

It's stupid and it will almost definitely end with all of us in jail. But what if I gave it a go? One big push to give Dad and me a fresh start.

Dad's life could be saved and mine could begin.

Chapter Three

So that's how I find myself the next evening, after a day that's passed predictably slowly at a shit temp job I've somehow been doing for three years to fill the gaps between cinema shifts, driving to meet Miles and Chaz.

Stuck in traffic, I can't think about the ridiculousness of what I'm doing, so I pass the time fretting about my dad. If I force myself to be honest, something I hate to do, he's been odd for a while. Then again, it's hard to know what 'normal' looks like.

My mum's parents warned her against marrying a 'no-hoper' like my dad. He owned a little shop when they met, selling fishing tackle and shotguns for clay-pigeon shooting. Mum didn't like the guns and live bait in wriggly boxes, and trade was drying up anyway, so he sold up, started working as a handyman for a firm.

But he got injured on the job when I was a teenager; blamed his own clumsiness, although I've never seen him clumsy.

Signed off work on long-term sick leave, he was just ... stuck. Fortunately, 'people like him' don't 'get depressed'. They simply 'get on with it'. So that's lucky. Around that time, he took up gambling, which looks so shiny and carefree in the adverts, and Mum started to drift away. And so began the first spiral.

We've had cycles of up and down ever since. He's tried working again on and off, but too much exertion just results in another health crash. A setback a few years ago caused another swoop into the addiction abyss, but we clawed our way out. I really dared to hope things would continue.

But now I admit it: he's been different recently. Normally mild-mannered to a fault, Dad snapped at me the other day when I asked what he wanted for dinner. He barely reacted when the new *Bridgerton* season came out, even though he loved the last one. We've not had a charity shop antiques trip for ages. Since we sold the last chair he restored for less than we hoped, he's had the same upcycling project on the go for over a month, even though he usually works on them obsessively until they're finished.

At least he has his weekly routine to ground him: coffee morning at the community centre on Tuesdays, film club on Wednesdays, meet-ups with his weird friend Gerald for a stroll on Thursdays. Gerald always sends me a thumb-like selfie of the two of them by some anonymous patch of greenery, taken from below to showcase their chins. I always reply something excessively cheery: **Looking good, you two!** or **Good day for it!**

Although now I think of it, Gerald didn't send me anything last week. The realisation makes my heart stutter, then race. This sounds like nothing, I know. But routine is important for my dad. Routine makes me trust that he's doing OK. That he's not lying. That he's fine.

I've been too busy, or too cowardly, to question it. But what if I've dropped the ball and it's already too late?

I pick up Chaz and drive until Maps takes me straight past the turn for Felborough and on up the hill to, apparently, the middle of nowhere; nothing in sight but hedges and fields. I have no idea why Miles asked us to meet here. I pull over at a passing place anyway, wheels spinning in the mud, and park.

'Hi there.' Miles, wearing a loose linen shirt and sunglasses, leans against his car, hands in his pockets as he watches us climb out. All his clothes look so chill and unintentional they must have been outrageously expensive. 'Thanks for coming.'

We look at each other for a moment, ignoring the sounds of Chaz slipping briefly into the hedge as he clambers around the car bonnet. Like yesterday, Miles reminds me irresistibly of a racehorse: skittish and glossy.

After enough of a pause that I tug at my jacket just for something to do, Chaz brushes off his hands in Miles's direction and announces, 'Anyway, hi, we're all here.'

Miles gives a slight start and says, 'Right. Shall we?'

He leads us through a gap in the hedge signposted as a public walkway. We stride uphill along a path that edges a muddy field, some crop or other growing in rows. It's cloudy and humid. The one benefit of my office job is the lack of dress code, a pleasant change from my dreadful cinema regulation polo shirt. But I'm quickly too warm in my jacket and belted black trousers as we walk, like a goth gentleman pirate who forgot to check the weather.

Miles seems content with silence, or he's playing mind games to freak us out. Chaz seems relaxed too, if it weren't for the mud and general nature. This is the closest to hiking he'll have done in . . . ever. We follow the field around, the path now sloping upwards more steeply. I sling my jacket over my shoulder. Miles shows no sign of effort, apart from a slight dampening at his forehead, visible when he turns.

'Almost there,' he says.

I raise my eyebrows and concentrate on not tripping over the clods of mud a tractor has carefully laid out directly where I'm trying to walk. We crest the hill and stop, looking out over the view.

Below, nestled in a valley, is Felborough. The huge building is made up of three sections of warm yellow stone, the two wings sweeping away in a horseshoe shape. It's pocked with hundreds of windows and balconies, topped with crenelations and towers like the best sandcastle ever.

Around it, the gardens stretch for miles: a pool of vivid green lawn with a circular fountain big enough to be visible from here, a sprawling walled garden, patches of trees and bushes and flowerbeds. At the back, partly hidden by the surrounding forest, are the glasshouses. A glimmer of smooth glass is visible through the trees, and a sense of bulk.

Miles is watching for my reaction. 'What do you make of it?'

It's impressive, honestly. It's as big as I remember, unusual for things that you see as a child and return to as an adult. Despite its enormity and the scaffolding masking a section of its façade, the Hall manages to give the effect of symmetry and grace. It's the kind of stunning stately home where a man-with-a-good-fortune-in-want-of-a-wife would live if, as I learnt yesterday from the website, it hadn't been turned into laboratories and offices in the fifties after the family who owned it finally sold up and moved out.

I school my face into neutrality. 'Not a bad view.'

Chaz shrugs, bent over with both hands braced on his knees as he catches his breath. 'I'd take it.'

Miles nods, smiling slightly. 'Good, isn't it? Even with the scaffolding. It's been closed to the public for renovations for a few weeks and to accommodate the settling of the orchid. But they're going ahead with the grand reopening next month.'

'So what's the plan?' I ask as we wander on.

'I have this contact: a collector. Kind of a tough guy, but he's set his heart on the orchid. He's willing to pay a significant sum for it.'

I raise my eyebrows. It's amazing what rich people will spend their money on. 'What makes this orchid so special?'

'Just that it's a brand-new species,' Miles says, his voice casual, 'never grown in captivity. Quite famous though. Darwin mentioned it in his diaries, although he never found one. And—'

'Sorry, *Darwin*?' I interrupt. Chaz, who's red-faced and out of breath from the climb, finds the energy to give me a sardonic look. 'What? He's a famous guy! A history guy.'

'Can't believe this is the moment that piques your interest, you awful nerd,' Chaz wheezes.

'It flowers every ten years, they think,' Miles continues, as though Chaz hasn't spoken. 'If they manage to time their reopening to coincide with it blooming, it'll be a real coup for Felborough. And, of course,' he goes on, his tone just as light, 'it would be a huge embarrassment if something were to happen to it. They'll have people coming from all over for the event.'

The Hall looks placidly back at us in the distance.

'What if, in the very moment of the unveiling, the curtain was drawn back to reveal . . .' Miles lifts a hand to sketch in the air. 'Nothing. A blank space where the flower was.'

For once, I'm lost for words. Miles sounds . . . I suppose it technically makes sense.

'So,' I say, 'where do we come into this?'

'I knew I wouldn't be able to do it alone,' Miles says. 'And, believe it or not, there isn't huge scope for renowned organised heist teams in this town. So when I found an article about Chaz and his . . . skills, I got in touch.'

'Ah,' I nod. A while ago, Chaz got caught in a stupid hacking stunt. Like a hackathon but less legal. None of us knew until he was hauled into the police station early one morning, still wearing his PJs. He always wears a matching set, like an old man or an Edwardian child.

29

'Why didn't you hide your tracks?' I asked when I phoned to tell him what a stupid idiot he was. 'Isn't that, like, hacking 101?'

'My sweet Phil,' he'd crooned, back home, his keyboard clicking in the background as he did something else devious, probably. 'Then how would they know it was me?'

I later learnt he'd hacked the police database to demonstrate how easy it was and changed all the officers' names to *his own*. They were so embarrassed they let him off with a job offer to fix their shitty security. Chaz refused but photos of him strolling out of the police station in his PJs were published in the local paper and online, with a short article using the phrases 'wunderkind' and 'tech prodigy'. Chaz was irritated at being called a wunderkind, aged twenty-six. But his baby face has always been misleading.

We've reached the end of the field. Miles offers me a hand over the stile, which I decline.

'I've checked their security system and any fool could hack it,' he says as I hop over. 'So that'll be easy for Chaz. But the other information doesn't exist online. Where the orchid is stored, how to keep it alive for the sale. So we need another team member. Someone to do some recon. And that's where you'll come in.'

I bite my lip. 'Why me?'

'We need you, Phil,' Chaz says instantly. 'You're good at talking. You can get people to do stuff for you.'

'Being called manipulative isn't the compliment you think,' I say.

'Listen.' Miles rests a hand on the fence, exchanging a glance with Chaz. Clearly, it's his turn to tag in. They probably planned this. 'Felborough isn't just any old botanic garden. It's the precious gem of the UK botanical scene, or whatever they love to call it. Why else do you think this orchid's there? Nowhere else in the country, probably the world, is better equipped to take care of it.'

'Sure,' I agree. This isn't doing anything to help his point but is, at least, definitely true. A lovely, certain fact.

'And that means it's hard to get into, it's well-protected and *people love it*. Chaz has the brains, I've got the connections, but we need someone to charm their way in, get on their good side, make them trust you. Make them like you. There's no one better for the job.' He smiles. Miles's jawline is as strong as his conviction. His fingers wrapping round the fence post are elegant, the fingertips disarmingly blunt-edged.

I clear my throat and look away. 'I mean, thanks for the compliment. But you don't even know me.'

'But I do.' Chaz has tagged in again. 'Phil! We've done this before. You can talk your way out of anything. Remember Choco-dealers?'

I'm unable to prevent a sigh of laughter. 'Seriously? Choco-dealers?'

He's staring at me intently. I shake my head, grinning. This is the stupidest angle they could have chosen. Chaz is referring to a brief but very special period when healthy eating became something schoolkids did in the UK. Thanks, Jamie Oliver.

I was new to the school; we'd moved after my dad's shop

closed. In the playground, trying to figure out which group to join, I was in a perfect position to witness a blonde girl I'd already identified as Queen Bee or Queen-Bee-Adjacent, screech, 'Eww, gross,' and slap away the hand Chaz was holding out to her. 'Why is it sticky?'

'It's wrapped,' I heard Chaz point out calmly. 'Even if it was sticky, it wouldn't be on the chocolate, would it?'

'You're such a weirdo.'

He shrugged. I watched in amazement at his total lack of discouragement as he turned to another girl and asked, 'How about you, Denise? Can I interest you in a Bounty for a quid?' Screams of disgust followed him across the playground as he ambled over to me. 'Bounty for a quid?'

I pointed out that this was a rip-off, given that, before all the chocolate and sweets had been replaced with apples and cereal bars, the vending machine used to sell them for 60p.

His eyes crinkled. 'They don't any more, do they?'

The open-hearted audacity of it. I couldn't help laughing and he laughed as well, sudden and surprising. Looking into his eyes, a deep, sparkling brown, was like falling into a cha- otic abyss – my first glimpse into Chaz's soul. Clearly a loner, but in no way downtrodden, he gave the strong impression of being very difficult to bully.

I befriended most of our year in the end, but I kept coming back to Chaz. He was then, as now, just a weird little guy. And I was desperate for fun and silliness, an escape from my sad, quiet household where my parents didn't speak to each other and if I wanted jokes I had to make them myself. With an amoral chaos demon like Chaz around, there was never a shortage.

Choco-dealers was our first (and last) business venture. By the end of its career, Chaz was buying multipack chocolate bars with his mum on her weekly shop and bringing them to school tucked into his inner blazer pockets. He'd dramatically fling open his jacket to reveal the loot and I'd approach our customers to do the talking.

'It was so good! You were such a strong business partner,' Chaz says now, perched on top of the stile. 'Choco-dealers would have been nothing without you. Remember when Mrs Hopkins found us selling during English and instead of giving us detention you got her to buy three Twixes?'

I shift my weight to the other leg and sigh. It was all so long ago. 'She was obviously having a bad day. Didn't I give her one for free?'

'Oh yeah. Not that strong a business partner, actually.'

'The point is,' Miles says, presumably keen to head off any more nostalgia trips, 'we need *you*, Phil, because you'd be good at this. And I hear your research skills aren't bad either. That's important too. We need someone who's observant and interested.'

'I bet as soon as you got home last night you started Googling Felborough and making notes,' Chaz chimes in. 'Didn't you?'

'Shut up,' I say, without malice. I haven't made any notes. Just a couple of lines on my phone to remind myself of key points. There's a lot more to do. Or there would be, if I was going ahead with this.

'And,' Miles clears his throat, 'Chaz says he won't do it without you.'

I laugh. There it is.

'Here's the plan,' Miles says, 'so you have the facts. Felborough are bringing on volunteers to get everything ready for the grand reopening. You'll be one of them. You'll find out about the orchid, the security, the care: everything we need to know in order to steal it.'

Chaz jumps off the stile as I digest this. Felborough has several hundred employees, according to its website – gardeners, scientists, volunteers. So at least blending in wouldn't be too hard. But this *volunteering* sounds an awful lot like working without being paid. Which I can't afford to do. Then again, if the outcome is a huge payout it might be worth it. Could Dad and I scrape through, just for a few weeks? His benefits barely cover anything, but my temping is flexible and I could let the cinema know a change in my availability.

I can't believe I'm seriously considering this.

Ahead, a little terrier comes nosing round the corner. It's dark blonde and hairy with a luxurious moustache and eyebrows, busily snuffling through the undergrowth. The sight makes me smile, a welcome distraction from this stressful heist talk.

Miles curls his lip as the dog wanders into the middle of the path. Miles tries to go round and the dog moves right too; Miles goes left and so does the dog. Chaz hiccoughs with laughter.

'Shoo!' Miles makes a jabbing motion at the dog, who braces its stocky legs and growls at him.

'Eva!' comes a call, followed by hurrying footsteps. 'What are you—'

Someone appears and abruptly stops, seeing the stand-off. A funny flicker twists in my stomach.

It's the woman from the pub. She's wearing a dark green fleece today and no makeup, her hair plaited away from her face, but it's definitely the same woman. Her eyes flare in recognition as they fall on me.

Miles snaps, 'Call off your bloody dog!' just as she clicks and says, 'Eva, here.'

The dog throws Miles a filthy look and returns. Miles shakes his head. 'What a menace. You can't have a dog going round growling at people.'

He rolls his eyes at me as though I'm going to back him up. I look away, embarrassed for some reason.

The woman gives him a look reminiscent of the one Eva just shot his way and says, 'You're the first person she's growled at in months.' She makes eye contact with me. 'And fancy seeing you here, *not a teeth guy*.'

I can't believe she remembered that. 'Nice to see you too,' I say, deciding the best approach is to pretend everything is totally normal.

'Keep your boyfriend under control,' she spits as she walks away.

'Keep your dog—' Miles starts to yell, but she's gone before I can dissect my urge to shout, He's not my boyfriend!

We walk on in a slightly awkward silence. Maybe Miles is scared of dogs. To be fair, none of us were at our best in that interaction. It must be exhausting for that woman to be so enraged all the time. I'm way too tired to keep that up. Eva's a cute name for a dog, though.

The path continues through the woods, following the hill down. Felborough recedes out of sight.

Miles's plan, although basic, does technically make sense. And, if the security system is as old-fashioned as he makes it out to be, a heist might not be that hard.

But . . . 'Why do you want to steal this orchid, anyway?' I ask. 'There must be quicker ways to get your hands on a heap of cash if you're willing to break the law.'

A moment passes. Then Miles stops walking and says, 'It's not just the money . . . Where do you think Felborough gets all these rare plants?'

'Um.' I can't tell if he's taking the piss. 'You tell me.'

'They steal them,' he says simply, his voice resonant with suppressed anger. 'Maybe you know this from your research,' he raises his eyebrows and, for some stupid reason, I blush, 'but this orchid is from the Darien Gap. It's an area filled with narcos and violence. And this explorer just goes in there, entitled as anything, and takes one of their orchids? As if they don't have enough problems. It's fucked up.' He shakes his head. 'And then what do Felborough do?'

I shrug. He's not really asking.

'They lock them away.' He kicks at the ground, unearthing a stone with his shoe. 'No one else is allowed to grow them or own them or look at them without permission. They're literally privatising plants. And they charge *us* our hard-earned money to visit.' It crosses my mind to ask what Miles does for a job, but he continues before I can. 'And all the other countries where the plants actually grow? They're being deforested and destroyed. But Felborough doesn't care about helping with any of that as long as they have their display plants.' He laughs, as if in disbelief. 'Which are *stolen*. It's not right.'

I think my expression of deep scepticism is obvious because he smiles ruefully. 'I know not everyone cares about things like this. But it's morally wrong. But more importantly,' he turns to me. I squint up against the brightness of the sky. His hair really is so glossy. 'They're profiting while people like you, Phil . . . Your dad's in debt, right?' He holds his hands up when I flinch. 'That's all I know, promise. Chaz said you're private and I respect that. I'm the same. But you've been working to fix it, haven't you?'

He waits. I don't know where he's going with this. But I can't deny it. Eventually, I nod.

'But no matter how hard you try, doesn't it feel like everything is rigged against you?'

The hours I've spent becoming an expert in the system. The hoops they make you jump through to access basic dignity. The humiliating, dehumanising disability assessments that my dad won't – can't? – do unless I force him, that we spend months dreading, then months recovering from, just to keep his joke of a 'benefits' package. The money we're disqualified from because I 'earn too much', although to describe my wages like that is laughable. The impossibility of ever digging our way out of this pit.

Miles's voice is insistent, his handsome face leaning closer. 'Felborough is rich and successful and it doesn't care about the people in the community. You've seen the way our town's being gentrified. They're working to uphold the rigged system that's never, ever given you a break.' He tilts an eyebrow. 'So why not help dismantle it?'

Chapter Four

A surprisingly short time later – a few days, if that – I'm sitting in a light, airy, incredibly grand office wearing a smart white shirt and a sycophantic smile.

A gentle breeze drifts through the window, which has been propped open with a book. The walls are lined with bookshelves crammed with leather-bound tomes so aesthetic that they could easily be a mural. I'm showing no outward sign that this interview is the first hurdle to clear before we can start properly planning an actual *heist*.

I clear my throat and take a small sip of water from the tiny glass I was offered. As long as I don't think too carefully about what we're doing, it all continues to make perfect sense. And I can still turn back at any moment. It won't matter to Felborough if I bounce from this interview; five or six other wannabe volunteers are waiting outside.

The elderly woman at the huge desk wears an expression you might describe as formidable, if you were so inclined, as she unfolds the piece of paper I've just handed her. Her shiny green name badge says *Ms Lenson, Head of Operations*. She's wearing a cream blouse and a lanyard and – like everyone who wears lanyards – she means business.

'Anthony and I have never actually met,' I explain, smiling as though this is a funny coincidence. 'But my great-aunt was an old friend of his grandma's, so when she realised Anthony worked here . . . She knew I've always wanted to as well.'

Ms Lenson nudges her reading glasses up her nose as she inspects the paper: a printout of the email from my 'great-aunt'.

The issue with Felborough being all famous and amazing and so on is that everybody wants to work here. The fact that they're using the orchid excitement as an opportunity to do some renovation works in our favour. But, as Chaz put it, no one was going to hire me based only on my smile and my house-plant-murder background. We needed an *in*.

'Miles, you seem like a nepo kind of guy,' Chaz said, when we were trying to figure this out the other day. 'Have you got any connections we can rinse?'

But although Miles frowned briefly as if about to get defensive (thus confirming Chaz's diagnosis), he just said lightly, 'Sadly not.'

I suggested Chaz did some kind of gentle hacking. But then he had this idea: if Miles didn't have a way to make me stand out in the interview, we could always just invent one.

After scrutinising the Felborough organisational chart, we chose a gardener called Anthony Fitzwilliam. We judged him most likely to have the kind of aged relative who would try to pull in a favour for a friend, based purely on his surname and him having gone to a public school we'd all heard of. Admittedly a punt, but snap judgements are quite literally all we have.

A bit of research and Chaz had Anthony's entire family tree. Then it was easy: impersonate a friend of his late grandma with a few choice personal details to add plausibility, name-drop Anthony in the interview, hope my charm carries us the rest of the way.

It's obviously a risk. But we had no other choice. And Anthony's unguarded social media and rugged website photo suggest he's not someone obsessed with data protection, so he hopefully won't follow up. He's probably too busy being hot and getting laid.

'That's very admirable, Phil,' Ms Lenson says, scanning the email. 'You're certainly not alone in wanting to be part of the Felborough story. Can you tell me a bit about your qualifications?'

'Of course,' I say, smiling. 'I'm a team player and very driven. I studied history at university, so I'm fascinated by the stories Felborough can tell.' My own voice comes out of my mouth smoothly and calmly, like a well-oiled robot who's just learnt to bullshit. 'I have a lot of customer service experience so I'm confident I can bring that to the team.'

I keep talking, telling her about the times I've organised events at the cinema, been promoted to manager of the bar I worked at. My interest in history and my desire to learn more about botany. I hint at a bit of a sob story too: dropping out of university for mental health reasons but never giving up on my dream of working somewhere as fabulous and renowned as Felborough. Just getting my foot on the ladder as a volunteer would be an honour.

Ms Lenson is nodding and smiling, her reassurance clear. I'm almost alarmed by how well this is going. The weird thing is, most of what I'm saying is true. I do have a lot of customer service experience. Most of the jobs open to me when I dropped out of uni were service jobs, so there I went and there I've stayed. I don't even mind customer service. The issue, of course, is that it's not going to result in a surprise six-figure Christmas bonus, which is the other fantasy I dabble in when the lottery one gets old.

'You'd be needed for five volunteer shifts a week, just until the grand reopening.' Ms Lenson consults her clipboard. 'Including two weekends a month. So it's rather a commitment.'

'That's fine,' I reassure her, suppressing the flutter of panic at the thought of all this unpaid labour.

'In that case,' she looks up, her direct gaze meeting mine, 'welcome to the team, Phil Hart.'

'I got the job?' I exclaim, my professional façade slipping.

'You did.' She smiles. 'Well done. We're bringing on lots of new staff and today's cohort has been very strong. It's always a pleasure to hire people on the spot.'

'Thank you.' I grin back, unable to hide my relief. It's been ages since I've had a job interview I've felt anything

42

about other than listless. But as soon as the relief flickers, it's replaced by a crunch of anticipation in my stomach.

If we're really going to do this, that's step one complete.

I text the group chat with Miles and Chaz as I follow the gaggle of other new hires down the corridor, some of them jostling to get as close as possible to Ms Lenson.

Mission: You Know What is a go.

Surely you can think of a better name, Chaz replies.

No mission names! Miles sends, moments later. **But good job, Phil ;)**

I repress a shudder at the winking face and shove down the embarrassing flash of pride. Who cares what Miles thinks of me? He's not even hot. Not at all. Not one bit.

'These are the kitchens,' Ms Lenson announces as we enter. 'The servants would have spent a lot of their time here when this was a working country house.'

We're in a spacious whitewashed room with high ceilings and a fireplace big enough for several underfed Victorian children to stand abreast. A massive wooden table dominates the centre of the room. It's easy to imagine the kitchen full of people, sweating over a roaring fire, the table laden with food.

But instead of the platters of plastic meat and fruit I remember from a school trip to Hampton Court, to hint at the Tudor vibe, the table is covered with neat piles of papers, name badges, a couple of computers and, hilariously, right in the middle, a floor plan.

We need one of those for the heist! I won't make a grab for it now. That would be premature. And a bit of a giveaway.

'This is the central meeting point for the volunteers,' Ms Lenson tells us. 'The scientists have a common room upstairs and the gardeners tend to meet by the stables as they have a base there. Now I'll just get your contracts printed and we'll find you uniforms.'

I drift round the kitchen while we wait, inspecting the woodwormed cabinets and poking my head into the rooms leading off it – a pantry and a washroom. Everywhere has the look of the modern laid firmly over the ancient: a printer sitting incongruously on a draining board; a MacBook left at one end of the table.

I'm big enough to admit that this is the kind of place I'd have loved to work in the olden days. On my freshly started history degree, I'd imagined myself one day researching old manuscripts, finding undiscovered gems, sharing the details of the past with other people so they could be fascinated by it too. But that world wasn't for me. I was home again a few months later.

At least I get to be in a big old house today, looking at their nice shit. The table has curly engravings on the legs in the shape of plants, flowers and an animal with four paws and a long tail. Someone must have carved all that by hand.

'All set,' Ms Lenson intones, looking up from her seat at the computer. She hands around papers and takes us off to the cloakroom.

'We may as well take the opportunity to introduce you to a few people,' Ms Lenson says, once she's selected a variety of black and green polo shirts (will I never escape the tyranny of the polo shirt?) and slung them over our outstretched arms.

She marches briskly onwards through the warren of corridors. We've gone up a set of stairs and down another two but we still seem to be on the ground floor. I really need to start paying attention so I can create a visual map.

We emerge, blinking, into the daylight, quite suddenly through a side door that I didn't notice at first.

'Ah, Hiwot,' Ms Lenson says, giving a polite nod and a wide smile to a stocky woman standing thoughtfully on the other side of the courtyard. She's surrounded by a cluster of people wearing gardening clothes in varying stages of dishevelment. 'Everyone: this is Ms Gyamfi, our head gardener.'

At her words, the woman turns. She has short salt-and-pepper hair and a clear gaze that takes us in at a glance. 'Good morning, Mary.'

Given that an important goal of mine here is to present as both calm and cool, I try to disguise the involuntary flex of my shoulders with a casual stretch. I've met minor celebrities before. People pass through our town on their way to Felborough all the time. And sometimes they do the kinds of events where mere mortals like me queue up outside the Felborough gates for a glimpse of the celebs. A murder mystery was filmed here a while ago and sometimes the Hall and parkland is used for high-budget period dramas. It does a lot to make this town less irretrievably dire.

But this is my first time seeing the woman who's done so much to promote Felborough. She joined as Director of Gardens five years ago. In that time, the research output has doubled. Doubled, I tell you! Or so their website reports, at least.

Importantly, it's the kind of research that makes the actual news, not just niche botanical publications, which is why it sometimes pops up on my social media – like one of her articles last year. I don't know what it was about; it mentioned flowers and featured frequent use of the word 'splicing'. Obviously, nobody else really understood it either, but that didn't matter; the local news was mainly reporting on the fact that her article had made national and international news. It definitely had 'groundbreaking' in the headline because I remember trying to make some incredibly weak gardening-based joke when talking to Chaz about it. He waited impatiently for me to be done and then told me it hadn't been worth the wait. It's so important to stay humble.

Anyway, Hiwot Gyamfi has made some changes around here and they're working. She's also the first Black woman to have had the role, which is kind of amazing given the crusty white-male-dominated world of botanics. Or, at least, I assume. My lack of knowledge of the world of botanics is probably the key challenge I'll have to overcome in the next few weeks. I set my shoulders and try not to think about it.

'These kind souls are going to be joining our team of volunteers. That's Emilie, Alice, Audrey, Phil . . .' Ms Lenson rattles off everyone's names as I listen in amazement. What a memory trick. 'Everything going well, I hope?' Ms Lenson finishes, as we nod our greetings.

46

Ms Gyamfi inclines her head calmly. 'Absolutely. We're just considering our move with the pleached hornbeams along the wall.'

This statement sets off another hushed conversation among the gardeners clustered nearby. They might as well be speaking another language. I'm distracted by the sight of a scruffy little blonde shape nosing into the courtyard.

'Eva?' I mutter under my breath. It probably isn't. Dogs aren't allowed in here.

The little dog stops and looks back at someone coming through the archway in the courtyard wall before continuing its snuffling.

'Ah, Lily,' Ms Gyamfi says, 'good.'

Oh, fantastic.

The figure looks up from the wheelbarrow she's pushing and says, her voice deferential but confident, 'You wanted to see me?'

She's wearing mostly what she was wearing when I saw her in the field a few days ago – hard-wearing trousers, sturdy boots – but her fleece is off, hung over the side of the wheelbarrow. Her dark green T-shirt sleeves are rolled up to reveal the kind of wiry muscles you get from doing a physical outdoorsy job. I tear my eyes away quickly.

I guess this explains why she was nearby the other day. She must have been taking Eva for a post-work stroll.

One of the other gardeners starts to say, 'I was thinking, Ms Gyamfi, it might be good to—'

'Not you, Benny,' Ms Gyamfi says without looking at him.

'Lily is one of our senior gardeners,' Ms Lenson tells us. Shit.

'Hi,' I blurt as Lily's eye, scanning across our group, falters on me. She looks me up and down.

I bend to greet her dog, who's come to investigate my shoe, but Lily clicks her fingers, ruining our bonding moment. Eva looks up at me once, then pads away. Tossing her hair, Lily turns back to the head gardener. 'How can I help?'

I suppress a sigh of irritation. I was ready to extend an olive branch but clearly that's not happening.

'Lovely,' says Ms Lenson, oblivious. 'I think that's everything for today.' She puts a gentle hand on my arm as she looks round at the new volunteers. 'Why don't I give you a quick tour of the toilets and then you can head off? I need to sort out the rota but your first shifts will be next week.'

'Great,' I say. Lily is watching me, smirking.

'Enjoy the toilets,' I think I hear her mutter as we shuffle away.

Chapter Five

Felborough's storied history

Felborough Hall once belonged to the Mountjoy family, who lived here until the mid-twentieth century. Always a botanical polestar thanks to its unparalleled glasshouses, the family sold the property after the Second World War to be used in the interests of science and conservation, creating Felborough, the institution we know today.

Although its rich botanical life is Felborough's main attraction, the property contains a number of little quirks that enchant visitors. When the Hall was refurbished in the seventies, several secret passages were discovered. In the ha-ha, for example, a now blocked secret passage led all the way to the stables – presumably used for playing jokes on unsuspecting shepherds tending the sheep just outside the grounds.

In the Orangery, afternoon tea is served in the quaint, mismatched crockery used by the Queen when she spent a

summer here as a young child – and it can also be rented out
as an events space.

Honestly. It's all so whimsical. I take another swig of wine. If
I wasn't such a heartless cynic by dint of my circumstances, I
would be eating up this stuff. Which I am certainly not doing
already. We're here to rob the place, not to get invested. That'll
be the first thing to remember.

'Hello, calling Phil.' Chaz's voice and a finger-clicking
sound break into my thoughts. 'Are you even listening?'

We're sitting at the glass-topped kitchen table in Miles's
flat. This place is swanky as hell, all spacious Scandi chic
with high ceilings, white everything, and no dust anywhere,
in a way that surely means he has a cleaner. It's 'only' one
bedroom but it has a view over the nicer part of town and a
bathroom bigger than our living room. There's a garage in the
building's basement where Miles keeps his car, as he informed
Chaz, under the mistaken impression that this would be of
interest. Chaz would only notice a car if it literally ran him
over.

'Sorry, yes.' I lock my phone, the Felborough webpage
blinking away, and slap away the clicking fingers Chaz is
waving in my face. 'What was that, Miles?'

Miles smiles at me indulgently. He's at the head of the table,
his fingers steepled, looking like a Doctor-Evil-style crime
boss but sexier. I wish it wasn't true. But his hair is tousled and
he's wearing a deep red corduroy shirt that I'm really enjoying.

Also, I've had one and a half glasses of high-quality white

wine. The kind of quality I never normally experience. It's bathing the tastefully minimalist lines of the flat in a warm, rosy glow.

'I was just saying,' Miles explains, spreading his hands grandly, 'that step one is complete.'

'Actually,' Chaz says, his cheeks slightly flushed as he sits opposite me blinking at his laptop, 'we've all seen the films. Step one of any heist is getting the team together.' For once, Chaz has allowed himself a small glass of wine too. This is so rare that one or two sips might just do it for him. I'm hoping he'll get up on the chrome breakfast bar and start twerking. 'So we're already further ahead than that. Maybe step two was getting inside Felborough.'

To my utter surprise, he shuts his laptop and pulls out a notebook and fountain pen.

'You're not serious,' I say, as he scribbles the word 'Notes' and underlines it, transporting me instantly back to our schooldays. He'll probably write his name and date in the top right corner too, possibly adding a love heart. 'I think this is the first time I've ever seen you voluntarily write with a pen.'

'This is how they do it in the films,' Chaz insists. His handwriting looks like a drunk spider fell into an ink pot. 'I've got some red string in my bag, too, for the noticeboard.' He gestures over at the corner, where a corkboard sits incongruously on a stand. 'And I've ordered a grappling hook just in case we need one.'

'Isn't red string for solving murders, not heists?' I ask,

my brain meandering along with his words. 'Wait.' I sit up straight. 'You've ordered a *grappling hook*?'

'Oh, is it?' he asks, interestedly. 'I don't know. But at least this way we have it. And people are always using grappling hook for heists, aren't they?'

A helpless laugh bubbles out of me as Miles says, 'Good work, Chaz. I appreciate the commitment. Shall we discuss our next step?'

Aside from it being laughably premature to order a grappling hook, the thought of Chaz using one to smash into a glasshouse, probably while wearing his silk PJs, has gripped me now. This is it. I'm sunk.

'Shut up, Phil,' Chaz says. 'We're focusing now. Stop laughing. Our next step is to identify the victim.'

'Not the *victim*,' Miles cuts in. 'That sounds awfully devious.'

'Fine.' Chaz barely looks up. 'The fall guy. The idiot we'll pump for information so we can actually pull off the robbery.'

This quenches my laughter abruptly. I fiddle with the stem of my glass, twirling it on the polished surface. 'And remind me who we're going for again?'

I already know and that's the issue. I think this whole conversation might be redundant.

'Someone senior enough that they can help us because they'll know things more junior staff will be kept away from,' Miles says. 'But not so senior that it's a risk to get close to them. A happy middle ground.'

'You've met some people already, haven't you?' Chaz asks me. 'Have you got an idea?'

'Maybe,' I reply, not looking up.

'Who?' Chaz says, impatiently. From the corner of my eye, I catch Miles making a calming, shushing motion at him. Maybe he can tell I'm getting skittish.

I take a breath. Lily's scornful expression sits with me. She's just so unpleasant. I wouldn't expect planning a heist to be fun, per se, but does it really have to be her? I bet there are loads of other senior gardeners who are close to the head gardener. I can probably find one of them to ingratiate myself with instead.

'I have an idea,' I hedge, 'but I'm not sure yet. This person might not be the right fit for the heist.'

'They don't have to be a perfect corporate candidate, Phil.' Chaz rolls his eyes. 'They just need to know the shit *we* need to know.'

'Yeah, yeah,' I say, downing my wine. 'It'll be fine. I just need a day or two.'

'Don't wait too long,' Chaz chides. 'We've only got a month until the orchid does its thing. And the collector only wants it after that, right? Otherwise it's not valuable.'

'Yes. When it blooms for the first time in ten years,' Miles says, his voice taking on a mysterious note. 'What a sight it will be.' He grins, his eyes crinkling into malice. 'Felborough will never see us coming.'

A slightly strained silence follows this announcement. Miles is very intense sometimes. And yet he's so relaxed, sitting here. He gives the impression of total confidence that it's going to work out. I'd love to share that. It's kind of hot.

To avoid going down this train of thought, I drum my fingers on the surface. What else do they use in heists?

'We'll need blueprints,' I suggest, in a flash of inspiration. I've never seen a heist without them. 'I saw some in the Hall today.'

'We can just get those online, can't we?' Chaz asks, as he writes in little letters in his notebook: OBTAIN BLUEPRINTS. Just above it, he's written CASE THE JOINT. 'These huge places always have them publicly available.'

'Felborough doesn't,' Miles says. Of course. That would be too easy. 'But this is where we're relying on you, Phil. Maybe break into the office or something? We definitely need a proper map.'

Miles gets to his feet and wheels the corkboard over from the corner of the room.

'We'll add to this as we gather documents and so on, but for now . . .' He taps the one item on the board. He's pinned up the stylised tourist map of Felborough from its brochure: a featureless expanse of pale green parkland, a cluster of circles for the glasshouses, a simple brown rectangle depicting the bulk of the Hall.

'Oh good, we already have a map,' I say. 'Why not just use that?'

'Yeah, it's got such nice pictures of ducks.' Chaz points at the light blue lake, with its cartoon ripples and a tiny illustration of a pedalo.

'Very good,' Miles says. 'Obviously this isn't going to cut it. But one thing it does show us is how far it is from the glasshouses to the entrance. It takes about twenty minutes to walk between the two.'

I consider and then dismiss suggesting that we all hire Segways for the night of the heist. It might not lend the sense of grandeur we're after. Also, I've definitely had too much wine to be able to contribute in a useful way. My brain keeps getting stuck on the fact that . . . we're not *really* doing this, are we?

But Miles's expression is steady and serious as he turns to face us both. 'This is the kind of scale I'm talking about. A lot can happen in twenty minutes and Felborough security is tight. But we need more information. So, Chaz, you're obviously on hacking duty. Find out what security system they use. Start to make your way in. And Phil, we need you for the things that aren't online. We won't even know what we need until you find it. Let me know if I can help with anything.'

Chaz is nodding as he earnestly writes, ACCESS SECURITY.

'Wow, what a helpful list,' I say. 'How could we have remembered we'd need to break into Felborough's very powerful security system without that note? Seriously,' I turn to Miles, 'is this all we have to go on? Because it's never going to work.'

'Don't worry, babe,' Chaz says. 'I'll do a list for you too.' He rips off his page and starts a fresh one. 'Number one . . . is obviously get the team together. Then . . . number two: set up an amazing plan. Then number three . . . Easy.' Scribbling as he speaks, he rips off the page and hands it to me. 'There you go. Should help you remember.'

Against my will, I read the scrap of paper.

THE GREAT ORCHID HEIST:
1. **THE TEAM**
2. **THE PLAN**
3. **THE HEIST**

'You're not funny,' I tell him, scrunching it up in my fist and shoving it in my pocket.

'I've never once heard that before,' Chaz says, pushing out his lower lip in mock sadness.

Miles holds up both hands and adopts a soothing tone. 'I understand your concerns, Phil, but this is all a normal part of the process.'

His composed expression is a welcome change from Chaz's smug face.

Miles places a hand fleetingly on the corkboard, over the cartoon glasshouses. 'We're just starting out, taking stock. And I hesitate to say Chaz's list is helpful, but I think the first step really is getting the team together and taking it from there. It's OK that we don't know everything yet.'

I sigh, letting out a breath. Surely he would need to have done several heists before now to have the authority to comment on that. But he is quite commanding. *Maybe* we can do this.

It's good to have a plan. And we can always decide based on the information we've gathered that it's not going to happen. Can't we?

Miles waits until I nod and then treats me to a flash of a

smile. I push away my wine glass as if that's the cause of the warmth in my cheeks.

'Is everyone clear on what we're doing?' he asks.

Despite myself, number two on Chaz's list – THE PLAN – skitters across my mind. 'I suppose so,' I say. 'I basically just need to figure out what's going on in Felborough, right?'

'Exactly. Chaz, you're clear too?'

'As crystal,' he says, tapping his list.

'OK. We'll meet back here in a week.' Miles stretches as he stands, revealing a sliver of taut skin between his shirt and waistband, which I – and Chaz – quickly look away from. 'Good work, team.'

'Do you want to fuck Miles?' Chaz asks, conversationally, as he fastens his seatbelt and settles back in his seat a couple of hours and a strong coffee later.

'Excuse you,' I comment, as I pull out of the turning onto the main road. I'm giving him a lift home, as usual; we live close together and he can't drive, legally or emotionally.

'What, I'm just asking,' he says. 'I don't, but I can see the appeal.'

This is high praise indeed from Chaz, who's never shown any romantic or sexual interest in anyone. He claims to be far too busy.

I shrug. 'I can see the appeal too. Miles is non-controversially attractive.' There's no need to act coy with Chaz. I mean, there's a danger he'd repeat this to Miles by accident in pursuit of being funny. But I can always turn it round on him if he does.

Chaz nods, solemnly. 'Tale as old as time: a tall, well-built white man with a strong jaw and great hair. Strong jaw for now,' he adds. 'Let's check back in twenty years. And on the hair as well.'

'Please don't ruin this for me,' I say. 'It's nice having a godlike person to hang out with.'

We fall into silent contemplation as the familiar streets float past our windows, the grey of concrete interspersed with the occasional flash of green glowing in the spring evening sunshine.

'Look on the bright side,' Chaz says, a few minutes later as I pull up to his house. 'If the heist fails, you can always try to seduce Miles.'

'Important to have a backup plan,' I agree. 'I could be a kept woman.'

'Or he could be yours,' Chaz says, getting out, 'given there's no way you'd give up control over anything in your life.'

He waves as he slams the door and strolls off, cutting off my protest. I roll my eyes as I drive away.

I'd be lying if I said I hadn't considered it. My hunch is that Miles is too hot to be any good in bed. He's never had to try, so is probably the type of man who thinks sex finishes when he does rather than when all parties are satisfied. But he could learn, and being gorgeous does get you some of the way there.

And life isn't just sex, is it? Miles could drive me round in his silly little sports car with its own parking space and pour delicious wine for me and pay his own bills. My life would be ten times more secure.

Of course, I literally can't imagine him and my dad in the same room. Miles sitting on our old, worn sofa in his pristine linen shirt, manoeuvring himself around whatever mangy piece of furniture my dad's currently working on and the corresponding pile of tools and paint tins. Attempting a family holiday to, like, Crete in a villa where Miles and I sit around drinking Aperol spritzes and my dad ... splashes in the pool? Makes a sandcastle?

No. The imagination glitches away, like trying to hold two matching magnet ends together. They wouldn't have a single thing to say to each other. But maybe that's fine. I could just always go to Miles's flat, in this alternate reality.

I shake my head to rid myself of this ridiculous train of thought as I park outside my house. I can't let Chaz get in my head. It literally never ends well.

Chapter Six

'So what's the deal with this orchid, then?' I ask, wringing out my sponge. It's my first day at Felborough and I'm working by the newly refurbished cafe with some other volunteers and gardeners. And thank you, yes: this *is* a very cunning and sneaky opening gambit to learn about the object of our heist.

Today's job is to set up the outdoor seating area. We're scrubbing dirt off the picnic tables, hanging fake wasps' nests in the trees (apparently these deter the actual IRL wasps) and making things look nice. I do like things to look nice but I rarely know how to make it happen. It's the potted plant situation all over again. I buy it, it looks good for a few brief, beautiful days and then the wilting begins. Fortunately, I have a new little gardener friend to help.

'Oh, the *orchid*,' Benny squeals. 'Phil, you wouldn't believe how secretive the whole thing is.'

'Really?' I say, scrubbing at a stubborn bit of bird poo on a bench.

'Highly classified.' Benny taps his nose with a dirt-encrusted finger. I met Benny earlier, when we were thrown together in our task. He's short and stocky and his dark hair sticks straight up, like a nail brush. So far, he's told me a lot about himself – he loves women, salsa (music or dip, unconfirmed), white teeth and summer fruits – and almost nothing of any use to me. He's quite sweet though. I can't quite tell if he's hitting on me or if he's just . . . like this.

'Have you seen the orchid then?' I ask him.

'No!' he laughs, as though this is an idiotic question. 'None of us have, except the senior gardeners. And even they don't get much time with it. The only person who knows everything about it is Ms Gyamfi.' Benny grunts as he hauls a barrel of earth over to a picnic table. 'She doesn't tell anyone her full plans. She tells the senior gardeners some stuff, I think, but she swears them to secrecy. I'd love to be a senior gardener,' he adds, rolling the barrel to a standstill, 'but I'm not committed enough.'

'Aren't you?' I ask. 'You seem very committed to me.' When I suggested earlier that we knock off for a tea break, Benny said something about how HG wouldn't like it and how it would probably be best if we just kept working.

Oh, also they all call her HG. HG for Hiwot Gyamfi; HG for Head Gardener. I have to admit I like it.

'She demands the best of the best, Phil.' Benny's face turns solemn, his eyebrows slanted into utter seriousness. 'The crème de la crème.'

61

'Right,' I say. 'And what does this crème de la crème look like here?'

'Sorry?'

'How can you impress her?'

'Oh,' Benny grins at me, 'not that easily. She only likes a couple of people.'

'Who's she a fan of then?' I ask, heart sinking. I can guess the answer, according to Sod's Law. Who's the one person in this workforce I don't want to spend time with?

'She likes Anthony and Sanj, two of the senior gardeners,' Benny tells me, earnestly. I appreciate how seriously he's taking this information-gathering mission of mine, although hearing Anthony's name sends a clench of nerves to my throat. Fortunately, Benny continues, oblivious. 'But her favourite is Lily Francis,' he adds, for my benefit. This guy is truly so helpful. 'She's like her protégé. They've worked together on publications and research and stuff. And HG hates animals but she lets Lily bring Eva round the gardens whenever she wants. It's not really fair,' he shrugs, 'but Lily's kind of scary so we can't really question it. You know?'

'Yeah,' I say, helping him dust off the barrel, resigned to my fate. 'I do.'

'She never wants to come for a drink. And she won't join our quiz team, even though she knows loads.' He sighs wistfully. 'Lily's super driven. She wants to be head gardener someday and that's all she thinks about.'

'Sounds like you might have a little crush on this so-called Lily,' I say, to test his reaction.

He stares at me, shocked. 'Phil! No way. She'd never be interested. She hates everyone.'

Later, I'm assigned to another task with a different under-gardener. This one is called Diego and, much like Benny, he takes things very seriously. His hair is also dark but swept back in a ponytail and he has large brown eyes that dart around like a nervous bunny.

'We're redoing loads of stuff,' he tells me, while we sweep out what could be several decades' worth of dust from the old stables. Another volunteer has already been led away to have her coughing fit in private. 'Felborough is never shut for so long normally, especially at this time of year. But with the orchid here, they're making the most of no visitors and we're doing a spring clean and stuff, and the electrics. The wiring in this place is ancient. It's a death trap,' he adds, giving a slightly manic laugh.

'Ideal for a workplace,' I say.

'But it's worth the risk,' Diego gushes, his nervous expression softening into pride. 'There's nowhere else in the country where you work with such amazing plant life. And HG is world-famous. It's a dream come true.'

'Yeah, I suppose,' I agree, hoping I sound more enthusiastic than I feel. This is a valuable reminder of the workplace's vibe. I need to act more grateful; everyone who works here bloody loves it. I suppose it is nice to be doing this different kind of work in picturesque surroundings. It makes a change from shovelling popcorn and sweeping up old nachos.

I straighten and lean against my broom to stretch out my back. As I do, Lily passes the hole in the wall leading to the vegetable garden.

'Working hard in there?' she asks, her hand resting on the vine-encrusted archway. She's wearing gold wire-rimmed glasses today. And, fine, they look good on her.

'Yes, Lily,' Diego chirps, jumping about a foot in the air. His broom acted as a sort of pole vault, I think.

'Let me know when you're done,' she says, looking directly at me. I stare back, hoping my look is intimidating. From the slight curl of her lip, it isn't. 'I've got a job for you in the pumpkin patch.'

She walks off. I pull a face after her. What the hell kind of place has a pumpkin patch? Are we in an American cartoon?

Diego and I hardly talk after that. Instead, he whizzes round the stables like a whirling dervish, furiously sweeping. I trail after him with a dustpan on a long handle, coughing at the clouds of dust, until he drags me off to find Lily.

She's not in the pumpkin patch when we arrive. It's hard to decide if I'm disappointed or relieved. What I am disappointed by is the location.

'What kind of a pumpkin patch do you call this?' I ask. There's a tangle of thick greenery in rough sections across the raised beds but not a pumpkin in sight, dashing my hopes of a *Gilmore Girls*-style pumpkin fest.

'It's just called that because we do special autumn and Halloween events here. But the pumpkins are coming,' Diego hurries to reassure me in a portentous tone. 'They won't be ready for a few months, but look.' He darts over to one of the raised beds and crouches excitedly. 'Here they are.'

I nod politely at the little green tufts spaced around the bed. Kind of wild to imagine vegetables springing up out of nowhere.

Diego points out a few pumpkin alternatives as we wander between the beds, his enthusiasm bubbling through his previous reserve in a way that I must admit is adorable. It's nice to see someone really caring about something.

The rows of assorted veg clearly started off lined up but they've exploded into a riot of green over time. Dutifully, I admire the growing courgettes and summer squash, the runner beans. They're surprisingly cute in their baby forms.

We get to the end of a row to find Lily has left instructions for us in the form of a gardening fork and a couple of trowels stuck in the dirt. A section of the plot, where the tools are, has been meticulously cleared of weeds and the greenery off to the side looks as though it can finally breathe again. The message from Lily is clear.

I'm not convinced this is part of my job description, but Diego is smiling wryly and saying how clever Lily is to show us what to do like that. So I grab one of the trowels and start digging at a patch of green. Diego scuttles to the other end of the row and begins there.

I've never weeded before. But how hard can it be? I can recognise a weed. Easy. It's satisfying too, feeling like you're clearing space for the veg to grow. Some of these little growing guys are so choked up with stuff they probably haven't breathed in months. I feel quite mindful, actually.

'Oh my God!' comes an exclamation, ten minutes later. Lily is standing over me with genuine alarm in her voice.

I squint up at her. I was just starting to get into it.

'What in God's name are you doing?'

I spread my hands. 'Weeding.' The *obviously* is implied.

'Weeding?' Her voice lifts an octave.

I'm offended by the tone. I might not be a gardener but I know some things. 'You know, clearing space so the plant has room to grow?'

She's staring down at the patch I've cleared. 'Have you ever seen a plant before?'

I almost laugh at how rude this is and am about to thank her for her concern but, yes, actually, I have. But she continues, her voice rising still higher, 'Have you ever *heard* of biodiversity?'

'Right.' I brace my hands on my knees and stand, facing her. She's got about an inch on me, annoyingly. 'Why don't you tell me what I'm doing wrong so I can fix it?'

As soon as I've squared up to her, she drops to the ground and starts to sort through the small pile of weeds I've pulled so far, muttering.

'What?' I say, crouching again. I never realised gardening would be murder on the knees. But she ignores me, her fingers quick and sure as she starts to separate the stems and leaves of the indiscriminate plant stuff. They fall into their separate plants in her hands. If I was doing that I'd be tearing them to bits.

I notice idly that her nails, which have dark half-moons of soil under the tips, are short, like mine; although, unlike me, I don't think she bites hers. The phrases 'massacre' and 'bloodbath' are just audible under her breath as she works. I'm no plant expert, but this doesn't sound ideal.

Eventually, she sits on her heels, shaking her head. 'This is why I tell HG we shouldn't let volunteers into the gardens. Just an absolute bloody menace. And whose head will be on the chopping block when she sees this?' I'm about to protest – it's hardly my fault that I've not been properly trained to do my job, is it? – when she clears her throat. 'Right. Phil, was it?'

'Good memory,' I tell her. I know this won't help but I can't resist.

'You're wearing a name badge,' she spits.

'What's your name again?' I ask, even though I know perfectly well.

'Listen here, *Phil*,' she says, picking up one of the plant piles and brandishing it. 'I'm going to give you a very simple lesson in *growing things*. So see if you can keep up, yeah?'

I plop backwards from my squat position so I'm sitting on my bum on the earth. My knees can't hold it any longer and this seems like more of a learning pose anyway. 'I'll do my best,' I say, false sweetness dripping from my voice.

She gives the handful of plants a shake. 'These are what we call *weeds*,' she says.

I gesture at them. 'So I did it right?'

She throws them down onto the ground. 'And these,' she

picks up the pile next to it, her hands careful despite her barely suppressed rage, 'are not.'

Ah.

'Clearly you know nothing, so you won't have heard of companion planting. And that's on me, really. I should have lowered my already rock-bottom expectations. But,' her voice takes on the sing-song tone of a primary school teacher explaining that, No, Timmy, one plus one does not equal one, 'companion planting means we put other plants *near* the ones we want to grow that will *help* them.'

She sorts through the bunch. 'So this, that you've so help-fully ripped out, is oregano. It makes good ground cover and attracts hover flies, which feed on aphids. That's good because aphids *eat* young vegetable leaves. Do you see?'

I'm torn between fury at how much she's patronising me and genuine interest in what she's saying. I also can't believe I didn't spot oregano. It looks different in the packet. 'How about that one?' I realise I've asked.

She rubs the bridge of her nose, her finger bumping against her glasses and leaving a smudge of earth on her skin. 'Mar-joram,' she says eventually. 'Pollinators like it. And this is basil. It's good for the soil and keeps mosquitoes away.'

'And they eat young leaves too?' I hate the edge of neediness in my voice.

'Wow, top of the class.' She turns away, straightening up. 'Thank God you didn't rip up the nasturtiums as well. Although that would have taken a special kind of stupid.' She indicates the vine trailing up the short poles dug into the ground along the central row of the pumpkin patch. 'Hang on, I spoke too soon.' She stoops and pulls out another plant from the pile of weeds. 'Here's one that didn't make it.'

The full ridiculousness of what I've done is starting to come home to me. Gardening aside – and to be fair, I am a little regretful about destroying these innocent plants for no reason – I've just further ruined my chances of a normal, friendly relationship with this person. Which means the heist is fucked before we've even started.

'I'm sorry,' I blurt, scrambling to my feet. Lily eyes my ungainly movements as I inadvertently crush another plant. 'I didn't mean to,' I say. 'I'm actually not always an idiot. I'm just new to this.'

'Please go,' she says, waving a hand at me. 'I need to sort out this mess.'

My heart thuds suddenly. 'Are you . . . firing me?'

She snorts. 'I can't fire you, dillweed. Luckily for you. If I had firing powers, the workforce round here would look very different.' She throws a dark look around the garden, catching Diego in its line of fire.

I dig my trowel into a patch of ground that looks safely free from any plants, companion or otherwise, and brush the dirt off me as best I can.

'Try not to trip over and ruin anything else important on your way out,' Lily calls after me as I leave.

Chapter Seven

'I've not found out much new stuff yet. We've just been doing a big tidy-up, basically.' I sit back on my bed and jiggle the mouse on my laptop. 'Is this right? The screen's gone black.'

It's a few days later and I'm reporting back to Chaz and Miles over FaceTime. While I fill them in, Chaz is talking us through downloading a secure messaging service. Miles seems to be struggling a surprising amount. It's almost like he's not used to taking instruction.

'Felborough never closes to the public so they're all excited to have this time,' I finish. 'Oh, the screen's back on. How about yours, Miles?'

'Have you been in the Hall yet?' he asks eagerly.

'Not much, apart from my interview,' I say. 'Most of it is offices. They do tours and stuff to the old bits, but the volunteers don't do much of that unless the staff are super busy.'

'And the glasshouses?' Chaz asks. 'When are you gonna see this sweet, sweet orchid?'

'This is the stupid thing,' I say, rearranging the cushions behind my back. I'm in my childhood bedroom which, of course, regrettably, is also my adulthood bedroom. The single bed is too short, but I don't think we'd fit a bigger one in here. Even if we could afford one, I'd have to work through what that would mean emotionally, with its implication that I'd be fully, genuinely committing to living with my dad long-term. 'I think we might have underestimated how seriously they take this.'

'How so?' I can hear the frown in Chaz's voice.

I fill them in on the security situation and how none of the junior gardeners have even seen the orchid. 'And no one knows anything about it, except the head gardener and, like, her favourite minion.'

I tried Googling the orchid again earlier when I got back from work, a desperate move brought on by the fact that I've hardly learnt anything useful so far. But the only information was on the Felborough website, plus a few brief articles announcing it had been discovered. The rest of the search results related to the grand reopening and the red-carpet event they're holding in a few weeks.

One article named HG as an important figure in orchid botany, or whatever the phrase. The author was optimistic that HG would be able to figure out the outrageously complicated and difficult-to-replicate conditions the orchid needs to grow because she's a 'plant codebreaker'. But that was all.

'I'll do some digging,' Chaz says, after I've finished relaying this. 'There's always more on the internet.'

'I'm not sure there is,' I say. 'I spent a while searching.'

Chaz kindly restrains himself from scoffing, although not enough that it's not evident in his voice. As if I'd dare to suggest his precious internet won't have the answers.

'Good stuff. And even if you can't find much, this is why we have you, Phil.' Miles sounds cheery. 'You're going to befriend the minion, aren't you? And find out all about the orchid.'

'Yeah, about that,' I say. He doesn't understand the depth of the issue. I'm about to point out that Lily is the owner of the little dog Miles fell out with in the field the other day, when—

'Phil?' My dad's voice. He's coming up the stairs.

'Nothing!' I blurt out. Panic fizzes through my veins as I jolt back to being seventeen and hearing my dad approach and knowing there's nowhere to hide the joint I'm smoking or the partly clothed, tattooed older girl I'm sharing it with.

'Sorry?' he says, muffled through the closed door.

'Gotta go,' I hiss, jabbing at the end-call button. I slam my laptop shut and strike a no doubt highly convincing relaxed pose as my dad knocks and pops his head round the door.

'All right, love?'

'Yep, fine.' I force myself to take a breath. 'How are you?'

'Just off to bed.'

'All right, sleep well.'

He fiddles with the door handle, keeping his voice casual as he says, 'I'll be out tomorrow night.'

The alarm bell in my head clangs so loudly that I look

round to see if he heard it too. Out? On a Tuesday evening? This is a deviation from scheduling. 'Where are you going?'

'Just meeting up with an old pal.'

'Which old pal?' One time, my dad met up with 'an old pal' when I was a teenager and my mum had to go and collect him from a park after a big win; he and the pal were celebrating after a few pints by splashing around in the pond, terrorising the geese. Another time, he lost several thousand on what ended up being not a dog race, as I thought, but a duck race. I didn't know you could place bets on those or in fact that they existed. It's not exactly a baller way to plunge your family further into debt. That was shortly before my mum reached the end of her tether and left.

All I'm saying is, there's precedent for me to be worried.

But my dad waves an airy hand. 'You don't know them.'

'I really don't think you should be seeing those guys from before,' I say, unable to stop myself, 'if they're who you're meeting.'

My dad gives me a look that says quite clearly, Thanks for the opinion I didn't ask for.

'I just think,' I protest, 'maybe it's not a good idea.'

'I won't be late,' he adds, as though I've not spoken. A classic tactic. 'But don't wait up. Night, love.'

He's gone before I can formulate something that has a hope in hell of him answering. Shit.

My mind flits again to the ashes in the fireplace. I've not seen any more suspicious letters, but it's only been a few days. Any bill-chasing institution would surely wait a week or two before they sent any more. But how can I monitor it? It's not like I can lie in wait for the postie.

I listen to the familiar sounds of my dad pottering round the bathroom, the tiny room next to mine: brushing his teeth, lifting the toilet seat with a clonk, failing to replace it, giving his hands a cursory rinse, clicking the soap dish against the basin. It's way too intimate. No one should be this clued up on their own father's nightly routine. Sometimes the desperation to be somewhere else, with privacy and peace and no responsibilities, is so strong it's an ache in my stomach.

Stifling the urge to flip onto my front and groan long and loud into the duvet, I wait until my dad's shut in his bedroom, then rejoin the call. 'Sorry,' I whisper. 'Just my dad.'

'How is he?' Miles asks.

'Fine,' I say. I don't think Miles is really interested. But nice that he made the effort. 'Where were we?'

'Talking about the gardener,' Chaz says, as though he's reading off the minutes sheet. Which, to be fair, he might be. 'You said "about that" when Miles mentioned it.'

But my suspicions about my dad and the reminder of both the threatening letter and my own living situation have solidified things. I just need to make it work. I can't give up on this yet, the one and only ticket to freedom I've ever been offered. And if it means grovelling and sucking up to Lily, the rudest person in the entire Felborough vicinity, then so be it. I can do whatever menial shitty tasks she wants to get her to trust me. Even if it means learning how to garden.

'Don't worry,' I say, confidently. 'We had a rocky start but

I just need a bit more time to get close to her. But it's going to be fine.'

Miles's voice breaks into a chocolatey smoothness. 'I knew she'd do it,' he says, as though talking only to Chaz. 'Didn't I say?'

'Hmm, what?' Chaz replies, obviously looking at something else on his screen. 'Er, yes. Phil can definitely do this. We all know that,' he adds, as though this is so obvious there's no point mentioning it. A typical Chaz compliment.

'We just need some basic details and then I can start hashing out the plan. So over to you, Phil,' Miles says. 'Our hopes are resting on you.'

We ring off, my mind buzzing with plans and desperation and a little tinge of gratification that Miles and Chaz, at least, believe in me. I may not be able to do much, I may not have achieved anything in my life at all so far, but I can do this one thing. If they think so, why can't I?

Chapter Eight

Despite my grandiose promises, the next week at Felborough flies by before I have a chance to grab it. The other volunteers are nice: a vivacious elderly woman named Ethel with lilac hair; a gangly teen called Taylor with about a hundred badges pinned to their regulation fleece; an unfeasibly gorgeous angel called Martina with a PhD in neuroscience. It would all be very enjoyable in other circumstances.

But no matter how much I rack my brains, I can't think how to convince Ms Lenson of the necessity of me being assigned to jobs with Lily. Everyone I meet simply confirms Benny and Diego's opinion: Lily is the apple of HG's eye. She's the one HG talks to and she's the one helping with the orchid.

This makes it all the more frustrating that so far I've utterly failed to get any closer to her. Since the unfortunate pumpkin patch incident, I've mostly seen her in the distance, hurrying past intent on a task. She's always wearing some fleece, T-shirt and boots combo, with her hair the only part of her appearance that changes: one thick blonde plait down her back or braided in a crown round her head. Once, space buns. But she's always striding with a sense of purpose I can't imagine experiencing for a job.

Even when not working, Lily might as well be walking around carrying warning signs that flash *fuck off* if you get too close. She sits alone at lunchtime, her dog lying at her feet. They leave as soon as she's finished. She didn't join the quiz night Diego organised at the pub nearby, even though loads of us went, and she gives a strong vibe of someone who knows stuff about things so would be an asset to any team.

In spare moments, I plot wild situations that would engineer emotional closeness. Could I fall in the lake when she's passing and pretend to drown? Could I fake-kidnap Eva-dog and then rescue her? Could I bribe another volunteer to do some aggressively bad gardening in her vicinity and loudly tell them off to prove to Lily how expert I now am?

No, I know. It's not convincing.

Meanwhile, my dad is still being odd. The night he went to meet up with his 'old pal' I lay awake waiting for him to get back. At about one-thirty, I woke to scratching at the door; the unmistakeable sound of someone trying and failing to quietly break into their own house. I waited a minute, willing him to succeed, until I couldn't handle it any more and went to let him in.

'Thanks, pet,' he said, not meeting my eye as he pushed past. I tried to ask about his night but he was having none of it, so I gave up and went back to bed. He's refused to discuss it since, other than saying it was a 'good catch-up'.

He's not been out like that in a long time, not since a few years ago when we heard his benefits were being cut after another awful disability assessment. We argued after I tried to convince him to appeal, although I wasn't even sure if he should; we'd appealed once before and the months of waiting, the bewildering admin and the relentless dehumanising questions nearly destroyed us both. Instead, in just one impressively destructive night, he got back in touch with his old gambling friends, went on a spree with them, added thousands to our debt and then, in a remorse-filled panic, cut up and flushed all his credit cards – which, alongside everything else, was an administrative and environmental nightmare.

At least that short, sharp spiral was better than a long drawn-out one. And, against my expectations, it didn't lead to further months or years of chaos. He seemed to get it together again. That time.

But just the memory is enough to fill my body with grinding tension and a need to act. A peek inside his wallet finds his one bank card is still there, intact. He asked me to hide the others once we'd replaced them after the flushing debacle, so at least they're safely out of reach. But when I log into his bank account, easier than it sounds given that all his passwords are just my name and birthday, I find he withdrew over a hundred pounds that evening. He's not a big drinker. There's no bar in this town fancy enough that you can spend a hundred quid and it be a chill, elegant night. You need quantity to make up that cost.

I'm used to spending time worrying about him. It's familiar, almost comforting. The difference is, I guess, that I have other things occupying my mind. The heist has stalled before it's begun and even if by some miracle I do manage to get the information we need, it still might never happen.

And then fate hands me a trump card.

'You're assigned to the woods today, Phil,' Ms Lenson tells me as the volunteers loiter in the kitchens that morning awaiting instructions. It's a sunny spring day, the first properly warm weather we've had this year, hinting at golden summer days to come. Or so we hope.

'The woods?' I repeat. I'm sitting by the window, my face turned towards it to bask in the sunshine, T-shirt sleeves rolled up to the shoulder. It's almost soothing. I can't remember the last time I felt soothed.

'The woods,' she taps her clipboard with a Felborough-branded pen. 'By the lake. One of the senior gardeners has something they want help with.'

'Which senior gardener?' I ask, in a tone as casual as I can manage, sitting up straight.

Ms Lenson, who's already turned to the next person on her list, looks back vaguely. 'I'm not sure Ms Gyamfi said.'

'It'll be a nice surprise when you get there,' Ethel says bracingly. 'Hope it's that Anthony.'

'Hope not,' I say, laughing. 'He's too strong and silent, it's unsettling.'

Anthony, my ticket into Felborough after unknowingly acting as my nepotism connection, has so far only crossed my path once. He approached while I was cleaning the cafe windows and asked me where Ms Lenson was so quietly that I had to ask him to repeat it three times. It's been easy to avoid him otherwise, especially now I've learnt he's like a spider – more scared of me than I am of him.

'He's a snack,' Ethel states, her fluffy lilac hair bobbing as she leans in to confide in me. 'My granddaughter taught me that word. Have you seen that boy's guns?' She whistles. 'He could throw me around no trouble.'

'Shoot your shot, Ethel,' I say, as Ms Lenson finishes today's orders and motions us to get moving.

I walk down the path through the fancy flowerbeds, past the fountain, and skirt the rose garden to head towards the lake. Everything's glowing luscious and green and it's surprisingly nice working here. But I can't forget my goal. Which is why when I approach my destination to see Lily's familiar figure standing very upright, looking out at the lake, my heart skips a beat, then starts to thud.

Here we go. Today's the day: it's got to be.

She turns as I stride towards her through the grasses. This part of the grounds hasn't been mown for months; the morning dew dampens my trouser legs to the knee. The lake lies in the morning air, glassy smooth, fluffy white clouds reflected in its surface. A duck striking out into the middle leaves a trail of ripples that fan out behind, widening until they reach the bank.

'There you are,' is Lily's greeting. Eva twitches her tail.

'Morning,' I say brightly. 'Such a nice day, isn't it?'

She regards me with suspicion, as though I'm trying to trick her. Then she says, begrudgingly, 'Yeah.'

I tuck my hands into my pockets as I come to a halt. 'What's the plan, chief?'

'Come with me.' Lily spins on her heel. Eva and I trot after her as she heads round the lake and follows the path into the woods.

Lily might not be in a chatty mood. But she and I need to actually talk today, so, at the risk of getting things off to a bad start by reminding her of my total incompetence, I ask after a minute or so of quietly tramping through the trees, 'So . . . what are we doing here?'

Lily flips her plait over her shoulder. 'We're going to the perimeter. We need to make sure the fences are secure. And start to break in the paths again as no one's been this way since winter. And pick up litter.' She points at a cigarette butt. 'That's one for you.'

'Oh cool, thanks,' I say, walking over. I look back. 'I'll just fill my pockets, will I?'

She pulls a bin bag out of her trouser pocket. 'Or you could use this.'

We wander along. The deeper we get into the woods, the more we have to fight the nature that's crept across the path. Lily goes first, whacking at it with a stick she's picked up. I'd quite like one too but all the options I can see are either way too small or stupidly massive. I'm glad I wore combat boots today, despite the heat. My feet would be soaked by the dew otherwise.

'So, how's your day going?' I ask, after another few minutes of silence.

'Magnificent, thanks,' she replies.

'Mine's good too,' I say, once it's clear she's not going to ask. 'If you were wondering.'

'I wasn't.'

So she's still thinking about the weeding incident. Fine.

Eventually, we reach what must be the perimeter: a towering hedge lining one side of the path. We follow it round to the right, still not talking.

Eva trots ahead, sniffing the hedge. Sometimes she stands stock-still, staring intently, before Lily clicks at her to come. Lily runs her hand along the leaves, occasionally snipping with her shears. I pick up the odd bit of litter and stuff it in the bag while I rack my brains about an opening gambit that won't enrage her further.

The hedge is prickly and dark green, almost Christmas-tree-like, and off-puttingly thick. It grows around a sturdy fence that must have been built before the hedge was planted. It's an effective barrier. To break in, you'd need to cut your way through the hedge before being confronted with the fence, which seems to be laced with barbed wire. This is useful intel, to be fair.

I make a note to tell Chaz and Miles. We'd struggle to make our escape with the orchid this way. But first, to keep trying with Lily.

'I can help with,' I make a snipping motion at the hedge, 'the trimming. If you want.'

'Have you got shears?' she asks, turning to look at me. Her expression isn't even annoyed now, just bored.

I wave my hands at her. 'Just the ones God gave me.'

She frowns, wiping away any trace of a smile before I can be sure it was there. 'I didn't peg you for a religious sort.'

I sidestep the urge to reply 'you pegged correctly' and instead say, 'No, you were right first time.' After a moment's passed, I ask, 'Are you a religious sort?'

It's quite hard to judge what's an appropriate conversation topic with Lily. She's so prickly it's as though all my chatty attempts are barbs she deflects without difficulty. I doubt she'll answer this, which is partly why I ask. But to my surprise, she responds after a moment, 'No, not really.'

Before I can probe, a rustling starts up in the hedge further along. We walk towards it, Lily going first with her hand out behind to indicate that I should keep quiet. I could probably have worked this out for myself. As we approach, the movement, which started gentle, ramps up to a wild thrashing.

'Fuck,' Lily says, apparently involuntarily, coming to a sudden halt.

'What?' I peer around her. There's a gap in the bottom of the hedge which Lily, now in a crouch, is edging towards. I bend down too and try to see.

Inside – the thrashing coming to a frenzy now – is the biggest rabbit I've ever seen. Its eyes are wild, its fur matted, and it's hooked on a bit of barbed wire that's come undone and curled into a tangle on the ground.

'Oh God,' Lily says. 'Shit. The poor thing.'

'OK,' I say, for want of something more helpful. We clearly need to free the little guy. But going closer might scare it even more.

Lily's stooped in a crouch nearby, seemingly torn between wanting to reach out to soothe it and staying away.

'Right. OK,' I repeat, as if by speaking random words I'll keep a semblance of control. Then, when Lily doesn't respond, I prompt, 'What shall we do?'

'I'm not sure,' she says, wringing her hands in a desperate movement.

'This is your ballpark,' I remind her. She might be about to panic, which wouldn't help anyone. 'I'm sure you know what you're doing.'

Lily rounds on me from her crouched position. 'I'm a gardener, not a vet!'

'It's all nature, isn't it?' I exclaim.

'It's all na—' she repeats, as if this is the stupidest thing she's ever heard. 'Did you grow up in some metropolitan nightmare, like a World War Two evacuee?' she hisses. 'Have you ever seen an animal before?'

'I grew up just down the road actually,' I tell her. This is good; the panic has been replaced by irritation. 'A suburban nightmare. I've seen an animal *and* most of my formative experiences took place in this town's one nightclub.'

Her eyes flare wide. 'Wait, really?'

'Yes?' I say, my voice turning up at the end. I don't know why this would be interesting.

We're both distracted by the sudden absence of sound. The animal's frozen into stillness.

'Eva, *no*,' Lily snaps, as the little dog comes trotting down the path, looking interested. 'Grab her!' she tells me and I obey without thinking, scooping up the dog.

'I think you can free it,' I say to Lily, absently patting Eva. She's hairy and surprisingly sturdy, like a warm brick wearing a fur coat. A comforting weight. 'Rabbits are stronger than you think. It looks like it's just caught in one place, so you could unhook that bit of wire.'

'Do you think?' She shuffles forward. After a moment, I hear her crooning nonsense under her breath. 'Hey, it's OK, I'm coming to help you. Yes, I know, it's scary. I know.'

Her movements are calm and smooth. The rabbit lies there, pinning her with one huge dark eye. But it stays still. I hold my breath as Lily gently, slowly, reaches forward and takes hold of the leg that's caught.

'There we are, there we are,' she soothes. It kicks once, then lets her guide the leg around. 'It's a bit stuck,' she murmurs, I think to me. 'And it's not a rabbit. It's a hare.'

Oh. That'll be why it's so huge. 'Either way,' I say, 'you've got this. It trusts you now, look.'

The hare isn't freaking out any more; it's just waiting in poised, strung stillness. Lily carefully lifts the wire and curls it away, leaving a gap in the fence. 'Nearly there,' she says, 'nearly . . .'

In a move so sudden it makes me jump and Lily let out a small yelp, the hare is off, streaking through the hedge to the other side and freedom. Lily sits on the ground and looks up at me. The façade of toughness is missing and vulnerability is writ large in the relief on her face.

'Yikes,' she says.

A small laugh escapes me. 'Pretty much,' I agree, plopping Eva down as she struggles in my arms. She trots over to Lily, who scratches her beardy chin. 'That was good,' I say, because it was and she might need to hear it. 'You did great. Very nurturing.'

She laughs.

'Really,' I protest. 'The hare was vibing with you. You could see it.'

Lily shakes her head. 'I'm only laughing because "nurturing" is a new one. My ex once accused me of being unable to feel human emotion.'

'Are you serious?' I exclaim, partly in surprise at the sentiment, mostly because I can't believe she's actually volunteered this information. She must be more shaken up than I realised.

She nods. 'Not a great guy, as it turns out.'

'No shit,' I say, before I can stop myself. But Lily smiles slightly.

I reach out a hand to help her up and after a moment's hesitation she takes it, gripping my wrist. I pull her to her feet and we stand face to face for a split second before she steps past. Her eyes are a clear grey. I hadn't realised before.

The Great Orchid Heist

'Anyway,' she says, picking up her stick, 'we've found at least one place where the hedge needs repairing.'

I poke at the damaged area. 'It kind of looks like the barbed wire's been cut.'

'Might just have rusted. But it's still something to report to HG.' Lily frowns, a little wrinkle appearing between her eyebrows. 'We do sometimes get people trying to break in. But not often. We need to be on top of security for the orchid. That's why we have this inspection team coming in.'

'Inspection team?' I ask, not making any sudden movements. This is the longest speech I've ever heard her make.

The wrinkle deepens as she pokes at the wire. 'They visit every week to make sure the orchid is safe, check the conditions, the security. HG hates them. She knows how to do her job.'

Lily straightens, then gives me a surprised look and shuts her mouth abruptly.

We continue round the perimeter: Lily snipping at the hedge and me picking up litter. We don't talk much, despite a couple of attempts by me. But that was definitely progress.

When Lily makes me go in front to give her a rest, I mention that it would be good to have a stick to slash at the overgrown path. She finds me one and I whack away, feeling as though we might be getting somewhere.

87

Chapter Nine

That afternoon, I'm assigned to work in Felborough Hall. The majority of the building is permanently closed to the public; most of it is the research centre, filled night and day with clever-looking scientists. But they need more office space, so the current renovations involve finally opening up the section of the Hall that used to belong to the family and clearing it out.

The task, Ms Lenson explains in her lunchtime briefing, is to sort through the remaining items from the family which have been languishing in a couple of huge attics for the last forty or so years. Felborough will put them on temporary display for the grand reopening, to give everyone a chance to pay their respects – or place their bids. Then they'll get rid of them by donating to museums and such or selling to the highest bidder.

I reckon this could go one of two ways, as Ethel and I pant up the twelfth flight of stairs and pause to catch our breath. Either the attics are filled with valuable, fascinating artefacts, unseen and unloved for decades, which we'll have the privilege of bringing to light. Or everything in them is worthless, flea-ridden and probably quite stinky junk.

Only time will tell. So Ethel and I, along with the dozen or so other volunteers assigned to the task, gird our loins and get stuck in. The first step is to sort through the piles of endless stuff in the attics.

The word 'attic' doesn't really do them justice; the low, sloped-ceiling rooms stretch the full length and width of the Hall. Whenever I catch a glimpse out the small, panelled windows of Felborough's grounds unspooling into the distance, the soles of my feet tingle with vertigo. I'm not exactly scared of heights. But the floorboards don't feel like they've been redone for at least a few centuries and they're bowing under the weight of the stacks of furniture and boxes that were shoved in here when the Hall was given to science.

We start at one end and burrow inroads into the pile, handing things out to each other. Ms Lenson and a few senior volunteers are on hand to guide us with cataloguing and decision-making – toss or keep. Some things are obviously to be tossed: a pile of mouldy cushions, a bench with a hole in it, a wodge of highly suspect insulation padding that we're not allowed to go near. Others are less certain: piles of artwork stacked against an upright piano, velvety drapes that *might* fit the windows of the display room downstairs, a set of blue and white crockery in pristine condition.

Chaz couldn't have predicted this when he was trying to sell me on the heist, but it's what he'd have meant about me 'loving historical shit'. Trawling through dusty old artefacts, sifting the interesting from the mundane: it makes you feel like an investigator. It's good to remember this when you're confronted yet again with what was once a rats' nest. The air does not taste fresh up here, to put it delicately.

'I've been dead keen to see inside this for years,' Ethel tells me, as we make our way through piles of old rugs, each one approximately the weight of my car. She's volunteered at Felborough ever since retiring from her job as a terrifying primary school headteacher. 'We hardly get to see inside the Hall. It has Cluedo rooms, you know.'

I'm entertaining myself with a fantasy of how I'd use this attic space, if it were mine, so this takes a moment to sink in. When it does, I frown. 'What do you mean, Cluedo rooms?'

'Ms Lenson knows more than I do.' Ethel gives a mischievous grin to someone behind me and I whip my head round, suppressing my guilty urge to deny all interest. This is a normal question. No one's going to arrest me.

Ms Lenson, who's strolled up to check on our progress, smiles with loving condescension. 'That's just what the volunteers named them. When they were renovating the Hall in the sixties to turn it into a lab, they found several secret rooms that weren't on any maps.'

'No way,' I say. Not on any *maps*? Oh my God. Cluedo rooms!

She nods. 'The family who lived here were a bit eccentric.'

I love it when people describe unhinged behaviour as eccentric. 'What happened to the rooms?'

Ms Lenson scratches her head with a biro. 'They turned a couple into cupboards and so forth. But they weren't sure they found all of them. No one in the family was very forthcoming. They hinted of at least one more that no one had discovered yet. But, as you can imagine, it wasn't a priority for the Research Centre.'

'Very fun,' I comment lightly. 'Very murder-mystery.'

'Isn't it just?' Ethel says eagerly. 'Just the other day, I was playing an escape room with the girls in my Crime and Smut-tishment book club and we were saying how all books should have at least one secret passage. Of one kind or another.' She tips an exaggerated, unnecessary wink, in case any of us missed her double meaning.

I nod, barely listening. Where would you hide a Cluedo room? Definitely the library. That's a classic. Or the billiards room. But damn it – there is no billiards room any more. It'll just be, like, the propagation room. Or the DNA room. Or whatever.

Either way, I'll find it.

As I walk to the car park that evening, a little dog trots along from an adjoining path. Sure enough, a moment later Lily appears. She must be heading home too.

'Hi,' I say. This is an unexpected bonus.

She nods and we fall into step. I'm about to ask how her day was, in case the last time I asked after her day and she shut me down was an anomaly, when she speaks.

'So ... you know Elements then?' she asks, her eyebrow twitching upwards.

I gape at her.

'What?' She tugs at her plait. 'It's just, you mentioned ...'

'No, that's right,' I say, absurdly pleased that she's bringing up an offhand comment I made. She was paying attention. 'You know it too? My condolences.'

Elements is – or was – the town's one club. It was exactly the type you'd expect of a place like this: small, dank, sold three Jägerbombs for a fiver. None of the toilets had doors, let alone seats, and one year the actual ceiling fell down, but no one was injured so it was generally agreed to be fine. It got closed a number of times for boring reasons relating to 'the law' and 'violating every single health and hygiene regulation' or some such. But it kept bouncing back until it finally bit the dust a couple of years ago.

'I spent every weekend there the year I turned eighteen,' she says. We regard each other for a moment.

'How old are you?' I ask at the same time as she says, 'What year were you born?'

'Same question but yours requires maths,' I say. 'I'm twenty-seven.'

'Me too.'

'Huh.' I guess this isn't such a weird coincidence. But a lot of the workers come from further away, specifically for Felborough. I assumed that's what Lily did, given what Benny said about her wanting to be head gardener. 'Maybe we bumped into each other at some point,' I muse.

'I doubt you'd remember. I'm not very distinctive.' She tugs at her plait again, an unconscious action.

I snort. 'You're kidding, right?'

'What?' She looks genuinely surprised.

I roll my eyes and decide to take the bait. I hold out my spare hand and count off on my fingers. 'You have hair like a Disney princess and biceps that could crush a man's ego without even trying. I've seen you chopping wood.' Only from a distance, but the force and speed with which she wielded the axe was memorable. I've thought about it several times since. 'And you're scary enough that everyone in your vicinity is terrified of you. That's pretty distinctive.'

Lily glares at me for a moment. Then, 'Shut up,' she says. 'I'm not scary.'

I shrug. 'Sorry. Too far?'

She gives me a sidelong glance. 'I can't believe you think I am.'

'I didn't say *I* did. I don't, actually.' I realise as I say it that this is true. 'It's just something I've noticed about your general vibe. And how you interact with people.'

'People are just annoying,' she huffs, kicking at a stone on the ground. 'I haven't got time to be all fluffy and nice.'

'Hey,' I say, trying to hide my amusement at the sulky turn this has taken. 'I'd never tell you to be fluffy. Do I look like a fluffy person? What about this haircut and outfit screams fluffy to you?'

Lily looks up at me, her gaze landing on my hair and then, for some reason, skittering away from where my T-shirt sleeves are still rolled up, revealing my tattoos: a pirate ship in full sail on my upper arm, a mermaid wearing a cowboy hat, a stylised sun. 'I'm *not* scary,' she insists again.

'Anyway,' I say brightly, realising things might have veered dangerously close to being too unprofessional to claw back. 'I should be going.' I jingle my car keys. I've offended her. I knew it would be too much; I shouldn't have said anything.

'Thanks for noticing my biceps, anyway,' she says a few seconds later, as we walk towards the car park. Her tone is so dry, so normal, that it takes me a second to realise what she's said. 'We should arm wrestle sometime.'

I'm surprised into a laugh. *Now* who's being unprofessional? 'Not until I've done a lot more manual labour,' I reply. 'My ego's too fragile to let you near it at the moment.'

'I'm sure your ego will be fine.'

Something makes me want to push it further. This side to her is unexpected and intriguing. 'OK, if you're willing to risk it,' I say. 'We'll put it in the calendar. Arm wrestling: you and me.'

'I'll pencil it in,' she nods.

'Great.'

When I sneak a glance, her lips are twitching, one side curving as though she's fighting a smile. I want to make her laugh, a proper belly laugh. She seems like she hasn't done that in a while.

'Anyway, good job on the hare rescue today,' I say, as we part. 'We make a good team.'

'Hmm,' she replies, but her eyes are smiling even if her mouth isn't. 'Have a good evening.'

And she stalks away, Eva at her heels.

It takes me almost the entire drive home to identify the strange feeling in my body. I hum along to the radio as I drive, my arm resting on the open window in the sunshine. I explored an attic full of weird old shit. I got a little closer to Lily. We rescued a hare. Also I *saw* a hare for the first time. All this nature is on our doorstep and I had no idea.

As I park and stretch out my shoulders, I realise the feeling is satisfaction. I had an interesting day at work. It's not usual for me to have that, but today I did. It crosses my mind how nice it would be to work at Felborough properly, without ulterior motive (and plus salary). Just helping out, learning about its history, getting to know people. I could see it for myself.

Maybe, if we called off this whole ridiculous plan, I could get a weekend job there. I wouldn't have to keep seeing Miles, who's so sure of himself that it makes me nervous. Lily might warm up to me. I wouldn't have to risk orchid jail.

I chew my lip as I nudge the front door open and step inside to a quiet house. All my worries thud back into place, dispelling the fantasy in a moment. No one's here. I'm already panicking that my dad's out somewhere odd again without letting me know, and then telling myself off because of course he is allowed to leave the house without my permission, when I discover on hurrying to the kitchen that the back door's open. He's in our postage stamp of a garden, sitting on one of the kitchen chairs facing away from the house.

It's a little jarring going from Felborough to this: a patch of scrubby grass surrounded on all sides by a ramshackle wooden fence. A quarter of the space is taken up by an old shed that was here when we moved in and that we've never used, due to the sheer quantity of miscellaneous shit in there. In my mind, if we open it, thousands of spiders will pour out. Which would be neither pleasant nor relaxing.

Anyway. It's nice to see my dad enjoying the sunshine. I'm always telling him he should get outside more.

'No, but just listen a moment,' he says, tapping his fingers on his knee. He's on the phone. 'You say it's fine but that's not what I'm seeing.'

Torn between wanting to let him know I'm here and wanting to know who he's talking to, I hesitate, looking down at the kitchen table. And there, in literal black and white, is a letter.

It's the same font that was on the scraps of burnt paper. Before I consciously decide anything, I'm scanning the letter at the frantic speed I've learnt over the years of reading things not intended for me.

Further advance received several months ago ... Fourth repayment now missed ... Call us at your earliest convenience ... House may be repossessed ...

I grip the back of a kitchen chair, my knuckles stark white. Blood rushes in my ears.

My dad is still out there in the garden, face in the sunshine. How has he kept this hidden?

I know what a *further advance* is, from my private Googling late at night when sleep is held at bay by the nagging worries. It's like remortgaging; you take out more money against your house. But where's the extra cash, if that's what he's done? Not in his usual bank accounts. I'd have seen a transaction like that.

House may be repossessed flashes before my eyes again. I try to go back, reread the letter, but my vision is blurring and it makes no more sense than before. If you don't keep up the repayments, they can take back your house. The one thing we had that was safe. Gone.

'OK.' My dad's voice comes from the garden. 'So I just wait and see then?' A pause. 'Right. You'd better not be wrong about this. I need that money.'

I stand frozen, my mind racing. I don't know what to do. Whenever I try to force him to face up to things, he goes all silent and stubborn. 'I am your *father*,' he said, one memorable time when I was trying to get him to admit how much he'd lost. As if that was relevant; as if that meant he had it all under control.

Outside, my dad is off the phone. He sits for a moment, looking out at the one bit of green visible to us – a horse chestnut tree at the end of the garden. Even I can recognise a horse chestnut. It drops conkers over our wall every year. For now it's in full glorious bloom, holding its white candles aloft like hundreds of chandeliers.

There's a strange moment of unnatural calm as my dad stares up into its branches and I watch, wondering if by some telepathy he'll know I'm here, and turn, and come inside and tell me it's all going to be fine. And have it be true.

I release my grip on the chair. But then my dad does turn. He raises a hand.

'Hi, love,' he calls. He eases himself up and wanders inside. I back away from the table so I'm standing in the doorway. 'Good day?' he asks.

I nod, speechless. His eye flits to the letter. He knows I've seen it. And I know he knows.

I could ask him; I could try and make him talk. But I don't need to see the future to know how it will spool out. He'll feign misunderstanding. Then he'll walk away. I'll follow and say we have to talk, he could let me help. He'll say it's under control. He's the grown-up in the room. I'll get upset about how much I want that to be true. He'll get upset for the same reason. He won't tell me anything else and he'll leave and maybe he'll turn to his favourite crutch and things will just get worse.

Or instead, I can shove it deep, far down where the feelings can't hurt anyone. And I can focus on the one thing I can control: our escape route. Via one very small, very secret orchid.

I clear my throat. 'Yeah, it was good thanks. Yours?'

His grateful look is like someone on the deck of a ship as it starts to go up in flames. They hold out a hand to you and, side by side, you watch the fire start to lick up the mast and smoulder at the sails. It's just the two of you, no lifeboats in sight. You can't abandon each other now. So you stand there and you grit your teeth, and you watch as the ship breaks apart.

'I thought we could get a Chinese for tea?' He goes to the fridge and looks inside.

'That would be nice.' I clear my throat again; it seems to have thickened a little. My heart is fluttering fast. 'I'll be back in a bit. Just going upstairs.'

In my room, my hands find my phone. Miles and Chaz, both chronically online, reply quickly. I tell them I've made contact with Lily and I think I can get the information we need. I have some stuff to tell them.

We'll meet tomorrow evening.

I know I can do this.

Chapter Ten

We're sitting in a semicircle in the living room of Chaz's flat, which is a funny mix of cosy and careless. Half of it is pale yellow walls, colourful cushions and his collection of jigsaws. The other half is a godforsaken cave of an office, all blinking screens and blackout curtains. Chaz divides his time roughly evenly between the two atmospheres.

Chaz suggested meeting here in case it started looking suspicious that we were always going to Miles's. I was happy with the idea, not least because Chaz has two older sisters, Ravi and Nevindie, who I've not seen for a while. They often drop in to take the piss out of his lifestyle and fill his freezer with Tupperwares of home-cooked curries and sweet treats from their mum, who (rightly) believes Chaz incapable of taking any interest in feeding himself regular meals. It's always funny to watch Chaz revert to his teenage self around them.

'So,' Chaz claps his hands, 'I've got an agenda.' He presses a button on his laptop. A second later a bullet-point list is beamed onto the wall, presumably in lieu of the corkboard which is still at Miles's flat.

'This is organised,' I comment. 'Got sick of the notebook and pen, did you?'

Sliding a hand into my trouser pocket earlier, I was confronted with a scrunched-up piece of paper which, when I unwrapped it, revealed itself as the stupid three-item heist list Chaz made. We're still on item two, THE PLAN, so that's about as useful as predicted. I re-scrunched it and shoved it back into the pocket of my Felborough fleece, which I found abandoned in the storage room the other day and adopted.

'If a thing's worth doing,' Chaz says, with dignity, 'it's worth doing in the way you find most fun.'

'I don't think that's the saying.'

He motions at the list. Item one is, *Update on Felborough personnel*. 'This one's yours, Phil. Take it away.'

'Right,' I say, taking a deep breath. 'So the good news is we have our target. As in' – this is all a bit dramatic – 'I know who I need to get close to. Things are very secretive, like I said, but this person knows all about the orchid security, or as much as anyone does other than the head gardener, and they're well in there with HG. Like, they have special dispensation for their dog to come to work, even though no one else is allowed. And they know a lot about plants,' I add.

'What's their name? And do they use they/them pronouns?' Chaz asks, typing notes as I speak.

'Er,' I say. I hadn't realised I'd been doing that. 'No. They don't. She doesn't. She/her, as far as I know.'

'And her name?' he prompts.

'Right, yes.' I clear my throat. The thought of Lily innocently working at Felborough with no idea what's coming gives me an uncomfortable feeling around my ribs.

But it's not like telling Chaz and Miles her name will make any difference; it's not more of a betrayal than anything else I'm planning. And anyway we've just had one nice conversation, that's all. I don't owe her anything.

'Lily.' I force the word out.

'Right.' Chaz looks over at Miles. 'Promising start. Miles?'

'Absolutely. Terrific work, Phil.' A slight quirk of his mouth hints at a smile just for me.

I look away, clearing my throat again, more forcefully this time. I need to get over this praise kink or it's going to embarrass me.

'So next you get this Lily to show you the orchid?' Chaz goes on, all business.

'I guess,' I say, thinking it through as I speak. 'None of the volunteers and no junior gardeners have seen it, so it's got to be her.'

'Do you think you'll manage?' Chaz asks. 'Because item two,' he gestures, circling with his mouse pointer, 'is orchid care. And it's a much shorter item than we'd hope.'

'You couldn't find anything either?' I ask, trying to hide my smugness. It's obviously not ideal, but I did tell him.

'It's not that I couldn't find *anything*,' he fires back. 'I found lots of stuff.' He brings up some images. 'Here are some pictures of orchids.'

I lean closer, resting my elbows on my knees. There's a huge amount of variation. Different colours, shapes. Some of them seem to be growing right out of trees; others are actually underground.

'What are we looking at?' Miles asks, frowning. 'Are any of these the Splendid Paradise Orchid?'

'These are just some ideas of what it could look like,' Chaz says, haughtily. Bless him. He hates to admit he doesn't know something. 'What we know is, the Splendid Paradise Orchid was discovered in Colombia recently by someone called Richard Hook. He seems to go by Hook though, as a mononym. Like Cher.'

'Not a lot like Cher,' I say, as Chaz pulls up a photo of a guy with a handlebar moustache and an oiled hairdo, who's literally holding a pipe. He looks like a man out of time. Pop him in baggy trousers and make the photo sepia and he could be a colonial-era explorer. How are these people still in existence?

'He brought the orchid to Felborough because of his links with the place. He was briefly head gardener there before he went travelling.'

Miles leans closer to the image. Maybe he's imagining what he'd look like with that kind of moustache. It would probably suit him.

'He looks a bit like you, Miles,' Chaz comments, looking down at his notes.

'No he doesn't,' Miles says, stiffening. 'And what kind

of fool name is Hook anyway? He's not a children's book character.'

Chaz and I exchange an amused and slightly alarmed glance. That was out of nowhere.

Miles, intercepting it, adds quickly, 'I bet that's not his real name. He probably changed it to try and be all . . . stylish.'

There's a pause. For some reason, I find myself filling the silence by saying, 'Chaz's real name is Chathura. He rebranded in primary school. To be more stylish.'

Chaz is frowning slightly. 'Do you know this guy, Miles?'

'How could I possibly know him?' Miles laughs. 'I don't hang around with dinosaurs. Or gardeners.'

'Right,' Chaz says, giving his head a little shake. 'Anyway. You also rebranded in primary school, *Philippa*, so you're one to talk. The point is, that's all we know about Hook. But I can look into him and his probably devious past, if it would help.'

'I doubt it,' Miles says. He sits back against the couch, which is incongruously decorated with a pink and yellow crochet blanket that Chaz's sister made a few years ago in a crafting phase. 'We need to focus on the now. What do we know about the orchid?'

'What we know is that . . . we don't know what it looks like.' Chaz clicks and the images merge to become just one: the line drawing on Felborough's posters for the reopening. 'Or what kind of care it needs. Phil confirmed it's kept in the glasshouse but that's basically all the information we have.'

'They're so bloody secretive,' I exclaim. 'It's just a normal flower. Just an innocent flower.'

'Honestly, I'd be surprised if we were the only ones interested in heisting it,' Chaz says. 'It's a delectable prize.'

'You've got such a way with words,' I tell him. 'Like a tacky supervillain.'

'I'm allowed to enjoy language,' he says with dignity, 'you *Phil*istine,' he adds, ruining the effect by sniggering. 'Anyway, if we move to item three.' He clicks and the slide changes again to show: *Item Three: Now What?* 'Let's discuss next steps.'

'Great.' Miles taps at the crochet blanket. 'We basically need to know three main things: how to get to the orchid; what to do with it when we get it; and what to do with it after we get it.'

That does make it sound nice and simple. But I'm getting sick of these three-item lists that wildly understate how difficult everything is.

'Neither of you need to worry too much about the third part.' Miles assumes a sombre, assertive expression. 'I'll take care of that. As you know, I have a buyer lined up. I'm ironing out the details with him. Transport and so on.'

Chaz and I exchange glances. Miles has said this before. But even now, having committed to this heist, it still feels intangible and paper-thin, as though a slight gust of air could disperse the entire operation.

'Are you sure, Miles?' I press. 'And it's definitely worth what you said?' The letter about the repayments spooked me badly. Plus, this volunteering has meant my income has taken a huge, terrifying hit. I've been working a few evenings but, as luck would have it, a rota fuck-up at the cinema means I'm on hardly any lates for this month and without me earning, our bills don't get covered. My dad's benefits barely cover the interest on his debts, not that he's technically 'allowed' to use them for that, let alone anything we actually need to live. So, you know. I need to be sure.

'Phil, don't you trust me?' Miles says, spreading his hands.

'I don't really know you,' I point out, softening this with a shrug. Even if I do like how you talk to me.

Stop it. Not now.

Miles folds his arms, looking slightly put out. 'I have a buyer, OK? For the amount we said. It's not like I can get him to sign a contract, but he's not backing out. He's got the money and he wants the orchid. You have my word. And we may not have many things in this life but we do have that.'

'Fine.' I shake my head. People like Miles think 'their word' means everything. So I have to believe *he* believes it'll be fine.

'So,' Miles continues, waving a hand as though to dispel the negative atmosphere, 'Phil, you're working on getting to the orchid and Chaz will help.'

'Should be easy enough getting inside Felborough's network.' Chaz hauls himself up to sit cross-legged on his seat. 'I've not managed to hack the main system yet, but it's old as fuck. I've already made some moves to get in.'

'Oh, about that,' I say. 'They have people coming in to do weekly checks at the moment. To make sure everything's secure with the orchid. So . . .' I trail off. 'It might not be as easy as we think.'

'Good to know. But don't worry,' Miles adds. 'These big

old institutions have to be dragged kicking and screaming into the twenty-first century. It'll be fine.'

My mind flits to Ms Lenson, working away at a careful list on her clipboard, avoiding technology at all costs, and Ethel dutifully memorising the new office security code by writing it on her own arm. Miles could be right.

'We'll keep an eye on it. But the glasshouses' security and what to do with the orchid when we get it are down to you, Phil,' Miles says.

'Plus,' Chaz adds, giving me a pointed look, 'we need to keep the orchid alive long enough to flog it.'

'I don't know why you're glaring,' I say. 'I know.'

'It's just,' he smirks, pretending to look worried, 'your capacity for plant murder precedes you. It's a big responsibility and you don't always pay attention, you know?'

I'm briefly taken straight back to a group project with Chaz in school. We had to make a poster about a historical event; our group was assigned the Spanish Armada. Chaz made us spend so much time planning and critiquing that the rest of us were driven nearly mad with impatience. Chaz wouldn't let me write anything on the poster in pen, as he said I'd ruin it with my lack of attention to detail. So, behind his back, I illustrated the poster with big, colourful felt-tip ships and wrote *Chaz is a dick* in very tiny writing on every one of the masts. On the deadline, we handed it in and then didn't speak for several days.

I roll my eyes at the memory and at Chaz's comment. 'Yeah, well, I'll probably try a little bit harder not to murder the plant if thousands of pounds are at stake, won't I? Anyway,'

I say, bracing my hands on my knees, 'I should get going. But I think I'll focus on figuring out the location. We still need a map and I haven't even seen the glasshouses yet. They've been shut to everyone except senior gardeners. So that'll be my next move. OK?'

'You need to case the joint,' Chaz says, nodding furiously. I get the impression he's been brushing up on heist films with the express purpose of picking up vocab.

'Sure, if you want,' I say.

'Sounds good.' Miles gives me a warm smile. It does a little to ease the knot of tension in my stomach and my sudden irritation with Chaz, but not much.

'Great.' I stand up to leave.

'Want to go for a drink?' Miles asks as I pull my jacket on in the hall.

'Er,' I say, kicking my feet into my boots. 'With Chaz?'

'Just us,' he says. He looks down at me, dwarfing me with his height. He raises an eyebrow in a question. I look back at him, considering.

It's been a while for me but I don't normally go for Miles's type. Men, for a start. But also ... his vibe reminds me of people I met in my brief stint at university: the smooth talkers, arrogant thinkers. I know on some level, even if not consciously, he believes he's better than me – an uneducated woman with a dead-end job and an addict father.

And yet, something about him is compelling. Maybe it really is just his confidence. *Back yourself* is the subtext to every statement. And because he believes it so strongly, you find yourself starting to go along with it too. Maybe I should be more like that.

I open my mouth to reply, wondering what I'll end up saying. 'Ah, no it's OK,' is what comes out in the end. 'It's getting late. I should get home to my dad.'

'You sure?' he asks.

'Yeah.' It's not worth jeopardising the heist. And I'd hate to confirm my hunch about what he's like in bed.

'Another time, then.' He holds my gaze.

'Definitely,' I reply, looking away.

Chapter Eleven

Over the next week, Ms Lenson assigns me to at least a morning or afternoon in the Hall every day. This frustratingly reduces my chances of a Lily encounter. But, as Miles points out, it's still an opportunity. I'm not just helping with the endless cleaning needed before the Hall can be reopened to visitors. I'm *casing the joint*.

So I swallow my impatience and take up my disinfectant supplies. I soon learn the place is large enough that, despite the scientists in their labs and the hordes of volunteers rushing about, I can go minutes at a time without crossing paths with anyone. As I work, I keep an eye out for any intel that could help. You never know what might come in handy.

I've not given up hope of finding a secret room, either. On my way down from the attic to empty the hoover one day, I duck into the library. So far, I've felt my way round the crevices of every toilet, empty lab and – in one nerve-racking experience – a cupboard under the stairs that turned out to be so full of boxes of glassware labelled FRAGILE that my hasty retreat almost caused an explosion of smashing.

But my heart says if it's anywhere it'll be the library. It's one of the few rooms that kept its purpose in the original refurbishment. Disappointingly unlike the leather-bound books that line Ms Lenson's office, this library is more technical. It's filled with files, papers and stacks of shelves, the originals built into the walls plus dozens of extra stacks and filing cabinets arranged in a maze, making it almost impossible to get from one side of the room to the other.

A large sepia photo on the wall by the door shows what the room used to look like. There was once a huge wooden desk at the end opposite the fireplace, with a sprawling family tree tapestry behind, and walls and walls of ancient books. That's more like it.

I press along the varnished-wood built-in shelves feeling for a button, a lever, anything out of the ordinary. But everything is smooth, well cared for, unyielding.

A quiet throat-clearing makes me whip around. HG is standing in the doorway. I don't know how long she's been there. She just looks at me.

'Hi,' I blurt. 'I was just . . . having a look.'

'A keen reader, are you?' she asks, her voice giving nothing away.

Several options thunder past. I could try to style it out, say I'm after some light reading. But she'll see right through me; surely it's obvious I have no idea what these books are about. I could say someone sent me to look for something. But then if she asks, I'll have to come up with a name and a person, which is doable but too easy to verify. So I go for option three: double bluff.

'I was actually . . . looking for the secret room. Ethel told me about it. I thought I'd have a quick look.'

HG raises an eyebrow.

'You know,' I say, 'it's always the library, isn't it? Or the study. Anywhere you might get murdered by a candlestick.' I haul the reins of my thoughts and my brain kindly agrees, jamming my mouth shut.

'Sometimes it's the billiards room,' HG says, after a long pause.

'Right,' I exclaim.

She nods. 'I do see that it's interesting— What was your name?'

I supply it.

'I see that, Phil. But please, try to keep your crime-novel research outside of business hours. I'm sure you have a job you're meant to be doing. I can find you one, if not.'

Chastened and slightly dizzy with relief, I scuttle away.

We're making headway in the attic, but there's still a huge amount left. I poke through drawers and cupboards, find faded documents, old keys, knick-knacks from long-gone holidays. An entire thimble collection is rolling around loose in one drawer; another has what looks like the pelts of several unwell rodents sewn together to make a very nasty hat.

The enormous family tree tapestry I recognise from the photo of the old library has just been unearthed from where it was jammed behind a wardrobe. I pause to examine it, the frame now propped against a wall.

The lines of family relationships sprawl across the fabric in stitches so tiny they're barely visible, names and dates picked out in cursive thread. The lower left corner is blank, in a fabric of a slightly different colour, like it's been patched.

The tapestry's faded colours and embroidery style make it look ancient, like something in a fusty museum about medieval nobles. But the family tree's lowest branches depict birth- and death-dates in the twentieth century, so it was in use not that long ago. A couple of us drag it towards the exit, ready to be carried downstairs and displayed again. We've tackled most of the bigger items now, which has cleared some reassuring paths through the junk.

That afternoon, I sit by the door with an empty box to sort through a display cabinet crammed with odd artefacts. The few labels with dates show they were acquired over decades, all by people with the surname Mountjoy. Adventuring clearly ran in the family – unless it was just one keen and prolific ancestor doing the whole clan's vital trinket-collecting work. Among the selection of pottery, glassware and jewellery, there's a bone labelled as the tooth of a sabretoothed tiger (unlikely) and a medallion on a chain. It's labelled as 'worn by the dread pirate Blackbeard'. I snort as I read this.

'Something wrong, dear?' Ms Lenson asks.

'It's just,' I show her the label. 'Really?'

She comes over, a faint smile washing across her face. 'Ah, yes. Possibly a little fanciful.'

I pick up the coin, holding it carefully between finger and thumb, and rub it against my T-shirt sleeve. 'This wouldn't have been worn by anyone, let alone Blackbeard. Look.' I pull a few links of chain through the hole in the centre. 'It's just a normal coin that someone's decided is a necklace.'

Ms Lenson makes a *hmm* of agreement. 'You may be right.' She gives me a piercing glance. 'Are you interested in this kind of thing, Phil?'

I replace the coin, carefully; even though it's a fraud, it's still several hundred years old. This gives me some time to plan my answer. As with HG in the library, my first instinct is to lie. I'm in the habit. My whole existence already feels like one big web of fakery, even though most of the lying so far has been by omission.

But I guess I don't need to lie about this. 'Yeah, I am interested,' I tell her. 'I actually studied history. Nothing came of it, but it was still nice.'

'Knowledge for knowledge's sake,' she agrees, her wavery voice firm. 'It's never wasted.' She nudges the chain into place with a finger. 'Perhaps we need to update that label. Ah, Lily,' she looks over my shoulder, 'good.'

I spin to see Lily hesitating in the doorway a few feet away. My stomach twists strangely at the sight. I haven't seen her since our walk to the car park the other day. She ducks her head at me as she comes towards us. I might be imagining it

114

but she looks a little embarrassed, as though we've caught her doing something she shouldn't.

Ms Lenson is shuffling through papers on her clipboard; she retrieves one and holds it out to Lily. 'Here we are.'

I crane my head to catch a glimpse as Lily takes it, but she holds it against her chest.

Ms Lenson potters towards the door, saying, 'I'll be going then. Phil, if you'd like a little break, I'm sure Lily will have a job for you.'

I raise my eyebrows at Lily. Another handout from the gods of fate. 'We meet again,' I say.

Her hair is twisted into a low bun, a few strands escaping to frame her face. She tucks one behind her ear.

'Looks like it,' she agrees. Our voices are quiet, muffled against the chaotic array of stuff in the attic. The other volunteers are out of earshot.

'Well,' I add the coin to the pile in the box and straighten up to stretch, 'do you have a job for me?'

She's scanning the paper Ms Lenson handed her and doesn't answer for a moment. 'What? Oh. No, I don't think so.'

I lean around, subtly trying to see what's on the sheet. It's a table with a few columns. From my upside-down reading, a few things jump out: a date column, a wider column for notes of some sort, and the word 'orchid'. My heart thuds at the sight.

Lily isn't paying attention, still reading.

'So, a secret message from Ms Lenson,' I comment, rocking back on my heels. 'Anything interesting?'

'Depends who you ask,' Lily says vaguely.

'Say I were to ask you,' I suggest. I want to know what's on the paper. And I also want her to pay attention to me.

She looks up, her expression distant. Then she focuses on me. 'Yes,' she says. 'Pretty interesting.'

'Is it about plants?' I ask. 'What? Just a guess,' I add as she rolls her eyes.

'I'm not only interested in plants.'

I hold up my hands. 'I have no doubt you contain multitudes. You probably like lots of things. Do you have weirdly wholesome hobbies, like ... wild swimming? Baking? No, wait,' I say, enjoying this too much to stop, 'rock climbing?'

She looks dismayed. 'How did you—?'

'Lucky guess.' I shrug, hiding my deep amusement. No one whose hands are as strong as hers wouldn't use them for rock climbing. She'd make a killing doing lesbian thirst traps on TikTok. I probably won't mention this for the moment, or ever.

She presses her lips together and fires back, 'What are your hobbies then? Apart from being pushy and overfamiliar with people you hardly know.'

I scrunch up my nose. I will certainly not be telling Lily the truth, which is that I don't really have any hobbies. I discard a couple of rejoinders – 'What is this, a GCSE French oral exam?' – and decide on a shrug. 'Nothing that good. I'm enjoying all the new plant info I'm learning from you, though. Maybe that can be my new hobby.'

Lily sniffs and mumbles something that sounds a lot like, 'When hell freezes over.'

We start to walk towards the door. Lily holds up the paper again, then turns and immediately catches me in the act of trying to get a glimpse. 'You're very nosy, aren't you?' she comments, frowning and hiding it once more. 'Why are you so interested?'

I back away, heart racing. 'Sorry, sorry. I just find you very fascinating,' I add, giving her my best, sweetest smile.

To my surprise, a faint flush paints her cheeks a light pink and she fumbles and drops the paper. 'Stop it,' she scoffs, reaching to pick it up.

Before she's got to it, I'm there. Swiftly, I scan the page, taking a mental snapshot before Lily snatches it out of my hand and, giving me one final glare, hurries off. I stand, hands on my hips, highly entertained by this reaction to my bald attempt at flirting. I'm having too much fun. But it's working, isn't it?

Before I forget, I get out my phone and open the secure messaging app to text Miles and Chaz as much as I can remember from the paper.

Inspection notes
Orchid flaccid. Wilting on left.
Decreased soil pH by 2.
Temp between 25–30 °C. Humidity too strong?
Unsure if on track to bloom as hoped.

'Give me strength,' comes a plaintive grumble as I pass the door to the right of the gardens after lunch. It has a big sign saying PRIVATE, which to someone in my position basically reads COME ON IN. I'm on my way back from emptying the bins (small) into the mega bin (huge) and I'm in no rush. The only thing entertaining me was the vague hope of seeing Lily, who's disappeared again.

Looking left to right, I wait to see if anyone answers the voice. But the path is empty. Another groan emanates from the room. I've never had a reason to go inside before, despite looking for one, as I've got my suspicions about this particular office. Before I can overthink, I knock and pop my head round the door.

A large man in a black polo shirt is sitting at a bank of screens, in the posture of one who's seen the end of days and welcomes them. He's holding his phone close to his face as though he can't believe he's meant to be able to read it.

'Everything OK?' I ask, clenching my hands behind my back in excitement. Suspicions confirmed. This is the security centre.

He turns, revealing wisps of greyish hair, a kindly wrinkled face and an expression of deep loathing. 'Bloody thing!' he exclaims.

'Phone trouble?' I ask sympathetically, taking a step inside.

He brandishes it. 'My daughter insists on sending these voicemails. Do you get voicemails?'

'Sometimes,' I say. 'But I never listen to them.'

The bank of screens shows shots of different areas around the grounds: the front entrance, the Orangery, the corridor to the kitchens. The images are grainy but live; as I watch, someone bustles through in jolting motion and enters the kitchen. I look around, trying to take in as much as possible before I'm chucked out.

The man throws both hands in the air. 'Exactly! Why did I even make all that effort learning texting if we're doing *this* now?'

I step a little further in. The desk is covered with four or five empty mugs, a small pile of pistachio shells and a litter of pens, pencils and scraps of paper, on one of which is drawn a startlingly accurate and well-shaded outline of a horse. The security guy is a horse girl! Who knew.

'Need a hand?' I ask. 'I think we've got the same kind of phone.'

'Would you, love? I just need to tell my daughter to give it a rest.'

I pull up one of the wheelie chairs and he places his phone in my hand. I quickly see the issue: his daughter has sent a series of short voice notes.

'Have you listened to these?' I ask. Her most recent written message says, **Easier to just tell you about it, hold on.**

'It took ten minutes to get through the last one,' he exclaims. 'Kept stopping and starting every time I looked away. I'll never hear what she's on about. Might as well just give up now.'

'They do that,' I agree. This guy's cheerful nihilism is endearing. 'Look.' I show him how to hold the phone to his ear. 'Try it like that. If you move it away it'll pause, but you just press play again.'

His expression clears from suspicion to delight. While he

119

listens, I surreptitiously keep staring around. What Chaz said about the security must be right. The screens built into the wall are nineties-looking: lots of chunky black plastic, curving glass and pixelated images. The jackets strewn around the place and general mess don't suggest great commitment to tidiness and discipline.

A couple of minutes later, the man lowers the phone, grinning. 'You'll never guess,' he says. 'Zoe's found a wedding venue! Not far and she'll get it for cheap because her friend knows the owner.'

'Great news,' I hold out my hand. 'I can show you how to send one back, if you want.'

He beams, apparently still riding the high from hearing his daughter's voice. 'Oh, go on then.' A moment later, he's speaking loudly into his phone. 'That's great, darlin', glad you'll be getting me a good deal on the venue, ha ha! I've been having a devil of a time listening to your voicemails but a nice young lady who—' He stops short. 'I never asked your name.'

'Phil,' I say.

'Phil,' he repeats into his phone. 'She's been a world of help. Now, thanks, love, and speak to you later, all right? And I'll see you for tea tomorrow. Now, I just need to ... how do you hang up?' He lowers his phone, then raises it again. 'I'll just ... end my message ...' He stares blankly at it. I gently indicate the send button and he taps it triumphantly.

'There you are,' I say. 'Your first voice note. You're a natural.'

'Cheers, Phil.' He beams. 'I owe you a cuppa.' He starts

to get up, then slumps, annoyed. 'But we're out of milk here. I've gotta get some from the main house. My name's Ted. I never said, did I?'

'Nice to meet you, Ted. And don't worry,' I say. 'I'm on my way to the kitchens anyway.'

'We can have that cuppa there then.' Ted nods. 'Just a tick.' He turns back to his desk.

While he's distracted getting his black Felborough windbreaker off his chair and pulling it on, I whip my phone out of my pocket and, quick as a flash, snap a picture of the room. I don't know if it's enough for Chaz, but it's got to be a start.

Chapter Twelve

A few days later, things are going well for the team. Chaz has used my photo of the security centre to figure out the brand and type of camera-operating system and to inform us that they are indeed as old as they look. Miles has made progress on the details of transferring the orchid to the buyer and has set up a bank account for the funds.

Everything is ramping up towards illegality extremely fast but they both seem completely fine and comfortable, so I've decided that's how I feel as well. Easy-peasy. The extensive heist research I've been doing has helped too. If thieves can steal Rembrandt's only ship painting in an art heist from an extremely secure gallery in 1990 causing uproar and chaos and *still not have been caught*, we can steal this one small plant. It'll be fine.

In the kitchens one morning, one of the other volunteers – a string-bean teen who hangs around with the equally lanky Taylor – is complaining about being assigned to the potting sheds. 'I'm too tired today,' they whine. 'I don't wanna be lugging pots around.'

'I'll swap with you,' I offer, seizing my chance. It's all hands on deck to transfer plants to the rose garden for the new borders. And you know what that means.

'Are you serious?' they ask, clutching their skinny chest in relief. 'You're a lifesaver.'

'No problem.' I wave them away. 'I'm just an everyday hero,' I say to Martina, the one with the neuroscience PhD, who's finishing her coffee and who just laughs dismissively and says, 'OK, Phil.'

I hurry to the potting sheds, filled with anticipation. Anthony, the stoic senior gardener whom I am now confident will never voluntarily speak to me, is directing the stream of plants bobbing towards him between the sheds and the rose garden, carried by a production line of under-gardeners and volunteers traipsing back and forth.

I spot Benny and Diego as I follow the line towards the sheds. They're wearing matching red socks and blue shorts today, which makes them look like a cartoon duo. When I open my mouth to greet them, Benny interrupts with, 'We didn't plan it! It just happened!'

'It's really working for me,' I tell them both. 'You should plan it next time.'

'Do you think?' Benny asks, brightening.

Diego just sighs as I nod seriously.

'What's going on here then?' I ask, gesturing at the line of volunteers.

'HG decided to change the rose garden design as a special surprise for the reopening,' Benny says immediately, his arms full of plants. 'So we're planting out all the annuals now.'

'May is a little late for planting,' Diego adds, biting the inside of his cheek as he balances his own tray of plants, 'but we're meant to have lots of sun over the next few weeks. And April was so cold that HG decided we should wait.'

'Does she often change stuff around here?' I ask. I know from HG's Wikipedia page that she grew up in Ghana and has Ethiopian roots. Also, she said in an interview once that she was inspired by her mother who was curious about the world and loved studying and travel. And that's the beginning and end of the personal information I could find about her. She's almost as enigmatic as the orchid.

'She likes mixing things up in the gardens,' Benny says, with the air of one imparting an important secret. 'She's making her mark on Fells, big time.'

'She loves it here,' Diego chips in, the human embodiment of the heart-eyes emoji.

They hurry off towards the rose garden and the queue moves along enough for me to see the blonde, hairy shape of Eva. She's sprawled on the gravel outside the potting sheds, the sight filling me with hope. I give her head a little scritch, which she tolerates with a wave of her feathery tail.

I've not been in this bit before: a neat row of sheds filled with plants in various stages of adulthood. And there's Lily, working in one. I wait behind Ethel as Lily shows her, with surprising gentleness, how to carry several baby plants at once.

When Ethel toddles off and I step inside, Lily looks me up and down.

'Morning,' I say. I hold her gaze, one eyebrow slightly raised, waiting to see what her mood is today.

'Morning,' she replies, shoving her hands into her pockets. Her hair is in one French plait, strands already escaping. 'Welcome to the potting sheds.'

'Thank you very much.' A welcome! This is a pleasant surprise. It prompts me to comment, 'It's nice in here, isn't it? Cosy.'

It's a cool, cloudy day, no sign of yesterday's sun. But it's warm inside the shed; the plants make it calm and somehow alive.

'You can hear things growing,' Lily says, her tone matter-of-fact as she looks affectionately at the pots. It's such a sudden hint of vulnerability and so close to what I was thinking that I stare at her. Who *is* this person?

The moment lengthens as I struggle to find something to say. I can't make a joke out of that; it was too pure and sweet.

She turns to the table, clearing her throat. 'Here, take these. Anthony will show you where they're going.'

She carefully piles the pots into my arms, leaning closer as she arranges the leaves so they don't get crushed. I can see a smudge of dirt on her glasses and her breath brushes against me. Heat rushes to my face, out of nowhere. The shed is suddenly stifling.

'Thanks,' I say, shifting the pots, 'got them.'

I hurry out into the refreshingly cool air. Eva watches me

pass, her expression doleful. I need to get it together. I'm *supposed* to be getting closer to Lily. I can't be running away from her.

On my second trip into the sheds, I'm ready. I'll ask about her favourite potted plant. This will be a good way to ingratiate myself because Lily famously likes plants and I might be able to steer the conversation to the orchid.

But when I get inside, I'm just starting to say, 'So which of these—' when Lily, at the same time, asks, 'How's the rose garden looking?'

'Er,' I say, thrown off track. 'Nice?'

'You didn't notice, did you?' Her voice is dry as parched soil.

'What would I be looking for?' I enquire. This line of questioning doesn't seem that useful, but any conversation with Lily is good. 'Other than pretty flowers.'

'Well, that,' she says. 'But also how the plants are looking. What pattern he's chosen. I just wondered how Anthony's getting on.'

I sigh inwardly. She probably fancies Anthony, as everyone does. The idea is annoying. What has Anthony got, apart from height and good looks? Surely the bar isn't as low as that. Anyway, I'm tall for a woman.

'Are you worried he's messing up?' I ask, expecting her to blush. 'That he's just a pretty face?'

Instead, she mutters, 'I wish,' as she reaches for another plant.

'Really?' I ask, interested. 'Do you not like him then?'

'I don't dislike him.' Lily gives me a sidelong glance.

'High praise indeed.' I want to explore this further. I assume Lily disliked most people, but this seems specific. 'Have you got, like, a plant nerd rivalry going on?'

She rolls her eyes but doesn't deny it.

'Is that it?' I bet this is it. 'Are you worried he's more muscly than you and that if you got in a fight he could take you?'

'Always with the muscles.' She shoves a pot into my arms with more force than necessary. 'Seems like you've got a real thing about them.'

'Maybe I have,' I reply, shrugging. It's harder to pull off with an armful of delicate cargo, but I just about manage. 'You haven't, then?'

'*No*,' she emphasises, a faint blush tingeing her cheeks.

'All right. Noted,' I say. Lucky for me.

I'm about to leave when she says, from behind me, 'He thinks he's so clever and he deserves the promotion, no question. But people only listen to him because he's a tall, handsome man.'

Lily looks suddenly bleak as I turn back. A jolt of defensiveness surprises me. I don't want her looking bleak. Given that I can't deny that tall, handsome men enjoy a pre-smoothed path through life, I don't know what to do except try to distract her.

'I believe that,' I say. 'I saw Ethel trailing after him with a watering can earlier, asking how to use it. When I, an almost professional watering can user, was right there and would have been happy to show her.'

'Surely *you* have never used a watering can in your life,' she says, momentarily diverted. 'You act like you've never seen a plant before.'

'Hey, I have house plants,' I tell her. 'Several, in fact, and not all of them are dead.'

'Careful, you're impressing me almost too much.'

'*And* I'm a quick learner,' I continue. 'So I've remembered everything you said about not ripping up nice healthy plants, which I had no way of knowing before. Anyway,' I say, backing towards the door, 'I should take these to their little sleeping bags. That's what they're called, where plants live, right?'

'They're called *beds*,' Lily shouts after me.

'Like I said,' I call back.

Benny is outside next to Eva, who's still lying guard on the gravel. They're wearing matching expressions of confusion. 'Was that . . . a joke?' he whispers as I stroll past. 'With Lily?'

'She's in a good mood today,' I say. His face brightens.

As I leave, I hear him say cheerily as he enters the shed, 'What's it to be, boss? Choose me a good one!'

I just about catch Lily's reply, which sounds like, 'Please be careful, Benny. We don't want you tripping over again.'

I don't have another chance to talk to Lily as by my third trip we've got to the big trays of plants. Several of us form a chain and pass them out to a waiting wheelbarrow. These trays hold little green sprouting things, indistinguishable from each other. Benny whispers that they're sweet peas. He seems to be keeping his voice down so as not to incur Lily's wrath again.

Diego, undeterred by Benny's failed attempt at chummi-ness, is trying to engage Lily in conversation when I return trundling my wheelbarrow.

'HG said we'd be basing one of the designs in the rose garden on the glasshouses, is that right?' he asks. My heart gives a jolt of anticipation. I couldn't have planned this better if I'd fed Diego those lines.

'Yes,' Lily says shortly. 'Over here, please.'

She hefts a big sack of earth into his arms. Diego sags but rallies. 'What's it going to look like?'

She eyes him. 'HG hasn't decided.'

'I wonder if it'll be the colours of the national flags for the plants,' he muses. 'That could be good. The visitors would get a little clue about what's in the glasshouses, wouldn't they?'

Lily doesn't answer, apart from piling another sack into his arms. Taylor, the volunteer who seems to have taken a shine to Diego, gives Lily an angry look as Diego staggers away. Lily, either not noticing or not caring, gives Taylor a sack as well and they hurry after Diego, probably to pat his wounded pride.

I edge up to her. 'Not a fan of the flags idea?' I ask. 'I think it could work.' I have no idea what Diego was on about, but sometimes if you pretend to know more than you do, people believe it.

'He's an idiot,' she says shortly.

'Is he?' I ask mildly. Diego seems like a hapless, quite sweet person to me. 'He seems harmless.'

'He keeps bad company,' Lily snaps.

OK, so we won't follow that line of questioning to conversation-shut-down central. But back to the matter at hand. I might as well just go for it. 'Are the glasshouses opening to employees soon? I'd love to see them.'

'Really? An accomplished gardener such as yourself?' Lily's voice is sarcastic, but it lacks the biting edge she adopted with Diego. This must be a good sign.

'Will you ever let me live that down?' I ask.

'When you've planted and nurtured some new nasturtiums, we'll talk.' She hands me a broom, taking one for herself too, and gestures for me to start sweeping where earth from the plants has scattered.

We work in silence for a bit. 'It's just,' I say, feeling for the words I need, 'the way you talk about this stuff. It's kind of . . . compelling.'

'Are you taking the piss?' Lily eyes me, then makes a little motion with her fingers. In response, Eva grumbles under her breath in her best approximation of a growl.

'No,' I exclaim. 'There's no need to set your hound on me. Why would— The point is, it's interesting. I'd like to know more.'

'Hmm.' She doesn't say anything else, but I get the impression, as we continue to work, that she's thinking about it.

I take a few deep breaths to try and control my heartbeat, which is faster than usual. I want Lily to show me the glasshouses. I really meant it when I said it was compelling. I've never thought about botany before. The way she cares about it is kind of fascinating. There's an entire world out there I

130

know nothing about. The part of me that used to be curious and want to learn, that's been lying dormant for years, is stretching and waking up. I need to know these things for the heist, but I *want* to know them too.

The problem is, I realise as I wash my hands at the end of my shift, with these feelings – and with Lily – it's hard to know what's real and what's not.

Chapter Thirteen

A gala is being held to mark Felborough's reopening. Just a couple of weeks away now, it's a soft launch before Felborough throws open its doors to the public. It will be an intimidatingly high-budget, red-carpet chance to show off the renovations to a select group of interested celebrities and VIPs, and do some fundraising. Crucially, it's also meant to build orchid hype as we approach the moment when it will bloom.

The closest I'd have got to an event like this previously would be as a groupie lurking outside Felborough's gates to watch the celebs arrive. Strangely now, as a volunteer, I get a legitimate invitation. Felborough is democratic like that.

This would be lovely and exciting, apart from the fact that unfortunately we've agreed I'll use the gala to try to get into the glasshouses. As Chaz comments every time we meet to discuss plans, we should really be grateful that Felborough's staggering its reopening into two stages. It works nicely for heist purposes.

So: I'll attend the gala, as is my right, then use the cover of the crowd and general mayhem to do a recce to the glasshouses. We need to at least see what'll be in our way, what to expect. Then, a week or so later, when the orchid flowers, Felborough will open to the public. That's when we'll make our move.

My shoulders tense every time I think about it. But, 'You've got this, Phil,' Miles says as we leave Chaz's flat after another planning session. 'We know you can do it. We just need to get the final details of the picture. Then we'll be set.'

I just grimace and reply, 'That's the plan,' with as much confidence as I can muster. I'll fake it until I make it. Or until I get arrested. Whichever comes first.

Work is ramping up at Felborough to get things shipshape before the gala. Platoons of volunteers wash windows, sweep floors, polish everything in sight. In the Hall, we move furniture, hang paintings and create displays with the newly found exhibits, which will be available to view the night of the gala.

When I offer to make the new labels for the artefacts I was sorting through the other day, Ms Lenson agrees. This is nice, partly because it's quite interesting and means she trusts me, but mostly because it lets me address the missing link in the heist plan: get a proper map so we can case the dang joint.

Or finish casing it, I mean. I feel like I've already been casing quite hard. But there's plenty more joint to case. I make a mental note to check with Chaz if I'm using the phrase correctly, not that he'd know.

Ms Lenson gives me the password to the kitchen computer, then wanders off to oversee something else, leaving me alone. It's almost too good to be true.

'If you have any issues, just shout,' she says, kindly. 'That computer is a little temperamental.' She gives the screen a pat as she goes, like it's an old but troublesome family pet.

'Will do.' I smile through gritted teeth. Such a sweet person to be caught in the crossfire of my deception.

As soon as she's gone, I minimise my document. This might be my only chance to be on this computer legitimately and there could be any amount of useful information: plans of the house and gardens, security details, contracts. I start digging.

There's a lot of boring stuff: names of contractors, insurance policies, invoices for repairs and bills. The filing system is as organised as I'd expect, given the number of lists Ms Lenson has on her clipboard and the way she has a handle on everything everyone's doing all the time.

Eventually, I find a file called 'Felborough architecture'. When I click into it, the floor plan of the House, which was spread over the kitchen table on my first day, pops up. Gotcha. It's more detailed than I remember, spidery labels picking out what might be hundreds of rooms. There's a level for the ground floor, first floor, second floor, and various turrets and towers.

Someone could be back any minute but, for now, the kitchen is deserted. Without pausing to second-guess, I click 'Print'. Then I wait. Nothing happens. I dash to the printer which squats enormously at the other end of the table and jab a few buttons. It groans into life and I sprint back to try and figure out how to make it do my bidding.

Following the directions to link it up, I realise suddenly that this computer isn't connected to the internet. This is why Chaz hasn't been able to hack into it yet. It's literally just a screen and a keyboard: a glorified notebook.

Should I hotspot it? But if I connect to it for the first time ever, there's no way it'll be subtle. You'd get pop-ups and alerts and notifications. But I might never get this chance alone again.

Standing up now, desperate, I spot a loose USB cable. At random, I poke it into the computer's dock and give the process over into the keeping of any interested gods.

Astonishingly, the printer whirs. At glacial speed, a piece of paper starts chugging through.

Footsteps are approaching along the hallway. I used up all my luck on the printer. I close all open documents except the one with my labels and sit tight. The printer clonks and grinds. For a few heart-stopping seconds, it falls silent and motionless; I consider thrusting my entire fist in my mouth to stifle my screech. Then, in one smooth movement, it spits the paper out and I've grabbed it and thrown myself back onto my chair, the paper tucked underneath me, just as HG strides into the kitchen.

She fixes me with her gaze. I brush my hand across my hair and look up from the screen, as though for the first time all afternoon.

'Have you seen Ms Lenson?' she barks, her eyes resting on me. She must be able to see how out of breath I am.

'I think she went to oversee some stuff in the East Wing,' I gasp, trying to sound mature and normal.

'Hm,' she acknowledges. She hesitates a moment, as the printer emits one final death rattle.

Then she marches off and I sag in my seat.

Got the map, I text the group. **Printed out.**

Great. Can you drop it off tonight? Miles writes. **I can start combing through it ASAP.**

Their security system is a shitshow, comes the next message from Chaz. **Just a big joke tbh. I'm actually laughing rn.**

I roll my eyes, leaning on the sturdy kitchen table. **Glad you're enjoying yourself.**

When are we meeting? Chaz sends. **You've got to see this.**

The day after the gala, Miles replies. **To hear the new glasshouses intel. All ready, Phil?**

I guess, I type. Then I delete that and instead send, **Absolutely, I was born ready.** I almost forgot to fake it, for a moment. The gala is not going to be what I'd call a chill evening. But at least I'll get to see everyone all dressed up.

Good luck, Miles replies. **Keep us updated.**

Send pics of u in your tux, Chaz says.

I send a thumbs up. This is fine. Everything is fine.

Later, I find Lily as she's walking past the rose gardens, Eva at her heels. On my break, I ostensibly came to see where HG was; Ms Lenson is now looking for her.

'Where are you both off to then?' I ask, having ascertained that, in a true farce fashion, Lily doesn't know where HG is. Eva allows me to give her a little pet as Lily watches, her expression slightly confused.

'We . . . have some stuff to do.' Lily hesitates as I scratch behind Eva's ear. Then she blurts, 'Did you mean it, before?'

'What?' I ask. 'About being a watering can professional?'

Lily shakes her head. 'About . . . finding plant stuff compelling.'

'Yeah,' I say simply as I straighten. Eva noses against my leg for a moment before padding away.

'Why?' Lily suddenly glares at me, as though to pre-empt mockery.

I shrug to hide my amusement at her obvious suspicion, which is so endearing that I want to laugh. 'I'd never thought about it much before. There's a world of stuff I know nothing about and other people do. It's your whole life, isn't it? So it must be interesting. It makes me want to know more.'

Lily bites at her lip. I wait. Then, to my never-ending amazement, she asks, as though despite herself, 'Do you want to see something cool?'

I smirk, unable to let this go. 'Can I just check we have the same definition of cool?'

She rolls her eyes. 'If you call me a plant nerd one more time, I'm—'

'Just kidding,' I say. 'If you think it's cool then it will be. And I like the plant nerd stuff.'

'I think you're lying to be nice,' Lily sighs. But her lip is quirking slightly, as it does when she's pretending she's not enjoying something. I want to push my thumb into the dimple it makes. 'Come on then.'

She grabs my elbow and leads me into the wildlife walk. The sky is blue and the air is clear, and I'm slightly too warm in my Felborough fleece now the weather's turned nice again. Even through the thick material I'm conscious of Lily's fingers pressing into my arm. *Grip it harder,* I want to tell her. *Show me you're really there*. But this is one of the first times she's ever voluntarily made physical contact; now's not the moment to freak her out.

She tows me down the path, into the trees. 'This is the way I prefer,' she says, as the path narrows. 'The main entrance is over there, but there's a side door.'

The path curves to the right and I suddenly realise that this is not a drill: we're going to the glasshouses. The main reason Felborough is so famous. The things I've only seen on the cartoon map and the orchid flyer. The place I was going to attempt a recce to get even slightly close to at the gala.

Lily takes a key from her pocket to unlock a gate, ushering me through. My stomach twists in anticipation. This is where the orchid is kept.

We round the corner and, abruptly, there they are. The glasshouses.

It's one titanic building constructed of several distinct but connected parts, forming a kind of cross. The parts all lead towards a central glasshouse, whose gracefully curved roof towers higher than I'd have believed. The drawings don't come close to doing them justice. Countless panes of glass interlock to form the walls, through which a thick, rich canopy of green is visible, rising several storeys high as I crane my neck towards the roof.

The glass is a strange, greenish blue colour. I run my hand over it as we approach along the side, admiring the tiny bubbles in the glass. 'It was all blown by hand,' Lily says.

'No way.' I gaze at the sheer wall soaring into the sky. 'How is it so huge?'

Lily looks satisfied at my reaction. 'It was carefully made. And it cost an obscene amount. It actually bankrupted the family who built it.' She looks upwards too, sounding almost pleased at the idea. 'This is where we keep the plants that need climate control. There are five buildings. This one's my favourite.'

'Why?' I manage to ask. This colossal glasshouse has left me stunned. I've never seen such a beautiful building.

'This is the South American one,' she replies. 'The Cloud Forest House. It's replicating the climate of a rainforest. I'll show you.'

She walks along to a section that looks the same as the rest. I follow and discover a tiny keypad stuck to the glass, camouflaged with the same greenish blue. Lily enters a four-digit code, then pulls a key from her pocket.

'HG doesn't trust technology,' she informs me, sticking the key into a section of the wall. 'So we need this as well.'

The part of my brain that's not trying to memorise the shape of the code registers this with alarm. Will we need a key for every door to get to this orchid? Another part watches with nothing but pure anticipation as Lily pushes the wall and it becomes a curved door.

Eva flops to the ground with a sigh as I follow Lily inside. We're hit immediately by a wall of damp heat.

I release an involuntary 'Ugh' that makes Lily turn and smirk at me.

'Nice, right?'

'I'm not built for this,' I say, as she closes the door. The heat is so oppressive it's like wading through a quagmire.

'My ancestors were Vikings,' Lily says. 'I'm not built for this either.'

'Of course they were,' I mutter as Lily leads us towards a rickety spiral staircase. I'm not sure why I'm pretending to be grouchy. This is one of the most amazing places I've ever been.

There's so much lush, vegetal greenery that the glasshouse is bursting with life. Enormous trees soar towards the sky, pressing their leaves against the glass roof far above. Vines and creepers loop over their branches, vivid pink flowers bursting out in patches on the trunks. A small sign by the path announces that 'Plant Theft is a Crime', which makes my stomach lurch as though I'm seasick. It's not like I didn't know that.

As we ascend the spiral staircase, glimpses of the iron-grating floor disappear under a thick layer of ferns and plants. At the top is a small metal platform with a bench. A walkway joins it to others on our left and right, connecting all the way round the very top of the building.

'They've only just finished redoing this,' Lily tells me, as

I traipse up the last few stairs panting. She's lightly out of breath too, a thin sheen of sweat or humidity glowing on her brow. 'The walkways were rusting.'

'Thanks for waiting until now to show me then,' I say, peering over the edge. It's actually less vertiginous than I thought, as we're high in the tree canopy. If you fell, you'd probably be able to grab a branch on your way down.

It's so *green*. More patches of flowers spring up the more I look – not just the bright glowing pink but fiery orange, cerulean blue, burning red. I almost expect to see a puma crouching in a branch, monkeys swinging between the vines. Jets of water suddenly hiss from the foot-level pipes spaced all around the walkway, spraying a fine mist over the plants below. It makes me jump back, then laugh.

'They do that every few minutes.' Lily's watching me take it in. After a few moments, she says, 'What do you think?'

'What do I *think*?'

She shrugs, clearly trying not to appear too pleased. 'You said you wanted to see it.'

'Lily,' I say, deciding on candour for once. 'It's stunning.'

She laughs, relief clear in the sound. 'Pretty great, right?'

We stare out at the bold vegetation. Everything is on a huge scale: massive ferns the size of double beds; a huge leafy guy taller than me that I recognise as a cheese plant. I know because I had a potted one once which, you guessed it, I accidentally killed.

It's hard to take in. I could sit on the bench up here, but I somehow want to get closer. 'This would be a good place for a date,' I say without thinking.

'It's a bit sweaty, isn't it?' Lily pushes her sleeves up and flips her hair over her shoulder, airing her neck.

'Sometimes that's OK,' I say. Just to see.

She snorts and flicks my forearm which is resting on the parapet beside hers. 'Don't be cheesy.'

Fair enough. 'So, where's this super-secret orchid then?' I keep my tone light. 'It's in one of these glasshouses, right?'

'Yeah.' Lily nods. 'The main one. This is one of the four outer ones. They all connect.'

'Have you seen it?' I ask.

Lily presses her lips together and I think she's not going to answer until she tilts her head just slightly and says, 'Yeah.'

'Is it as splendid as they claim?' I ask, after a moment's silence. I truly can't think of anything else orchid-related to ask, given I know nothing about it.

To my endless relief, Lily laughs again. 'It's actually annoying that they're advertising it as the Splendid Paradise Orchid,' she says. 'Not very descriptive. Although I agree with the marketing decision not to pitch it as the Hook Orchid. Which is shit, even if, unfortunately, it's kind of the official name. *Calanthe Caerulissimus Hookiae.*'

'What would you rather it was called?' I want her to keep talking. That complex Latin name just rolled off her tongue like molten silver.

'*Calanthe* is just the genus of orchid, but *Caerulissimus* means bluest of blue.' Her face takes on a dreamy expression. 'Which is perfect for this orchid, we think.'

'I guess it could be the Blue Orchid or Indigo Orchid,' I suggest. 'But that doesn't really get at the magic, does it? It's like you need a word for bluer than blue.'

Lily gives me a funny look. 'Exactly.'

The misters start up again, hissing their fine sprays over the glasshouse below. A rainbow shimmers for a moment in the haze.

'HG must trust you,' I say lightly.

'She does.' Lily looks at me and frowns.

I cast about for a distraction and find one that's both a great and a terrible idea. 'Have you, er,' I lean back against the railing and stare up into the spiralling roof, 'brought anyone else here?'

'Who would I bring?' Lily turns too, reaching for a vine that's dropped from a thick branch above our heads. She loops it around a twig so it's secure. 'Everyone's after my job. They're just waiting for me to slip up so they can get promoted above me.'

'Aren't you worried I'm after your job?'

She lets out a 'Ha' of what you might call derisive laughter. 'I've seen your work, so I think my job is safe. Or you're doing a pretty convincing job of leading a double life.'

I laugh because I have to. That's the reaction it warrants and it's the only one that will give me any deniability. It hurts more than I expect. But I'm in far too deep to back down now.

So, 'That's me,' I say. Time to make a joke and hide behind

flirting. It's never failed me before. 'I'm secretly an amazing gardener. I was just pretending so you'd have an excuse to tell me off.'

'As if I'd need an excuse to tell you off.'

I turn towards her just as she straightens and looks at me. Her gaze is very direct, her grey eyes more piercing than ever against the background of all this green. I realise I'm biting my lip; her gaze flits to it. The moment stretches.

Then it breaks. 'Anyway,' she pats the railing once, then starts to move away, 'I need to water the bits in the middle where the jets don't reach. We should get going.'

'Already?' I ask, leaning over for another look. I shouldn't be encouraging this. I should be getting the information and getting out of here. I was stupid not to think of the cost. But this is too good an opportunity to miss. Clearly Lily trusts me enough to show me this place, somewhere special to her. I've hardly learnt anything about the orchid and I need to make the most of it, even if it feels like the worst thing I could be doing.

'We shouldn't really be here,' Lily says. 'We're not opening to the public for a while yet.'

She's closed off again. I don't know what I've said. Maybe it was pushing about the orchid. I keep forgetting to take it slowly. This tightrope between talking to her easily, normally, like someone I want to know, and remembering that I have an ulterior motive – it's messing with my head.

Chapter Fourteen

The time in the glasshouse with Lily was so enjoyable that I feel kind of strange when I think about it. Warm, almost. It feels a bit like showing up to a competition you've won a thousand times, whose every part you can predict, except this time there's a new competitor who's at least as good as you, who might even beat you. And they challenge you to be better, to take an interest again. They wake you up.

When I check the rota the next day and learn that today is Lily's day off, disappointment drops in my stomach. No chance to see her all day.

Plus, there's a work social this evening. I was hoping we'd get a chance to talk; it would be the perfect scenario to loosen up, keep figuring her out. But there's surely no way she'll come if she's not already at work, given how much she dislikes everyone. Damn.

But this feeling makes sense, of course it does. I'm just disappointed I won't get to progress the heist today, that's all.

At least thanks to Lily, I don't need to use the gala for a glasshouses recce any more. Leaning against the wall, I check my phone. I told our group chat about it this morning before I left for work. I didn't fancy it last night, for some reason. Instead, I just slid the tightly folded blueprints into Miles's letterbox and scurried home before he could invite me in.

Dad and I had a quiet night watching a new adaptation of *Persuasion*. It was peaceful, as far as either of us can achieve peacefulness at the moment. He didn't go to film club yesterday and for the third or fourth week in a row no unappealingly angled selfie from Gerald has arrived on my phone, making me sure my dad's been skipping their weekly walks. He's isolating himself and it freaks me out. Maybe I'll sign him up to some kind of course, force him to do a new hobby. He might like pottery. I've never tried it, but the idea of sitting quietly in a room where no one's asking you to do anything except focus on making your vase sufficiently bulbous does sound calming.

Omg, Chaz has replied. I swipe away from my half-arsed research into local pottery courses to read his messages. **You saw the glasshouses????**

EXCELLENT work, Miles replies.

I grimace, my shoulder involuntarily twitching as though to brush this off. I only got to see them thanks to Lily's kindness. Even though obviously that was my goal and I encouraged her.

Anyway.

I tell them I'll update them tomorrow. Before I can put my

phone in my pocket, another message comes through from Chaz.

So what will you do at the gala if you've already done that now?? Hey, why don't you break into the security centre, see what's up.

Great idea, Miles agrees, **or you could get back on the computer? We could do with more info about personnel.**

I rub my nose. These ideas are significantly more stressful than just wandering towards the glasshouses while everyone else is occupied. And even that didn't sound relaxing.

Gotta go, let's discuss later, I send, as Ms Lenson bustles in, holding – what else? – her trusty clipboard.

'Ah, good,' she says, seeing us gathered. It's just a small group of volunteers in the kitchen this morning. 'The gardeners are busy today,' Ms Lenson informs us, as I notice this. 'We have a special visitor. Colonel Hook.'

I control a twitch of my eyebrows. The Cher-like explorer! He's here?

Ms Lenson removes her glasses and lets them hang on their string round her neck. 'Hook is a very important man,' she tells us. 'He discovered the Splendid Paradise Orchid and presented it to Felborough. He's our honoured guest, so please treat him as such.'

I'm reminded of a pep talk before a school trip. She doesn't need to worry, though. No one here would do anything to jeopardise Felborough's reputation. Except me, obviously. But that's not for today.

*   *   *

I don't glimpse the explorer until lunchtime when I take my sandwich outside. It's a cloudy, mild day, no need for my Felborough fleece, and I'm very into the pumpkin patch ever since I, you know. Learnt about it.

My favourite bench is by the broccoli and runner beans, which are doing well, but I hesitate at the end of the path. HG and a stocky man around her height wander slowly between the vegetables. His head leans towards hers, his fingers linked behind his back. I don't need to be introduced; that handlebar moustache would identify him a mile off. I inch closer as they round one row and head up the next.

'How's the temperature?' Hook's asking, his voice beaming self-confidence. 'It may require more variation than you think.'

'I've considered it,' HG says, sounding slightly strained. I follow at a distance, hidden by the trellises of beans. 'But I doubt that's the issue. The right stamen has a small browning patch and the roots aren't growing in the usual three-sixty pattern.'

'Perhaps,' I catch sight of some moustache-stroking through the leaves, 'the soil pH is too high?'

HG makes an impatient noise. 'We've decreased it already. I'll try again the day after tomorrow if there's no improvement.'

'And the humidity?'

'Monitoring it,' she says shortly. 'Ah.' They round the corner and come up short. 'Phil, was it?'

'Hi,' I blurt, 'yes. That's me.'

'Phil is one of our volunteers helping with the reopening,' HG announces. I'm astonished and slightly concerned that she remembers my name.

'Ah,' Hook exclaims. 'Terrific. Enjoying yourself? Happy camper working here?'

'Um, yep, thanks,' I say, waving my sandwich in the direction of the bench, in proof that I was having a normal time and not, in any way, eavesdropping. 'Just going for lunch. It's nice out here.'

'Splendid.' Hook beams. 'Nothing like a vegetable garden to stimulate the mind as you take a well-earned break.'

'Er.' It seems wise to just go along with it. 'Exactly.'

'Let's go this way,' HG suggests, giving me a quick glance as she leads Hook away.

They were discussing the orchid, of course. It sounds terrifyingly complicated. That was a strange dynamic though. I don't know why HG was so irritable. It could just be Hook's grating personality. But she's a professional. She must be used to shit like this all the time.

Musing on how I'll report the conversation back to Chaz and Miles, in case it adds up to anything useful, I don't notice until I get to my bench that it's already occupied.

'Oh.' I stumble.

Lily looks up. 'Hi,' she says, her eyes crinkling in a smile or against the brightness of the sky. I hope the former.

'I thought it was your day off,' I say. Eva is lying under the bench, a bone-shaped biscuit between her paws. She pauses in her gumming to regard me calmly, twitching her tail in greeting.

'It is,' Lily agrees. 'But HG wanted me to meet Hook and his security team. So I came in.'

I rock back on my heels. She looks settled, a packet of crisps on her lap, an apple beside her. If she was anyone else, I'd offer to go somewhere else. But I shouldn't, for the heist. And I also don't want to.

'Were you going to sit here?' she asks, looking at the sandwich in my hand.

'I can go somewhere else,' I say.

'No, it's fine. Loads of room.' She shuffles to the end of the bench, giving me more space than necessary.

So I sit. She doesn't say anything else, so I unwrap my sandwich and start eating. Lily's fleece is thrown across her shoulders, lying softly against her neck. Her hair's in one long plait, one of the most wholesome of her hairstyles.

I lean back as the clouds part to allow a welcome glow of sunshine. I thought it would be awkward to sit with Lily in silence but oddly it's not. My normal urge to fill every moment with chat and bluster seems to have left, for the time being. I can't find it in me to discuss the orchid. She crunches a crisp. I eat my sandwich and bask in the sun, like a lizard on a rock who's thankful it remembered to take a hay fever tablet this morning. The air is thick with pollen.

When Lily offers the crisp packet to me, I check the front. It's green, so I can't tell the flavour. 'Cheese and onion?' I ask.

'Please. Salt and vinegar.'

'Thank God.' I take one. 'Thanks.' A robin lands on a twig nearby, its eye beady-black, then flits away. 'Are you going to the social tonight?' I ask, voicing the question on my mind.

'I don't think so.' She tips out the last crisp.

'Why not?'

She shrugs. 'I'm bad at darts.'

'Shame. I was hoping you'd be there.' I stare out at the garden. 'I could do with a win. Given I've clearly got no chance in our upcoming arm wrestle.'

She smiles slightly. 'I don't think anyone wants me there.'

'I'm sure they'd be happy to see you.'

Lily folds the packet into thirds. 'Doubt it.'

'They're pretty welcoming,' I say, watching her surprisingly dextrous crisp-packet origami. 'Maybe you just got off on the wrong foot.'

'Why?' she asks, her fingers stilling. 'Has anyone said anything?'

'No,' I reply quickly. 'What would they have said?'

'I don't know. Just that I'm an ambitious rude bitch or something.'

'Hey,' I protest, trying to scrub all trace of honesty from my face. 'Definitely not. They just want to get to know you.'

She sighs, then laughs, as if against her will at something not that funny. 'You sound like my mum.'

'Oh God, really?' I say, involuntarily.

'Not in a bad way. Just that she's always trying to get me to be more sociable. More likeable. Put on a nice face.'

'Gross.' It's hard to imagine having a mother who'd tell me

151

to do that. My mum, before she left me and my dad to fend for ourselves, used to warn me away from men and tell me not to trust them. Quite a different way to mess someone up, really. 'I'd hate to put on a nice face,' I say, instead of any of this.

'Right?' Lily replies. 'Me too.' She gestures at me after a moment has passed in comfortable agreement. 'I don't know. Your face is just . . . nice, anyway. Friendly, I mean. You don't need to put on a different one to make people like you.'

My mouth quirks into a smile. I do have the kind of face that's approachable. I know this because despite my tattoos and cropped hair and piercings, which you'd think a lot of people would interpret as fuck-off signs, I often get asked for directions. People strike up conversations in toilets and tell me about their bad days.

Maybe that's what made it all the more surprising when Lily lashed out at me the evening we met. I'm not used to it. I have resting talk-to-me face. Which is ironic, really, given how rarely I tell people real stuff about myself.

'You should see me when I'm alone,' I say. 'My face goes all horrible.'

'Sure.' Lily tucks the crisp packet between the bench slats. Eva, lying beneath, lifts her nose to poke at it for a second, then returns to her biscuit. She really is an amazingly chill dog. Dogs take on the characteristics of their owners, don't they? Lily doesn't seem anywhere near as chill. But it reflects well on her, anyway.

'Come to the social,' I say, as I get up to leave. 'It might be fun.'

Lily looks up at me, her forehead creased. 'If I do, can we be on the same team?' she asks.

'Of course.' I don't know if darts is a team sport. But I'll obviously do anything to make it work.

Chapter Fifteen

At my last work social, the cinema manager ordered a few pizzas and we watched a film. We all had to clock off before it started so we wouldn't get paid for the time, and a few people smuggled in beers or a hip flask, and the night ended with us sweeping the aisles for litter as usual.

The Felborough social, in comparison, might as well be at The Ritz. The darts place, recently opened on the non-Felborough side of town, is nothing like the dingy shops flanking it. Its exposed brick walls, hung with dartboards and burnished metal surfaces, make it look like a very small warehouse. The bar has a complicated arrangement of pipes, as though the drinks are plumbed directly into the taps. It's surprisingly dark given that it's only half-five and people will shortly be flinging around pointy objects.

A few people start up a chaotic game while the rest of us cluster around some tall tables. Ms Lenson organises drinks while HG stands stiffly by her side, frowning slightly if anyone comes too close. Felborough have taken over the whole place for the evening and it's heaving.

Right up until I'm settled with my pint, I'm convinced Lily won't show. But suddenly there she is. Ordering a drink, cramming in beside the rest of the gardeners because we've run out of stools.

The conversation sputters, then restarts with extra vigour. I'm squeezed in on the other side, but we share a quick smile before she turns to her neighbour and determinedly, as though it's a big effort, asks how their day was.

Ms Lenson and HG finish their lime and sodas and leave with ill-concealed relief, HG opening the door for Ms Lenson and guiding her with a chivalrous hand on the small of her back. The atmosphere gets noticeably rowdier thereafter. Benny goes to the dartboard and starts throwing two at once. Martina flips her hair and pretends to blindfold him. The muscly Anthony, his tongue loosened by his first sip of beer, is chatting to Ethel and Diego in an enthusiastic way I know I'll hear about tomorrow. Ethel isn't giving up on this cause. And all power to her, honestly. Nothing but respect for those who identify the people they fancy and then go for it. Talk. Flirt.

Instead, some of us have to pump them for information and feel increasingly conflicted and have quiet little freak-outs when no one is watching.

All good clean fun.

'Nice that Lily showed up,' Sanj says, helping herself to a peanut. She's a senior gardener and therefore Lily's rival for

HG's attention. Not that Sanj seems particularly bothered. 'I didn't think we'd be worth her time.'

'She used to come out.' Diego turns to us, twiddling the straw of his pink cocktail. 'In the olden days.'

'Yeah, you knew her before, didn't you?' Sanj asks interestedly. I look to the corner, where Lily's watching a game of darts. Her shoulders are a little tense but she laughs and claps when Martina throws a good one; Martina laughs too, saying something to her.

'We did our training together,' Diego explains. 'Me, her and Nathan, before he went off to work abroad. You met him didn't you, Sanj? Nathan was Lily's ex,' he adds to me.

My stomach jolts.

'Just that once, when he came to Fells for an interview.' Sanj nods, as Benny flops into a seat beside her. 'Obviously HG wasn't keen or he'd have got the job.'

'Are you friends then?' I ask.

'Haven't seen him in a while,' Diego says, the corners of his mouth turning down. I'm irresistibly reminded of a sad basset hound. 'I didn't realise what he'd done to Lily, to be honest. Men can be so cruel.' He takes a sip through his straw.

'So true,' Benny chirps, clearly not listening. 'Hey guys, what do you reckon?'

'About what?' Sanj asks.

'Martina! Am I in with a shot?'

The group focus turns to Benny's relative chances, with general consensus being they're slim to none but he might as well have fun trying. I drift away to get another pint when Lily wanders to the bar.

'Hi,' she greets me. She's probably not fooled by my casual walk over. But that's OK. This will be our third drink, so things are gentler and fuzzier anyway. I can't stop thinking about this *Nathan*.

'Having fun?' I ask to interrupt my rambling inner monologue.

'You know,' she says thoughtfully, 'I might be.'

'Told you.' I lean against the bar. For this brief, glorious moment, I'm just another worker relaxing with a colleague after a day's work.

'Are you bringing anyone to the gala?' Lily asks, watching the bartender adding tonic to the gin already splashed into her glass.

'No, are you?' Most of the gala guests are VIPs, but staff can bring a guest, if we want.

'My parents,' Lily says, in a tone suggestive of great suffering.

'Are they interested in botanical stuff?' I ask. In my head, Lily's parents are a quiet couple who enjoy Radio 3 and gardening, or a terrifying pair of landed gentry who live in a castle and own dogs specifically for the purpose of yelling at them.

'My dad is,' she says, tapping on the bar. 'My mum's had to get interested, what with being married to him for thirty years.'

'That's cute,' I comment. Her hand is close and I watch,

unable to tear my eyes away, as it inches closer to mine. 'My mum never made an effort with my dad's interests. Or vice versa.'

She gives me a sideways look. 'They didn't want to come, then?'

I laugh. The idea of my dad bumbling about Felborough trying to make conversation with celebrities is outstripped in ridiculousness only by the thought of Mum being there. She'd make a beeline for the most exciting celebrities, try to engage them in witty conversation, then pick a fight with Dad, make a scene. If she even came. I'm not actually sure she's in the country at the moment. 'I've not extended the invite.'

'I'll probably end up wishing I'd done that,' Lily sighs.

'Why do we need a gala, anyway?' I ask, as the bartender starts pulling my pint. 'We're doing a launch for the general public too. Can't the celebs just come to that?'

Lily laughs. 'They're too fancy for general admission. And they need wooing to make them dig deep because Fells always needs more investment. Ticket sales are OK, although stuff like the orchid helps bring in more guests.'

I nod, knowledgeably. 'A one-of-a-kind orchid flowering is a very sexy event.'

'I agree,' Lily says seriously. 'But even with those, we don't get the funds we need to cover all our research. And we partner with botanic institutes all over the world, so we try to foot the bill as much as we can, particularly in poorer countries.' Her voice takes on a strident tone that both intimidates and, I can admit it, makes me need to tug at my collar. 'The global south will be hardest hit by climate change yet have contributed the least to it. We should be pouring resources into this.'

'Have you considered starting a cult?' I ask, to distract her from commenting on my reddened face. 'You're very inspiring. I'd join.'

Lily eyes me. 'This work is crucial, Phil. *Vital*,' she emphasises, poking me in the side.

'Lots of things are "vital",' I say, in an obvious attempt to defuse the intensity in her stare. And pretend it's no big deal that she just touched me, voluntarily.

'This is part of the attempt to avoid a mass extinction,' Lily says. 'Which we're on course for, sooner than any of us are willing to realise. Trying to preserve the potential to keep *living* on this planet is the most important work any of us will ever do. In the history of humanity, probably.'

God. The bartender blinks, then jumps as beer pours over the top of the glass and he quickly closes the handle. The total lack of drama or ego in Lily's voice makes this statement a hundred times worse. I'm starting to see why she's so serious all the time.

I clear my throat, suddenly sure I can't engage with this right now, or how an *orchid heist* places us squarely in the bad-guys role. So instead I say, 'Thank you for your service.'

She frowns, but when I say, 'I mean it,' she rolls her eyes and smiles.

As we're wandering back to the others, a pool table in the corner catches my eye. That looks more fun than darts. 'How are you at pool?' I ask Lily.

'Not bad,' she says, then laughs. 'Quite bad.'

'Want to play?'

'Sure.'

I used to play a lot with friends from school but it's been a while. I pass Lily a cue, then arrange the balls while she watches somewhat doubtfully. I lift the triangle. 'Want to break?'

She twists her mouth. 'OK.'

She lifts the cue and aims. I can see immediately she's not entirely sure what she's doing. If I were a toxic man on a date I'd already be standing behind her, positioning her fingers. I shouldn't do that. I know I shouldn't.

Her first shot is a good attempt; it hits the other balls at least and sends them rolling gently in all directions. 'That's about the level we're working with,' she notes, stepping away.

'Not bad,' I say, moving up to take my shot. 'Have you played much before?'

'Not recently. But I lived in Melbourne for a bit,' she says, watching as I line myself up. 'It's full of stuff like this.'

'Try-hard bars that are really out of place in their small towns?' I ask, tapping the cue against the white. It clinks into a red, which smoothly drops into the corner pocket. A shiver of satisfaction tingles in my fingers. I forgot the incredible ASMR of the *clock* of pool balls.

'Dark bars with fancy whisky and pool tables. And everyone has an impressive beard and tattoos and dresses in that kind of . . . effortless style. You'd fit in there.' She inclines her head at me, focusing on the table as I line up my second shot.

'Because of my great beard?' I say, to distract from the fact that I think she just paid me a compliment. I *clink* another red into the same pocket as before.

'Yeah, that's what I meant,' she says, still not looking up. 'Sorry, you didn't mention you were good at this?'

'Don't let my general air of incompetence fool you,' I reply, taking my third shot quickly and stepping away. There's no rush. 'How long were you in Melbourne?'

'Just a year. It was good. A nice place to live. Sometimes I wish I'd stayed, honestly.' She lines up another shot, then takes it, blunting the edge of this admission. The white hits one of my reds instead of the yellow. 'Uh-oh. That's another shot for you, isn't it?'

'We don't have to play that rule,' I say. She gives me a look that says, Don't you dare patronise me. I look at the ceiling. 'Pretty sure I can beat you without it.'

She frowns, then laughs. 'Fine. Your go.'

I pot another, then try to line one up so she'll have a yellow in the firing line. I slightly misjudge it – I'm really not that good – but maybe it's for the best. I doubt she'd appreciate my help.

I also don't actually know what my plan is here. This is all part of the bigger game, right? Of trying to get close to her for the heist? But I keep not asking her about the orchid. Thinking about the movement of her strong fingers on the cue. I quickly look away.

To be fair, this is my first heist. No wonder I'm not great at it.

'Why did you come back if you liked Melbourne so much?'

I ask. She doesn't seem to have taken to living here again but I'm not sure why.

She pauses and I wonder if she's going to tell me to piss off. Eventually, she says, 'My family's here. And I was there with . . . someone. And it fell apart so I came back.'

'Not the same ex you mentioned before?'

She throws me a quick look. 'Maybe.'

I'm surprised by my desire to know what happened. But sensing not to push, I just watch as she stalks around the table trying to find her angle.

The problem with getting to know women – getting close to them, spending time together, feeling a connection – is that you never bloody know where you stand. Are we becoming gals being pals – or *gals being pals*?

Here's the thing: Lily has mentioned one ex, a man. That points to her being straight. It's definitely what you would assume, if you hadn't thought about it much and didn't really care.

But it's not a definite. It's not quite enough to make me suppress all hope and shove it down with all the other times I've had a crush on a straight woman. I'm a tragic optimist. For that to happen, I need her either to tell me outright there's no chance, which she's unlikely to do because women are polite and hate hurting your feelings, or to wait a few weeks or months until she gets another boyfriend and then they get engaged and married. And even then I'd probably check in every few years on social media, just to make sure.

The point is, a male ex doesn't make you straight. I have a

male ex. It doesn't mean anything. It doesn't mean I don't feel irrepressibly drawn to Lily in a way that actually doesn't make sense because she's been nothing but prickly and nervous around me so far; or that I haven't wondered if the smooth skin of her throat is as delicious as it looks or what her lips would feel like against mine. I rub my temple with my pool cue, then take a long drink of my beer.

I need to chill out. Everything is absolutely fine.

'Fuck's sake,' exclaims Lily. I turn back from replacing my pint to see her ball rolling futilely away from the pocket. 'All right. What am I doing wrong?'

'This feels like a trick,' I say, stepping away round the table. If I just avoid her immediate vicinity I won't have to be so aware of her forearms, which are lightly muscled and tanned, and the end of her plait, which has curled into a fishhook shape over her shoulder. I imagine it drawing me in.

'Not a trick,' she says, holding her cue towards me. 'I'm serious. How are you doing this so easily?'

'A misspent youth,' I admit, not taking it. 'While you were having new experiences in Melbourne and breaking up with unsuitable people, I was right here: playing pool and wasting my time dating them.'

She tilts her head slightly. 'Are you dating anyone now?'

'No.'

'You also spent your time breaking up with unsuitable people then, didn't you?'

'I think I *was* the unsuitable person, most of the time.'

'Either way.' She comes round the table. The dim glow

from the stupid fake lanterns glints off her cheekbones. 'I want to learn.'

I shake my head, unable to prevent a laugh slipping out. 'You've got to be kidding.' Are all my resolutions *not* to be that dickhead for nothing?

'Why? Come on.' She taps me on the shoulder with the cue and I catch it with my fingers. Two-and-a-half-drinks Lily is more relaxed than I'd have imagined possible, having seen what she's like the rest of the time. 'I've taught you something, you say.' Lily doesn't let go, the cue connecting us. 'It's your turn.'

I sigh. These things are sent to try us.

'Fine.' I take the cue and demonstrate the grip. 'You see? You just hold it there and balance it. And then you just line it up and . . . slide.'

She watches intently. 'I'm actually already doing that.'

'Evidently not,' I say, leaning to set up a shot and gently bumping her aside with my hip, 'or you'd be able to do . . . this.'

I slide the cue to just tap the ball and it rolls fluidly to knock another red into the pocket. Relief floods me. I was about to look like a real asshole.

Lily snorts. 'How embarrassed would you have been if that hadn't gone in?'

'Can you imagine?' I shake my head. 'I'd have had to just keep hitting and hitting it until it did.' I straighten to hand her the cue to find she's a lot closer than I realised. She takes it but doesn't move away.

'I've been meaning to say,' she starts, meeting my gaze steadily and causing my heart to thud a little. Clearly it's not been updated on the whole *Lily will never be interested* situation. When will it learn?

'What?' I ask. Our hands are both still on the cue. She's only an inch or so taller than me. If I just raised my thumb a little, it would brush the underside of her finger. I keep it still.

'Sorry I was so rude to you that night.'

'What night?' I ask, although I know the one she means.

'When we met.' She frowns.

'Oh, in the *bar*,' I say, enjoying myself as she rolls her eyes. 'Seemed like you were having a bit of a weird one.'

'Yeah, well.' She finally takes the cue and turns for the chalk. 'I was.'

'Why?'

She hesitates and I can almost see her battling her impulse.

'You're about to say, "I don't have to tell you anything about that," aren't you?'

Lily widens her eyes, then smiles, just slightly. 'I was actually gonna go for, "None of your business."'

'That's the same.'

She presses her lips together. I'm about to start a new topic about her next shot when she says, through gritted teeth, 'I met my ex that night.'

'Oh.' There's a pause. I reach for the chalk myself and press it against the end of the cue.

She watches, eyes narrowed. 'Not *oh*. Not anything.'

'That's why you were grumpy.'

'I wasn't *grumpy*. I was just . . . processing.' She shrugs. 'You know. Men.'

'Not really,' I say.

'No?' Lily raises her eyebrows a fraction, her expression curious and . . . something else.

'Hardly ever, to be honest. Not really my thing.' I might be imagining the jolt of understanding that passes between us. I could be totally misreading; maybe she's so deeply straight that this small confession passed her by. But maybe not. 'Why did you meet up with him?' I ask, wanting to hold onto this new intimacy.

'He thought we could try being friends. But turns out it was way too soon. Like,' she laughs mirthlessly, 'ridiculously too soon.'

'Why do you even want to be friends if you left Australia to get away from him?' Everything I've heard makes him sound like a total dick.

She shrugs. 'Guess I wanted to see if he'd changed. Or if he felt guilty. And we do have stuff in common. He's a plant nerd too.'

I suppress the totally insane stab of jealousy to my stomach and say lightly, 'To be fair, that's a very sexy trait.'

'Yeah, well,' she shakes her head, 'turns out he hasn't changed and doesn't even regret *betraying* me. So. Maybe fine not to be friends.' Her light tone belies the force behind her words.

I consider offering to punch this guy in the face, but I suspect a show of violence wouldn't soothe Lily's skittishness. I take a deep breath.

'Would it help if I said a platitude about how you're better off without him?' I ask, leaning over to gently, with a nudge of my finger, correct her grip. She looks at me from under her eyelashes.

'I don't know. Am I?'

'Obviously.' I rest my arms on the table beside her. Her eyes flick to my shoulder for a second and the tattoos on that arm: a bird with wings outstretched about to peck at a pomegranate; a vine wrapping around my bicep; a strawberry; the words *Good luck, babe.* I wonder if she's going to say something.

Instead, she turns back to the table and, with her newly corrected grip, takes a shot. The ball rolls, *clocks*, and a yellow sinks neatly into the pocket.

'Yes!' she exclaims, raising both arms in the air.

I whoop and clap her on the back in an unthinking celebration that I instantly regret, as it means I'm confronted with the skim of her shirt across her skin and I now know what her lower back feels like: firm, warm, forbidden.

'Another drink?' I ask, to hide my panic. It's just a back, for God's sake. Calm! Down! 'HG would want you to celebrate.'

'In a minute,' she says, leaning to the table again. 'Gotta do this one first. This is the best feeling ever.'

Chapter Sixteen

The day of the gala dawns grey, rainy and inauspicious. Miles calls our group chat as I drive to work, to confirm we're meeting tomorrow to problem-solve the plan he's been working on.

'How much problem-solving will we need?' Chaz asks, his voice tinny over the speakers in the cocoon of my car. Drizzle splatters the windscreen and I amp up the wipers another notch.

'I'm going to suggest we use the hole in the perimeter to break in,' Miles says.

'Wow, spoilers,' says Chaz. I roll my eyes, although neither of them can see.

'We know from Phil's map that there's a direct path with just one gate from that hole to the glasshouses. And now Chaz has pretty much cracked the security system we also know there are no cameras until we get inside.'

'Right,' I say. 'But we need a key to get in there. Plus, the security guards—'

'Exactly,' Miles interrupts. 'We need to know their shift pattern which, thanks to the head gardener's stupid technophobia, isn't online. They probably carve it by hand into stone tablets.'

'Ms Lenson prints out the rotas every day,' I point out, wondering why I sound defensive. 'So it must be on the computer somewhere.'

'Ah yes, the non-internet-connected computer,' Chaz scoffs. 'My favourite.'

'So it's agreed,' Miles says. 'The computer is your goal this evening, Phil.'

I grip the steering wheel. 'Fine,' I say, after a moment.

My heart has started fluttering unpleasantly at odd moments of the day: when I walk past the potting sheds; when I think about creeping around Felborough's huge grounds on the big night, just a week away now; when I see Lily. It's not a sustainable way to live. But I'm in too deep now.

Worse, Dad is alarming me further. A couple of days ago, I walked in on him clearing out all the kitchen cupboards. This sounds like nothing, or even something positive. But not if you know him like I do. This is an impending crisis, a panicked search. He took everything out of the cupboards and left it all over the house. I don't know if he found what he was looking for. I can only hope it wasn't the bank cards he asked me to hide; if it was, he didn't find them tucked under the loose carpet down the side of my bed. By the time I got back, everything was tidy again, tidier than before. He was out when I got home last night and I didn't have a chance to interrogate him before I left this morning.

At least I can bury myself in gala prep. There's an air of excitement at Fells today as we finish preparing the front lawn and rose garden, where the event is being held. The rain finally stops and a glimmer of sun pokes through the clouds as we set up tables under the marquee and add finishing touches to the decorations.

Lily directs a parade of under-gardeners carrying fresh flowers and sprays of greenery. I try to ignore the pleasant flush of recognition when I see her, distracting myself by looking up at the Hall's façade. It's as stately as ever, its numerous windows glinting in the dull afternoon light. They'd better – I spent enough time this week cleaning them. I'll surely never work somewhere like this again.

The thought is surprisingly unpleasant. My heart thumps in the way that's now familiar.

I turn back to the garden to see Lily, alone among the staff in looking pale and tight-lipped, snap at Diego to, 'Pick that up quickly before it stains.'

He hurries to pick up the knocked-over vase, looking wounded. I don't blame him. Lily's stressed again today, after the glow of the other night. I wonder if I'll get to meet her parents. Under no circumstances would this fall under the remit of things it would be useful to know for the heist. But maybe I'm just interested.

We finish early so we've got time to go home and change before the event starts at seven. My hands shake as I button my shirt and slide on some silver rings and I have to stop to take some calming breaths in front of the mirror. I can do this.

I get a lift with Diego, who lives nearby. We arrive to find the Felborough gates flung open and members of the press crowding around, clicking away on their enormous cameras. We show our passes and go straight through.

A temporary walkway has been built to lead us to the Hall, decorated with the strewn vines and plants that Lily was directing earlier. There's no roof, but a thin wire zigzags along the length, from which hang hundreds of origami shapes, spaced at intervals and made of glossy green and blue paper that glints in the evening sunshine. At first glance, they look like paper cranes. But . . .

'Orchids,' Diego coos in delight. I reach to brush my hand against one as I pass. I make a note to congratulate Ethel. She and her team have been folding for days.

A real, actual red carpet adorns the front steps of the Hall, turning the terrace into a makeshift stage. To the right, a photo opportunity has been set up: beautifully draped wisteria framing a wooden door. It glows golden in the warm light and is already home to several influencers posing.

Diego points out everyone he recognises, friends and celebrities alike, tugging on my arm as we walk. TV presenters, film stars, A- and B- and C-listers. They're all here. The place is rife with national treasures. There's the white-haired old man who's been presenting nature documentaries longer than most people have been alive and who made them appeal even to someone like me. I've always thought of him as like my grandad, if my grandad was a lot nicer. There's the young girl who's done so much to fight the climate crisis, who always fills me with guilt that she's years younger than me and yet so much *better.*

I've underestimated how strange it would be to mingle among these people. I'm almost used to working at Felborough now; it's easy to forget how important it is. But the other day, my ex from school – who moved to London a few years ago and who Chaz and I are still friends with – sent a photo of a tube advert for the Felborough orchid. She was asking, incredulously, if I was attending the red-carpet event; she'd heard from Chaz I was volunteering there now.

The ad had the image of the glasshouse and the orchid, emblazoned with the news that it would be opening to the public in just one short week. When I confirmed that I was, my ex asked, in a way that suggested she wasn't joking, if I got a plus-one.

I lied and said no. Of course I can't bring a plus-one if I'm busy with heist shenanigans. But it would be another lie to suggest that was the only reason I didn't want to take someone with me.

A slight prickle under my skin reminds me there's no sign of Lily yet. I want to see what she's wearing this evening. She's gorgeous all the time. But I've never seen her in this setting before.

At least I'm dressed OK. Not in a tux, to Chaz's disappointment, but I'm wearing a slim black suit that I got from a charity shop a couple of years ago for twenty quid. I'm smugger about this purchase than anything else in my entire life. It fits bizarrely well, as if I've had it tailored even though

I haven't, and it gives me a little boost of confidence, which I've never been more grateful for.

'Looking lovely, HG,' says a familiar plummy voice. I turn to see Hook, the explorer, wearing a dinner jacket and big red cummerbund.

HG, passing, gives a terse nod and takes a minuscule sip of champagne. She's also wearing a suit, but hers is crumpled, with visible dirt on the cuff, as though she couldn't resist stopping for a bit of weeding on her way here.

I do a round of the lawn, chatting with my colleagues, who introduce me to their plus-ones. Everyone's delighted to be in such a fancy setting on this beautiful, sunny evening, drinking free champagne and fraternising with celebs. This could be very much my vibe too. These are people I'd easily be friends with. If we all lived in another reality where I wasn't planning a laughably enormous betrayal, I mean.

At least the others are making the most of the event. Benny dives on the canapés every time a tray passes and I'm pretty sure Sanj is on her second glass of champagne ten minutes into the party. I guess none of us have to do things that require fine motor skills later.

Except me, obviously. I take a deep breath, blow it out through pursed lips, and stride across the lawn. It's time to get this show on the road. I'm so focused on my striding that I almost bump straight into someone, a nature documentary presenter in fact, with a craggy brow and kind, earnest smile. Finn something is his name.

We stop ourselves in time, apologise, and I look up once

he's passed to be confronted with Lily, standing just a few metres away in a floor-length, sleeveless, deep-crimson dress. There's a slit up the side to the thigh, hinting at the smooth skin beneath, hugging the delectable curve of her hips. I briefly wonder if I'm going into cardiac arrest.

I clear my throat as we make eye contact and she smiles. The neckline is cut in a deep V that I am not going to look at, not at all. Keep it together, Phil. I carefully hold her gaze as I step towards her.

'You look fucking stunning,' I hear myself saying. I don't remember giving my brain permission, but fine. I press my lips together to avoid further blurting. Jesus.

Her cheeks flush, a hint of pink colouring her neck. I think that's because of me. 'Looking pretty good yourself,' she says.

'This old thing,' I reply, absently, as I drink her in. Her hair is plaited around the sides and looped up in a twist at the back, a few strands falling to frame her face. I can't stop myself from reaching to tuck one of them behind her ear. She bites her lip, her flush deepening.

I clear my throat. 'Sorry,' I say. 'Thought I'd just . . . help you out.'

'Thanks for . . . helping. How generous.'

I nod. 'I can be.'

Her eyebrow raises just a fraction and she says, 'Good to know.'

Someone else clears her throat and I become aware of two people flanking Lily – surely her parents. The woman has blonde hair like Lily's, in a crown plait around her head that Lily's worn once or twice. The man is shorter than his wife and is leaning to peer at a rose bush a few metres away, making gentle exclamations.

'Hello,' I say, giving my friendliest smile. 'You must be Lily's parents.'

'Indeed. Mr and Mrs Francis.' The woman looks me up and down. Her gaze falters on my suit, lingers on my nose ring.

'Phil's just joined Fells,' Lily interjects, after swallowing a gulp of champagne. 'She's learning a lot about gardening. Aren't you, Phil?'

'I sure am,' I say, amused. She must be drinking to take the edge off and I'm starting to see why. Her mum is still staring at me as though she can't quite believe what she's seeing. To be fair, my look is a mile away from her tasteful, high-necked navy dress and pointy beige shoes.

Lily's dad, on the other hand, stops staring into the distance and fastens his eyes on me. 'Is that right,' he says. 'Are you a keen gardener too?'

I smile at him. 'I didn't know much before I worked here, actually. But I've learnt a lot from Lily.'

I turn to see Lily looking at me with an odd expression.

'That's our girl,' her dad says heartily. 'Takes after her old man. We're so proud of her, aren't we, Helga?'

'Of course.' Her mum doesn't smile, but her eyes narrow very slightly. 'So ambitious, our Lily. Sometimes we think it would be good for her to take a break, don't we, Charles? Spare some time for her relationships.'

My eyebrow twitches involuntarily. This comment, paired

with her dad's reaction – which is to shuffle and look into the sky – gives me one of those lightning flashes of insight, as though seeing their relationship laid out in front of me.

'Yes, well,' Lily says, twiddling her champagne glass, 'I'm not *in* a relationship any more, Mum, and this matters to me. And it's paying off.' She's defiant as she meets her mum's eye. 'This is very new, but HG's put me in charge of one of the glasshouses. Not Anthony, *me*. And . . . it's the important one.'

Her dad leans forward eagerly. 'The important one? Lils, you don't mean—'

Lily raises her eyebrows significantly as she takes another sip of champagne. My heart thuds again. *The important one.*

It's got to be where the orchid is kept. And Lily is in charge.

I check over my shoulder. HG's on the other side of the garden, her head bowed towards Ms Lenson next to her as they mumble together. She definitely can't hear us. Not that Lily would say anything she shouldn't hear anyway, obviously.

My stomach is churning. Is this good or bad news? I have no idea. It will surely help me, while also making it much harder. For Lily, it's good. Until I ruin things for her.

'That's exciting.' I find my voice. 'HG has a lot of faith in you.'

Lily grins, her eyes shining in the evening light. 'It just bodes really well for my promotion,' she says, her enthusiasm bubbling past her usual reserve. 'She's testing to see if I'm ready. So I need to show her I am.'

Her mum looks pained, in a genteel sort of way. 'Let's not

discuss promotions at a party, Lily. It's not polite.' She turns to me, maybe to try out my potential as an ally. 'Work isn't everything, is it, Phil? One must have a balance.'

I smile sunnily back. 'I'm impressed by Lily's dedication, to be honest.' I meet Lily's eye as I add, 'It's inspiring to have a passion and go after it like this.'

Instead of looking away, Lily holds my gaze. Her eyes crinkle slightly at the corners. I try to send her a telepathic message in response to this clear thank you, but I wouldn't know where to start with my mix of emotions.

So I just smile and hope it's enough for now, even though it won't be forever. The timer is already ticking down on our relationship.

Chapter Seventeen

At about eight o'clock, the crowd flows towards the terrace for speeches. The documentary presenter I almost bumped into is standing by the waiting mic, relaxed and smiling down at us. Finlay Slater, I remember suddenly. That's it.

'All right everybody,' he's saying in his soft Scottish accent, 'gather around.' He waves at an individual, then points at a group. 'How are you doing? Having fun?'

The crowd ripples closer as though drawn by magnets. This guy has been on our TV screens for at least the last ten years; he's in his mid-thirties but he's already travelled all over, bringing natural wonders to us back home. That's how the programmes pitch him, anyway.

There's something about celebrity. It's more than charisma. Just that tangible sense that this person is bigger than I am; the things they've seen will be hard for me to understand. Even Lily, surely the most down-to-earth person I know, is drifting over, eyes fixed on him.

Finlay Slater spreads his arms to welcome us. 'Good evening, everybody.' His voice beams out, echoing around the trees. A few people yell 'Good evening' back; others cheer. 'What a joy it is to be here for the reopening of these sensational gardens. The most wonderful institution in the world.' He looks around, smiling beatifically.

The sheer positivity radiating off him makes me smile too. It *is* a joy to be here, I find myself agreeing. I am hashtag-blessed to be here in this moment.

'I'm lucky enough to have worked with Felborough on a number of projects. Their work leads us to new scientific discoveries, ways of conserving our planet. It offers a chance for hope.'

People are nodding. I look over to Lily, who's staring at him fixedly as though if she moves she might miss a second of the experience.

'I like to sit in the glasshouses when I need inspiration. They help me remember that even when the state of our warming planet seems hopeless we still have to try; there's still work to do. I'm between projects currently, so you can imagine my relief that they're reopening next week. My agent would like to thank you as well.' Everyone laughs politely. 'And, Ms Gyamfi, I am available for weeding services.' He raises his glass to her and everyone laughs again.

'In all seriousness, these botanic gardens are a powerhouse of research and conservation. They are leading the way. We're honoured to have any part in that journey, whether we're lucky enough to work in partnership with Fells, or as a visitor experiencing it for the first time. Thank you for the work you do.'

There's a pause for some genuinely emotional applause and much shutter-clicking from the photographers.

'Without further ado,' Finlay continues, 'we're going to hear from Colonel Hook, the man responsible for discovering the Splendid Paradise Orchid all the way on the other side of the world and bringing it safely back to Felborough. Where we'll soon be able to view it for the first time! Over to you, sir.'

Hook beams genially as he bounds over. 'Thank you, thank you all. I never imagined when I was held hostage in a guerrilla fighters' camp in the rainforest all those weeks ago that I would end up standing here, drinking champagne. It's never tasted so delicious.'

There's a ripple of uncertain laughter. This is new. I thought the explorer just went and got the orchid and came home again.

Lily is shaking her head. 'He is not meant to be talking about that,' she whispers.

'But the good old reliable Panamanian and Colombian governments did magic work and here I am today. And it was all worth it,' he says, his expression switching at breakneck speed to utter seriousness. 'For the beauty of that orchid, I would do it all again.'

I sneak another glance at Lily. Her face, so open and filled with delight as Finlay Slater spoke, has hardened to stoniness. While I watch, she looks to HG, standing equally grim-faced a few feet away, and they share the kind of moment that says, We'll discuss this later and there will be a lot of shit-talking.

I want to intercept it. But it's not for me. I won't get to be there. I'm not part of their world at all.

Oh, I am such an idiot.

The explorer is talking on about something: the beauty of the rainforest or the magic of orchids or whatever. 'Back in a minute,' I whisper to Lily. I ease through the crowd towards some clear space, ending up at a refreshments table on the other side of the lawn.

I can't be jealous of Lily and HG's closeness, for God's sake. I'm here for a bloody heist, not to fall for someone totally out of my league.

An old gentleman corners me as a server refills my glass with sparkling elderflower. 'What's the name of those columns?' he bellows, gesturing in the direction of the Hall's façade. 'Damned if I can remember who designed them.'

This is a welcome relief from my own thoughts and the voice of Hook, whose amplified speech is still booming out over the lawns. And I do actually know the answer.

'The columns are Ionian,' I tell him. 'And the house was designed by Nicholas Hawksmoor in the early seventeen hundreds.'

'Is that right!' he exclaims. 'My guess would have been Chris Wren. Seems like one of his jobbies.'

'He was actually second choice, so you're not far off,' I agree, hiding my amusement at referring to Sir Christopher Wren as 'Chris', like an old friend rather than a world-famous, long-dead architect. 'And he did have some input into the design. Hawksmoor worked closely with him on lots of his buildings.'

'Yes, yes.' He strokes his ample beard. A woman who's wandered up to refill her own drink is listening in. 'When was this?'

I set my glass on the table. 'The Hall was designed in the early eighteenth century but wasn't completed until 1720.'

The man nods, still staring up at the building. The woman holds her glass to her chest, nodding too. They seem genuine, so I might as well continue. Chaz and Miles were totally uninterested when I tried to tell them about this bit of my research the other day.

'It has elements of Castle Howard, like the scale and the big Baroque façade. But Hawksmoor used Classical elements like the columns and the overall size to give it this amazing drama.' I point up towards the Hall. 'Blenheim Palace was built around the same time as Felborough and there are some obvious similarities.'

I'm pointing out features to the small group that's now gathered when I turn at another question to see Ms Lenson.

'Er,' I say, suddenly wondering if I've broken some unwritten rule of the gala. No impromptu lectures! No uncouth tour guiding! But Ms Lenson just flaps a hand at me to carry on. So I do.

Ten minutes later, people have used up their questions and the main speeches have finally finished. Ms Lenson selects a canapé. 'That was interesting, Phil,' she says. 'You're good at explaining things.'

'Thank you,' I say, taken aback. I'm surprised by how much I enjoyed having people hanging on my words like that, as though they're important.

'Have you ever considered being a teacher?' she asks. 'You clearly enjoy sharing knowledge.'

'Um,' I say, stumped by this: the first time Ms Lenson has offered a personal comment. I wonder if she's tipsy. She doesn't seem to be drinking at all though.

'You have a good memory for facts,' she continues, when I don't elaborate, 'and a thoughtful approach. It could suit you.'

It's not just the suggestion that's surprising, although truthfully this is something I've considered once or twice. It's also the fact that while I've been observing Felborough, she's been observing me too.

'I— I'm not sure,' I say in the end. 'Maybe.'

'Something to consider, perhaps,' she says, as someone else comes up to chat to her. 'Oh hello, Sandra.'

'Mary, darling, I've just been having a little snoop around the grounds,' the woman greets her, her face bright with vigour. 'Did you know the gate into the stables is quite broken? You can push it right open!'

I control the urge to shush her. Mind your own business, Sandra. Some of us are relying on these security lapses for plans of our own.

But Ms Lenson, rather than looking worried, pats her arm. 'That's kind of you to notice. But we're getting it fixed in time for our reopening.'

Sandra tuts, still looking worried. 'Just that gate? There might be other issues too, if there's one.'

'No, everywhere. Hiwot wasn't keen, but Hook has insisted on an overhaul. So we've been working with Hook's security team and a company we've contracted. We finalised the plans today.'

Hang on. They've contracted a new security company?

'That's a relief!' Sandra flaps her hands. 'Because, dear, I hate to criticise, but it really is looking rather lax.'

Instead of looking offended, Ms Lenson smiles equably. 'It does make sense to renew the security now we have the orchid. You know, we've been getting these phishing attacks recently.'

'Phishing attacks?' I say. My own voice sounds distant.

Ms Lenson tuts. 'Hard to believe, isn't it? Somewhere like Felborough. But we've received a number of suspicious emails and when I forwarded them to our IT department, they were absolutely clear I shouldn't answer them.'

Sandra nods, tutting again. 'You can't be too careful these days. Just last week I received an email inviting me to a website to meet some bizarrely buxom young women. I didn't know where to look.'

But I've heard enough. This is very, very bad news.

We have a problem. I'm standing outside the Portakabins messaging the group. **They're updating the security system. They were tipped off by some phishing emails.**

Fuck, is Miles's succinct reply. **Phishing emails?!**

The easiest way to get into a system is to be invited in, Chaz writes. **It's not glam but it works.**

Like a vampire, I think but don't say. I sometimes know when to shut up. I can just picture Chaz's defiant expression.

Great, Miles says. **Nice one, Chaz.**

If you want to take over hacking the security please be my guest, Chaz sends back, so quickly that he's obviously in defence mode. He hates it when the veil is lifted on his IT work.

All I know is they're installing new security, I say. **So back to square one.**

Miles is typing. Then he's not. Then he's typing again. I stare at my phone, waiting. He's our leader, the one who pushes us forwards. He's got to have a backup plan.

After all our work, is what he eventually goes with. That wasn't worth the wait. No words of reassurance or at least gratitude that I've found this out?

I rub my forehead with the heel of my hand. We have one week until the orchid blooms. Whether that will be enough time for Chaz to crack an entirely new and far superior security system, I don't know. None of us do, judging by the silence ringing through my phone.

Eventually, another message arrives from Chaz. **Let's still meet tomorrow. Just find out what you can tonight, Phil.**

See if we're as screwed as it seems, Miles adds.

I shove my phone in my pocket so hard I nearly rip the lining. I've risked so much for this heist: compromised my morals over and over, lost income, jeopardised my ability to get a job ever again, and therefore my dad's and my entire future. Yet the payout is further away than ever.

There's no point trying to break into the kitchen to get on the computer now; the information will be out of date by next week. I might as well go back to the party.

Chapter Eighteen

Lily finds me at the canapé table, mainlining salmon blinis. If these are my last few days of freedom before I either go back to my no-hoper lifestyle or get thrown in jail for botanical treachery, I may as well enjoy myself. I've got some champagne too.

'That bloody explorer,' is Lily's opening line. 'Did you hear?'

'Yeah, what was he on about?' I ask, swallowing my mouthful. This is a welcome change of topic.

She checks no one's in earshot before leaning in. I catch a whiff of what might be her perfume, or possibly just *her*, and grip the edge of the table as she murmurs in my ear, 'Part of the deal was the Colombian and Panamanian governments would rush through the bureaucracy. And, in return, he wouldn't mention the whole "captured by rebel fighters situation". Which he now has, in front of the press. It obviously doesn't look great for them.'

'Yikes,' I say. That puts a new spin on the Hook situation. I always thought he was a regular entitled prick, and he is. Good to have it confirmed.

Lily leans away again, disappointingly.

'No Eva this evening?' I ask.

'She couldn't make it,' Lily says. 'Nothing to wear.'

I laugh, despite the feeling of the ground spinning away that the salmon blinis have done nothing to help.

A new security system will make the already difficult plan almost impossible and the grand opening is only a week away. My dad is refusing to speak to me about a potentially life-ruining financial and/or gambling relapse situation. The volunteering job I got for the purpose of stealing this bloody orchid is more fulfilling and interesting than anything else in my life, and I'm going to lose it. I can't afford to work for free, plus I won't ever be able to come back here. Everything I've learnt will stay rent-free in my head.

Stupidest of all, the most consistently good thing in my life these days is Lily. She's funny, interesting. She's gorgeous. It's not just how unattainable she is, no matter how much I try to pretend that's why I feel this connection. I just really like her. And I think she likes me too.

'Are you OK?' Lily asks. 'You went somewhere just then.'

I look up, realising I've been staring at my glass for the last few seconds. 'Sorry. No. I mean, yes, I'm fine.'

'What's up?' Lily selects a cheese straw and takes a bite with a snap of her teeth.

This might be the first time someone's properly asked me

this in . . . more time than I'd care to admit. I've pushed people away for so long, trying to carry everything alone, that most have stopped trying to be let in. How long have I been lonely? I wonder suddenly. How long have I been putting off trying to be happy, believing I can't be until all my problems are solved?

Surely it wouldn't be so bad if I talked to Lily. Everything else is fucked anyway.

'It's just . . . I don't know.' I gesture round at the party. 'I sometimes feel like I'm getting everything wrong.'

Lily raises her eyebrows, her expression full of kindness. 'Ah. One of those.'

'That old chestnut,' I agree. Her joke eases the admission, making it lighter.

'Want to go and sit over there?' Lily asks. 'If you need to do some unpacking.'

We find a couple of spindly metal chairs in a secluded corner of the open-sided marquee, shielded by the hedge. They're still warm from the afternoon sun. Conversations from the party reach us, blurred by distance.

'Go on,' Lily says.

'You're not seriously interested,' I reply.

'I am.'

'Why?'

She bites her lip, a hint of a blush on her cheek. 'Why wouldn't I be?'

Because you're prickly and closed off and someone actually told me once that you hate everyone, is what I could answer. But her blush gives me new courage and I don't want to ruin any chance I might have. Even if it's only a fraction of a chance.

So instead, I say, 'Because it's boring. I'm just killing time, like any drifter who peaked in high school and fucked up as soon as they left.'

'You didn't peak in high school,' she says.

'Lily, I'm twenty-seven. I don't have any skills; I've never had a good job. Apart from this, I mean. This one might actually be good.' Apart from I'm not being paid for it and I've only got it for another week. 'I've not dated anyone for ages. My last girlfriend broke up with me because I worked too hard and had nothing to show for it. That's not exactly what she said,' I clarify, seeing Lily's expression. 'But it was implied. And my family's too messy to bother mentioning.'

The Hall looms over us, stately and beautiful. Lily sits, just listening. She rolls the edge of the tablecloth between her fingers. I want to move closer but I don't. She's just being a kind friend. I expect her to fill the silence but she doesn't. We stare out over the lawn.

Some more words bubble to the surface to fill the space and I release them into the still evening air. 'Getting to volunteer here . . . I guess just makes me realise I'm not where I thought I'd be. Like I'm trapped on the world's most boring rollercoaster, trying to keep things moving. And I'd forgotten that there could be more. Because I actually . . . love working at Fells,' I tell her, finding some honesty that I can actually share, that doesn't relate to my dad or the heist or Lily herself. 'And I'll have to leave once it's reopened and they don't need

190

so many volunteers. But this whole other world of, like, the glasshouses and history and plant stuff, and the way you love what you do . . . It makes me want it or at least,' I search for the words, 'want how it makes me feel.'

'How does it make you feel?' she asks. I'm not imagining it; she's shuffled slightly closer.

'Curious,' I say. 'Like there's more out there. And like I might actually be able to grab it.'

I force myself to meet her eye. Her expression isn't mocking, like she's gearing up for a joke, or waiting for me to stop talking until it's her turn to speak. She's listening, her face inscrutable.

Then she says, 'I wouldn't have thought you'd feel like that.' Anticipating my next question, she continues, 'I don't know. You seem so sure of yourself. People find it easy to talk to you. You're charismatic.'

I shake my head, dismissing the compliment. Liking to talk to people is very different from being sure of myself.

Lily still hasn't looked away, her eyes bright and compassionate. It's uncomfortable being seen like this, after such an honest admission. The vulnerability hangover is predictable but still stunning in its intensity.

'Anyway,' I say, 'sorry. I haven't said congratulations yet.'

'For what?' She frowns.

'The new glasshouse responsibility. That's amazing.'

Lily nods. 'It's what I want. And I beat Anthony,' she adds. 'You know, not to be a wanker about it or anything.'

Lily throws me a sidelong glance and I laugh and say, 'Please, be my guest.'

'Well,' she goes on, cheeks going red, 'he actually joined Fells before I did. And he definitely thinks getting this promotion is, like, his due. So this is even more of a win. A win against straight white men everywhere, in fact,' she finishes, triumphantly.

I smile as she knocks back the rest of her champagne. Is it normal to find ruthless ambition so charming? And hot? Let's not worry about that.

'Well done you,' I say. 'You deserve it.'

Her profile is neat and elegant as she looks across the lawn, her hair shining gold. The night is young and I'm feeling relaxed in a desperate "the abyss is just over there and I'm barrelling towards it" kind of way.

I find myself blurting out, 'Your hair's so lovely. With the plaits. I like how you,' I wave a vague hand around my head, 'always make it look nice.' It's excellent to sound this pathetic, even if I do mean it.

'Thanks.' Lily twirls a curl around her finger ruefully. 'I don't really like it. But it keeps it out the way.'

'You don't like it?'

'I don't recognise the person in the mirror sometimes. It doesn't . . . reflect how I imagine myself. You know?' She glances at me. 'You don't.'

'I do,' I insist. I remember this feeling well. 'I felt like that non-stop until I was about seventeen.'

'What happened after that?'

'I took control of it.' I remember it vividly. I saw a butch woman in an advert, with short hair and a sleek suit. It wasn't exactly what I wanted to look like but it was enough to plant the seed of realising: there's another way to be, different from the options I'd been told were available. 'I cut my hair, stopped wearing skirts. And whenever I felt badly about my body I did something that made me like it more. My nose piercing made me like my nose. My tattoos made me like my arms.' I hesitate. This feels important to say. 'You can always change things. You get to choose.'

Embarrassed at this speech, which Lily very much didn't ask for, I slip off my jacket and sling it over the back of a chair; roll up my shirtsleeves. The last rays of evening sun warm my skin. No point overthinking it now anyway.

'I like your tattoos,' Lily blurts out. I squint at her. She looks slightly surprised and quickly tears her eyes away from my forearms. 'I've always wanted one.'

'Why don't you do it?'

She shrugs. 'My mum would be a bit . . . you know.'

'Scandalised?' After meeting her mum, this is only too easy to imagine.

'She'd think it wouldn't help her goal of me settling down and giving her grandkids. As if getting a tattoo would make me less likely to go back to my ex.'

It's not my business and I shouldn't get involved. But that's not fair of her mum. The one good thing about my mum leaving is not having to deal with that kind of boomer shit any more.

'It's your body. If you do get one,' I twist my champagne glass in my fingers, 'I could come with you. If you wanted.'

'Would you?' She looks at me from under her eyelashes.

'Course.' This isn't some huge, generous offer. 'I'm in the market for another one. What would you want to get?'

She looks dreamily into the distance. 'Maybe a fern. A fiddlehead.'

I can picture it: a fine-lined botanical tattoo. She's so beautiful already. It would be perfect. I clear my throat. 'I got most of mine at my friend's place. They often have guest artists.'

'I'll think about it,' she says.

That's a no, then.

'I mean, I genuinely will think about it,' she adds, as though she's read my mind.

'All right,' I say, stupid warmth flooding my body at the fact that she wasn't rejecting me. I'm about to tell her more about my friend when I pull up short with a jolt. I can't take Lily to get a tattoo; what am I thinking? I'm going to *betray her trust* any day now. She won't want something permanently on her body that reminds her of me. For God's sake.

'You know,' Lily says hesitantly, as I take a sip of champagne and stare into the sky, which is fading to a soft pink in the west. 'You're the first person who's persevered with me in a while.'

'What do you mean?'

She shrugs. 'I kind of swore off work relationships a while ago. So people don't like being around me. They find me rude and . . . and needlessly aggressive.'

194

This cuts through the turmoil of emotions in my head. I raise an eyebrow. 'I don't find you needlessly aggressive.'

'You're the exception.'

'You know,' I start, choosing my words carefully, 'you could give people another chance, if you wanted. Like with Diego or the others. Clear the air. Just something to think about,' I suggest, as Lily looks sceptical. 'You couldn't have such a nice dog if you were a horrible person,' I add, to bring us back to earth.

Lily shakes her head, but smiles. 'That wasn't me. Eva did that all by herself.'

Chapter Nineteen

As the sun sets, the fairy lights strung through the trees flicker on, speckling the place with flashes of gold. Servers light candles on every table and the band on the veranda starts to play gentle, fifties-style tunes, easy to bop along to. People dance on the lawn, lit by the strings of lights that mark the edge of the dance floor. The glow and the music and the warm chatter lends a sparkly romance to the scene that does nothing to help me, personally.

I'm considering finding a bucket of cold water to dunk my head into. I've had too much champagne and Lily's sitting close beside me now, her leg touching mine, and we're laughing at the sight of HG and Hook dancing. HG is holding herself so stiffly, her neck at a rigid forty-five-degree angle, that it couldn't be more obvious that she was strong-armed into it.

To my alarm, when HG spots us she leads Hook over and firmly invites – orders – Lily to dance with him.

'Not long until you need to check the glasshouses,' HG says bracingly, clearly barely restraining herself from brushing off her hands as she palms Hook off on Lily. 'So just time for a short dance.' She hurries off.

Surreptitiously pretending to scream over her shoulder at me, Lily consents to be pulled away. I watch as she and Hook awkwardly circle the dance floor. They move in and out of the couples. Martina is swaying with Benny, towering over him in her heels as they hold each other in a clinch. Ms Lenson and HG are dancing together, their postures very formal. Anthony stands beside Diego on the opposite side of the lawn, both happily watching.

When Lily appears in the throng looking even more uncomfortable than before, I give her two thumbs up and mouth, 'You look good together.'

She rolls her eyes, lips pressed together to stop herself laughing. Hook turns her in a spin. When she faces me again, she widens her eyes and jerks her head subtly towards me, then back. I frown, pretending not to understand that she's calling me over.

She grimaces, then, after another spin, lifts her hand from Hook's shoulder and very clearly beckons with one finger.

Shaking my head, as if this is all in a day's work, I shrug on my jacket and tug the lapels to straighten them. Then I stride towards the dance floor and tap Hook on the shoulder.

'Mind if I cut in?'

I've always wanted to say that to someone. It's in every period film with a dance scene that I've watched with my dad. Until now, I've never been in a situation where it was called for or where I'd be confident the other person would understand.

But, 'Not at all,' Hook says, stepping away as Lily grins in disbelief.

I step into his position and take Lily's hand, resting my other hand gently against her waist. Her dress is silky and my fingertips graze the bare skin revealed by the glorious low-cut back. She swallows and rests her hand on my shoulder.

'Now what?' I whisper, looking into her eyes.

She gives a mischievous grin, like a baby monkey. 'Is he gone?'

I turn us slowly. 'See for yourself.'

Hook has disappeared into the crowd and immediately found another attractive young woman to dance with.

'You're such a knight in shining armour,' Lily says, flexing her fingers on my shoulder.

'Thank you.' I nod. 'I've been desperate to be that for you ever since you bravely saved me from that hare.'

We turn slowly again. I adjust my hold on her waist, nudging her a little closer. She responds instantly, moving towards me.

'I'm glad you remember me as heroic,' she murmurs. 'Given the main danger was one of us getting too upset and having to leave.'

'A modern fairytale,' I say.

'It does seem like it sometimes,' she says mildly, looking fixedly over my shoulder. Her back rises and falls under the flat of my hand. I think it's faster than normal. I'm not imagining it.

The dance floor is so crowded I have to hold her closer. This will be the excuse I use when she throws my hand off and reels back. But she doesn't; she leans in, folding herself into me until we're standing so close there's no space between us. I spread my hand, my thumb reaching up to her shoulder blade, my little finger following the delicate curve of her spine. Her warmth brushes against me, sending a bolt of anticipation to my stomach. Her cheek touches mine.

My heart is pounding, but not in the horrible way it's been doing recently. More in the teenage way: when you're close to someone you can't stop thinking about. You get sweaty behind the knees and your limbs fill with buzzing and you know that, surely, you're the only person in the world ever to have felt like this.

She looks into my face. I take a breath. I could be about to make the stupidest mistake of my life.

Then again, as stupid mistakes and my life go, this might not even make the top five. I glance around, checking if anyone's watching. But we're hidden by the darkness and the dancing; everyone's occupied. No one's looking.

My head is racing with every conversation we've ever had, combing them for scraps of meaning. She had an ex who was male. But she didn't even like him. She *does* like my tattoos. She thinks people enjoy talking to me. She thinks I wouldn't have noticed her when we were at school.

'Lily,' I say, breathing her name like a question. She inhales shakily. Our hands are still intertwined. I use that to draw her closer as I lean in, moving slowly, giving her the option to leave. To stop me. But she doesn't. Her eyes are on my lips and, as we move together, her free hand moves from my shoulder to the side of my neck and rests there, delicate as a butterfly against my skin, her thumb just brushing my pulse as though wanting to check I'm real.

This is a bad idea, I know it, but the voice of reason has receded to the very back of my mind. At the front is just Lily: her hair, her cheek, her long, pale eyelashes that curl at the tips, lit by the strings of fairy lights. At last, gently, I press my lips to hers.

As they touch, it's like coming home, like fireworks, like every stupid cliché. She tastes like champagne and evening sun, glowing bright and comforting. Letting go of her hand, I press my left hand against her back too, pulling her still closer. She reaches into my hair, her fingers cupping my head. The contact is unspeakably tender. Despite the chill of the evening, everything about her is warm, radiant. I slip my fingers under the fabric of her dress where it curves at her lower back and stroke her skin, soft like silk.

The kiss deepens just for a moment, becoming less gentle, more urgent. She tightens her fingers in my hair, making me let out a little sigh of surprise and longing, our bodies pressed flush. Our similar heights fit us easily together.

When we break apart, we're both breathing hard. Her face is flushed in the darkness of the evening, her eyes shining. 'Phil,' she says, like a prayer.

'Lily,' I agree, resting my forehead against hers.

'We're in public,' she says, her voice on the brink between laughing and frustrated.

'No one's watching.' I lean to whisper in her ear. 'Are you nervous?'

'Yes.' She clears her throat. 'Are you?'

I shake my head. 'No.'

Her eyes darken as I speak, her gaze on my lips.

'Oh God, Phil, I want—' she breathes. Then a wisp of laughter escapes as she murmurs, 'Am I creating a hostile work environment?'

I run my thumb along her cheekbone, watching it paint on a blush like dye into water. 'Lily. If anyone's being hostile it's me. I want to take off that dress,' I add, in a whisper. In for a penny in for a pound.

Lily runs a hand across her face, doing nothing to make her cheeks less pink. She's so beautiful I can't look away. That kiss has unlocked everything I've been suppressing the last few days and weeks, and I can't think. I want her alone, away from here, straddling me, spread out for me. Any way she wants.

'Fuck,' she says, as if casting about for a lifeline, clinging to my shoulder. Then, to my despair, she catches sight of her watch. 'Oh God. I have to go. Not like that,' she adds, seeing my expression. 'It's just, it's half-ten. I have a job.'

'Do you need help?' I ask. If this was anyone else, I'd be certain they were making an excuse to get away. But Lily's face is pure, naked emotion. She's not lying to me. She couldn't, not like this.

'I need to check on the glasshouse.' She pauses. 'You wanted to see, didn't you?'

'You've shown me already,' I say uncertainly. This can't be what she means. Surely not now, at this of all moments.

'The orchid.' She looks at me under her eyelashes. The word makes my heart thud. 'I need to check on it. I can show you, if you want. It's not bloomed yet but it's still beautiful.'

I'm struck into silence. For the last few minutes, unlike all the minutes in the preceding weeks, the orchid hasn't crossed my mind. Not once. It was just us. I didn't realise until I heard the word again how freeing it had been to be so fully distracted.

This is exactly what we need for the heist. If Miles was here, or Chaz, they'd already be screaming acceptance.

But this offer from Lily is so genuine, so sweet in its wish to share something beautiful with me, that the idea is suddenly unthinkable.

Of course I can't see it, not like this.

The heist has been hanging over me, dragging down my every step, making me overthink my words, actions, responses to everything normal. But Lily like this, her kiss still fizzing through my limbs, makes me stop and wonder. It's a skylight opening above me, a beam of sunshine onto a different path.

What if I didn't have to do this?

'I'd love to see the orchid,' I say, blindly feeling my way. It's true. I can't believe a plant can be so valuable and can occupy so much of people's time, including my own, without me ever having seen it. 'But I'd rather ... spend time with you. If you wanted.'

Lily tucks her hair back, defiant, taking a deep breath. Then she says, 'We can do that. We can do both.' She leads me off the dance floor. 'This orchid is so beautiful, Phil. You probably don't get it, as you're not a plant guy.' Her smile takes the edge off her teasing and I laugh.

'Is that your official job title?'

'But it's the most amazing thing. There might be less than fifty left in the entire world and it's never been researched before.' Her face is so alight with passion that I catch my breath. 'It's barely bigger than my hand but it could be the key to a new medical treatment or give us new insight into how plants adapt, or anything. But, more than that, orchids are so delicate, so in tune with their environment.' She pauses, her expression unutterably sad. 'They're the canary in the coalmine for the climate crisis. If biodiversity is lost or an ecosystem is damaged, orchids are the first to disappear. So we don't yet know what properties it has or what it might do. For now, it's a beautiful flower that we might have found just on the brink of extinction.'

Silence blooms between us after this pronouncement. The noise from the party feels far away and Lily's still holding my hand. Unconsciously I squeeze it, her words swirling through my mind. For the first time, I glimpse the depths of the orchid's significance. And I wish I didn't.

It's like finding an undiscovered painting of immense historical importance in someone's attic moments before it went up in flames, or bulldozing a car park and braking just in time to solve a centuries-old mystery of where a king was buried.

It's a pure, unadulterated desire to save and cherish something invaluable, so nearly lost forever.

'I think I understand,' I say, when I can speak. 'More than I did, anyway.'

'Meet me there?' she asks. 'I need to change my shoes. I'll tell you the gate code.'

I meet her gaze. I can't do this, surely I can't. And yet Lily wants to show me the orchid and I want to be where she is. So I nod, brushing my finger once across her palm as she whispers the code before walking away.

Chapter Twenty

I steal through the night towards the glasshouses, hands in my pockets. The trees are silhouetted against the slightly paler sky, their leaves so dark they look almost navy. No one is around; no one's allowed in this section except the senior gardeners.

The whispered code for the gate rings in my ears. This was what I wanted, before. If I'd got it a week ago I'd have been triumphant. But my plans to find more heist intel have fallen apart. I'm just not doing it.

And I don't want to hide from Lily any more. Not now the heist is probably screwed anyway with the security updates and especially not now there could be something *there* with Lily. Something I haven't felt for years, if ever. It's easy to pretend to be cynical and close off your heart. But it's much harder to keep that up when a back-talking, angry person with a cute dog and hidden heart of gold just . . . yanks the feelings out of your chest and shoves them in your face.

It's stupid to do this. My dad needs me. But maybe Lily

will understand or sympathise, even. She knows what it's like to have a family connection you can't escape, no matter how old you are or how hard you try. My dad and I are linked; we have been ever since Mum left. Lily understands a complicated family dynamic.

The only sound is my feet rustling against the path and the occasional crunch of gravel. If I wasn't so highly strung, I'd be able to appreciate the beauty of the surroundings. As it is, I jump at every slight movement. When a pigeon coos nearby, I nearly trip over my feet and yell, Who's there?!

I catch myself in time and force my breathing into slowness. People like Lily who are at one with nature probably love stuff like this. The natural world holds no fear for them. Especially in the UK, when the scariest thing out there is a smallish deer or maybe a medium badger.

I type in the gate code and it unlocks without a hitch. As I round the corner, the dark glasshouses rear up ahead. The night makes them look like they're bearing down on me, like I'm treading water in the sea as a cruise ship approaches. They could run me down without even noticing.

A few lights are on inside, gentle greenish blue ones at ground level like glowworms, quietly lighting the way. The effect is beautiful and eerie: not a cruise liner but a spaceship, one that touched down years ago and has been breathing and growing by itself ever since.

I creep towards the door Lily led me to last time. Then, in case she's watching, I stop creeping and force myself to walk upright. Ideally I'd at least appear confident and sexy, even if the thought of seeing her, admitting my plan and begging forgiveness is making me want to throw up or run away, or both.

The wall is as smooth as I remember. I run my hand along it. The thickness of the glass is evident, cold and impenetrable. After some feeling around, I reach the keypad marking the door. There's no sign of Lily. I should wait here; she must be nearby. It's almost eleven. I trace the door's outline and idly try to open it, a half-conscious motion.

That's how I'm standing when a torch beam flashes across my face.

It's coming from inside and it scares me so much my heart almost leaps through my mouth. A dark figure stands on the other side of the wall.

I press a hand to my chest. 'Fuck, Lily! If you're trying to give me a heart attack that'll be ten out of ten for effort.'

But as the figure lowers the torch and approaches, something is wrong. They're shorter than Lily, stockier. The door swings open.

It's not Lily.

It's HG.

She marches out and shines the torch right at me. I flinch, covering my face. I want to say something but, for once, words fail me. I'm not allowed here. She's caught me in the act.

'Phil,' she snaps. 'What on earth are you doing.' It's phrased like a question but it doesn't sound like one. I don't know what to say. I can't throw Lily under the bus. If I'm not allowed to be here, she's not allowed to help me be here either.

So I hoist the remnants of my courage off the ground where they've scattered and say, 'HG! I was just . . . looking around.'

'Looking around.' She glares.

I try not to visibly cower. 'Yes. I . . . wanted to see the glasshouses. I've not seen them before,' I add. Why not add another lie? 'They're so famous. I wanted to know what they were like.'

Her gaze doesn't waver. There's no way she's buying this. I can see the moment she decides she doesn't believe me but isn't going to engage. 'You understand you're not allowed in this area. And late at night, trying to break in?'

'I wasn't trying to br—'

'You seem like a bright person, Phil. You must understand we take misdemeanours very seriously, particularly in the current situation.'

I nod, miserably. I seemed like a bright person to myself at one point too. I can't believe this is how I get caught. Not because I was casing the joint; not because I was doing my best to find the information we need to get this bloody heist done and save my dad from a ruinous fate. No. It was because I couldn't control my stupid idealist fantasy of baring my soul to Lily and her being totally, unbelievably fine with it.

'Go home. I'll speak to Ms Lenson about this.'

An image of Lily waiting here alone flits across my mind. If I go, she'll think I stood her up. But if I protest and stay, she'll get caught too. My choice is clear.

* * *

I get a taxi home, the orchid origami fluttering in the breeze behind me, wondering if anyone in the world is as ridiculous as I am. What's Lily doing now? How long will she wait?

I want to get in touch, explain. But my hands are leaden and I can't bring myself to reach for my phone. I struggle down our garden path and lean against the doorjamb, unable to find the energy to open it.

Then the door opens. My dad is shrugging into his jacket.

'There you are,' he exclaims, as if this is surprising news.

'Here I am,' I agree. His face is so indescribably dear, so familiar, that I nearly cry.

'Good party?' He steps aside to let me in, nearly knocking me against the door as he loses his balance.

His odd, tense energy breaks through the fug in my head as I step inside, steadying us both with a hand on his arm. I eye him. 'Are you going out?'

'Just, um.' His hands shake as he ties his laces. 'Off to see my pal.'

Another visit to this so-called pal he won't tell me about. I try to moderate my voice to sound inquisitive rather than anxious. 'Are you OK? You seem a bit frantic.'

'There's something I need to do. But I just need some more time.' He scans the hall, his mind clearly elsewhere. 'Can I take the car?'

My instinct is to say no, but I can't think of a way out. I pass him the keys. 'I'll need it tomorrow morning, remember.'

He nods, fumbling them into his pocket which is already half full of what looks like a letter. It falls to the floor and I stoop to grab it, gripped with intuition. Before he can stop me, I'm holding it up, my eyes flicking across the top.

Notice of possession hearing.

'Phil!' He snatches it and tucks it under his arm. 'That's not your business.'

'Dad, what's going on?' Despite my efforts, my voice shakes as though I'm about to start crying. Maybe I am.

'I've got it under control,' he insists. He roots around on the coat hooks and pulls out the old blue scarf I bought him for Christmas years ago. 'Things are a bit . . .' He clears his throat. 'I'm just—'

The scarf. He wears it when he's gambling. He says it's lucky.

'Dad,' I start, trying to wrench the atmosphere in the hall back to steadiness and calm. If he's going to the betting shop, I need to not panic. I need to help him. But I can't think; dread fills me. I take a shaky breath. 'Where are you going?'

'To meet my pal, I told you.' He flips the end of the scarf around his neck, his forehead creased deeply with what might be determination. 'Don't worry. And don't wait up.'

I'm left in the empty hall, the door closing behind him.

A possession hearing. My chest squeezes and I gasp for breath as I slip my phone from my pocket to find out what this means. Maybe it's not as bad as I think. Or maybe it's much worse.

A possession hearing is part of the eviction process, the website tells me impassively. I scroll, but the page is blurred.

I seem to have forgotten how to read and my fingertips are fizzing with adrenaline. I lean against the door.

He must have fallen further behind on payments than I realised. My heart is thundering but the rhythm running through my head is, How could I have been so stupid? We're nearly out of time. Things are so desperate that my dad's trying to win money back. It must be a last resort. He promised me he wasn't gambling any more.

And what have I been doing? I've jeopardised the one thing that *was* certain about our finances; first by taking a job volunteering, where you famously earn zero money, and then throwing that away in a moment of stupid teenage horniness.

Like, what did I think was going to happen this evening? I'd explain everything to Lily and she'd say, 'Oh, don't worry, Phil, that all makes total sense. I support you! I don't mind that you're going to steal the most beautiful, meaningful plant any of us have ever seen or that it'll ruin my chance of career progression, AKA the driving factor of my life. You go for it.'

Yeah. I don't think so.

Chapter Twenty-One

The next morning, I hardly dare look out the window in case the car's not back. Dad could've left it in a field, used it to drive to London or Glasgow, crashed it. It was in Glasgow I had to go and bail him out that first time, aged nineteen. That was also the time I accidentally yelled at him about how he was ruining my life.

To be fair, that was the wake-up call he needed. You have to hit rock bottom before you can climb back up. He gave up gambling, joined his support group. I thought everything was solved, then. I didn't realise that was just one battle in the war we're fighting. Not to sound all militant about it. I can't imagine anyone feeling less militant than I do right now.

But when I twitch aside the thin curtain, there's my Fiat, squatting outside as though it never left.

The straggly little tree across the road is thick with new leaves and the sky is an aggressively pleasant blue. The neighbouring house has its bins out, one big black and one small green, which they never take in. The lamp post is covered with layers of stickers, calling for protests or advertising gigs. I've been waking up to this view for most of my life. It may not be exciting, or beautiful, but it's steady. Safe. We have nowhere else to go, no relatives to call on any more. Losing it is unthinkable.

He'd been doing so well, too – calm and chatty, going antiquing with me, working on his upcycling, making peace with his new lifestyle. Maybe that should have tipped me off. We seem to only be able to manage a couple of peaceful years at a time before things go tits up, and I was living in denial. I should have predicted we'd end up at this current moment: a lucky scarf and a repossession hearing.

Movement from downstairs indicates he's up, at least. I brace myself for a walking-on-eggshells conversation to try and get him to do something positive today, and go through the motions of my morning routine. It just about lets me hold it together enough to avoid fully, massively freaking out.

But when I get downstairs, Dad, to my astonishment, is at the stove flipping a pancake. He's wearing a jazzy purple jumper that I've not seen in years. For him, this is the equivalent of a full face of makeup and heels.

'Morning.' He nods, sliding the pancake onto a plate. 'Hungry?'

'Um,' I say, standing there. Pancakes are one of Dad's repertoire of three meals. The other two are toad-in-the-hole and, oddly, salmon en croûte. It was Mum's favourite. Her fancy upbringing gave her a taste for it; her family used to have it for Christmas dinner.

Her side cut us off when Mum left, which meant no more visits to my grandparents' house in the countryside and salmon en croûte just once in the last few years – one evening shortly after Dad stopped gambling for the first time when we were both feeling powerful and defiant. Very unlike the current moment.

If I'm honest, it's not quite as simple as Mum's family cutting us off. Her parents didn't mind *me*. Dad was the problem. When she tried to get me to come with her, one look at Dad made me realise that would remove the last shred of hope from his life. So I told her where to get off. I would fix it; I could take care of Dad and I didn't need anyone to help, least of all someone who barely showed interest in me for the first seventeen years of my life until she flitted out of it.

Oh God. What have I done.

In a daze, I sit at the table, where Dad has laid out brown sugar and a lemon. He must have bought it on the way home last night. What the hell.

Dad hums as he pours another ladle of batter into the pan. 'Busy day?' he asks.

'Not sure,' I say. I don't know if I still have a job. So it's hard to tell. 'How about you?'

'Thought I'd go for a stroll,' he replies, poking at the pancake. 'Nice day. Maybe I'll come and visit you at your Felborough sometime.'

'You can't,' I blurt out. I wasn't sure Dad was even aware

of my new job. He looks slightly offended. 'I just mean ...
it's not open yet. But it will be next week.'

He nods, back in his silent world again as he focuses on
the pan.

I eat quickly. It's a shame; the pancakes are probably nice.
But I'm too on edge to taste them. It's hard to believe how
badly last night went. Not only did I kiss Lily, adding layers to
my forthcoming betrayal, I then *stood her up*, something that
in any circumstance would be unthinkable. I'm the stupidest
idiot in the land. I don't deserve to walk on the same soil as
her.

The thought of going back to Felborough to face Lily and
(worse?) HG is dwarfed in awfulness only by the idea of *not*
going back and knowing there's nothing I can do for my dad.
This new state of cheerfulness is almost as concerning as last
night's desperation. I can't risk the heist again.

I need to tell Miles and Chaz what happened but I'll
wait until I know what it means. My shift starts at nine
and I've not heard from anyone at Felborough. HG said
they'd be in touch, so who knows? Maybe they're planning
to throw me in the dungeon that they probably actually do
have available.

Or, more conveniently, maybe they'll just fire me. I wonder
if a volunteer's ever been fired before. I can't lose this job.
There's no way we can pull off the heist with our current
information, not now they're updating the bloody security
system.

For want of anything else to do, I leave the house at half

eight and drive to work. No one yells at me and the person on the gate waves as usual when I pull up.

The feeling of tentative normality lasts until I walk into the kitchen and find Ms Lenson at the computer.

'Phil,' she regards me over her glasses, 'there you are. I wanted a word, please.'

A few other workers are finishing morning teas or getting supplies. I clear my throat, which seems to have a part-inflated balloon lodged in it. I don't remember eating one. 'Sure.'

I follow her to the office where she conducted my job interview, several weeks ago. Not to be a big cliché, but it might as well be a lifetime. The view from the window is different: greener, more vibrant. The trees are doing their thing. Clouds are scudding across the sky. It's a wholesome setting to watch my life fall apart.

'Ah, Hiwot,' Ms Lenson says warmly as she motions me to sit.

I spin as HG stalks in. She plops herself into another chair so we're in a triangle. Her expression, soft as she looks at Ms Lenson, hardens as she turns to me.

'So, Phil.' Ms Lenson straightens her glasses. 'You'll know what this is about. Would you like to explain what you were doing around the glasshouses yesterday evening?'

I close my eyes. It never gets nicer being told off. It's exactly the feeling of being hauled in by a teacher to explain yourself after you'd been caught purposely blocking a toilet with paper towels or doodling dicks in a textbook.

Ms Lenson, with her pale, kind face and her wispy hair,

is the kind of teacher figure I wouldn't have understood as a teenager. I'd have thought she was bland and boring and way too trusting. Like Jane Eyre warmed up, just asking to be bullied. But it's different as a grown-up. She looks wounded, as though I've let her down. It's hard to look her in the eye. Sometimes empathy is a bad thing. Is that the lesson I can take from this?

'I'm sorry,' I say. 'Really. I've heard so much about the glasshouses. I was just looking. And I was planning to . . . meet someone there. But they didn't show up, so I was about to leave. That's when HG found me.'

'Oho,' says HG, like a Victorian gentleman. 'Meeting *someone*, eh?'

'Yes,' I reply simply.

HG leans forward. 'And are you going to tell us who you were meeting?'

Ms Lenson taps a pencil on the desk. 'It would help your case if you did,' she encourages.

I look between them. I'm not giving them Lily's name. 'No,' I say, apologetically. 'Sorry.'

For a second, approval gleams in HG's eye. Then it disappears. She pierces with me with a gaze so vicious I unconsciously put my hand to my cheek to see if it's as hot as it feels.

'If I ever catch you snooping around my glasshouses again,' she whispers, her voice low enough to be truly terrifying, 'you will not be getting away with a slapped wrist. Is that clear?'

'Yes, sir,' I say, unintentionally. 'I mean . . .' I clear my throat. This woman has really fucked with me. 'Yes, HG.'

'Good.' She sits back. 'Mary?'

Ms Lenson sighs. 'You're an excellent volunteer, Phil. I was hoping to ask you to progress to tours soon, to stay on once we've reopened. You're a natural at public speaking and you have a way with people that's hard to teach. But if I can't trust you, it's not to be. So you'll stick with just your current duties for now.'

She looks so downcast that I can't stop myself. 'I'm really sorry, Ms Lenson. I—' I don't know what to say, but the words keep coming. 'I really appreciate that you were going to do that. It means . . .' What does it mean? In comparison to previous jobs where I was told off for using my brain and talking too much and trying to suck up to people when I was just being friendly, doing anything to get through the day without losing my mind with boredom? 'It means a lot.'

'Right. Off you go then.' She waves a hand at me.

I back out of the room. HG watches me go before shuffling her chair closer to the desk. 'Well, dear,' I think I hear Ms Lenson say as the door closes behind me.

I waft back towards the kitchens. Ms Lenson calls HG *dear* in private, my brain tells me, as though that's useful in this moment.

Blood is racing in my ears and the adrenaline has nowhere to go. Is that really it? I just got told I'm not getting the promotion I didn't even know was on the table and sent on my way? I mean, I'll take it.

A giggle of hysteria bubbles in my chest and I slap my hand over mouth, forcing it down. I don't know if I want to cry with relief or stress, but now's not the time to lose control. Not when I've been given a second chance. That's been by far the nearest I've come to screwing everything up. And it wasn't even in aid of the heist.

As I pass through the corridors, footsteps tapping quietly against the old stone, I curse myself for being so pig-headedly stupid. I can't lose focus again. I'm going to keep my head down and ear to the ground. The opening is a week away. We need to figure out the new system, confirm our routes in and out, finalise the details. No more faffing around. And absolutely, definitely, *obviously* no more kissing.

Chapter Twenty-Two

I manage to avoid Lily the entire day of the gala clean-up. I see her a couple of times in the distance, at which point I scuttle in the opposite direction like a mouse fleeing a very sexy hawk. I desperately want to explain what happened, but I don't dare. She has to think I stood her up. The thought makes me feel genuinely sick, but I can't see another option.

If I try to explain that HG busted me, Lily will march straight to HG and confess, which will mean Lily losing her chance at promotion for nothing. It's not like once we've cleared that up I can fall into her arms, no matter how much I want to.

The truth is, I've already let it go too far. I've made it so I can't avoid hurting her. Either it happens now – a clean break. Or, alternatively, we have a few blissful days of romance, followed by me stealing the orchid and ruining her life. Which I'd argue is worse.

And if I tried to lie and claim not to be interested, I just can't see myself convincing her. She'll stare at me with her beautiful, honest face and her clear eyes and her way of making me tell her things, and the truth will come blurting out. It's better this way.

So I avoid her eye and the couple of other times she tries to talk to me and, instead, I watch her woefully from afar, like a told-off dog. I clock off work one minute after my shift ends and drive to Miles's flat.

In Miles's building, I hold the door for his neighbour: an elderly woman with a scrunchy, kind face who's struggling with her shopping. When we realise we're going to the same floor, I help her carry her eight or so bags of incredibly heavy tinned cat food to her door, which is just opposite Miles's.

'Do you need a hand taking it in?' I ask. I'm in no rush to get into Miles's and one thing I *can* offer society is a new ability to carry quite heavy stuff.

'Thank you, dearie, but I can manage,' she smiles.

'If you change your mind,' I say, 'I'll just be through here.' I think she grimaces as I go to knock on Miles's door but she gives me a sweet smile as she unlocks her own.

I square my shoulders in preparation for the next thing. But when Miles opens his door, he pulls me into a surprising and, I hate to admit, comforting hug. I try not to lean into him. Am I that desperate for physical contact? I got a taste of it from Lily and it only reminded me how long it's been. Fantastic.

'Holding up OK?' Miles asks.

'I'm fine.' He smells nice too, although it's nothing on Lily. 'How are you?'

'Great.' Miles bounds into the open-plan living room, beckoning me to follow. The place is as clean and minimal as ever. It's actually kind of weird, like no one lives here. Maybe he hides all his shit in a cupboard before we arrive every time and it all piles out again after we leave. I doubt it, somehow.

'Glass of wine?' He goes to the fridge. 'I've got the sav blanc you liked last time.'

Well, that's nice news at least. I had no idea what that wine was and had resigned myself to never experiencing it again. 'Yeah, go on,' I say, dropping onto the tasteful beige sofa. 'Just met your neighbour. She seems nice.'

To my surprise, Miles scoffs so hard as he opens the bottle of wine that I fear for the integrity of his throat. 'Please. She's rude. You know,' he lowers his voice, although it's just us, 'they had to open up that side of the building to social housing. And we were all for it of course, but they've been nothing but trouble.'

'Right,' I say. 'I just gave her a hand with her shopping.'

He shakes his head, raising his eyebrows and giving what I imagine he thinks is a worldly grin. 'Careful, Phil. Give them an inch and they'll take a mile.'

Fortunately, the buzzer goes after this bizarre statement so I don't need to respond. Miles retrieves Chaz, who stalks into the room a few moments later in the manner of a leopard come face to face with a larger, slightly glossier leopard. Feline, is what I mean. Wary.

'Welcome, welcome,' Miles says easily, as if the last time we spoke wasn't the most miserable update of the heist so far. He bustles around settling us on the couch with drinks, then takes a seat across in the matching beige chair and raises his glass. 'Team. Thanks for coming.' He waits until we raise ours too, then says, 'We're all upset about the security news. But it's not over till it's over.'

'Really?' Chaz says.

'Of course.' Miles leans back, relaxed. 'I let the stress of the mission get to me, let the doubts in. But,' he holds up his hands, 'that's not your fault.'

'We're the ones putting ourselves on the line,' Chaz fires.

'Yeah,' I agree, swirling my wine around my glass. 'With my . . . family situation, I can't afford to mess this up.'

'I understand.' Miles nods, his expression serious. 'I do, Phil. My family's gone through troubles too. It takes a toll.'

It's hard to imagine what kind of family troubles Miles is talking about. Probably nothing anywhere near this ballpark. But maybe I shouldn't be judgemental. There was no trace of flippancy in his words. 'Thanks,' I say, after a moment.

Miles raises his glass again. 'So let's have some supper and, once we're fed and watered, we can re-evaluate.'

The place smells delicious: garlicky and warm. The thought of a home-cooked dinner is suddenly the most appealing thing I can imagine. 'OK,' I say, nudging Chaz until he nods. 'We can do that.'

Dinner helps, as food often does. When we push our plates away an hour or so later, after coq au vin followed by lemon tart, things seem marginally less bleak. Miles tops up our glasses and I tell them all I know about the new security system – that is, nothing.

'We'll just have to break in once it's set up,' Chaz says. 'I'll put the word out on my message boards once we know what system they've gone for. See if anyone's hacked it before. That's quicker than hacking it myself.'

'Yes,' Miles says. 'That's what I'm talking about. We can still do this. We're so close and them putting up this new barrier is like . . .' He casts around. 'Like peasants building a flimsy defence out of straw around their keep. But we're knights and we can ride right over it once we've armoured up. It's going to be fine.'

'Er, OK,' I say, after a moment to let this absolutely batshit image sink in. We're not fucking *crusaders*. 'Once more unto the breach.'

Miles beams at me. I'm finally getting his rhetoric right.

Maybe I don't need to tell them about nearly being fired after all. No harm, no foul.

'You OK, little buddy?' Chaz asks, as I drive him home. 'You seem . . . sadder than usual.'

'Thanks for noticing,' I say, braking jerkily as a traffic light turns from green to amber just too close for me to go through. Typical.

'Really, though,' he presses. 'What's up? Not just heist stress.'

I grunt non-committally.

'Is it your dad?'

I sigh.

'It *is* your dad,' he says triumphantly. 'Go on, tell Uncle Chaz. What's Mr Hart done now?'

Nothing will convince Chaz to just call my dad Pete, like everyone else does. I don't bother correcting him. I just sigh again.

This would usually be the moment when I tell Chaz to leave me alone, it's none of his business, I don't need his help.

But I'm so tired. I don't know if it's the high and low of last night or the emotional pummelling I've taken today but my barriers are on the floor and I can't find the energy to raise them.

'I think my dad's gambling again,' I blurt. 'He remortgaged the house without telling me and now . . . we might lose it.'

We drive in silence for a couple of minutes. Even Chaz doesn't have a snarky response. He's seen second-hand the things my dad has done over the years. But this exceeds them all. If I think about it too much, I'll absolutely fly off the handle with panic.

'This heist has to work,' I say simply. 'I don't have another option.'

Chaz nods. He pats me on the shoulder. Then he says, 'We could always restart Choco-dealers.'

I hiccough a laugh. The simplicity of that time feels further out of reach than ever. To stop myself crying, I say, 'How many Bountys do you reckon we'd have to sell?'

'Quite a few,' Chaz acknowledges. 'And they were never as popular.'

'I don't know why you insisted on stocking them.'

'I like them.'

'You're the only one.' I indicate and turn, taking the familiar road to Chaz's flat. I don't know how many times I've driven this route. Five hundred? A thousand?

'Want me to talk to your dad?' Chaz asks, surprising me.

'How would that help?'

He shrugs, fiddling with the window. 'You're always complaining he's a man's man. If he won't talk to you, maybe he'll talk to me. And I might be able to help. As Miles would say, I have a certain set of skills . . .'

This is an unprecedented and kind offer. But Chaz didn't do anything to get us into this mess. 'Thanks, but it's not your responsibility to solve my problems. You should focus on breaking into Felborough.'

'You're my friend, you dick. Your problems are my problems.'

'That's nice,' I say. 'I appreciate it. Really,' I add, his sceptical look burning into the side of my head as I keep my eyes on the road.

'You appreciate it but you won't let me help. You always think you know best. Have you ever considered that other people might also know things?'

'I don't always think I know best,' I say.

'Yeah, you do.'

'So do you,' I shoot back. This is so rich coming from Chaz, honestly.

'That's different,' Chaz says, as I pull up outside his place. 'I do know best.'

Chapter Twenty-Three

Back working at Fells, I just need to avoid Lily forever; or at least for the one remaining week until the orchid blooms. We haven't talked since the night of the red-carpet event. She tries to call after me a few days later but I stride past, scrunching up my face to avoid her expression and ignoring Eva, who's toddling over to say hello.

I can't think about what it must be like because if it's anything like the heart-wrenching pain it is for me, being the cause of that is unbearable. I hate myself for being so cowardly; for all of it.

In the Orangery one morning, I'm gathered with some other volunteers to tidy the greenery growing in natural wreaths around the ceiling, in preparation for a wedding there soon after the reopening. When Lily asks Anthony to come and hold one of the ladders, he looks at her and then, quietly, says, 'You're not my boss yet.'

Lily jerks back as if slapped and Diego, nearby, gasps and

starts to speak. But Anthony scowls at him and then very pointedly turns his back, shoulders hunched, and walks away.

Diego flinches, his lower lip pushing out. He and Lily share a wide-eyed look. Then, to my surprise, she mouths, 'You OK?'

Diego nods, unconvincingly, and they morosely return to the task. It's sad girl vibes all round. I haul my gaze away, which has already drifted back to Lily there by the panelled glass doors of the Orangery with her hair in a scruffy ponytail, looking more beautiful than anyone has a right to. Me mooning around like a lovesick teenage idiot is helping precisely no one.

I've not earnt a proper wage for weeks, longer than I can remember; I've still hardly been able to do any evening shifts, thanks to the cinema manager being a dickhead; and my savings are almost gone. Without the orchid takings, I'm not even sure how we'll make it to next month, let alone address the Main Issue, as I've taken to calling it.

My dad seemed a bit brighter after our pancake breakfast but he's withdrawn again now, spending most of his time in the house watching *Downton* and biting his nails. His schedule is totally shot. And, needless to say, he's not volunteered any further information, on anything.

I keep Googling possession hearings and reading the same webpages over and over, trying to make sense of it. It's almost impossible to imagine that information applying to us. My brain slides away. The heist is the one thing that can save us and that, at least, I have some control over.

The new security system is in place, moving as quickly as threatened. It took a team of ten men in black two full days to install. They zipped around the property with bags of tools and Thermos flasks of tea, as though they didn't trust us to provide refreshment. After they left, it was even worse than we thought.

All the volunteers received key cards today. They unlock certain doors only. For example, we can open the door to the Orangery, because we might need to show visitors around. However, we can't get into the gardening sheds, which now have key card access too, or the stables; and we certainly, absolutely, cannot get anywhere near the glasshouses. If we lose our key card, it's ten quid to replace it.

'How are the key cards programmed?' Miles asks keenly, once I've finished explaining that there are now locks on pretty much every door and gate.

We're at Chaz's flat this time, sitting around in the living room. A plate of his mum's butter cake sits on the coffee table in fluffy, blonde slices. It's not a relaxing atmosphere to enjoy it, unfortunately, although it's one of my favourites. Miles is slipping his signet ring on and off his finger in the now familiar fiddly, nervous movement that makes me want to grip his hands into stillness. Everyone's talking about fifty per cent faster than usual.

'Chaz could code you a new key,' Miles suggests, 'couldn't you, Chaz?'

'I've seen them being done,' I tell them. I overheard Ms

Lenson talking Ted, the security guard, through the process. 'You need access to the system.'

'Worth a try,' Chaz says. 'Have you got the card?'

It would surely be a huge, unlikely oversight on the part of the security company to make key cards that could be easily overridden by someone with no knowledge of the system in just a couple of days. But I keep this to myself.

'Er, it's a tenner to replace though,' I say, as I hand it over. 'So . . . how long do you need it?'

Miles reaches for his wallet and opens it. 'I've only got a twenty,' he says. 'Will that do?'

I hesitate. He holds it out impatiently. 'He *is* bankrolling the heist,' Chaz reminds me.

'Right.' I take the twenty. 'Thanks.' It feels wrong to accept money from anyone, let alone Miles. 'I'll give you change next time.'

But Miles has already lost interest and is gazing at Chaz. 'Well?' he asks intently. 'Can you do it?'

'I said I'll give it a go.' Chaz doesn't sound as cocky as usual.

'If we have that, our problems will be solved,' Miles exclaims. Seemingly unable to sit still, he leaps to his feet and starts pacing.

'Did you forget what I told you?' I wave at him. I don't want to shit on his parade but, once again, he's totally missed the reality of the situation. And I have simply no time for men who don't listen. 'HG doesn't trust security systems. We also need the key code. Or one of us needs to get really good, really quickly at breaking and entering.'

'Right,' Chaz says. We muse for a while.

'I have an idea.' Miles's eyes light up. He picks up his phone and starts typing, then turns the screen to show us a gadget. 'How about this?'

'Maybe.' Chaz peers at it. I guess it could work. Better than nothing. 'Are you searching on that secure browser I showed you?'

'Oh, oops.' Miles grins. 'Always forget. Anyway,' he puts his phone down and chooses another piece of cake, 'I'll order one. Let's talk about the getaway, shall we? I'll be waiting outside with the van—'

'Why do we need a van?' I interrupt. 'Why can't we just use a car?'

'Because,' Miles says, 'we'll need enough room for the loot.'

I look up at him. 'Miles, if there's one thing I know about this orchid it's that it's a tiny fuckin' flower. The flyer is misleading. You can use my Fiat 500 if you want.'

Miles looks intrigued, then regretful. 'Sorry, Phil, we can't. They'll trace it back to you.'

I suppress an eye roll with so much difficulty that I crick my neck. That'll teach me to make jokes. Sad to find that the more I get to know Miles, the less attractive he is. There's no quicker turn-off than a failure to commit to the bit.

'So I'll hire a van,' he continues. 'We'll split up, to make it harder for anyone coming after us. We dump the van, reconvene, and head out to meet the buyer.'

'We need to check we can get out where we planned,' I say. That gap in the perimeter that Lily and I found with the hare, all those weeks ago, is still our best hope. 'The hole was going to be fixed anyway but now there's been all these security upgrades. There's no way they missed it.'

'So we unfix it again,' Miles says. 'Just need some wire cutters.'

'Cool. Who here has wire cutters?' Chaz asks. 'Because I certainly don't.'

Even in this mood, I smile faintly. The only nod to a toolkit in this flat is what Chaz and I affectionately christened the 'glamour hammer', which his mum gave him for Christmas a few years ago. It has a fluffy pink handle and glitter. Chaz isn't exactly a handy guy.

'My dad will have some,' I say, suppressing my mockery for now. 'But one of you needs to do the snipping,' I add, 'because if I get caught messing around before the heist, it's over for all of us.'

'You know I don't do manual labour,' Chaz replies patiently, rolling up his sleeve of what I think is a raw silk shirt. 'It's very much not what I'm paid for. Miles, you can do it.'

Miles grimaces. 'I'd really rather not.'

'One of you is gonna need to stop being a baby,' I say. We eventually agree that Chaz will go and make the hole in the fence bigger, and Miles will drive him there, to show willing.

We go through more details. I push cake crumbs round my plate as Miles and Chaz pore over the blueprints, pressing them into a pile with my forefinger. The more we discuss, the more holes we find. This is surely the least plausible, most ridiculous plan in history. But it's all we've got.

'What do you reckon?' I turn to Chaz when Miles goes to the bathroom. 'Will it work?'

Chaz tilts his head, that characteristic gesture. His sleeves rolled up, his cheeks slightly flushed, he looks livelier than I've seen him in months. 'No idea. But nice to have a challenge, isn't it?'

I start laughing, then have to pull myself together when I realise it's a struggle to stop. It must be nice to be Chaz.

'Hold on,' Miles says a few minutes later, leaning forward over the blueprints. He taps a spot on the lowest part of the floorplan cross-section: a small square floating just on the edge of the diagram, unlabelled. 'What about this? It could be one of your special secret rooms, Phil.'

'If it's on the map, it's not a secret,' Chaz says, with the air of one repeating an easy instruction for the millionth time.

'Still,' Miles shrugs. 'Worth checking?'

If I'm honest, my excitement about the secret rooms has waned recently. But sure, why not take on yet another difficult and stressful task? 'I'm on it,' I say, with a sigh.

Chapter Twenty-Four

A couple of days later, I've found a new spot for lunch beside the lake under a weeping willow – suitably melancholy and dramatic. At least there's a nice view. I settle onto the grass to eat my sandwich. The calm lake stretches into the distance, ringed with trees bursting into endless green as spring hurtles headlong into summer. The lake edge is tangled with weeds but a narrow, rickety jetty leads into the centre, giving the wooden rowing boats clear access to the open water.

I take a bite of my cheese and Marmite pitta, which I scraped together from remnants in the fridge, cupboard and freezer – what you might call the bottom of the barrel – and return to my usual pursuit of musing on the upcoming impossible task.

My peace is disturbed by voices and I twist from my seat on the grass. A group of gardeners are approaching in their green polo shirts, lunch boxes in hand, Benny and Diego at the front.

'Phil!' Benny waves. 'Is this where you eat lunch too?'

'I thought I was first to discover it,' I say, as he capers over.

'We always eat here in nice weather,' he says, plopping himself beside me, his bottlebrush hair as gravity-defiant as ever. I move my stuff out the way so he doesn't kick it into the lake.

'Benny!' Diego chastises him. 'You should ask first. Sorry about him,' he adds, with the remorse of a parent apologising for a toddler who's not yet learnt you shouldn't grab someone else's ice cream and shove it whole into your mouth.

'Please,' I smile. 'More the merrier.'

They settle around me in a straggly half circle, facing the lake. A snuffling at my elbow makes me jump and Eva is suddenly there, nosing at my pitta. Lily's standing behind. She must have been at the back of the group.

'All right if I sit here?' she asks quietly. She looks tired, the bags under her eyes a delicate greenish blue, but her hair is in the familiar two French plaits and her chin has a determined set. Oh God. She's worried I'm going to snub her.

'Of course,' I say, moving to give her space. My plan was to keep being cold but that resolve melts at the sight of her. The fact that she's having lunch in a *group* is a sea change from her usual approach. Is she making friends? 'Did you all hear that alarm earlier?' I ask, to distract from the fact of Lily settling onto the grass to sit cross-legged just centimetres away. The alarm startled me: a wailing siren that pierced right through my dejection and edged me towards high-level panic. 'What was that about?'

Benny drops his Meal Deal onto the grass and, tutting, opens all three items at once: sandwich, chocolate bar, smoothie.

'Benny can explain,' Sanj says, her expression carefully blank.

'It's hardly my fault,' Benny begins, taking a long drink of his smoothie and lowering it to reveal a fruit moustache, 'that their stupid new system is so hard to use. Tell me how that's my fault.'

'Most of us have managed not to set off the major glass-houses alarm system already,' Sanj comments.

'Yes, well.' Benny picks some grass and throws it at her. She bats it away easily. 'Some of *us* are very smug.'

'What happened?' I ask as the others grin.

Benny looks fixedly into the distance, so Diego steps in, carefully squeezing a lime wedge over his home-made, per-fectly boxed lunch with every appearance of deep satisfaction. '*Someone* was doing some routine maintenance in glasshouse three and tripped the new alarm, which—'

'To be fair,' Benny interjects, 'how was I meant to know they've installed actual lasers in there? Lasers! I mean,' he turns to me, entreatingly, 'lasers, Phil. What is this, *Ocean's Fifteen*?'

No, it certainly isn't that. 'Seems excessive,' I say, carefully controlling my face. 'Are they over the actual plants?'

He nods dejectedly. 'If you step onto the flowerbeds or reach more than half a metre over them you trip the alarm.'

OK. So we won't do either of those things. Fine.

'And then,' Benny continues, 'if you reset the alarm but

don't know the master code, you have to keep resetting it every thirty seconds or it goes off again.'

Wait. Once we've broken into the glasshouses we'll need to reset the alarm *every thirty seconds*?

'And Benny had no way,' Diego gestures with his fork, oblivious to my inner crisis, '*no way* of knowing this, apart from the security briefing all the gardeners attended where we were told it.'

'It was a very long briefing!' Benny exclaims.

'Luckily, Lily was there,' Sanj puts in. 'Weren't you?'

Lily nods as I look up, intrigued in spite of myself. Quiet until now, I wonder how Lily will react to being put on the spot. But she's smiling. 'I had the pleasure of seeing Benny trip the alarm, reset it once, then freak out when the main siren went off thirty seconds later. Sorry!' Lily adds to Benny, while everyone else laughs and Benny scowls. 'I thought you had it under control.'

'That's OK, Lily, I forgive you. But the rest of you are on thin ice,' Benny says, brandishing his sandwich in a not noticeably threatening way.

They keep talking but I barely hear them. As usual, my snooping reveals almost exclusively bad news. All I've learnt is how to recognise the sound that, if I hear it on the night of the heist, signals I should go ahead and start preparing for jail. If we'll need to reset the alarm every thirty seconds, I can't do that alone.

So now what?

* * *

The gardeners look up pleasantly as I get to my feet at the end of my break. They're talking about the birthday tea HG organised for Ms Lenson the other day, where we gathered in the kitchen to sing her 'Happy Birthday' in classic, droning fashion. Ethel presented her with a Victoria sponge cake, which fitted her vibe perfectly, and Diego presented a chocolate caterpillar cake, blushing that, 'Benny insisted.' Ms Lenson had no idea how to react to the latter – 'I'm surely not supposed to cut off his poor chocolate face?' – which was sweet.

'I'd better be off,' I say, stretching. 'Nice to see you.' I'm not even lying. Aside from the security bombshell, it's been lovely letting their chat wash over me, feeling like I'm part of their weird little plant nerd group.

'Bye, Phil.'

'See you later.'

Lily scrunches her sandwich wrapper in her hand. 'I'll come with you,' she says, not meeting my eye. 'I need to get back to work anyway.'

'You really make the rest of us look bad,' Sanj comments and everyone laughs, including Lily.

We fall into step as we walk away, following the path that curves around the lake and back towards the rose gardens. The place is verdant and beautiful, the path freshly wood-chipped, the air clear and clean. As Lily would say, you can hear things growing.

Her being so close is driving me up the wall. I have no idea why she's come. I'm braced for her to yell, or at least demand an explanation; I wouldn't blame her.

As usual, she surprises me. 'How are you?'

'How *am* I?' I repeat.

'Yes.' She clicks to Eva, snuffling in a bush. 'How are you. Just a normal conversation starter.'

'I'm—' Barely holding it together? 'Fine. How are you?'

'I'm fine too.' We walk on a little further. I consider throwing myself into a hedge but decide against it, on the grounds of it being overly dramatic and needlessly sharp.

I sneak a glance at Lily. Her face is pale but determined. Oh God. What's she being determined about this time? I'm not emotionally stable enough to make sensible decisions. I check the vicinity in case any hedges are available but there are just brambles and nettles nearby. Damn this rewilding business.

Lily eventually breaks the silence. 'I've been doing some thinking,' she says, not looking anywhere near me, 'and it's OK that you didn't show up. I get that you had cold feet.'

'No, I—' I shake my head. This is so shit. 'I didn't get cold feet.'

The usual internal argument kicks off. I *could* tell Lily that HG caught me that night and that I got lightly told off and demoted before I'd even been promoted. What would be the harm?

Just that Lily is clearly the type to throw herself on her sword. She'd go to HG and get in trouble too. And it would just be an *amuse-bouche* of me ruining things for her before the main course of full ruin later on. It's better left alone. I've already spectacularly failed to stay under the radar. Now I'm just firefighting until the heist.

But she deserves a half-truth; it's better than Lily thinking she's been rejected. It should be illegal to reject Lily. If anyone's breaking anyone else's heart, it should be her breaking mine.

'I just . . . can't tell you why, but please trust me, OK?' I hesitate, then add quietly, 'I really wanted to come. More than I can tell you.'

She turns her gaze on me, clear-eyed as usual. I suppress a shiver as she looks what feels like directly into my rotten soul. I'm sure she'll spot the lies and the fear.

But instead she asks, 'Is it family stuff?' I jump slightly, as she continues, 'Just because you mentioned your family was messy, before. It was just a guess, sorry.'

'Don't be,' I protest. It is family stuff, really. It's all family stuff. 'Yeah, it actually was.'

'Want to talk about it?'

I almost laugh at the generosity of this. First I stand her up; then she offers to make me feel better by being my emotional dumping ground.

'No, it's OK,' I say. She immediately looks wounded and I add, 'I would! If I could. But I can't, sorry. I hardly talk to anyone about it.'

'Maybe you should.'

'Maybe,' I agree. That's exactly what someone who was emotionally mature and not a disaster zone *would* say.

We're nearing the house now, where we'll go our separate ways. I can't miss this opportunity to say something. I'll probably regret it. But if I'm already set on my slippery slope to chaos town, I might as well be honest.

'I'm really sorry, Lily. I like you so much. But I'm just too much of a mess to be around you. I'm out of control, but if I stop, I'll sink. Like . . .' I cast around for an example. 'I'm the kind of person who hasn't had a bath in years.'

Lily raises an eyebrow.

I plough on. 'Yeah! A bath. Because they take too long and they feel too decadent and they require too much . . . time alone with your thoughts.' I laugh, hearing how stupid this sounds. 'Honestly, they're way beyond me right now. And if that doesn't give you an idea of the level of mess, I don't know what will.'

A slightly stunned silence passes.

Then, 'I don't care about your hygiene habits and I don't think you're a mess,' she says, stubbornly. I grimace at her. 'Or if you are, you're a hot mess?' she suggests, voice rising at the end.

I have to laugh again. 'Thanks.'

Almost unconsciously, judging by the dreamy movement, she reaches to take my hand, holding it between us as we face each other. I should drop it, let her go, run.

After a moment, she says, her voice quiet, 'Anyway, don't you think that should be my decision?'

I shake my head. Everything she says is another nail in the coffin of my feelings for her and my betrayal that's barrelling towards us like a high-speed train. 'I'd rather not hang around waiting for you to realise how terrible I am,' I say, aiming for lightness.

Her mouth twists in frustration. She doesn't like it when I'm self-deprecating.

241

We stand for a moment. Then she drops my hand and steps back. I'm braced for a goodbye, a final rejection – or, worse, an acceptance.

But to my surprise she just smiles, like sun through the clouds. 'I can't force you to trust me. But I'm not ready to give up just yet. Is that OK?' I start to argue, but she holds up her hand. 'That was rhetorical. Come on, Eva.'

And she strides away, Eva trotting beside her. A peal of astonished laughter escapes me and I press a hand to my mouth. I don't know what just happened.

But even though it'll be worse in the long run, it's hard not to feel triumphant as I walk away, hand still at my mouth to keep the feelings in. When I get to the small flight of steps leading to the kitchens, I take them at a jump, my heart leaping with me.

Chapter Twenty-Five

At a couple of days to go until the reopening, time is passing far too quickly and no one seems to realise but me.

We're on it, Miles replied when I messaged the group about the security lasers in the glasshouses. **Chaz and I can figure it out. You focus on investigating that bit on the map.**

Seems unlikely but I'm only too happy to give them the responsibility. And investigating, at least, is one thing I can do.

The final touches of readying the Hall involve tidying everything not meant to be on display out of sight. I stack boxes, artefacts and oddments all morning, until the pile is huge and I'm boiling. I dramatically fling off my fleece, which Martina, in charge of clearing the decks on the ground floor, insists I hang on a peg in the cloakroom.

'Just like primary school,' I say. HG, walking past, eyes me sternly but doesn't comment.

Once everything's piled, I seize my moment to helpfully – legitimately – move everything to the storage cellar. I pick up several boxes, piled on top of each other. 'Just through here?' I say casually, shouldering the door open.

Martina barely looks up before going back to scanning the multiple-page list in her hands. 'Yeah, thanks.'

I stumble through the door and trip, already flustered. I catch myself in time and stand, getting my breath back. The place is musty, low ceilinged and stacked with boxes.

If the bit Miles spotted on the floor plan the other day is right, the opposite wall is the one we need. I dump my armful and pick my way across, spirits sinking. I know the whole point of a secret room is to be hidden, but this wall is deeply unpromising: covered in grime and several feet deep in old crates.

I'm about to let out a dramatic moan of despair when I realise my hair is being blown back from my forehead. It's pleasant against my skin. Which is strange, given that we're in a cellar.

I lean precariously over the crates to brush a hand against the wall. There. Almost invisible, a thin groove runs vertically down it. My fingers brush away the dust, following it up to just above head-height, where it jinks to the right before turning another corner and going down again. Just like a door, in fact. A strange, door-shaped crevice.

Bracing my legs, I heave a stack of crates an inch or two away from the wall and there it is: a dusty, cobwebby, unmistakable handle.

I pause, but the place is motionless. 'Martina?' I shout, just in case.

'What?' she yells back.

'Nothing,' I call.

I quietly shove more crates aside. I just want to see if the door's unlocked. Quietly, trying to control my breathing, I grasp the handle, squeeze it for luck and turn it to the left. It doesn't move. Shit.

Maybe something's blocking it. Peering lower, I see it – another lock, a simple sliding one. I bend, trying to reach to slip it across. Curse my lack of flexibility. I don't know when I last did any stretching. Not recently enough, clearly.

With a final effort, I stretch the extra inches and slip the lock to the left.

This time, when I turn the handle, it opens. But instead of the tiny, square room I'm expecting, the dim cellar light shows a narrow path sloping downwards, disappearing into pitch-blackness. I flick on my phone torch to confirm. A definite draught whistles along it, ruffling my hair.

This isn't a secret room. It's a secret *tunnel*.

I was just going to see if there was anything here. But I obviously can't stop now.

'It's a bit of a mess down here,' I shout, trying to control my voice so it doesn't sound overexcited, out of breath or generally ne'er-do-well. 'I'll just find a place for these.'

'Great, thanks,' Martina calls, uninterested. Perfect.

Quickly, quietly, I slip through the door.

My phone torch illuminates a dusty tunnel, its cobwebbed corners thrown into harsh relief. I can't see where it leads; it follows a path straight down into darkness.

This is probably the most daring thing I've done since the time Chaz and I broke into the building works on our local church. Age seventeen or so, we climbed the scaffolding to sit on the highest platform, wearing stolen hard hats we'd found hanging in the entrance, giggling quietly. It was an adrenaline rush like a firework. For the first time in longer than I could remember, I felt free. Free from my family life – the one Mum had just left and Dad had started checking out of. Free from my schoolwork starting to slip through my fingers, from tangling through the hostile jargon of the benefits system for my dad for the first time. I was just perched high in the air on flimsy scaffolding, my feet dangling what felt like hundreds of metres above the ground. And no one knew where we were.

This is a similar feeling. I creep along, my hand instinctively running along the wall to remind myself I'm there, I'm real, we're fine. If anyone catches me here, I don't know what they'll do. This might not be a fireable offence if I hadn't already proved that I'm the kind of person who likes to sneak around and be suspicious. I might have set myself up badly there. And yet, on I go.

The tunnel right-angles and I follow it further into the creepy dark. I don't even know what I'm expecting at this point. The shadows are looming and if I think too hard about something jumping out at me, I'll scream.

Eventually, after probably no more than a minute or two, a shape rears up ahead. As I approach, footsteps speeding up as I get closer, I see it's a door. The same type as the one leading into the tunnel, with the same wooden handle.

I turn it. The door is unlocked. Easily, almost too easily, I push it open, something against it on the other side sliding as it moves. When the gap is wide enough, I step through.

This could be any depth underground but, strangely, the small, dark room is filled with gardening paraphernalia: plant pots, plastic sacks of soil, a gardening fork with a prong missing and a watering can without a head. Opposite is another door, outlined like the other one with dust and grime. A faded poster on the wall to my right shows an ancient Rosie the Riveter, her strong bicep announcing that We Can Do It. When I shine my torch on it, the colours fade, highlighting the peeling edges. That paper looks . . . old. Like, old-old.

Not just a storage room. A former air-raid shelter.

Excitement thrills through me, a feeling so close to fear that I instinctively clutch my stomach to suppress the butterflies.

Chaz can be as dismissive as he wants about the Cluedo rooms; if nobody cares about it any more, this still counts as a secret tunnel. And we can use it.

I creep towards the opposite door which is slightly ajar; muffled voices seep through the gap. I almost want them to sound conspiratorial, as though they're plotting. But the tone is calm, unhurried. One voice says something with the cadence of a question. I catch the words 'month' and 'seeds'.

Straining with the effort of silence, I apply my face to the gap as another voice replies, more clearly, 'Check the packet. Have we missed the season?'

'No,' the first replies, after a moment. 'Sow outdoors April to June.' There's a rattle, like tiny maracas. I adjust my position and finally get a clear sight line: there. A wooden table; rows of little seed trays. It's strangely familiar.

We're in the potting sheds.

'Hell yeah,' the second voice says. It might be Benny, I realise suddenly. 'Just in time. There are loads more in storage down there. How many do we need?'

I jerk away as the first person says, 'Dunno, I'll check.'

Unhurried footsteps approach as I scurry through the door I came through and pull it noiselessly shut behind me. Heart thumping, I half-sprint away, muffling my phone torch against my sleeve.

The journey back is faster. Before I know it, I'm stepping through at the other end. No more than a few minutes have passed. I straighten my shirt and run a hand through my hair to get rid of cobwebs, then head upstairs.

Martina looks up from her phone, vaguely. 'Sorted?'

'Er,' I say, my excuses about where I was (I was tying my laces! I fell and couldn't get up!) dying on my lips. 'Yep. All sorted.'

Chapter Twenty-Six

That evening, Lily and I walk to the car park after work. I loitered until I saw her pass because I have something to ask. Ms Lenson mentioned it to Ted the security guard in the kitchen earlier, while he dunked biscuits in tea and engaged her in cheerful chat.

And yes, I feel fine about asking Lily, actually, because it's not heist-related: it's everything-related. This is information of general interest. I could ask any gardener. I just want to ask Lily because she's my favourite. I mean, favourite gardener.

She said she was glad to see me today and it made me feel warm inside, as if my cold dead heart was thawing after a long winter. I don't remember giving it permission to come out of the deep freeze.

'Question for you,' I say, once Lily's finished laughing at my impression of Ms Lenson discovering a rat's nest behind the cistern in the toilets (genteel shrieking). 'Are they actually going to reschedule the reopening?'

'Unconfirmed,' Lily says, her expression serious again as we walk towards the gate. 'But I think so. We're worried about the orchid.'

'Why's that?' I ask, my voice neutral.

'It's not responding to the changes to its care. We're worried it won't flower on time. Which, to be fair,' she adds defensively, 'is kind of expected. We had to hedge our bets about when it would. And yeah, HG's got world-class knowledge but she can't read the minds of plants, even though it sometimes seems like it. So it wouldn't be that weird for it to take a little more or less time than we thought.'

'Makes sense,' I say, making a mental note not to express any surprise or irritation if the orchid doesn't flower the exact day HG reckoned. Even though, obviously, this will seriously inconvenience the heist and is therefore extremely bad news.

It was meant to be tomorrow. We're meeting later to go through final logistics.

'Plus,' Lily goes on, 'we need to harvest seeds from the flower when it blooms.'

'Really?' I ask, stepping aside to let her go through the barrier first.

I'm not adding much to the conversation. But the more she gives these snippets of information, and the more they directly contribute to heist planning, the worse I feel. So I just won't encourage her. Somehow in my mind, this makes the heist a more honourable prospect. I'm still going to steal the orchid, but I'll stop actively exploiting the person I'm possibly falling for and who really loves the orchid and do it passively instead. That's much better, right?

'This is a major part about the orchid, Phil!' Lily exclaims. 'Have we seriously not talked about this?'

'Er, no,' I say. 'You don't normally consult me about orchid matters. Which is weird, obviously, as I'd be so helpful.'

'We need the seeds,' Lily insists, her orchid passion clearly winning over her love of taking the piss out of my gardening capabilities, 'because otherwise we can't grow it again. Surely an accomplished gardener like you can understand that.'

'You mean you're not planning to create another orchid from scratch using just some soil and goodwill?' I ask, hoping this poor attempt at a joke will hide my unease. They won't be able to grow it again?

'Phil.' Lily turns to me, while we wait for Eva to catch up. Her hair is in one thick plait, so soft-looking that I want to grip it in my fist to see what it feels like, and her eyes are glowing with fervour. 'This is the only captive specimen in the world. Why do you think it's such a big deal?'

'Um,' I say. This feels like a test. But I do listen to her. 'Because it's never been kept in captivity before and it only blooms once every ten years?'

'*Because,* Philodendron, if that is your real name—'

'It's not.'

'—this could be our last chance to preserve these seeds for the future. This is what we do at Fells. And we only get those seeds when it flowers. We have no idea what properties this orchid could have. Do you even understand how important biodiversity is?'

'Woah there,' I say. I'm not the enemy here, or at least not in the way Lily thinks. I'm pretty sure she's asked me this before, when I didn't have an answer. 'I do now. You've taught me.'

'Exactly,' she says. 'This orchid is symbolic of everything that could be and will be lost due to climate breakdown.'

'Christ,' I say, involuntarily. I'm desperate to ignore this reality but it keeps kicking down my walls, barging into my consciousness. I do feel a kind of . . . bone-deep dread when I think about the climate. I am angry at the people in power. But I don't *do* anything about it.

And at least I was previously kind of net neutral on the issue. I'd never done anything actively good, like a climate activist or Lily. But other than generally being a consumer under capitalism, I'd never worked for its destruction either. Until now.

Lost in thought, it takes me a while to notice that Lily is chewing at her lip. She's as preoccupied as I am.

'What is it?' I ask, needing to know what's going on in her head.

She jumps. 'What's what?'

'You're worrying about something. Orchid stuff?'

'No, I— well . . .' I love watching that moment when Lily decides to tell me, rather than brush me off. The tension elapsing into a slump of the shoulders; the turn towards me. It never gets old. 'It's just . . . we were inspecting the orchid earlier, me and HG. I thought there were signs it would still bloom tomorrow or maybe the next day. But HG thought I was wrong.'

'You challenged her on something?'

Lily flushes a delicate pink. 'I didn't *challenge* her. I just . . . suggested a different opinion. Which she's usually open to!' Lily adds, defiant. 'She used to work in a big community of female botanists in the US who all shared their ideas. So she does like collaborating. But not this time.'

She chews her lip again, talking as if to herself. 'You get these little spikes where the flower blooms and this orchid does have one and it looks mature to me, and the leaves are getting to the colour they should be . . . but HG wouldn't miss an obvious sign . . .'

I wait to see if she's finished, then say, 'Maybe she thinks you're right but didn't want to say?'

'Or maybe she just thinks I'm being a bit of a Benny and doesn't respect my opinion.' The lightness of Lily's tone fails to hide the glimmer of uncertainty. I stop myself from squeezing her arm, telling her HG does respect her, thinks she's wonderful, how could she not?

I need to stop. Eva noses past and we follow her, pausing as we reach the main car park.

'See you tomorrow?' Lily asks.

'Yeah.' I reach to scratch Eva under the chin. 'Bye, little dog.' Eva tolerates this, then gives me a polite lick on the knuckle. 'Did you see that!' I exclaim. 'A goodbye kiss.'

'Lucky you,' Lily comments, raising her eyebrows. 'Lucky Eva.'

'Stop it,' I say, unable to hide my grin.

Later, I'm on the sofa in Miles's flat with Chaz sprawled beside me, watching Miles pace back and forth.

'So it's good news on the tunnel.' Miles is talking fast. 'But not the bloody timing.'

I've just explained what Lily said: the orchid could flower within a couple of days or, if HG is right, not for another four or five. So we don't know when the heist should be. Some of us don't deal well with uncertainty.

'I can't believe our lives are being ruled by a damn sissy flower. How the mighty are fallen.' Miles grips the back of a chair.

'We can't exactly schedule it in,' I say.

Miles pouts. 'So is our plan really just to wait around? Can't we just steal it now?'

'Doesn't the buyer want it as a flower though?' Chaz points out. 'If he's just some guy, he won't be able to make it bloom himself.'

'Unless he has a plant codebreaker as his personal assistant or something,' I say. The idea of someone else having the orchid slightly makes me want to cry.

Miles hesitates. Then he releases the chair and sighs. 'I suppose.'

'So all we can do is wait,' I say. 'And finalise our plan,

which is so far from watertight it's basically a sieve. We still need to check that security thing, don't we?'

'Hmm?' Chaz replies, after a long pause. He was gazing out of the window, lost in thought.

'Hello, are you listening?' I ask, waving at him. 'Or was there something more important we're distracting you from?'

His eyebrows twitch once but, to my surprise, he doesn't fling a comeback at me. He just says, 'What? Oh yeah. You're checking that for me tomorrow, aren't you? We might have a solution but we need a bit more time.'

I nod, sighing. Just a few more days.

And then ... whatever happens next.

Chapter Twenty-Seven

The morning before Saturday's scheduled grand opening, I loiter near the Hall as Lily gathers the gardeners on the lawn for an announcement. Anthony, her senior gardener rival, watches from the edges of the group, arms crossed. His expression is carefully blank, apart from his clenched jaw. Diego, at his side, keeps sneaking wary glances at him as though worried he's going to heckle.

Lily seems agitated too, twisting her hands behind her back. But when she speaks, her voice is steady.

'Thanks for coming, everyone. I have to let you know that we – HG and I,' she adds, 'now believe the orchid will not flower at the weekend.'

Anthony heaves a controlled breath, fingers clenching on his crossed arms. He's so jealous. Of course he is. If someone like *me*, a non-gardener and general idiot, is jealous of Lily and HG's relationship, then he definitely is.

'This means we've taken the hard decision,' Lily continues,

'to postpone the opening to Monday at the earliest.' She looks around, meeting people's eyes in turn. 'This is obviously inconvenient as it means we're on alert for the grand opening for a few more days. I'm sorry about this but, unfortunately,' she shrugs, 'we're subject to the whims of this exceptional flower. What can you do?'

There's a ripple of laughter and a few sighs of agreement. Ms Lenson already sent out an email to us all earlier, so Lily gives a couple more details before dismissing us.

'Nice work,' I say to Lily, hanging back as everyone troops away. 'You changed your mind then?'

'About what?' she asks.

'The orchid,' I say. 'You thought it would flower soon.'

She fiddles with the zip of her fleece. 'I must have been wrong. There are signs I missed and these rare orchids act differently from other plants.'

She wanders off, looking a little lost. Benny corners me as I stare after her.

'Phil,' he says, his tone devious.

'Benny,' I reply, regarding him with suspicion. If he's here to try and make me help him get Martina to go on another date with him, he's out of luck.

He sidles closer. 'Are you coming to the pub quiz tonight?'

'Um,' I hedge. My obvious instinct is to say no. I'm not particularly keen to pile on the layers of betrayal for these people.

'We need you on our team!' he whines.

'Who else is going?' I ask. There is still something I have

to do for heist prep and a pub quiz could be a much better place for it than running about in Fells today.

Also, I love pub quizzes and I'll likely never see these people again after this weekend and I just . . . like them. Chaz is busy trying to hack the key cards as Plan B, although he's not hopeful; Miles is organising the various gadgets he's ordered; and I am a hosepipe with a knot in it and the water on full blast. If I don't release some pressure soon I may explode and destroy something.

'You'll never guess,' Benny says, his eyes gleaming with triumph.

I tilt my head. 'Is it—'

'Lily!' he crows. 'I know! But I had to tell her you were coming,' he adds quickly, grasping my arm. 'She asked specifically and I said you were, so she agreed. So you have to come or I'll look like a real dickhead. Please. Please, Phil. Please. Phil, please.'

'All *right*,' I exclaim, giving Benny a gentle shove to release his iron grip on my arm. 'Good lord.'

Lily said yes because I was going. I try to ignore this rush of warmth. It's not sustainable, it's not helpful, it's not going to happen.

Later, I'm settled into a pub booth with a dozen gardeners yelling at each other about what colours the flag of Brazil is. As fate would have it, this is the exact pub where I met Miles for the first time. And Lily, of course.

I catch Lily's eye as Diego screams, 'It's definitely *not* red, Benny!'

Her hand rests on the table beside mine. Very slowly, she moves her little finger to brush gently against the side of my hand. A tingle runs down my spine and plummets like a bolt of lightning straight to my centre. I suppress a shiver.

'You OK?' she whispers.

I swallow. 'I'm fine.'

'Want to get another drink?'

'Sure.' I don't, but I could do with a break.

We shuffle out of the group and make our way to the bar, where she leans against it.

I rest my elbows next to her and take a few deep breaths in case it eases the spinny feeling of unreality permeating the evening. Everything's got on top of me all of a sudden.

Lily's warmth is present beside me, although we're not touching. She's wearing a soft russet-brown blouse and grandad corduroy trousers, like a dark-academia Pinterest board brought to life, and her hair is caught in a loose low knot at the back of her head.

'You look . . . different,' I say.

Lily nods seriously. 'I'm wearing a proper bra tonight. Thanks for noticing.'

I raise my eyebrows. 'And it's doing great work,' I say, allowing my gaze to linger on the creamy skin of her neck, the hint of the curve of her breast as her shirt is tantalisingly buttoned firmly closed. 'But it's not just that.'

'What then?' she asks, a whisper of flush starting as she

props her cheek on her hand. Her expression is open and relaxed, laughably different from the first time we crossed paths at this bar, and her skin is glowing with fresh air and hard work and . . . she's happy, I realise suddenly. Lily is thriving.

'You just look good,' I tell her. An understatement.

She twists her mouth in a suppressed grin. 'Thanks. So do you.' I wave a hand in dismissal and she gently flicks my wrist. 'I mean it.'

This is too much for me to know what to do with and I'm being pulled in all directions: drawn towards Lily, knowing there's no way it's allowed. I focus on the plant behind the bar – an aspidistra, as Lily called it that first time. It's doing OK. No worse than before. Maybe they listened to her advice.

When she says something, I have to ask her to repeat it, shaking my head to focus as she says, 'I spoke to Diego.'

'Oh?' I ask. 'What about?'

She shrugs. 'Just stuff about our past. Like you told me to.'

I frown, trying to round up my racing thoughts and bring them into line. Ah yes. The unsolicited suggestion I made about building bridges with the gardeners. I don't know why Lily listens to me.

She tucks a strand of hair behind her ear, smiling slightly. 'It turns out he's actually not friends with my ex any more. Hasn't been for a while.' Her smile broadens as though she can't help it. 'He's not one of those awful guys who always side with other men after all. So now we can be friends again. Who'd have thought?'

I try to smile. This is good news. And it's kind of lovely to know I've made a positive difference to her life, even in this tiny way. A small handful of change to set against the enormous price of the heist.

She looks up at me, tilting her head in a very Eva posture. 'What's on your mind? You seem gloomy.'

'Oh, you know.' I rub my forehead. My thoughts are too loud and seeing her like this while knowing it might be one of the last times she'll ever look on me with something other than contempt is almost too much. I *am* being gloomy. 'The old ennui,' I say, in the end.

'Are you annoyed Benny didn't let you name all the former members of One Direction?'

I laugh, surprised out of my own head for a second. 'Are you kidding? Seeing him smash that question was a joy.'

'What, then?'

'It's just—' I can't tell her anything real. But the way she's looking at me, a bit quizzical and a bit wary and genuinely interested – it's hard to stop myself. In my pocket, my fingers turn over my key card that I switched with Benny's while he was distracted with the quiz.

I can have a bit of emotional vulnerability, can't I, as a treat? In this no man's land of extra time between the orchid blooming and being stolen, I'm in limbo; nothing counts.

'I mentioned before about, like, not knowing what I'm doing. And family stuff.' She nods. 'The thing about my dad,' I say, 'is that I'm kind of all he's got.'

'Go on,' Lily encourages, waving away the bartender.

261

'So,' I add, already starting to regret it, 'it just makes it kind of hard. To make good choices or be selfish. Or prioritise things. Because in the back of my mind he's always there, needing me.'

I rest my chin on my hand. The temptation to tell her about the heist flurries up again. Would it be so bad? She might understand. She wouldn't let me do it, obviously. But ... maybe I could salvage some of our relationship. Maybe we could laugh about it, someday. Remember that time I tricked you into telling me about an orchid so I could plan to steal it and then I didn't? Ha ha! So fun.

I'd keep working at Fells and we'd see each other every day and as high summer came on we'd have hot, sunshiney picnics by the lake, or somewhere more private ideally, and we'd take Eva on walks and I'd go to her house and she'd come to mine and—

And it falls apart. Lily can't come to my house, where my dad is, where I wish I didn't live. Where we might not live for much longer, if I can't pull this off. Like, yes, I feel trapped there, but it's better than no home at all. There's nothing like having your problems slammed into perspective.

And I can't work at Fells forever. After next week – well, after Monday, now the grand reopening has been rescheduled – I'll need to stop being silly. The orchid money might save the house. I have to hope. But it's not a long-term plan. It won't keep us going for more than the five minutes or so it'll take me to find another job and my dad to knock my legs out from under us again.

'Phil.' Lily waves her hand in front of me. 'What's going on in there?'

There's no point. 'Honestly not much,' I say, looking around. There's a small table with two chairs near the back of the pub, away from the rest of the quizzers. 'Want to get a little bit drunk and form our own quiz team?'

She purses her mouth, her lips very beautiful. She's wearing that same lipstick from before. The one she apparently only wears on special occasions.

Then, visibly giving up, Lily holds up her hands. 'All right. Let's quiz. I'll have a cider, please,' she says to the bartender. 'And some crisps. Salt and vinegar,' she adds, throwing me a quick glance.

For the rest of the evening – through the next couple of drinks, our quiet success as a quiz team of two, the tipsy arm wrestle that Lily instigates when I try to grab the pen off her to write down an answer and she refuses to let go – I decide to just enjoy it. Pretend it's what my life is like. How sweet it would be.

Lily wins the arm wrestle. Of course she does.

Chapter Twenty-Eight

When I arrive at Fells on Saturday, I assume I'm imagining the air of intense anticipation. I'm projecting my own feelings. There's no reason for everyone else to be freaking out too; the orchid isn't flowering until Monday.

But people are rushing around, whispering. When I walk past the gardeners' offices, Anthony and Diego are huddled outside, faces close together. Diego has his arms crossed, looking up at Anthony, who's saying, quietly, 'I'm sorry about before, honestly. But this is what I want.'

Diego bites his lip. I hesitate, not wanting to interrupt but wanting to eavesdrop some more. But then Anthony's spotted me over Diego's shoulder and Diego spins round too, his expression guilty.

I wave, although I'm only a few feet away. 'What's up?'

Diego jumps and pushes Anthony away with a shove at his chest. Anthony stumbles, rights himself and . . . hides a smile? Diego opens his mouth to answer but, at that moment, Benny rushes past.

'Emergency meeting in the Great Hall! We're all needed there *now*,' he yells, his voice creating the Doppler effect as he sprints away.

I half expect this to be another of Benny's wild announcements, soon disproved.

But Diego nods. 'Let's go,' he says and his voice is so uncharacteristically assertive that I fall into step beside him and Anthony, whose face is so blank he must be working very hard to keep it like that.

'What's going on?' I ask, nerves roiling in my stomach.

'You'll see,' Anthony replies.

We get stuck behind the slow-moving Ethel, who's hamming it up a bit so Anthony will go to her assistance. By the time we make it, everyone's already there and an announcement has started.

I knew the place was big but it's still surprising to see the sheer number of people milling about. More volunteers have been called in today than usual.

HG steps forward, hands in her pockets, her brow furrowed. She's midway through a speech. 'We have decided not to reschedule the opening again. There is no point trying to pull it forward to tomorrow. It's too short notice and the public will be confused. Today is Saturday. We open on Monday, as planned.'

'How long does it flower for?' someone calls, amid rustling and whispering from the crowd.

Eleanor Vendrell

I give Diego a wild-eyed look. *Has the orchid flowered already?*

He nods, grinning, and looks up at Anthony, who smiles back and bumps him with his shoulder.

This wasn't part of the plan.

'We hope it will flower for several days,' HG announces, her voice firm. 'With luck, we will still be able to display it to the public.'

A trickle of dread thrills down my spine as I realise what this means. The heist must be tonight.

There are a few more questions and instructions from Ms Lenson, but I'm so checked out it takes me a moment to realise the crowd is dispersing and Lily's suddenly beside me. The air of anticipation has changed to one of buzzy excitement.

Lily grips my arm. 'When shall we go? Now?'

'Sorry.' I curse my lack of attention. 'Go where? What's happening?'

An exodus of volunteers and gardeners is streaming towards the double doors of the Hall.

Lily looks wistfully after them. 'To see the orchid, obviously. Everyone's going. But maybe it would be more special to see it later when it's quiet, even if it does mean the others get to see it first.'

My stomach feels as though I've missed a step. 'Have you not seen it already?'

'Bloomed in the early hours of this morning,' she sighs. 'And like some lazy slob, I've not been to the glasshouses yet today. I'm ignorant as anyone.'

266

'Not *anyone*,' I add automatically, my defensive instinct kicking in as always whenever Lily says anything even mildly diminishing about herself.

'Fine,' she agrees, her mouth quirking.

The room empties at incredible speed. The entire Fells population seems to have gone to view the orchid. If we were planning a heist of quite literally anything else in the estate, now would be a great time to do it. There would be no one to catch us at all. But it's probably too late to redirect the interest of Miles's buyer at this point, sadly.

I should try to see the orchid beforehand, anyway. And I do want to see it with Lily. If we were in a parallel universe this is what I'd be doing. We agree to meet later instead.

At four o'clock, not long before my shift ends, Lily and I go together to gaze at last upon the flower.

The glasshouses have cleared by now. Lily gets out her card to open the gate but a security guard ushers us through, saying, 'You're in for a treat.' He sounds as excited as any gardener.

We make it through the first set of glasshouse doors in the same way, then the second and final set. I follow Lily along the twisty path and around to the pond where, she informs me, we'll view the orchid from a safe distance across the water. Our footsteps slow as we get closer. A couple of other volunteers are ahead, Ethel and a friend, and they turn as we approach.

'It's magnificent,' Ethel says, smiling tearily at Lily. 'You must be so proud!'

'Thank you,' Lily says uncertainly. They potter away and she turns an anguished face to me. 'Was that weird to say thank you? I can't be proud! It's not down to me that it's beautiful.'

But I'm speechless. There, across the dark green water of the carefully built pond, is the orchid.

It looks nothing like the artist's impression on the poster. That's my first thought. After all our time fixating on it, the preparation, the hype – it's almost anticlimactic to realise just how tiny it is.

The flower is small, delicate, with sweetly pointed petals that soar upwards like uplifted arms. It's symmetrical, like all orchids. But most striking is the colour. Its outer petals are a subtle misty blue, almost grey at the very top. The grey-blue deepens and enriches as the colour sinks, until the bottom of the flower, where it meets the stem, is a deep, royal blue. It makes me think of the deep sea or the most beautiful sapphire I can imagine. It's magical.

'You can be proud, Lily,' I manage to say. 'You nurtured it. You did this.'

Beside me, Lily heaves a deep, satisfied sigh and, just gently, sways a little closer. Our hands brush, our fingers making the slightest contact. A delicious, excruciating shiver rushes through me and I close my eyes against it.

Around us, the only sounds are the gentle burbling of the water source feeding the pond and the occasional rustle of a branch. The air is thick with the hot, earthy scent of tropical plants. The orchid is beautiful. I couldn't be more devastated about what I have to do next.

Chapter Twenty-Nine

The three of us are clustered in Miles's living room for the last time. The corkboard is in front of us. The cartoon map has been replaced with the blueprint, and our notes from the last few weeks are pinned around it: information about the orchid, the glasshouses, the security cameras. It makes, from a distance, quite a convincing amount of information.

Miles stands in front of it, vibrating with nervous energy. 'OK, lads. One more time. This evening, Phil heads back to Felborough. You pretend you forgot something. You slip into the secret passage. There,' Miles spreads his arms in a kind of jazz-hands move, 'you *wait*. That will be fine, yes, Phil?'

I shrug. 'Hope so.' Now the orchid has flowered, I don't know whether anything will have changed with the security. We have to hope not.

'Step two. Midnight. Phil heads through the tunnel and out by the potting sheds. That takes you past the first level of defence.' Miles taps the corkboard, tracing the route. We've drawn it in red pen, running over the very faint, single line on the blueprint, barely visible after being scanned and photocopied too many times. 'Chaz, you wriggle through the hole in the perimeter and meet Phil as she gets to the second level.'

'The gate to the glasshouses.' Chaz nods. His knee has been jiggling against the couch this entire conversation. It's setting me on edge.

'You get through the gate and break into the glasshouse. Chaz is in charge of the alarm that needs resetting every thirty seconds.'

'It's not the alarm,' Chaz interrupts, impatiently. He had a breakthrough with this just yesterday, after I managed to get him the final puzzle pieces: the name of the new system, which I got by asking Ted the security guard; and an idea of the way it works, which I got by looking over Ted's shoulder at his security cameras, which he was only too pleased to show me. 'The CCTV is motion triggered. When you reset the alarm, you're actually resetting the motion trigger.'

Ted explained that, what with the enormity of the glasshouses and the antiquated computer system Fells still runs on, they can't be saving endless footage all the time. So they opted for the next most secure option: motion-activated cameras which only record when something sets them off. If you keep resetting the motion sensor, the cameras don't turn on.

'Are you sure about this?' I ask Chaz. I know Ted was telling the truth – he was chatting away as I made him a tea – but I don't dare trust we've found a solution.

Chaz nods. 'Hundred per cent. And thanks to the tunnels

we don't need to worry about the cameras in the Hall. So we're good.'

'Perfect,' Miles blusters on. 'So Chaz resets the thingy, Phil grabs the orchid with the snippers, bish bash bosh. In and out in twenty minutes. Half an hour, tops. Now, we've all got our headsets.' He taps the pile.

'We should test those,' Chaz says. 'Make sure they're working.'

'Already done.' Miles hands them out. 'Just check they feel OK, fit-wise. I didn't know how big your heads were.'

I'm too nervous to make a joke about big-headedness or about how Chaz famously has a very tiny head. I just take the headset, put it on, take it off again. It fits fine.

But oh God. I'm not sure about this.

'All right,' Miles says, clapping his hands. 'We're so close now. We've worked hard. Now all we have to do is do it.'

I exchange glances with Chaz. I'll be honest: it's not the rallying cry I was hoping for.

It's all right for Miles. All he has to do is wait on that country road in the van for us to meet him. We'll be in constant contact throughout, so at least he knows what's happening. He can tell us if anything goes wrong on his end.

We talk through more details, confirming timings and check-ins until, finally, we can't put it off any longer. It's time to go.

I take Chaz home, as usual. He's silent and preoccupied. I don't notice, because I am too, until he says, as he's about to get out, 'Are you sure you want to do this?'

'What?'

He shrugs. His face is pale, his eyes serious. 'I just mean . . . if you want to call it off, I'll back you.'

I can't believe what I'm hearing. Literally at the eleventh hour. 'You know my dad's situation. You know I have no choice.'

He hesitates. 'Are you sure he'd want you to do this?'

'Why are you even asking that? Are you having doubts?' This is the last thing I need; the only thing I totally failed to prepare for. Chaz is meant to be the one who isn't nervous, who helps me through. He's done stuff like this before, or close enough. He's meant to be the seasoned professional.

'I'm just worried about you,' he says. 'You've been so stressed. You're kind of acting erratically.'

I shake my head. 'If this is because *you* don't want to do this and you're trying to get me to back out too, then just stop. You got me into this and we're in far too deep now. So don't you dare. If you bail, I'll—' I don't know how we'd come back from it. 'I don't know what I'd do.'

He stares at me. Then he nods. 'Fine. Are you seeing your dad this evening?'

'Probably. I have to go home, don't I, before Miles picks me up. Why?'

'It might be good to talk to him.'

But when I press him for more, he clams up, ignoring all my efforts.

* * *

272

Back home, I sit on my bed, looking at the things I've laid out. If I'd been more prepared, I'd have stashed this at Fells days ago. Maybe part of me was still hoping a deus ex machina would swoop in to ruin the plan.

I'm about to put on the traditional all-black heist outfit but something makes me hesitate. Everything seems to scream at me to stop, wait, call the whole thing off. Chaz's words ring in my ears. I can't stop thinking about the deep blue of the heart of the orchid and the steelier grey of the tips, which reminds me of Lily's eyes.

Almost unconsciously, I head downstairs. I know my dad is here. I heard him fiddling about in the kitchen earlier. I'm suddenly desperate to see him. Maybe for a reminder of why I'm doing this, or for someone to talk me out of it. I don't know what I need.

I walk into the kitchen and he turns; his tired, drawn face softens as he sees me. 'Tea?' he asks.

'No thanks. Dad . . .' He clicks on the kettle. This has to be worth one last, desperate try. 'I just wanted to ask how you are. I know things have been tough recently.'

'I'm fine,' he says immediately.

I almost want to laugh. The fierce defiance.

'I've not been pushing you, I know it's your business. But . . .' I stop. His fingers are hooked through the cupboard handle, his shoulders tense. 'If it's my business too, I need you to talk to me.'

He's already shaking his head. 'It's not. I've got it under control.'

'The thing is,' I press, the first rumblings of frustration starting in my stomach, 'I don't know if you do. And I can't help if you don't tell me what's going on.'

'I don't need your help, Philippa.' He lets go of the handle and flattens his hand on the counter. 'I can handle myself. You've been my rock in the past, but at some point you have to trust me.'

'How can I when all you do is hide?' I exclaim, over the noise of the kettle building up. 'Something's going on and we both know it. We might literally lose our house and you still can't even look me in the face!' The rumbling turns into a roar as the stress and fear of the last weeks spill out. 'I'm doing my best to help you; I'm putting everything on the line *for you* and you don't even care! You don't even trust me enough to talk to me! You promised me you'd tell me if you're gambling again, but you're not even brave enough to come clean about that.'

The kitchen rings with silence as the kettle clicks off and the bubbling water subsides to stillness. My dad still hasn't turned, leaning on the counter with both hands.

'Dad?' I say, after a minute. My rage has dissipated as quickly as it rose, leaving only guilt behind. 'Sorry, I—'

I can't say I didn't mean it. We both know I did.

When he eventually speaks, his voice is so quiet I can barely hear it. 'I'm trying my best, Phil.'

I shut my eyes.

'I know,' I say. 'I— Yeah. I know.'

So that's that. That's my answer.

I take a long, unsteady breath. Then I let it out in a rush before heading for the door. 'I'm working late at Felborough tonight,' I say, pausing in the doorway. 'Don't wait up, OK?'

'OK, love,' he says, finally meeting my eye. The pain in his face hits me like a thud to the stomach.

I go up to my bedroom and put on the outfit.

Chapter Thirty

Miles drops me at Felborough so my car isn't left behind when we make a run for it. It's just before eight and the car park gate is still open, as expected, but the ticket office is shut and the place is quiet. A breeze wisps through the enormous oak trees that line the path. In a few months, they'll be dropping their acorns. Lily told me that the other day. Not that I'll get to see them.

A couple of people wander towards the car park and my stomach jolts, bracing for contact. Scientists who stayed late. But they stroll past, talking animatedly about an experiment, taking no notice of me with my volunteer's lanyard.

At the Hall, I say a silent and arguably hypocritical prayer, given my usual lack of religion, before holding my card against the door. It clicks open. I half-run through the corridors, following the now familiar maze towards the kitchens, until a scrape of footsteps makes me stop dead.

Hugging the wall, I creep forward. I can't tell where that

sound came from. My fingers curve around the corner as I reach the end of the corridor, scanning around. There's no one there. Shaking my head, I round the corner into the kitchen and smack straight into—

'Anthony?' I jump back.

'Phil!' he exclaims. He's red-faced, lightly sweaty. He's wearing a very nice burgundy button-down shirt that's definitely not Felborough regulation.

'What are you—' I find myself saying. Then I zip my mouth shut. If I ask him what he's doing, he'll ask me the same. I'll fall at the very first hurdle.

But Anthony is avoiding my eye. 'Better be off,' he mumbles. 'It's late.' And he scurries round the corner, as though pursued by a pack of flirtatious elderly volunteers.

I hesitate. Anthony is often rushing about. But that was weird. I don't have time to investigate though, and what would I even do? Make him explain himself? Garble an explanation as to why I'm here at the scene of the forthcoming orchid crime that he'll now be able to place me at? No, it'll only make things worse. I need to keep going.

I stand motionless until I'm certain the place is silent. Then I hurry to the storage room, edge into the tunnel and pull the door shut behind me.

And then I wait. At some point, I eat the sandwich I brought to keep my strength up, even though it tastes like nothing. The headset is working. I've got the orchid box and the snippers. Miles and Chaz talk a bit.

Somehow, the hours pass until, almost without realising,

it's time. I'm no longer lurking in the pitch-black passage but, like an out-of-body experience, creeping through the air-raid shelter and out of the potting shed exit. It spits me out past the first set of locked gates, close to the glasshouses.

I lift the latch and quietly, as quickly as I dare, steal away. The night is very dark, just a sliver of moon, and the woods rustle around me. I grit my teeth, trying not to imagine monsters lurking in the bushes. I don't need that. All the scariest things are in the open.

I follow the path, ducking to avoid the branches that have grown up even since Lily and I came through a few weeks ago. The walk is endless. Felborough is too big.

At last, I reach the second gate. A slight figure is waiting there: Chaz. He gives a tiny wave like a nervous child. Slipping Benny's card from my pocket, I tap it against the keypad, holding my breath, braced for a siren to rend the air. But the gate just clinks gently as it unlocks. I open it a minuscule amount to let us through. The vastness of the glasshouses looms above, creating that same mingled fear and awe as every other time.

Chaz puts a finger to his headset. His voice reverberates through mine as he says, 'We're in.'

I suppress an eye roll. He's been excited about saying that for weeks. When we reach the wall, I follow the path until, at last, we get to the door we need. Hands trembling, I pull out Benny's card again.

'There it is,' Chaz breathes. At least we no longer need an actual metal key to get in. That was a freebie from the new security system: key cards only, baby.

The door unlocks and we slip inside the glasshouse, the heat and humidity enveloping us instantly. I take a step or two before realising how utterly dark it is. The oppressive greenery means that more than a couple of metres from the door and you're deep inside a thicket of lush flowers and bushes. I take another step and a vine swipes at my face. Instinctively I swipe back, then freeze, heart thudding.

Did I trip the alarm?

No metallic beep. I stand another few seconds, trying to breathe. 'It's very dark,' I mutter to Chaz.

'Did you forget about the special torch?'

I press my lips together. 'No,' I whisper. 'Obviously not.'

OK, so I forgot about the special torch. Miles ordered us one each, even though he absolutely won't need one because he's spending this entire mission waiting in the warm, safe, unnecessarily large van.

Chaz sniggers. 'Shall I turn it on for you?'

I tune out Chaz's snide voice and pull out the torch. I feel for a button, then try to twist every part of it. Eventually, something moves and a soft red glow illuminates the metal floor. I'm further towards the edge than I thought. Just a couple more steps and I'd have walked straight into the low wall and probably had to catch myself with a hand landing on the flowerbed. Which would, of course, have raised the alarm.

I take a steadying breath. As I creep forward, placing my feet carefully, my mind wanders to my dad waiting at home. He'll be in bed, unless he's out again doing God knows what. What's he thinking about? Does he feel the crushing weight of his situation in the same way I do? How different is it for him, knowing he did this and being so unable to address it? The thought of him gripped in his own fear and despair just like me is enough to make me want to cry right here and now.

I don't, of course. That wouldn't help anything. If I can just grit my teeth and get this done, he won't have to any more.

We've followed the path winding in its serpentine pattern. Funny that it was designed to show off every area of the glasshouse floor and that, even now, it's forcing us to walk along like anyone else, taking it all in.

My red light beam, which I keep low so as not to draw attention, glances over what are probably very beautiful plants. In this dim bloody light, and the silent, waiting atmosphere, they're creeping me out. Like tendril-covered creatures, biding their time. A huge drooping flower at face-level nearly gives me a heart attack when I walk into it.

At last, I stop. 'This is the door to the main glasshouse.'

'OK,' Chaz says excitedly. This is another bit he was looking forward to. 'You've got the device?' I pull it from my pocket. 'You know what to do.'

I step closer and hold the blue-light magnifying glass up to the keypad. It hums gently in my hand. Through it, we can see which numbers have been pressed the most.

'Got it,' Chaz exclaims. 'The numbers are zero, two, five. But looks like more five. So probably start with that.'

Given what we know about Fells staff and their lack of interest in security processes, our guess is the code will be something easy to remember, or at least an intuitive shape on the keypad. We try a few variations. 0525. 2055. Each time, the device bleeps a quiet and firm *nope*.

'Fuck,' I whisper. It's dawning on me how stupid this idea was. There must be thousands of four-digit code combinations. 'How many goes do I have?'

As if in answer, the electronic display on the keypad flashes, *One attempt remaining.*

'Let's consider this,' Chaz's voice is musing, as though this is a calm and low-stakes situation. 'Who set this code?'

I'm jigging on the spot, hands flexing at my sides. 'Um. The security team?' But they wouldn't choose the code. The one who had final say would be— 'No, wait. HG.'

'What do we know about this HG?'

'Woman in her fifties or sixties, strict, enigmatic as fuck, doesn't trust technology,' I reel off, barely able to think. Time is ticking and if we get stuck here, the entire thing is ruined. 'Only likes about two people.'

I could be describing my dad, it suddenly occurs to me. And what does my dad use for passwords? My birthday. I tell him he shouldn't, but he always does.

'Could be a birthday,' I say quickly.

'Yes!' Chaz says. 'When's her birthday?'

'I don't know, but I'm not sure she'd choose her own ...' I take a step closer. A suspicion I've had for a while about HG is edging in, knocking on my consciousness. 'But might be someone else's.'

The way HG looks at Ms Lenson, as though she's the only person in the world HG doesn't think is a waste of time. How they always seem delighted to see each other; how they turn up to and leave events together. Ms Lenson calls HG *dear*. HG made sure Ms Lenson celebrated her birthday the other day. They're the epitome of discretion, but it's right there, if you're looking.

Taking a deep breath, I step up to the keypad. 'Wish me luck,' I murmur.

Then I lift a finger and, with the third and final attempt, type in the code 2 5 0 5.

The door unlocks with a quiet but audible click.

I suppress a screech of triumph and exchange a nod with Chaz. He takes up his position beside the door and I follow the path, heart like a hummingbird thrumming in my chest, increasing my pace as I hurry through the leaves. After all our scheming, all our high-tech equipment and hacking, this is what it's come down to. Me running through a glorified greenhouse to pick a flower.

The dark shape of the pond is just ahead now. I pause for a split second; my next move is to step onto the low wall and plunge into the knee-deep water.

In that moment, a gasp from behind, off to my left, makes me jolt. I spin on the spot, nearly overbalancing into the pond.

A dark figure is there, staring at me, out of nowhere. Taller than Chaz. They must have come through the inner door. How didn't I hear them?

I can't see their expression in the dimness, but disbelief and fury radiates from every inch of their tense stance, the hands reaching out palm down as if to say, *Wait, no.*

At their feet, a small, sturdy, four-legged shape. One that, even as I stand gripped by horror, hurries over to press a small, wet nose against my leg.

Oh God.

'Eva,' I breathe.

Chapter Thirty-One

The figure fumbles in her pocket, then switches on a torch and swings it up to point right in my face. I flinch, the glaring light stinging my eyes. She can't be here. She's not meant to be working tonight.

A gasp. 'Phil?' Then fury and disbelief in her voice. 'Eva, get back here right now.'

'Lily, wait.' There's a roaring in my ears.

But she's scanning the torch down my body, picking out my outfit, my backpack, my red torch. The pieces clink into place as I watch.

'I stayed late in the main office,' she says, almost wonderingly. 'HG told me I didn't need to, but I had a feeling . . . and then I got a call that someone was breaking in. But I never thought—' She looks at me, her voice breaking. '*Why?*'

I can't think of a single thing to say.

'Eva,' she snaps, harsher this time, and the dog finally stops nuzzling at me and potters away.

I find my voice. 'Lily, I— I'm sorry. I didn't want it to come to this. It's not—'

'Tell me why, Phil.' The torch beam is shaking slightly.

I look down at the floor. The freshly jet-washed iron grating, ready for tomorrow's visitors. The friendly vines, curling in all directions, growing peacefully over the low wall of their raised bed until someone hooks them back. I don't know what to tell Lily except the truth.

'I need the orchid,' I say.

I want to meet her eye, but she's in darkness and I can't see her expression. It's unhinged that I'm explaining rather than grabbing the orchid and running. But although she's not touching me, she's got me in a grip and I can't sprint for it like this. I just can't.

'What?' She's baffled more than anything.

'Phil!' Chaz's urgent voice in my ear makes me jump and swear.

Lily flicks her torch beam round. 'What was that?'

I raise a hand to my headset and flick the off button. 'Sorry. That was . . . nothing.'

She comes a step closer, peering at my ear. 'Is that a headset? Are you working with someone?'

'Lily, I beg you,' I whisper. 'Please.'

And then, in the distance, a siren. It sends a shaft of cold panic to the soles of my feet, pinning me to the floor. My first instinct is to swear at Chaz for fucking up the alarm reset. He had one job! Then logic kicks in. It's already been more than thirty seconds since we broke in and that's not the alarm that Benny set off the other day. It's further away, higher-pitched.

None of this is meant to happen. The night is slipping through my fingers.

Lily is breathing hard. 'You know I can't let you do this.'

I need to move, to decide, but my legs are filled with cement and all I can do is sway on the spot. The thought of fighting Lily is literally impossible. My mouth twists as I think of arm wrestling in that bright, cheerful bar, a thousand years ago.

Don't do it, Phil. For a second, I allow myself to imagine. Escaping, reconciling with Lily. Maybe she would forgive me eventually.

But how could she? And even if she did – my dad. Things would be the same; get worse. Both of us kicked out of our house, hopelessly broke. Destitute, even, if that word wasn't too horrendous an admission. Either way, I could never come back to Felborough.

But if I get the orchid and the money, at least my life can finally begin. The prospect is harder to cling to than several weeks ago, before I knew Lily. I try to summon the images I thought I wanted: the flat I'll move into, alone; the quiet, easy jobs I'll return to. The vision is missing the spark of life that's been ignited these past few weeks and the alarm drilling into my brain makes it impossible to think. But the thought of my dad free from worry, with time and space to heal, makes up for it. Almost.

I've come too far to give up now. She must understand. 'I have to,' I whisper, the words burning my throat.

'I thought I knew you,' she says. We hold eye contact and I don't dare look away.

The warm darkness rustles in an unseen draught. *You can hear things growing.* Truer than ever, in here. Ironic that it feels like a death.

I want to grab her, kiss her, apologise, cry. I want her to lead me away, tell me she forgives me, leave the orchid safe in its home where it's cared for and cherished. I don't want to uproot it, or Lily, or me.

But the alarm is only getting louder and I made my choice long ago. Without this final step, it will all have been for nothing. The planning, the deception, the sneaking around. The guilt and fear and stress. This is no time to grow a conscience, Philodendron.

I turn and in a quick movement hook one leg over the low wall and splash towards the middle of the pond. The alarm's already been triggered; it can't be triggered again. Behind me, Lily gasps, followed by a splash as she leaps in too. Eva barks.

Wading desperately, ignoring the water lilies I'm probably crushing under my feet – because what's one more plant destroyed in aid of this wretched plan? – I splash through the last couple of steps to the mound in the middle, to the tree, to the orchid itself. I'm already fumbling for the snippers, ready to burrow my fingers into the earth, to uproot the flower and take it away to be sold or dissected or whatever lies in store for it until I stop short.

Wavelets splash against the artificial wall as I freeze. Lily cannons into me and I fall to my knees, water soaking me to the waist. But all I can do is stare at the mound in the centre.

The place where just yesterday Lily showed me the fragile little flower – its bluish-purple petals, its delicate leaves – is now a patch of dark earth.

I run my fingers through it, stupidly, as though it will make it reappear. But there's no sign of the petals, the leaves, the greenery. No matter how many times I swipe through the earth, churning it to mud with my wet fingertips, it changes nothing.

The orchid is gone.

When a voice breaks through my stupor a moment later, I'm still staring dumbly at the place where the orchid should be. I must have sunk forward against the earth because something hard is pressing into my knees. But, as though I'm looking out from a fishbowl, the view is distorted, distant.

'No. *No.*'

It's Lily, I realise. She's still here, reaching for the patch of blank, stubborn earth.

'I was meant to protect it,' I think she whispers, too quietly for me to be sure.

The pain in her voice floors me. There was something I was supposed to be doing. But it's so hard to keep going. Everything I've done. Everything I've risked. Everything I've *lost* in pursuit of this goal. And for it to end like this.

The moments stretch on. The siren is still wailing. And

then another sensation. One of absolute wrongness in this botanical paradise.

'Can you smell that?' I ask.

'If this is a distraction technique, it's not fucking working.' But as she says it, Lily's eyes widen; she can smell it too. Smoke.

'Where's it coming from?' I spin on the spot, water dripping off me. My adrenaline, which I previously thought was racked all the way to full capacity, finds an extra level. I didn't know my heart could beat this hard.

It's difficult to see in the darkness, but wisps of movement are visible high above the glass ceiling. My hand involuntarily reaches towards Lily as I take a couple of automatic steps back. She doesn't notice, her head tilted up as well. Smoke is curling around the roof panels, as if trying to find a way in.

'We've got to go,' I say. Get yourself out. That's the first rule of a fire. 'Come on.'

Almost unconsciously, I reach to my headset and tap the 'on' button.

'Phil, what the *fuck*.' Chaz's voice in my ear, urgent and harsh, almost gives me a heart attack. He must have been yelling that whole time. 'Are you there?' I blink. 'You need to get out now. Now! There's a fire. You need to have been out of there ten minutes ago! Philippa! Do you hear me?!'

Chaz never freaks out like this. The strangeness of that, of all things, snaps me into action. I need to get out. *We* need to get out.

But Lily has turned to stare at me, pure horror in her eyes. 'What have you *done?*' she hisses.

'What are— You don't think *I* did this?' I gasp.

'I don't know what you're capable of!'

'Not *arson*,' I exclaim. Even in this terrible moment, the accusation hurts.

Grabbing Lily's hand, I pull her towards the door, charging through the pond to scramble over the low wall. Chaz is still yelling in my ear, something about the fire being on the east side, in the direction of the Hall. But my brain has tuned him out. For a couple of steps as we race after Eva, I manage to tug Lily behind me.

But as we cross the threshold to the central glasshouse, she yanks her hand away. 'I'm not coming with you.'

'Lily, please,' I say, trying to keep calm. 'We need to get out.'

Her face is a mask of terror, but she's shaking her head. 'I can't leave the orchid.' Ahead of her on the path, Eva whines.

'What? Lily,' I say again. I can't keep her name out of my mouth. I have to get through to her. 'The orchid is gone. We both saw. And your life is more important than some flower.'

'You've shown me exactly how important you think this flower is,' she spits. 'We clearly don't have the same priorities. Just go.'

'We can't discuss this now,' I yell, frustration breaking through. The fire must be closer to this side of the glasshouses; the upper windows have been left open and smoke has started curling inside. 'Does anybody even know you're here?'

It's a nightmarish vision at the top of the glass dome, smoke trailing around the tangled leaves and vines. The sight is so cartoonishly awful that it seems the leaves should wither and die as soon as the smoke touches them. But they stay steadfast, the insidious curls twining around them.

'It's too wet in here, nothing will burn,' I say, gripping her arm. 'Please, Lily.'

'The desert glasshouse,' Lily gasps. 'I need to check the sprinklers are on. They're not automatic.'

Before I can stop her, she's raced past. I hesitate for a single breath.

The orchid has gone. The place is on fire. Everything has gone to hell. I should get out. If I'm found here, they'll catch us all; they'll think I set the fire. I'll probably go to prison.

I run after Lily.

'Phil?' Chaz's voice is loud in my ear. 'Where the fuck are you? I'm coming back in. I can't see any flames,' he pants, as though running hard, 'but apparently it's the smoke inhalation that kills you.'

'No! Stay outside,' I yell. 'No one is going to die.' I suppress a hysterical laugh that could so easily turn into a sob. I've never had to say that before in a situation where there was any doubt. 'And your fire facts aren't helping.'

'If you die in there,' he scream-whispers, 'I swear, Phil, *I will kill you.*'

'I'm coming,' I say, coughing on the taste of smoke, a sharp pain in my chest. 'I just need to get Lily out.'

Ignoring Chaz's exclamations, I cross into the desert

glasshouse and stop in my tracks, last shreds of confidence draining away. The smoke is thicker in here; huge, spiky cactuses loom out of the dark. In front of me, Lily is coughing, clutching her sleeve over her mouth as she jabs at the fire alarm system. Behind us somewhere, Eva is barking, sharp and insistent against the piercing note of the alarm.

Then someone grabs my shoulder so hard I'm almost knocked off my feet.

Chaz. His face is sweaty and he's incredibly out of breath. This is probably the first exercise he's done since ageing out of compulsory PE lessons.

'What . . . the shit . . .' he puffs, 'are you *doing*?'

I reach for Lily's arm but it slips through my grasp as Chaz bends double, coughing, trying to drag me away at the same time.

'Lily—'

'Phil, I swear to God!' I've never heard Chaz sound like that before: ragged and frantic, gasping for breath. I'm torn between them: desperate to get Chaz and his tiny lungs out of here; needing to see Lily safe.

Then Lily, who's muttering under her breath, 'Come on, come *on*,' lets out a gasp of triumph as sheets of cold water drop from the ceiling onto our heads. The sprinklers are on.

With a final, desperate glance at me, Lily turns for the exit. I drag Chaz after her, faster and faster until we're sprinting. The specially designed orchid box bumps uselessly against my back. The main door is hidden by smoke, so we veer towards the smaller side entrance. Chaz pauses, coughing, but I shove him between the shoulder blades, urging him on.

When we finally break into the clear night air, it's like surfacing from under water. Blue lights flash through the dark in the direction of the Hall and urgent voices shout in the distance. All three of us run towards the gate, propped open how I left it. Apart from it isn't; the rock has slipped out and the gate is shut.

'Key card, key card, key card,' Chaz wheezes, as though this will make me find it faster. As I fumble, praying it's still in my pocket, and Lily turns, yelling for Eva, a tall figure rushes past on the other side of the gate.

My heart stops. It's the police or security, here to arrest us. But the approaching blue flashes illuminate broad shoulders, the back of a dark-coloured shirt flapping. The figure disappears into the smoke.

'What the fuck is happening?' I gasp.

'Who cares,' Chaz scream-whispers between coughs. 'Into the trees!'

I grab the card at last and slam it against the lock. The gate clicks open and I shove Chaz through, half-carrying him, and hold it for Lily. A small blonde shape darts through at our feet and sprints off, away from the fire – towards the blue lights. Lily runs after Eva without a backwards glance.

I can't follow her there, not towards the police.

'The trees,' Chaz croaks again. Into the trees it is.

I run and run, dragging Chaz with me. Through the panic, the smoke, at any moment I expect to hear shouts in our direction, cries of *Stop*. But none come and we hurry on through the dark woods.

When we can go no further, we collapse onto the ground, gasping for breath. I wait; trying to hear footsteps, someone else's heavy breathing, anything. But all is quiet.

Chapter Thirty-Two

The damp ground is solid under my back. I tentatively move my fingers one by one, leaf mulch chilly against my fingertips. I turn my head until my eyeline is level with Chaz's, flat on his back beside me.

'That went well,' he wheezes.

I press both hands to my face. The night sky bears down on us, heavy black above the canopy of trees which blankets us from the rest of the world. The reality of our situation is thundering towards me like an avalanche that started way up in the mountains.

Lily. Is she safe?

We should be here with a little box filled with one small orchid. Instead, the box is empty, the orchid's disappeared, the place is on fire and Lily might still be in danger. And I don't understand what happened.

Chaz draws in ragged breaths. It sounds less painful now we're away from the smoke, but not great, to be honest. He carefully pulls out his phone and holds it above his face. 'I'll check . . . Miles . . .' he rasps.

'Chaz.' I shake him. 'We need to find Lily.'

He locks the phone, then drops it, narrowly missing his face. Arms flat, he stares up at the sky. 'Nope.'

'What if she went back to the glasshouses?'

'Even if she did,' he says, between breaths, 'which she didn't . . . because we saw her, she didn't seem . . .' He pauses for a big rasp. ' . . . Interested in hanging out. Can you . . . please . . . focus.'

He turns to look at me, shaking his head. His words couldn't be less comforting. Or his whole vibe. Is he having an asthma attack?

'I am focused,' I hiss. 'The orchid was gone, Chaz. How!?'

He shakes his head. 'Fuck the orchid. Stupid flower. Never . . . liked it anyway.' He takes another deep breath. His voice is regaining its usual tone. 'We need to leave . . . through the nice hedge . . . Might as well tick off one part of our plan.'

He seems strangely calm now we're out of the glasshouses, not even bothered about the mission failing. A horrible suspicion creeps in.

Chaz knew the plans, the security, everything. He was being odd last night. Wanting to put me off the heist. Why would he have tried to get me to call it off unless he had something to do with the plan going so wrong? And he was distracted when we were planning it. Chaz never gets distracted. He's alarmingly hyperfocused when he has a project.

It adds up too perfectly. He couldn't be better placed to

have done it. I stare into his face, propping myself on my elbows.

'What?' he whispers. The abyss of his eyes is deeper than ever in the darkness. There's just no way of knowing the truth. He's always been a good liar, a good manipulator. I thought I knew him.

I do know him. What choice do I have, other than to trust him?

'Nothing,' I say, lying back.

My brain presents with sudden clarity the image of the dark figure running away through the smoke. I didn't get a clear sight. But the more I think about that shirt flapping in the wind, the more I think . . . Anthony hurrying away down the corridor earlier this evening. Clearly not wanting to be caught. Resentful about his lack of promotion, hardly able to look at Lily. Would he have?

I rub my forehead, shivering in the cold air. The orchid is gone. And Lily thought I set the place on fire. And now she's disappeared too.

'Why,' Chaz checks his phone, 'isn't Miles . . . replying?'

'Do you think he got caught?' Possible circumstances flit through my head, none of them reassuring: Miles in the back of a police car, in custody, being interrogated by HG.

It's hard to imagine how things could have gone less to plan. My mind has kicked in, trying to see other options, ways we can apply our Plan B and C and D. But there's nothing in my head but Chaz's rasping breaths and Lily, Lily, Lily.

Chaz shrugs, then coughs. I need to get him out of here. That's one thing I can do. Back the way he came in.

I relay this to Chaz, who nods once. We climb to our feet and follow the Felborough perimeter towards the gap Chaz crawled through a hundred lifetimes ago. The walk provides more than enough time for my mental state to spiral into further panic.

How could the orchid not be there?

When we come to the gap, I make Chaz pause, listening for anyone on the other side. Two or three cars go past and we wait until we can't hear any more before dropping to the ground. Chaz goes first.

I'm about to wriggle through when something damp and furry presses against my hand and I almost have a heart attack.

Pressing my lips together too late to fully muffle my scream, Chaz wheezes from the other side, 'What?'

From my prostrate position, she's right in my face. Eva's found us.

'Where's your parent?' I ask in a frantic whisper. She noses against my cheek; then, when I reach for her, presses her body into mine. She's shaking so much she's basically vibrating. 'I think she's terrified.'

Chaz huffs a sigh of frustration. 'No time for this.'

'Go back to Lily,' I hiss, making a shoving motion at her.

Trying to avoid rolling into the ditch, I wriggle through the hedge. But as I brush myself off, to my horror, Eva has followed. The grumble of an engine announces a car heading towards us. It's too late to dive back through.

'Just walk,' I say, at Chaz's expression of panic, 'purposefully. And hope it's not the police.'

We stride along the road, Eva following so closely against my side it's like she's been stuck there. She shouldn't be here and I don't know what to do, but my dread is growing at what this means. She would never leave Lily voluntarily. Something's wrong.

Rounding the corner, I'm brought up short. What should have been a dark, silent, country lane occupied by one nondescript, definitely non-suspicious orchid getaway vehicle is now . . . busy.

Several cars are pulled up on the grassy verge, illuminating the night with headlamps and brake lights. At least a dozen people stand at the stile atop the hill, staring towards Felborough. A couple have binoculars; some are in pyjamas with a jacket over the top; nearly all have their phones out. I send a quick but fervent prayer of thanks to any present deities that the gap in the hedge is far enough and that people are so obsessed with documenting things that no one noticed us emerge from the leaves. This explains why there's no sign of the van, at least. Miles must have had to scarper.

But my disorientation is total. People are chattering, pointing at the constellation of flashing blue lights sprinkled across the estate, the rising plume of smoke a lighter grey against the black of the night sky. Chaz pulls me aside as another car trundles past. Someone gets out of it, camera at the ready.

'Can you believe it?' the guy says, spotting us. 'Saw on TikTok.'

'Yeah,' I say quickly as Chaz starts coughing again. 'Us too. Looks bad.'

'It does,' he agrees, his eyes widening as he brandishes his camera. 'Gonna try and get some footage. I've never gone viral before.'

My mind hands me a half-formed thought about how bleakly dystopian this is. But his words have blurred and I must be seeing things because the next car pulling up now, neatly tucking in against the hedgerow, looks a lot like mine. In that, well, it's a Fiat 500 and it's black. And it has my number plate. I rub my eyes, but when I look again, it's still there.

I take hold of Chaz's jacket, pulling him to a halt. When he shrugs, I gesture frantically at the car. Not a jot of recognition. He's always had the equivalent of face blindness for cars. Bonnet blindness?

I'm about to yelp that we need to turn back, maybe run, but it's too late. Two people are getting out of my car, doing up their jackets. One of them is wearing a scarf that, if it was daylight, I'd be able to see was blue.

'Dad,' I'm calling, before I can stop myself. The urge to keep him away from all this, to protect him, is stronger than logic. But there's something else, too. Against the devastation of the last half-hour, our plans crumbling to ash – his posture, his face, the comfort of seeing him here, make me want to cry.

'Phil?' He turns.

I stumble over and throw myself into his arms.

'Is that Phil?' someone asks, after a few moments of stunned silence. A woman.

'Who the hell is that?' I mumble, my face pressed into my dad's jacket. He awkwardly pats me on the back.

'That's . . . my friend. Val.' He holds me at arm's length, looking into my face. 'Val saw the fire online. I knew you were here this evening so . . . we thought we'd come and check.'

'He was worried about you,' the woman says. I look at her properly. She has short, greying hair and square glasses through which her eyes peer, slightly magnified, her gaze direct.

'Mr Hart,' Chaz interrupts, voice still rasping as though he's been a smoker for forty years. 'Could you take us home? Phil's . . . not feeling her best.'

I almost laugh at how backwards this is; Chaz is the one who can barely talk. And there's no way my dad will go for it. He'll want to know what happened, why we're soaking wet, why – of all things – a small, hairy dog has followed us down the road.

But after looking between us, at Chaz's determined expression and my mask of desperation, he just says, 'Righty ho,' and opens the car door.

I hesitate. We can't leave without knowing how Lily is. But in the end, Chaz's small, wet, angry figure still wheezing, rubbing an unconscious hand against his chest as he glares at me to get in the car, makes me break. We need to get him somewhere calm. Crouching, I scoop Eva into my arms. We can't leave her. We'll find Lily. But first, to get away.

Chapter Thirty-Three

'Thanks for coming to get me.' The words aren't enough but I say them anyway as we get home. It's utterly quiet, the night air blanketing our silent street. I follow my dad and Val into the kitchen and pop Eva on the floor where she just stands, for once not going to sniff around.

'Hot chocolate?' Dad bustles about, filling the kettle.

'Yeah, all right.' I sink into a chair and rest both palms flat on the table.

The kettle boils. The spoon clinks. My dad puts three teaspoons of hot chocolate into mugs for Val and Chaz, one and a half for himself and me. Neither of us like it too sweet. The others sit, too.

It's nearly one in the morning. I need to know Lily's OK, not that she'll ever speak to me again. The thought is a fist squeezing my heart and I press my fingers into the table to hide my distress.

'There you go, love.' Dad places the mug in front of me,

along with several chocolate digestives. Something about the earnest way he's arranged them in a little triangle makes me want to cry. He perches on the side of the table, then changes his mind and pulls out a chair. 'I think we need to talk.'

I accidentally snap a biscuit. 'Sorry?'

He braces his hands on his knees, sitting very upright. For someone who just rescued his soot-covered adult daughter from a country road with a strange dog in the middle of the night, his energy is oddly ... bouncy. 'I've not been totally honest recently.'

'Yeah, no shit,' I say, putting a piece of biscuit in my mouth. I'm too knackered to be angry.

'I was handling it. But after what you said about—' he clears his throat, embarrassed. 'About the gambling.'

My eyes widen. We're not addressing things head-on, are we? Chaz shifts in his chair but Val sits perfectly still, hands wrapped around her mug.

'Wait,' I manage. 'Are we really doing this in front of them?'

I literally just met Val. I'd never heard of her before this evening. And now my dad is openly talking about gambling, something he's never voluntarily discussed in the last ten years.

Dad clears his throat again, then sighs. 'We don't like sharing our problems, you and me. But I dunno if we've been doing it right. So ... I'd like them to stay.'

'We want to be here,' Val says gently. 'Pete and Chaz have been worried about you, Phil.'

'Sorry, how do you know that?' I glare at Chaz, but he's picking at a crumb, avoiding my eye. 'Actually, never mind.' I don't care. The sooner Dad says his piece, the sooner I can get to Lily.

But my dad takes another steadying breath and I'm suddenly not sure I'm ready to hear it. I'm still wearing my heist outfit, for God's sake.

He holds up a hand. 'I'm not gambling again. I've just had a little bit of trouble with a . . . piece of business. I was led to believe it was a good investment. But it turns out—'

'It turns out it wasn't at all?' I suggest. Maybe I'm actually not too tired to be angry.

'I'm not some gullible fool,' he says, frowning.

'Course you're not, Dad.' As soon as the sarky words leave my mouth, I'm sure it's too far. He'll clam up, leave.

Instead, he still sits, his calloused hands braced against the table. It's a view into the future for me, my dad's hands. We have the same long fingers, the same blunt fingernails.

'I told you the truth before,' he says. 'I remortgaged because I *wasn't* gambling. I needed to pay off the debt. Show you I can take care of myself. You've been worrying about me for years and I'm sorry, Philippa.' He glances up, meeting my eye. 'I know it's not an easy burden.'

Philippa? Philippa and empathy? I suppress the urge to say, Who are you and what have you done with my father?

'It's not right that you live with an old man like me, love.' He nods, in a confirming kind of way. Like he's trying to give himself confidence. 'I can take care of myself.'

'You—' I say helplessly. 'You can't, Dad.'

Dad's tired eyes crinkle. 'I need to learn then, don't I?'

But I can barely hear him. 'It's not like this is what I'd choose. But it's how it works. I bail you out.' He's shaking his head, but I plough on, as if needing to convince him. 'That's what we do. Like when things were really bad that first time. And I nagged you to get help and you finally did.' I clear my throat. 'When I yelled that thing at you. You know. At rock bottom. Don't you remember?' I add, my voice desperate.

He's looking at me oddly. Then he says, 'That wasn't rock bottom.'

'Of course it was,' I almost shout. I can't believe he's arguing with me about this. He's always so stubborn; it used to drive Mum up the wall. It's not like I don't remember the bleakest moments of my life.

'That wasn't rock bottom,' he says, again. 'I was already planning my next bet; the voice in my head was still there. But a few days after that, I came into the kitchen and saw you standing right there,' he gestures at the counter, 'with a bag of shopping at your feet. Just standing. You looked so tired. And you were doing all this for me. And suddenly I just . . . didn't want to do it anymore. Or,' he shrugs, 'I still wanted to. But I didn't want to more than I wanted to. *That* was rock bottom.'

I just stare at him. So my whole speech about how he was ruining my life – none of that had any effect? 'But you made the change because of me,' I ask slowly. 'Didn't you?'

306

He nods. 'But not because of what you said. It was *for* you, not because of you. You do everything right, love. You always do.' He stands and comes over, reaching an arm out for me. 'But you'd been doing everything right for years. It was up to me.'

This hangs in the air. Biting my lip to stop it trembling, I let him gather me to his knobbly chest.

'What's been going on?' I ask, once my voice is under control.

'Don't panic, now.' He loosens his hold, stepping back. 'I got involved in this scheme. Cryptocurrency. They said that I just needed to invest a small amount, and—'

The alarm bell that lives in my head specifically for my dad chimes loudly. 'You're not serious,' I interrupt, all thoughts of his new self-actualisation whipped away. But Chaz is nodding and so is Val. They both knew about this?

'I said don't panic,' my dad says, as though this has ever helped anyone in history avoid panicking. 'I had to do something big to pay off my debts, like I said, so I remortgaged, got the sum to invest. Then the investment didn't pay off, because . . . well.'

He remortgaged the house to invest in an obvious scam. Right.

'So I was obviously . . . a bit worried,' he says, in a frankly stunning moment of understatement.

'Dad,' I say, enunciating very clearly in the way I know annoys him but I can't help at times like this. 'Why didn't you tell me?'

'Because you'd say I was a silly old man.'

'I wouldn't,' I protest, untruthfully.

He looks at Val, who nods reassuringly, then back to me. 'And it wasn't sorted yet. Chaz said I should tell you but I thought better not worry you with details till we knew it was fine.'

I gasp. It's one thing for Chaz to have known about something, but to have actually had a say in the decision-making?! I don't know whether to go for Chaz or to just start yelling in general. But the risk, of course, is that I wouldn't be able to stop.

'Chaz has been helping,' Dad goes on. 'We got talking the other day when he dropped by. He told me a bit about his line of work.'

'And what line of work would that be?' I glare at Chaz, trying not to imagine the various awful things this could be referring to.

My dad leans forward. 'Computers. He said you'd mentioned our situation. And he's a trustworthy chap or you wouldn't be friends. So I asked if he knew anything about crypto.'

'Dad,' I exclaim looking between them. 'Chaz? Dad!'

'Anyway, good thing I did because we heard just this evening. The scammer's given in! He's sending the money back!' He shakes his head affectionately at Chaz, who perks up.

'It worked?!' he exclaims.

My dad nods, grinning. 'Got the message an hour ago. Do

you need any sleep, son?' He turns back to me. 'He's been working non-stop. I was going to tell you tomorrow, but . . .' He trails off. 'We're all here now.'

'It was quite fun,' Chaz says, his voice more normal now. 'Almost a challenge. I might go into it full-time, actually.'

'Crypto?' Val asks, pleasantly.

He scoffs. 'Please. No, helping people who've been scammed by these lunatics.'

'OK . . . sorry.' I lean forward. 'Chaz has been secretly helping you. You're getting the money back, although I'll believe it when I see it. So,' I gesture at Val, 'no offence, but who the hell are you?'

She inclines her head calmly. 'This is a lot to take in. But I'm glad to meet you, Phil. I work at Citizens Advice. Your dad's told me so much about you. He's lucky to have such a caring daughter.'

'Citizens Advice?' I repeat. At this late hour, too. I didn't realise they offered such a comprehensive service.

'That's just how we met,' Dad puts in. 'I wanted help to not rely on you all the time. But now we're friends. You wouldn't believe how much Val's helped.'

'Helped with what?' I exclaim. If my dad had said he wanted to take up skydiving or learn to throw a javelin professionally I'd have been less surprised. Making 'friends' with someone called 'Val' who works for 'Citizens Advice'? A competent professional? Very much not his type.

My dad's face forms an odd, misty-eyed expression unlike

anything I've seen it wear before. 'She's a marvel. Val's even coming with me to the repossession hearing, aren't you, love?'

I would come with him to the hearing! I help him with this stuff. Does he not want me there?

'Phil.' My dad shakes his head. 'I don't know what I'd have done without you. But it's time for a change. Even when we get the money back, it's not a healthy way to live. For you, especially.'

This is not something my dad would say. It's something *I'd* say in a moment of stress and then he would ignore because he wouldn't know how to deal with it. I want to ask who he's been talking to. But it's obvious.

'So,' he says, with no variation in tone at all, smiling at Val, 'I've decided to sell the house.'

I can't speak. My mouth is open but I can't speak.

He's still talking. 'Turns out this house isn't half bad. When I bought it for a pittance in the nineties! We've already got some people interested. It's as good as sold.'

'*Dad*.' I need to check if I've slipped into an alternate reality. 'Are you saying you put our house on the market without telling me?'

He has the grace to look slightly guilty. 'I thought it would be better for me to do it. I tidied up, we had pictures taken.' Tidied up. That's why he was clearing out. Not to look for his bank cards. To *tidy up*.

'And Val tells me we don't need to worry about the repossession hearing,' my dad says earnestly, 'now we've done this.'

Val nods. 'If you show them you're selling up, they let you off with a bit of time to get the money.'

Oh my God. He's being scammed by Val too. A whole new spiral of debt and despair swims before my eyes. And Dad sitting there looking at me as though I should be reacting with joy.

'What does this all *mean*?' I exclaim. I wouldn't be surprised if my head was revolving like a spinning top. 'It doesn't explain . . . you've been so weird recently,' I insist, as though I'm the one who needs to defend myself. 'You weren't leaving the house! You stopped seeing Gerald!'

'I've been a bit stressed.' My dad's face sets into anger. 'And Gerald was thinking about walking out on his wife.'

'What?' I say blankly.

'He met another woman, thinks he can just run off with her. Bloody fool,' my dad scoffs.

'So he told you about it,' I say, carefully, 'and you fell out and that's why you weren't seeing him?'

'Of course,' Dad replies, like this is obvious. 'Wanted me to tell him to go ahead. Him a family man! Two kids!'

'Gerald's kids are in their thirties,' I say, as if this is of any consequence.

My dad shakes his head in contempt. 'The bloke needs to sort himself out.'

I rub my forehead. It's so far from my worst fears that it's like I've walked through a doorway only to find it's actually an outline of a door drawn on a wall and I've smacked straight into it. The ridiculousness of the situation: as if I'm the one being weird. I mean, why *wouldn't* I have assumed that rather than isolating himself in shame because he'd started gambling again, instead my dad fell out with Gerald because he morally disagrees with his views on the sanctity of marriage?

And also that he's selling our house.

Silence rings around the kitchen, pinging off the kettle, the toaster, the familiar dusty light fittings. Or rather, as I look at them properly, not dusty. They've been cleaned. Maybe my dad is telling the truth.

It's not that I think he'd lie. It's just. Everything.

And yet still all I see is Lily's face in the glasshouse. That terrible moment of stunned disbelief before it turned to anger. She didn't think I'd do something like this. She trusted me.

Looking at my life, it's hard to pinpoint the moment it went tits up. We have a few potential suspects: Mum leaving, Dad going off the rails. Me agreeing to a heist.

I kept going like I've always done. But no matter how hard I try, it's not enough; the goalposts are kicked further away. And now this. The goalposts have flown off a cliff and into the sea. And I'm *tired*.

Under the table, Eva paws at my leg and I jump. I forgot she was there. This is all monumental, impossible and ... I can't understand any of it while I don't know if Lily is OK.

Eva trots to my dad, who reaches to pull her onto his lap. 'Who does this little lady belong to then?' he asks, scratching her head.

If he'd only communicated with me. If I'd accepted Chaz's

offer of help. If my dad and I hadn't been in our parallel lanes – two lighthouses, shining in opposite directions, one of us lighting the other directly onto the cliffs.

The heist was for nothing.

I don't even know what I think. But I know one thing. 'I need to get to Lily.'

'Who's Lily?' Val asks pleasantly.

I grip the bridge of my nose. I don't know why Val's here and I want to hate her. But she's petting Eva now and she's helped my dad and Chaz trusts her. And she has a comforting, ample figure that makes me want to curl up against her bosom like a baby.

'Lily is—' I say. How to sum up Lily? 'Um. She's . . .'

'A gardener at Felborough?' Dad asks.

I frown. 'How did you know?'

'You talk about her sometimes. You're obviously very fond of her.'

'Yes, well,' I say, ploughing past this before it makes me sob. 'I need to make sure she's OK. At Fells this evening, she—'

I hesitate, eyeing Val. We theoretically trust her but maybe she has a legal duty to report any funny business.

Dad steps in. 'You can speak freely. Citizens Advice only have to report something if there's a safeguarding risk, which means,' he says very carefully, as though reciting something he's memorised, 'putting myself or anyone else at risk of harm.'

I stare at Chaz in manic disbelief, forgetting for a moment

that I'm angry with him. His eyes are wide with suppressed laughter. 'That was my thought too,' he mock-whispers. 'But it's fine. No conflict of interest.'

'You'd be amazed the things we hear,' Val says pleasantly. 'We get all sorts at Citizens Advice. Bless them.'

'Anyway,' I go on, 'Lily was at Fells tonight, at the fire.'

To my horror, tears thicken the back of my throat. I cannot cry now. I don't know when I started calling it 'Fells' like the gardeners do. As if I've earnt that right.

Chaz reaches a hand to me in alarm. 'Phil! Lily's fine: we saw her get out. And from what you've told me about her biceps, she can look after herself.'

'The glasshouses won't burn,' my dad offers. 'Can't start a fire in a rainforest.'

But if this were true and Lily is fine, Eva wouldn't be here. 'I need to know she's OK,' I say again, my voice wobbling further.

The wheels are coming off my sense of self and I scrunch my eyes to stop the tears coming. But it's no good. The floodgates, slammed and locked for so long, have been faltering for weeks. Now, as I watch Eva's hunched figure on my dad's lap, they fall. I rest my head on my arms and let them.

'Um,' Chaz says delicately. 'Mr Hart, Val – could Phil and I have a moment?'

The kitchen door shuts behind them. Eva, who stayed, presses against my leg.

'There, there.' Chaz pats my hand, thinly veiled panic in his voice. We've known each other nearly fifteen years and

I've never cried in front of him. I bury my face in my hands, making ugly heaving sounds as I sob.

After a while, Chaz says, 'I need to apologise.'

This is so unprecedented that I scrub a hand over my face and peer at him. 'What?'

His eyes are red-rimmed and his hair's a bird's nest. It has an actual twig in it. For the first time, I notice a couple of grey hairs at his temples. When did those arrive? When I see Chaz, I still see the boy I met when we were twelve.

'I'm just . . . sorry.' He twists his mug on the table. 'Seeing you like this has been kind of awful?' His expression has never been more serious and less Chaz-like. He takes a careful breath. 'It made me realise how much you have to worry about. And I've just been adding to your stuff. Like, I can't even drive! You always drive me around.'

'I don't mind,' I say, sniffing. 'And you failed your test too badly for me to feel good about you trying again.'

The memory of Chaz finishing his driving test by forgetting to brake and crashing merrily into a wall brings a weak smile to my face.

'I'm serious. It was time to pull my weight.' He shrugs. 'And it's obviously no big deal for me to do a bit of light hacking and blackmail to help out your dad. I just sent a virus and held the guy hostage until he repaid the money, plus interest.' He pauses. 'A lot of interest actually. All going to your dad too. Weirdly, knowing it was for a good cause made it,' he looks confused, 'more enjoyable?'

Chaz on his vigilante shit. The scammer becomes the scammed. I can't help laughing; everything is so stupid.

'I'm sorry for not telling you. We didn't know if it would work and your dad said we shouldn't until we were sure. And I'm sorry I got you into . . . all this.' He sighs. 'Can you believe after all that we didn't even get the orchid?'

'I know,' I say.

We sit in silence a moment. 'I wondered at one point if there even was an orchid,' Chaz muses.

'Maybe the real orchid was the friends we made along the way,' I say, in what the history books will call a valiant attempt at a joke. Benny's face pops into my head, shoving a handful of crisps into a sandwich. Diego flapping at a butterfly about to land on him. Ethel lusting after Anthony. Sanj laughing at them all.

Most of all, Lily. Holding a treat for Eva, laughing as Eva raises first one paw, then the other, desperate to do what Lily wants. Lily lying on the emerald grass, her hair in a halo. Sitting on the bench under the apple tree as she explains some minor point about composting and pH scales, like the best professor I've never had. On the dance floor, her face cupped in my hand, her body pressed against mine. Looking at me as though I was special, important.

'I tried so hard,' I say. 'And I've fucked it. Irredeemably.'

'Listen, this is fixable,' Chaz says. 'You've always been a fixer. And we're an amazing team.'

'We're not twelve-year-olds with chocolate stuffed up our sleeves any more. This is real life.'

'Come on,' he says, as though I haven't spoken. 'You never give up. It's one of your most annoying traits.'

I frown at him, despite the small ray of warmth his words plant in my chest. Time to admit something. 'I don't know what I'm doing,' I whisper.

He whistles. 'Can I have that in writing?'

'Shut up.'

'You've got this, Phil,' he says, squeezing my hand. '*We've* got this.'

I sigh. But he's right; I can't give up. I've had my hot chocolate. I've run my hands through my hair so many times it must be entirely vertical. My heart has been racing for three weeks straight and I have no idea what time of day or night it is. But it's not over yet.

When Dad and Val come back in, I'm ready, or as ready as I can be in this deeply unready state.

'Dad.' I stand to meet them. 'I'm sorry too. I was trying to help and it got out of hand. I do . . . trust you. But no more secrets, OK?'

He nods, then puts a hand on my shoulder and squeezes it. Good enough.

'Right,' I say. 'I can't process anything because I'm fully unhinged and there's no time, so we'll talk later. But for now, I need to go to Lily's house.'

My dad just nods. 'I'll take you,' he offers.

I consider declining; I can drive myself. But I'm tired. And it would be nice to be driven. To accept some help. 'Thank you,' I say.

Chapter Thirty-Four

Dad eases the car into a street of little terraced two-up two-downs, giving way to a police car. The sight is unsettling at this hour in a quiet residential street. Surely that wasn't anything to do with Lily? The grim-faced officer raises a hand in thanks and I turn away in an automatic and futile attempt to hide my face. This is my life now.

In my arms, Eva struggles free and places her front paws against the window. I only know the street because Lily mentioned it once; but not the house number. Our plan, as Chaz puts it, is to, 'Do a Hugh Grant in *Love, Actually*, but without the fat-shaming.'

But scanning the street as I climb out of the car, trying to hold the wriggling dog, I spot Lily's house immediately.

The other houses are cute, plain brick and neat. But ivy sprawls over one of them, curling around the square windows and the green front door. The tiny front garden is a bloom of colour, visible even in the greyish dawn light: oranges and yellows and reds, neatly tended and watered. Not a patch of clear ground is visible among the greenery and it has an air of barely suppressed exuberance. It has to be Lily's.

Eva struggles until I can't hold her, so I pop her down. She runs straight to the house and paws at the gate.

I turn to thank my dad, who says, 'Good luck, love. We'll wait down the road.'

The Fiat disappears around the corner. I gird my loins and follow Eva to the door, which has a brass knocker in the shape of a hairy little dog. Where on earth did Lily find an Eva-knocker?

The moments between me knocking and the door opening last about an hour. I run a hand through my hair yet again, no doubt doing nothing to improve my appearance. Until I see her, I won't dare believe that Lily made it out OK.

But then there she is. Her face and plaited hair are just as they were in the glasshouse, hours ago. Unharmed. She's clearly just got home; she's not even taken off her shoes.

Eva launches herself at her. She wriggles round Lily's legs, keening in a strange, high-pitched whine I've never heard her make.

'Shh, shh,' Lily is saying. 'I'm here, I'm here.'

Get a girl who looks at you the way Eva and Lily look at each other. If only.

Their reunion is so touching that I can't interrupt, so I just wait. I've always wanted a dog. But now I've met Eva I can't imagine wanting any other one.

'It was horrible, wasn't it,' Lily whispers, 'you got spooked by the smoke, didn't you? It's OK, you're OK.'

When Lily eventually surfaces, her expression is utterly cold. My slight hope, that the emotion of their reunion would warm Lily to me too, flickers and dies.

'Thanks for bringing her back,' she says. It's as though we've never met; I'm an incompetent employee whose name she doesn't bother remembering. As though I never accidentally ripped out her nasturtiums and she's never even called me a dillweed.

This is a wildly unpromising start, but I can't just leave. 'Lily, please. Can we talk?'

'I don't think so.' She hugs Eva to her chest.

'I know you're angry,' I say. 'Please let me explain.'

'I'm angry?' Lily bristles. She puts Eva down. '*Angry*? We could have died in a fire, Phil. A fire that the police suspect was arson. *Angry* is one word for it.' Her cheeks have flushed a furious pink, so similar in colour to the beautiful tone when she's blushing at something I've said. 'What are you even doing, Phil? You and your little team?'

I can't stop myself glancing over my shoulder at the word 'team', the unmistakable premeditation of it. The street is silent, just the first hint of sun warming the grey of the sky. If Lily's neighbours overhear this conversation, it would pour oil on the already crackling fire. A tasteless analogy, under the circumstances. But to be fair, I'm not sure my mind and mouth are functionally connected at this point.

'Someone could have died,' Lily hisses. 'And they thought it was *me*, that I'd be capable of something like that. Me!'

'Surely they didn't—' I begin to speak. It's too ridiculous to consider.

'And yet, they did.' She's properly furious now but crouches to feel gently up and down Eva's legs, along her belly, checking for injury. 'Did you think a police car was my preferred transport? They've been questioning me for hours.'

'I'm sorry,' I say, truly meaning it. If I could have protected Lily from that, I would. 'Please can ... can we not do this out here?'

She slaps her hand against the wall, just once. Then she steps back and indicates for me to come in.

I shut the door, the relief of being off the street almost making my knees buckle. A pain is pounding in my temple. 'I'm sorry,' I say again.

'I've been suspended from my job. My *job*. And, unlike you, I care about mine and was pretty interested in keeping it, actually.'

She's wrong. I care about Lily keeping her job more than I care about most people.

'Lily,' I say. The conversation is getting away from me. It's like being under a barricade of darts, Lily's aim unerring. I want to ask if I can expect a visit from the cops in the pressingly near future. But of course she'll have ratted me out. She'll want to save her glasshouses, see justice. I don't even blame her. Lily is my one exception to the rule about snitches.

'And worst of all, to find you there. I should have known you were too good to be true,' she says, as if to herself. 'I thought we had something—' She stops. Then she asks, her voice matter-of-fact, 'Was any of it real, Phil?'

The lack of emotion, the hidden betrayal, are worse than I could have imagined.

'Lily,' I say, unable to stop myself reaching for her, 'I didn't want— It was real! Most of it, and—'

But she shakes her head. 'It doesn't matter. All that matters is the orchid.'

Like a wave breaking over my head, everything rushes up to meet me. The orchid. We still don't know where it is.

'I can't stop asking myself, though.' She crosses her arms. 'Tell me, why did you "need" the orchid?' The sarcastic quotation marks are obvious. 'What could you possibly need it for?'

I press my lips together. She might not believe me. But, 'My dad's debt,' I say, on an exhale.

Her expression flickers, but she says nothing.

'I've been trying for years to earn the money we owe, but I've failed. We were going to lose our house. And I don't have any qualifications or rich relatives or lottery luck. ' I shut my eyes. 'We were going to fence the orchid and share the profits and all my problems,' I open my eyes, knowing what I'm saying is no longer true, 'would be solved.'

Lily is still motionless. Then she speaks. 'Did your dad ask you to do it?'

'Of course not,' I say. 'He didn't have to. But it doesn't matter. The orchid's gone and I don't know what happened and you probably won't believe me, but I didn't start the fire.'

We share a split second of eye contact. I know we're both thinking of the song. The fact that I can't acknowledge it breaks my heart. I've lost the right to share stupid references with Lily.

'Please go.' She turns away. 'I can't do this any more.'

The door is solid behind my back, but the rest of the world is unsteady. Or maybe it's me. But I can't stop here. The plan has been ripped up, burnt, sunk into the bottom of a bucket and then thrown off a cliff. But I know what matters now. It's Lily.

'I'm going to sort it out,' I tell her. 'If I didn't do it, who did? I saw Anthony there acting suspiciously. It's got to be worth looking into at least?! If we just go back to Fells and—'

Lily, who falters at the mention of Anthony, shakes her head. 'Sure,' she says. 'I'll go back to the scene of the crime, the place where they literally arrested me. You're not bloody *thinking*, Phil.'

She's right; she can't. But I can.

I'm going to find out what happened. I'll get her job back. I might have fucked everything up but it's not too late to de-fuck some things. It can't be. Because there's no way I can let Lily go until I've done everything I can to fix this.

Chapter Thirty-Five

Chaz and I have a new plan. I'll look for clues about the fire and Chaz will get in touch with Miles. We finally received a message from him in the early hours of the morning.

Had to abort plan. Sorry. Lying low for a few days. Suggest you do the same.

Neither Chaz nor I can lie low, so we part ways: him to his laptop for answers, me to Fells.

I feared I'd need to break in again; it's obviously shut today. But before I have time to really worry, an email pings into my inbox about the clean-up effort Ms Lenson is organising. Only experienced volunteers allowed. In a twist of guilty fate, that includes me.

Arriving at Felborough's gates at the end of its verdant, tree-lined avenue, I brace for a heavy hand falling onto my shoulder accompanied by shouts of *Got her!* But I just swipe my card and enter as usual. It's bright sunshine today. If we were doing pathetic fallacy, it would be pouring rain. Instead, the still smoking Hall is lit by vivid shafts of sunlight.

As I walk, I exchange quick glances with the volunteers I pass. The atmosphere is bizarre. Cleaning efforts are underway, but everyone is moving as if through treacle. The orchid is gone and the place has been attacked. I'm sure we all want to scream about *how* this could have happened; the wrongness of the small plume of smoke that, even now, drifts into the endless blue sky. But everyone else must be internalising their exclamations too and it's eerily quiet.

Ms Lenson gives us our orders in the courtyard by the kitchens, in a parody of normality. We're not allowed in until they've finished checking its structural integrity, but I peek past the police tape. The fire didn't last long and the kitchen looks oddly ordinary, just a few streaks of smoke around the ceiling. The old tapestry from the attic, which once hung above the desk in the library and that we so carefully displayed downstairs, has been laid across the table. The glass has smoked up but the tapestry is unscathed. From this angle, the bottom corner with its blank square of slightly different fabric is more obvious than ever.

'The reopening is postponed, of course,' Ms Lenson says, calling us to attention. 'But we're determined not for long. We're waiting for a full report, but we think the damage was concentrated in the front of the Hall as the fire started in the library.' She looks around, clutching her clipboard. 'The good news is the glasshouses suffered only minor damage. The wind carried smoke and burning material towards them but they didn't catch alight.'

Relieved chatter erupts among the volunteers clustered around her. After last night's horrors, this is more than I'd hoped.

There's been an outpouring on social media, Martina tells me as we get to work. The guy who was filming on his phone got his wish, or someone did, and the videos went viral. A fundraiser has already been set up to restore the Hall. Last time I checked, it was at well over thirty grand and rising fast. Multiple celebrities have pushed it. Finlay Slater has offered his services to come and rebuild with his bare hands, prompting many others to volunteer too, presumably in hopes of a good look at him doing some brawny manual labour.

Notably absent from Ms Lenson's briefing is any mention of the orchid. So I keep my mouth shut too.

When I encounter my group of gardeners at lunchtime by the lake, the fire is all they can talk about. It's bittersweet. On the one hand, I never thought I'd be here again, daring to be glad to see them. Then again, they don't know I betrayed them and I shouldn't be here at all.

'How can it have happened?' Diego keeps saying in frustration.

'Surely it was an accident,' Benny exclaims. 'Do they not know arson is a crime?!'

'Some people know things are crimes and do them anyway, Benny,' Sanj tells him, without her usual acerbic tone.

'I heard . . .' I say, clearing my throat. What I'm about to say is either very ballsy or irresponsibly stupid. 'I heard Lily's being blamed.'

'It's ridiculous!' Benny replies immediately.

'They just want a scapegoat,' Sanj mutters. Her dark eyes are filled with genuine concern. I saw her and Lily laughing together the other day as they walked across the lawns.

The gardeners sit for a moment, their vivacity dimmed. Before, when Lily was just a scary, irascible figure, they'd have been relieved that she's being blamed rather than them. But not any more.

'I think we should rally round, let her know we know it's not her fault,' I say, looking out over the lake as though it doesn't matter at all. It's choppy today, stirred up by the breeze. 'It'll be harder for the Board to pin something on Lily that way.'

'Good idea,' says Sanj, and the others nod too.

'It's kind of funny that Lily's our friend now,' Diego muses. Then he looks surprised. 'I mean, not that she shouldn't be. Just, before—'

'I know,' I say, to rescue him from his digging. 'But she likes you all so much. I know she'd appreciate it.'

'Leave it with us!' exclaims Benny, already reaching for his phone. 'Our Lily would never do anything to harm this place. She loves it more than she loves . . . any human, actually.'

The others laugh and I smile slightly. Maybe that's how it should be. My phone lights up with a message from Benny on the group chat he added both me and Lily to the night of the pub quiz, starting, **Lily!!!! We miss you!!!**

I spend several hours cleaning in the Hall, our previous hard work undone by the smoke. No one notices me slip away, pacing the corridors, checking in nooks. By late afternoon, I'm certain: no clues, no sign of a break-in with a broken window or door.

Time to pay Ted a visit in his security centre. I knock on the door of the PRIVATE office and pop my head round. 'Anyone home?'

'Phil!' he cries. 'You all right?'

'Fine,' I say. 'Came to see how you were holding up.'

Ted shakes his head. 'Mate. What a day. I've had that explorer bloke in here, getting on at me.'

'What's he been saying?'

'You can imagine.' He adopts a high-pitched, painfully posh accent: 'How *could* this have happened, and your team let us all down, and the like. If you ask me,' Ted murmurs, his voice lowering to a conspiratorial register, 'he's making things worse. Ordering people around as if we report to him. It's nothing to do with my team.'

'No?' I ask, leaning casually against the wall in the most casual wall-lean anyone's ever done.

'It's them bloody new security cameras, isn't it? Glitchy as all hell.'

'Really?' I lean a little further back. 'They didn't work last night?'

'I shouldn't really be saying this,' Ted says, raising an

328

eyebrow, 'but it's not my neck on the line, it's the new company. And their cameras biffed it, didn't they? Deleted all last night's files or never recorded them. Either way,' he snorts, 'no footage of the library or anywhere else in the Hall. Or the glasshouses, for that matter. It's a joke. After they spent how much on the new system? Should have stuck with the old one. At least it worked sometimes.'

'That'll show them,' I say, absently. My mind is churning. The footage is gone? That's good. It means sweet, genius Chaz was right about the motion sensors after all – we didn't set off the CCTV. We're safe.

The odd thing is the sensors *would* have been triggered once Chaz left his post and we all started rushing about because of the fire alarm. I'd forgotten the sensors by then, but the footage should have started up again. It's weird that the cameras didn't record anything. But lucky for us. The fire alarm must have overridden it or something.

But it's weirder about the library footage. It seems too convenient to be a mistake by the security firm. As I drink the tea Ted makes me and half-listen to him telling me about when HG came in last week wanting to be walked through the new system – which he's convinced was just a way to test he was paying attention when they set it up – I fret.

Once again, the thing I've been searching for has suddenly, out of nowhere, disappeared. This whole time, I thought we were in control. We had the heist all ready. But I'm starting to suspect someone else has been one step ahead all along. I just don't know who, or why.

Chapter Thirty-Six

Coming to Fells this morning gave me a false sense of purpose. By the end of the day, I've covered every inch of the Hall and still nothing. I was going to sort everything, get Lily's job back, but every time I stop moving for a second, everything drops more heavily onto my shoulders. Lily's face as she told me to leave. My dad explaining that it was all for nothing. Frustration nibbles at the edges of my brain.

My final task of the day is moving spare chairs out of the storeroom. It takes until I'm literally at the bottom of the steps looking at the far wall, when I realise the secret passage is the one place I haven't checked.

Once we've finished with the chairs, I drift back down to the cellar. It's risky; someone could pop down for something else. But I'm so good at being casual, as we know. And I need to make sure.

I slip inside the passageway, flick on my phone torch and follow the tunnel as I did last night. There's the patch of cold floor where I waited, eating my sandwich; there's the slope towards the potting sheds. Everything is exactly as it was.

On my way back, I go slowly, dragging my feet in despair. I should've known this would be a red herring too.

It's only because I'm training my torch on my footprints in the dust, too despondent to raise the beam further, that I see it. The footprints break away and disappear. I must have walked straight past the first time.

Stumbling to a halt, I spin and go back. And there it is: another passageway, barely wide enough for a person, branching to the right. The main passage widens, then narrows, and this bit is hidden behind an alcove.

Footprints definitely go that way though, or at least, the dust smudges look freshly made. I can't see the treads of a shoe. This would be a lot easier if life was more cartoonish.

On tiptoe, I creep along the narrow passage which slopes sharply upwards. It must lead to above-ground level. I have no idea where it'll come out. I was nervous that first time in the tunnel, afraid of being caught and forced to explain. But this is different. There's a roaring in my ears as I force myself to keep moving, one step at a time.

The person could still be here. I could be about to come face to face with them and I obviously have no idea what I'd do. I took two hours of martial arts classes when I was thirteen and I remember less than none of it. 'Solar-plexus-Instep-Nose-Groin' starts repeating in my mind, as if I'm going to take on a villain *Miss Congeniality*-style. My spare hand drifts along the cold wall, feeling my way through the dark.

Up ahead, the tunnel dead-ends, blocked by a flat surface which reveals itself as another door with a wooden doorknob, slightly splintery to the touch.

Heart thundering, I turn it very slowly. It's silent, but sound is probably muffled in here. I could be about to pop out in a random room of the Hall.

But when I open the door a crack, there's only darkness on the other side. I ease it open further, braced for attack. But none comes.

The door fully open now, I shine the torch into a small, cramped space, hardly big enough for three people to stand abreast. Am I in a cupboard? I still can't hear anything.

When I lower the beam, a tiny shaft of light from outside becomes evident, piercing the room at eye-level. Turning off my torch, I raise a tentative finger to touch it. It's a peephole.

Through it, a room of Felborough Hall is visible, slightly distorted like a fisheye lens. Tall windows on the facing wall, blackened with smoke; filing cabinets and shelves; boxes of documents.

The library.

Oh my God. A second fucking Cluedo room. I *knew* it would be in the library! Judging by the peephole placement, it's in the very bookshelves where I searched and failed to find it.

More importantly, it's empty: no arsonists in sight. Not any more, anyway. The library is where the fire started. This was clearly their route. They must have slipped out into the library, set the fire and made their escape back through the tunnel.

I can probably do that first part if I'm quick, as the library

The Great Orchid Heist

is deserted. It's been swept clean and emptied of damaged documents already and the peephole's fisheye is just wide enough to show a glimpse of police tape across the door.

Switching on my torch again to try to figure out how to open the Cluedo door – a lever or maybe a logic puzzle – something on the ground glints. I stoop to investigate.

It's a ring.

A gold signet ring, to be exact, thick and solid with a crest engraved into the flat side: a lion holding a snake.

It takes me a moment. But as I turn the ring in my fingers, the itch in my mind working away, I realise where I've seen it before. On Miles's little finger. The one he's always taking on and off. The annoying ring.

But Miles shouldn't have been anywhere near the Hall last night, let alone here. He stayed outside; he had no reason to come in. Unless.

Did he come inside the grounds in case something went wrong? Could the ring have slid off his finger during his incessant fiddling and ended up here, carried by the arsonist to frame him?

There's no way.

The ring sits there, shining yellow-gold. With numb fingers, I take a photo and send it to Chaz.

My phone lights up with the call. 'Chaz,' I whisper, without preamble, 'I think Miles had something to do with this.'

Silence on the other end of the phone. Then Chaz says, almost laughing, 'That fucker. Of course.'

I stand still as it sinks in. I didn't believe it. But Chaz's ready acceptance is a splash of cold water to the face. Why *not* Miles? We just don't know his motivation. But we will.

'I've found something too,' Chaz says. 'I was going to call you but I got distracted working on this. But I broke into Miles's flat earlier, and—'

'Chaz!'

'What?'

'You can't just—'

'Why not? He was ignoring us and we're meant to be a team. And what's a little bit of breaking and entering among friends? Anyway,' Chaz says, as though that's now covered and we can move on, 'he wasn't there. But I found this weird bit of material. I'll send you a picture. I don't know what it is, but maybe you will.'

A moment later, I'm tapping on the photo. It was clearly taken in Miles's flat; I recognise the minimalist furniture. Spread over the table is a scrap of fabric, a few inches wide, incongruously shabby against the glass-topped table. The edges are ragged but straight, as though cut a while ago and not hemmed, and it's sewn with darker coloured lines. It's not just fabric after all. It's a tapestry.

And the darker colour isn't just lines – it's names and dates. They're difficult to read, as the stitches are tiny, and there are only a few. But there it is, as I zoom in. The name Mountjoy, all the way down. Until the very last branch of the tree: an L. Mountjoy who, in 1993, married E. DeLancy.

DeLancy.

Miles's surname.

His hatred of Fells. His dark hints about the troubles his family suffered. The snipped-out section of the tapestry, so carefully preserved. I don't know how, but Miles is behind this.

'Chaz,' I state. 'We have to find him.'

'I'm trying to get his location,' Chaz sighs. 'He's blocked me, but I should be able to figure out roughly where he was last time he accessed the internet.'

I rub the lines in my forehead, trying to flatten them. My face can't remember what it feels like not to be frowning. We're so close to figuring this out but the more we talk, the less I know. I just want to lie down and sleep.

'I'm on my way,' I say.

Tucking away my phone and sliding the ring onto my forefinger for safekeeping, my hands creep over the door, searching for whatever will get it open. My finger slips past a small hole in the left-hand side. There.

I'm about to push the button when voices make me freeze. Heart thumping, I press my eye against the peephole again.

Hook has ducked under the police tape and strides into the room. HG follows.

'Hook, be reasonable,' she's saying. 'You won't find anything in here; the police have gone over it already. I keep telling you, Felborough's reputation can take this, you know it can. If anything, the fire is a good distraction.'

'No,' Hook snaps. '*You* be reasonable. It's too embarrassing. We can't have the senior gardener stealing the most valuable orchid in our history.'

'It wasn't her,' HG exclaims with frustration. 'Lily would never do this. I trust her completely.'

Hook raises a finger. He's clearly not listening. 'The orchid is gone, is it not?' HG starts to speak but he barrels on. 'Someone's head will roll, Hiwot. If it's not her, it's you. And I'd caution you against that.' He straightens his blazer, buttoning it at the front. 'I've asked Mary to call the girl in. She's on her way. Talk to her or I will.'

He marches out of the room. HG stands like a statue, one hand resting on a filing cabinet. The moment stretches.

Then I start frantically feeling around for the way out. No, no, no. This is not how it's going to be. Not for Lily, not today. Finally finding the button and jamming it as hard as I can, the bookcase slides open with a thud. I burst out of the Cluedo room and stumble to my knees on the floor.

HG, to my everlasting admiration, doesn't scream. She just reels back and presses a hand to her chest. Then she says very quietly, 'Phil.' Her stare could freeze a fully blown waterfall. 'No doubt you're going to explain.'

'You can't fire Lily,' I say. I'm still on my knees. All the energy's gone out of me and I'm not sure I could stand if I tried, but it feels oddly appropriate. 'You can't.'

She frowns. 'That was a confidential conversation. And, as to Lily,' she holds the back of her hand to her forehead, 'I don't know what choice I have.'

She's genuinely upset. She kept in her emotion in front of Hook but it's evident in her drawn expression; she doesn't want this for Lily.

And neither do I. Everything else is fucked. The orchid is missing, presumed dead; Miles is a fire-setting maniac; Lily hates me; and my horizon is dark. All this is one thing. But knowing Lily's life is destroyed as a direct result of my actions is too much to bear. If I hadn't helped Miles he wouldn't have been able to do this. We were all on the team.

I'm about to ruin my own life. But for the first time in days, a calm sense of purpose descends, lighting my way. I'm finally focusing on what's important.

'HG.' I clear my throat. 'You've got the wrong person.'

HG frowns. 'Excuse me?'

My bravado is waning, so I hurry on. 'I stole the orchid. I'll come quietly, I'll do anything you want. But it's not Lily's fault.' I've really done it now. 'It was me.'

My mind is already flitting to what Chaz will say, how he'll call me an idiot. Whether my dad will bail me out of orchid jail. My brain is twittering so fast I hardly hear HG's sharp intake of breath. I'm not expecting her next move, which is to sigh and shut her eyes.

Then she says, 'My office,' and motions me to follow.

Chapter Thirty-Seven

HG's office is part of the old stables. It's cosy, smelling of coffee. HG indicates for me to take a seat, then leaves. My movements dreamlike, I take the straight-backed chair in the corner.

A couple of excruciating minutes pass as I sit in silence, hands clenched. HG probably brought me here to wait for the fated orchid-police. Finally, my crimes catch up with me.

Should I say I have the right to a lawyer? I probably do. But pretty embarrassing if I'm wrong. Maybe I should Google it.

I spring to my feet and start to pace in a bid to head off the absolute freak-out heading my way.

The room is lined with shelves of textbook-like tomes, stacked haphazardly. A sheaf of stiff cardboard documents is shoved face-down on a shelf. When I ease one out and turn it over, it reads *Award for Services to Conservation*. It was presented a couple of years ago by a minor royal. There's another whole shelf of bound booklets that, when I pull one out, turn out to be dissertations. I flick through the acknowledgements. *To Ms Gyamfi, the best mentor: thank you for your life-changing support and inspiration.*

I shove it back in the bookcase, disgusted. If she's such a bloody shining light in the field, why can't she fix this? How could she let the orchid be stolen; how could she even think of firing Lily? How could she allow *me* to work here when I'm clearly a saboteur and a fool?

Gripped with the urge to do something, regain some control, I stride to her desk. Her orderly and structured approach to botany doesn't apply to paperwork – it's a mess of files, a laptop, pens. A framed picture of Ms Lenson holding a bunch of flowers and smiling very sweetly is propped against the lamp.

There are papers here from months ago. I carefully scoop up a pile and sift through. Information packs, safeguarding policies, a contract for the new security system. A contract about *Calanthe Caerulissimus Hookiae*—

About the orchid.

I grip it. It feels like finding someone's diary after they're dead: all their hopes for the future, come to nothing. Some self-punishing urge makes me flip through it anyway.

This contract has been agreed between Richard Hook ('the Collector') and Felborough Botanic Gardens ('Felborough') in accordance with Charity Commission guidelines ...

   This contract regards the Calanthe Caerulissimus

Hookiae ('the Orchid'), as gained by the Collector and presented to Felborough under conditions prescribed in this contract . . .

As an exempt charity, Felborough is subject to charity law. The overriding duty of Felborough trustees, as for all charity trustees, is to advance the purposes of their charity . . .

It's at least twenty pages long. Wild that there can be this much to say about one flower. Skimming the blocks of text, my eye is drawn to everywhere HG and Hook have signed – here, and here, and here. It's dated a few weeks ago; this must be the completed version.

I'm about to return it to the pile when I come to a page buried at the end where a short section jumps out as though ringed by flashing lights. It's bracketed in lilac highlighter with a big question mark and annotated so hard with overlapping scribbles that the printed words are almost illegible. It's all very aggressive.

There's a lilac highlighter in the pot on the desk. Even for a failed heist-snooper like me, it feels safe to deduce this as HG's work. But why she's done it like an angry toddler is less obvious.

I hold the page to the light, trying to read past the blurring.

On the Orchid's flowering, an embargo will come into force that precludes the free public sharing of information relating to it by Felborough, the Collector, or any

340

other party. Any informaiton will be held exclusively by Felborough and can be sold under agreed contract to interested parties, with 20% commission to the Collector. Any breaches of this contract will . . .

Wait. What? I read it again, but it still says the same thing.

I Google the word 'embargo' in case it doesn't mean what I think it means. But it does. An official ban.

Precludes the free public sharing.

Sold under contract . . . 20% commission to the Collector.

I drop into HG's desk chair, which is so ergonomic that it rolls away, knocking me into the wall behind.

Sharing any information about the orchid once it flowered would be banned? It doesn't make sense. That would mean all its potential to be a new source of medicine or unlock secrets of biodiversity – none of it would be shared for free?

This goes against everything Lily's told me about Felborough. They're a charity working for conservation, for God's sake. They don't sell information. They share it for the good of everyone. *It's the most important work any of us will ever do.*

But this contract has been signed by HG; it was done weeks ago.

I look more closely at the highlighted section again.

This time, I see it. *Informaiton.* A typo that a basic spellcheck would pick up. Surely that wouldn't happen in a contract like this, not in a clause this important? I rub my temple, trying to think past the buzzing in my ears. HG could be a devious supervillain type after all, secretly not caring about plant science, driven by greed and/or the forces of evil. She could be. Maybe she did this on purpose; maybe Felborough needs the money.

But it's like trying to jam a key into a lock that you know it won't fit. All those dissertations on the shelf thanking HG for being such a good person. The awards, tucked face-down as though they don't merit enough effort even to file them, let alone show them off. Her tireless work for Felborough, all her open-access publications. The fact that she spotted Lily's value and mentored her and defended her.

I don't believe she'd have knowingly signed this. And yet it has been signed. And the orchid has flowered.

What if HG only just realised? What if by the time they'd gone through the legal process to have the contract cancelled it would be too late? What might she feel she had to do to prevent this?

My stomach lurches, like a cannonball flung through my middle.

Footsteps outside. The door swings open as HG ushers Lily inside.

Lily falters at the sight of me. 'Phil?'

I look up, still in HG's desk chair, caught in the act. Lily's wearing her Felborough fleece. Her hair is plaited. I shake my head. I don't know what I can possibly say, but just the sight of her is enough to make me want to cry.

'What are you doing?' HG exclaims.

But I shake my head. The questions roaring through me have crystallised into a heavy, solid suspicion.

'HG,' I say, pushing myself to my feet. 'I know.'

Her eye travels to the contract in my hand, the highlighted page uppermost. Expressions flash across her face, too quickly to judge. I have no idea how old HG is, it occurs to me suddenly. Another layer to her air of mystery. Only a few wrinkles around her eyes and a slight line above her raised eyebrow betray anything; that and the way her closely shorn black hair, unchanging as ever, is speckled with white hairs that glint in the golden afternoon light.

If I'm wrong, I'm making things worse. They can add 'snooping through private documents' to my list of crimes, not that it's anything new. But I don't think I'm wrong.

Lily looks between us, starts to ask, but HG raises a hand. Just as the tension has become so thick that I consider screaming to break it, she speaks.

'Go on then.' Her usual assertive tone. 'Tell me.'

I take a deep breath. 'I told you I stole the orchid. But—'

'Wait, you told her *what*?' Lily cuts in.

I meet her eye. 'I had to. They were going to fire you. But,' I turn back to HG, 'you know what really happened, don't you?'

'Phil!' Lily exclaims. 'What the hell are you doing?'

But HG is still regarding me quietly, her posture like a tightly coiled spring. 'Go on,' she says again.

I don't know where to start. It's like juggling puzzle pieces that are morphing in and out of shape. Every time I grip one, another grabs my attention.

'The security footage from last night is gone,' I say, the words coming in a rush. HG's eyes are so piercing that they draw it out of me easily, this thing that my mind's been turning over all afternoon. Obviously the first thing security would do after a break-in is look at the tapes. But Ted hasn't seen them and nor has anyone else, because, according to him, the system malfunctioned.

'Indeed.' HG inclines her head.

'And isn't that just so convenient?' I say. 'That the brand-new system glitched just at the precise time, in the exact place, the thief needed it to.'

I pause. The atmosphere has thickened to the texture of golden syrup. Lily is gripping opposite elbows, her knuckles white.

'And then, there's the orchid.' I swallow hard, the word bitter in my mouth. 'The timing doesn't make sense. No one except Fells staff knew it had flowered. The public were told it hadn't yet, and the grand reopening was postponed for that reason. So either the thief didn't care if it was in bloom when they stole it. Or they knew it was. And that's why they chose that night to do it.'

'That doesn't narrow it down,' Lily says. 'Dozens of staff saw the orchid flowering. Pretty much the whole of Fells is a suspect.'

'No,' I say. 'I mean, yes. But also . . .'

Our conversation the other day. Lily *knew* the orchid was

going to bloom then. It was her job to nurture it, monitor it, predict when it would flower. And she did, she read the signs; it was the right colour and had the right little shoots or whatever. But HG didn't believe her; she got Lily to postpone the opening and stake her reputation on it.

Unless she did believe her. She knew Lily was right.

'No.' Lily shakes her head. But realisation is dawning on her face.

'HG,' I say. 'You knew it would flower then. You had to act before it was too late.'

Lily's hands float at waist-level as though trying to push something away, or hold it back. But I press on.

'You're the only one who could remove the security tapes and have no one realise,' I say, 'so you deleted the footage. Didn't you?'

HG holds my gaze. Then, slowly, inclines her head.

She must have seen me in the glasshouses. Obviously the motion sensor wouldn't just turn off if the fire alarm was triggered. God.

But wait . . . this means HG must have seen who set the fire as well, on the library cameras.

'Why did you do it?' Lily whispers, before I can follow this thought.

HG is Lily's idol, her role model. There's no relief in having someone else take the top spot as villain. HG must know this because her eyebrows crease together. For the first time, she looks almost pleading.

'Lily, as one who follows in my footsteps,' she says at last, 'let me explain. I know you will understand.'

HG begins to pace along the bookshelf wall. The confined space and the prowling remind me of a caged predator, biding its time until it's ready to break free.

'I've lived around the world, but I settled in the UK ten years ago,' she starts. 'Felborough called to me, as it called to you too, I believe.' She nods at Lily. 'These magnificent glasshouses hold some of the world's most wonderful plant life. And Felborough brings opportunities. The money for these places isn't available everywhere. Whenever a new species is discovered, when research is carried out – people come to us.'

She pauses, her eyes flashing as she pins me with her gaze. 'So imagine my excitement at the Splendid Paradise Orchid's discovery. Another spectacular find from South America's ancient rainforests. Another potential key to unlock new magic.'

HG stops pacing and leans against a bookshelf. 'Of course, the person to find it was Hook. I've known him for years. He travelled to the Darien Gap on his orchid-finding mission. He didn't care for bureaucracy, the legal requirements of importing flora internationally, the people who live there. All he cares about is reputation and money.' She narrows her eyes. 'Following in the footsteps of the Victorian orchid hunters. His colonial ancestors.'

Seeing my confused expression, Lily – who's barely moving – says distractedly, 'The Victorians travelled to the tropics for orchids and then burnt down the forests when they found them so other people couldn't collect them. Keep up, Phil.'

'Fuck off, is that true?' I splutter. Seriously, the more you hear about the Victorians, the worse it gets.

'When Hook found the orchid,' HG goes on, ignoring this, 'he didn't seek to learn from local experts or study it in the wild before he uprooted the specimen. No, once he had been released by the guerrilla fighters whose territory he was in, he . . . borrowed a private jet.' The words fall from her lips with utter disdain.

'Sorry,' I interrupt again. 'A private jet?' How much money is there in this orchid-hunting business?

'This is a man who professes to care about preserving the environment.' Her brows pull together, wrath emanating. 'He wants no such thing. Hook brought it back to Felborough in his friend's gas-guzzling flying machine and,' she pauses between each phrase, the heaviness of the words sinking in, 'he waited for us to laud him.'

'But why did you have to steal it?' Lily asks desperately. 'Even if Hook is like that, at least the orchid is *here*. It was under your care!'

I tap the contract on the desk. The embargo.

'Because,' HG says, choosing her words carefully, 'Hook didn't stop there. We are already leaders in the botanical world. But for Hook, it's not enough. He wants not to share knowledge, not to conserve our world, but to sell what we've learnt to the highest bidder. He saw this as a business opportunity. I realised too late. Mary realised actually,' she sighs, 'when she was reviewing our paperwork the other week. She's far more adept than I in that area.'

As always, her expression softens as she mentions Ms Lenson. Then it becomes grimmer than ever. 'Behind my back, he slipped a research embargo into our contract preventing us from sharing our work with outsiders, except for at a price that our board of investors – led by Hook – would set.'

Lily gasps.

'Felborough would become more exclusive. Hook and his investor friends would benefit. His reputation and influence would soar. When we realised, we asked a discreet lawyer friend if there's anything we could do. But the contract is binding. And then the orchid flowered. Hook's plan was about to come to fruition.' HG sighs, then says simply, 'I couldn't let that happen.'

Lily is nodding.

'Wait, you're agreeing?' I ask in amazement.

'I had no idea that was his plan,' Lily protests. 'I thought we were going to write up how we cared for the orchid and publish it. Why else would we have it?'

'But . . . now what? You're just going to keep the orchid at your house in secret forever? What if someone sees it? Or we report you to the police, HG?' I tuck my hands against my hips in a self-righteous expression. HG doesn't know I'd never report anyone to the police if I could help it. Although, looking at her shrewd expression, she might suspect that.

'I'll take care of it at my home,' HG says. 'And I'll continue the research alone if I must. It's too important not to.'

'Lily is going to lose her job!' I exclaim.

But Lily is shaking her head. I know what she's going to say before she says it. 'It's fine. The orchid is safe.'

'You've worked so hard!' I turn to her. 'Your job is your favourite thing!'

She twists her mouth and gives me a quick look, one that makes my heart race. Not now, idiot feelings.

I turn to HG, trying not to sound as frantic as I feel. 'You've got to at least get Lily's job back.'

'Yes. The fire complicated matters considerably. That was not part of the plan. So,' HG folds her arms, 'here is what I propose. The police said it was arson. But it might not have been. It could have been an electrical fault. Our wiring is old; it happens. It was an accident, so no need for an investigation.' She can't really be saying this. But her eyes are boring into mine again. 'The Board will listen to me, if I have time to convince them.'

'The other gardeners will rally round too,' I offer. 'If you want character references. Safety in numbers.'

'I don't know if—' Lily starts.

'They will,' I say firmly. 'They already are.'

HG nods once. 'About the fire. The library CCTV footage just shows a masked figure who, to me, looks male.' My heart thumps. 'On reflection,' HG continues sternly, 'from what I know of you, Phil, I suspect you had nothing to do with the fire and this wasn't for your own gain. I assume you don't make a habit of this kind of behaviour—'

A small noise of disbelief escapes my lips. This is one level below life and death, and she's talking to me like a strict but fair teacher who's always found that treating her pupils as adults gets better results.

'. . . So there would be little point putting you through this country's punitive so-called justice system. But I need to know this will never happen again. Can you guarantee that?'

'I can try,' I say. One last job. This could be better than I dared hope. If I can pull it off.

'I'll leave it with you, then. Both of you, I suspect.'

This strange interview appears to be at an end. I'm about to head for the door when I pause.

'HG,' I ask, casually, 'did you suspect me all along?'

She showed no surprise about seeing me in the security footage and she hasn't asked why I did it. She might never have confronted me if I hadn't confessed. And I thought I was hiding my tracks so well.

'I don't doubt your qualities, Phil. I understand you have many that Lily appreciates.' A slight glint in her eye makes me suddenly, fully, blush red. Oh my God, she's looking into my soul; she can see every smutty thought I've ever had. I daren't look at Lily. 'But among your – I'm sure numerous – attractive traits, you are not an effective criminal. And I am not an idiot.'

Excuse me?

'I did overhear you asking a lot of questions,' she says. 'That in itself wasn't suspicious, but I noticed. So I kept an eye on you. After I learnt about Hook's plan, I thought of that night I discovered you by the glasshouses. It gave me the idea that if I was clever, and lucky, I might be able to pin the orchid disappearance on you.'

I don't have time to parse how annoying and smug HG is about this because Lily gasps. 'So you did come that night! You didn't stand me up.'

'Of course.' I turn my back on HG, filling my vision with Lily. 'I'd never stand you up.'

Lily holds my gaze for a moment. Her eyes are clear and steady, and there's a hint of the old sparkle. I try to suppress the roaring in my ears at Lily's expression, her face. I still don't know if she can ever forgive me and yet, here I am, worried I'm in love. What a moment to realise.

'I assumed you were breaking in for the orchid then. Although, I must admit,' HG reaches into her pocket and withdraws a scrap of paper, 'I didn't expect my suspicions to be so fully confirmed when I checked your fleece pockets a few days later. So I have you to thank for that.'

She places the paper on the desk, smoothing out the crumples. Lily leans closer to read it. 'Oh my God,' she says, faintly.

But I already know what it says. Chaz's awful handwriting is unmistakable. And I know numbers one to three off by heart. It's not a long list.

The team. The plan. The heist.

I am going to murder Chaz.

Chapter Thirty-Eight

'Well,' I say, twisting my hands as we pause by Lily's car. We've walked to the car park in silence. But it doesn't feel hostile. 'I guess I'm off to make sure a pathetic master criminal gives up his life of crime forever. You don't . . . I can let you know how it goes.'

'Shut up,' Lily says. 'I'm obviously coming.' She jingles her car keys. 'Want a lift?'

She drives us to Chaz's flat. Chaz lets us both in with a brief, 'Hello,' as though he and Lily know each other well and the last time they saw each other wasn't in a smoke-filled glasshouse at outrageous heights of emotional intensity. 'Let's discuss the plan,' he says, rubbing his hands together.

We talk things through. I realise a couple of times that I'm glazing over, distracted by the strangeness of Lily being here, in Chaz's weird little flat. She's acting as though it's normal for us all to take down a criminal together. As though there's a chance she doesn't hate me more than she's ever hated anyone.

Maybe she's just keeping it under wraps until we've solved this problem. The hope is too painful to contemplate.

'Much better than Miles, aren't you?' Chaz comments, as we get into Lily's car an hour or so later.

She frowns. 'Not sure that's much of a compliment.'

'We should have had her in the team all along,' he says to me.

'It is absolutely too soon,' I say, looking in horror at Lily. But she just laughs and rolls her eyes.

The tension, which dissipated so blissfully for that brief period, crashes back as Lily drives us to Miles's. Chaz has traced him back to his flat. He had to come home eventually.

I grip my phone, unable to look away from the picture of the tapestry. Miles's signet ring loops around my finger, strangling it.

At his building, there's no answer when we ring the buzzer, but we slip in behind someone and hurry up the stairs to the fourth floor, unable to wait for the lift. When we reach Miles's door, I start banging on it.

'Miles!' Chaz yells. 'Are you in there?'

I give it a minute, then start banging again. 'We're not leaving until you talk to us.'

Our voices echo around the building, but I'm beyond caring. 'MILES,' Lily shouts, startling me. 'Open this bloody door.'

'He's not in, dearies,' comes a voice from behind.

I wheel around. It's Miles's neighbour, the little old woman I helped with her bags that time. The one who Miles said would take a mile, if given an inch. She's holding a book and a thermos and is coming down from upstairs, although she lives across the hall.

'Ah,' I say. 'Sorry about the commotion.'

'If it's himself you're looking for,' she says, raising her eyebrows, 'he's on the roof terrace.'

'Sorry?' I say. The building has a roof terrace. Of course.

She nods. 'I went up myself to enjoy the evening but didn't fancy it after all. He takes up a lot of space, doesn't he?'

'He does,' I agree, hurrying to the stairs. Chaz and Lily are already running up them.

'He's a pretty face but . . . goodness.'

I laugh. The mask has been stripped away and his neighbour is right: Miles *is* just a pretty face. I don't know how I ever got taken in by it. 'We'll try up there now.'

'Do you know the code?'

'Er, no,' I say, my heart plummeting. Not another hurdle. I can't be guessing any more codes. We're so close.

'Not to worry, dear. I'll write it down for you, shall I?'

Unable to believe my luck, I hold out my phone and she types it into the Notes app.

'There you are.' Then, to my amazement, she winks. 'Nice girl like you. Give him hell.'

Maybe she thinks I'm a jilted lover, or all of us are. That's fine; I can work with that. Thanking her profusely, I hurry upwards. The stairs go on and on but I take them two at a time, overtaking Chaz easily and catching up with Lily. I want to be facing Miles when I start yelling.

We burst onto the roof after a brief pause to ricochet off the closed door, having forgotten about the door release button. Shaken, out of breath and punch-drunk, I enter the code and almost fall, at last, out onto the wooden deck.

The terrace is furnished with loungers, a bench, some fake plants. In the corner, sprawled on a lounger, is Miles. What looks like an actual cocktail is beside him on the wooden slatted flooring. He is the *worst*.

I clear my throat. He turns, jolts and lowers his sunglasses. 'How did you—'

'Miles,' I say. 'What a pleasure. Did you know your phone seems to be off?'

I stroll towards him. Ten storeys up, the roof looks out across the town, lit with sunshine on this warm evening. In the distance, visible through the trees, is the golden stone of Felborough Hall. Miles can literally see it from his place. I almost laugh.

'We know it was you,' Chaz pants, pulling up the lounger next to Miles and dropping onto it.

'What are you talking about?' Miles's bluster kicks in. 'Why are you all here?'

'We don't know exactly how or why,' I say, brushing off another seat and offering it to Lily, 'but we know you set the fire.' Slipping the ring off my finger, I toss it onto his lap. It almost falls, but he catches it.

'Ah,' he says. He turns it, then slips it onto his pinky. Back in its usual place. 'I wondered where that went.'

He's suave as ever, as though nothing happened last night.

His hair is floppy as usual, freshly washed, and he's wearing that nice red shirt again, the one I liked before. In comparison, I feel like a sewer rat who's been put through a washing machine: mangy, unkempt, utterly confused. But also, crucially, furious.

'Weirdly,' I say, keeping my voice conversational, 'we found something else of yours too. I mean, we assume it's yours. Chaz found it in your flat.'

I want to get a rise out of him and we're rewarded by a slight widening of his eyes as Chaz, still lying back and panting, pulls the sliver of tapestry out of his pocket and holds it up. Miles didn't know Chaz had broken in.

'You probably shouldn't have given us your real address,' Chaz croaks. 'That wasn't very smart. Not very profesh.'

But Miles composes himself fast. 'How interesting,' he comments.

'What's your relation to Felborough, Miles?' I ask, my voice calm. 'We have our suspicions, but I'd love to hear it from you.'

'Oh, Phil.' Miles smiles. 'You love your history. Fawning over your Felborough research, as though you could tell me anything new. You only know their side of the story. I'd be delighted to share mine.'

I nod, suddenly wary of provoking him. I was wrong before. He's not suave; he's desperate. For the first time, a sliver of fear nudges down my spine. I'm grateful to have Chaz and Lily for backup.

'My family, the Mountjoys, owned Felborough once. My

great-great-grandfather was a well-known explorer. Just like Hook.' He spits the word. '*He* takes after him.'

My stomach flips as I understand. Hook. That's why Miles was so weird about him. That's why they look similar.

'My ancestor built the glasshouses. Yes,' he says to Lily's gasp, 'he thought it worth bankrupting the family for *plants*. Then we had a couple of feckless family members – a few bad uncles, gamblers. Nothing major, but the glasshouses set us on the path and they and the Second World War did the rest. And instead of offering support, do you know what the state did?' This has the cadence of a well-told tale, passed down through the family. He pauses, then murmurs, his voice low with fury, 'They refused aid. They "suggested" we donate it as a botanical haven. How many times in history has a great family run into trouble? And never would they lose their heritage because, in those days, they respected what was right.'

'But this must have been years ago,' I say, after several moments have passed in silence. 'When did your family last live in Felborough?'

'My grandfather was thrown out on his ear at the age of two,' Miles replies, haughty as ever.

'And then what?'

He frowns. 'What do you mean?'

'Presumably they weren't destitute.' The memory of Miles casually handing over twenty quid instead of the tenner I needed for the new key card, waving it off, rushes back. His extremely nice flat, swanky car, no sign of an actual job. From the way he lives, they've done all right.

'They moved to London, but I hardly see how that's relevant. Our family was taken advantage of at a low ebb. This country's been going downhill ever since. No one has any respect any more; no one values anything good. Britain's glory days are so far behind us no one even remembers them.'

'Jesus.' Chaz shakes his head. His expression is what you could plausibly call gobsmacked. 'You're really obsessed, aren't you?'

'It's not obsessive to want to right a wrong done to your family,' Miles sneers.

But Chaz is still exclaiming. 'Wow. How long have you been working on this?' He looks at me and Lily in disbelief, then back at Miles. 'It might be time to move on, mate.'

'What was your goal?' I demand. 'Did you even want the orchid?'

He snorts. 'I never cared about the stupid orchid. It was always just a means to an end.'

'So you could burn the place down?'

'Well, if you're going to put it so crudely. I just wanted revenge for Felborough. Our ancestral home, turned into offices and labs, filled with tourists. But I couldn't get access when security was so tight. So, obviously, I needed help from the team.'

I'm clenching my fists so tightly that my bitten-down finger-nails manage to dig into the palm of my hand.

'And the time had to be right, too. The orchid flowering was perfect: maximum drama, maximum embarrassment.'

'Can we confirm what you did, then?' Chaz asks. 'Just for fun.' When Miles nods, he says, 'When I went through the hedge, you gave it a minute, then followed. You went through the sheds, up the tunnel—'

'Which I obviously knew about; this *was* my family home,' Miles interrupts.

'—and up to your special little secret library room. Then you set the fire, made the call to tip them off that we were breaking into the glasshouses, and ran for the hills. Right?'

'Good plan, isn't it?' Miles shrugs. 'Their ruin and a scapegoat all in one.'

Chaz nods. 'I'm big enough to admit that.'

'Don't encourage him,' Lily whispers, rolling her eyes.

'But you failed,' I say, resisting the urge to click my fingers at Miles. I don't want him basking in any success. 'They're not ruined. All you've done is bring Fells more publicity. Have you not seen the fundraiser?'

'Their star orchid event is ruined and their Hall is destroyed,' he points out. 'I'd call that pretty good revenge. Or a good starting point, anyway.'

'Potato-pot*ah*to,' Chaz says.

'Oh my God,' I say, trying to keep my voice as calm as theirs. I'm desperate to wrap this up without anyone fully losing it. I'm pretty sure Miles went to some boys' finishing school for staying outwardly composed and making the person you're arguing with feel over-emotional and petty. But I'm not falling for it. 'Listen, Miles. I'm sure you want us out of your admittedly fantastic hair, don't you? So we'll be on our way just as soon as we know you'll never do anything like this again. We can trace it back to you,' I add.

'What, do you think the ring or that bit of tapestry will help?' Miles laughs. 'You found the ring in the secret passage where you weren't allowed anyway. Who do you think they'll believe? I admire the effort, but you've got nothing on me.'

'We have other stuff on you,' I say. 'We can go public with it.'

'You haven't got the guts,' Miles says, scornfully. He leans forward, his eyes fixed on mine. 'So nervous about the heist, all the criminal stuff. It was very boring. You, Phil, are too fundamentally law-abiding for your own good.'

I have to smile. He's got me there. My need to be morally above board makes me so much less fun. But he's wrong about one thing: my moral code doesn't always perfectly align with the law.

'Well,' I say. 'Lucky I have Chaz then, isn't it? I'm out-sourcing my immorality,' I explain, trying not to laugh gleefully, 'just for you.'

'So,' Chaz takes over, 'if you do go to the police, or if we hear a whiff of any other stinky business you're up to, infor-mation will be delivered to their system that proves you were there the night of the fire. They'll receive the messages from your accounts planning the heist and the fire, all traceable to your personal devices.'

Miles gapes. 'You can't do that,' he splutters, jumping to

his feet. 'Those messages planning the heist are to *you two*. You'll go down with me.'

But Chaz is shaking his head. 'That's where you're wrong, pal. Because Phil and I took the precaution of actually using that secure messaging system I got us to install, and you did not. Also,' he shrugs, 'and this is meaner, but I've *planted* – pun intended,' he says to Lily, who looks momentarily startled, 'some incriminating information somewhere on your personal records. Don't worry,' Chaz adds, holding up a hand, 'no one will find it unless they go looking. But if you go to the police, they *will* go looking. Because I'll tell them to.'

I suppress a slightly mad giggle. I can't tell if I'm laughing with relief that Lily's plan is working or hysteria that we've really resorted to blackmail.

'You'll pay for this,' Miles snarls, like someone in a film. It's more chilling than I'd have expected. He clenches his fists. 'How dare you threaten me? After everything my family's been through,' he adds, almost to himself. 'To be spoken to like this by someone like *you*.'

'What do you mean, someone like Chaz?' Lily asks, bristling. Seeing her square up to Miles, an angry lunatic, to defend Chaz, who she met mere hours ago, makes me want to kiss her.

'Never mind,' Chaz says, flapping a hand at Lily. 'I'm getting bored now. So, Fells had a minor electrical fault and that's what caused the fire, OK? End of. Oh, apart from one more thing.' As Chaz clambers to his feet, he tries and fails to control a twitch of his lip. He needs to work on his poker face. 'Miles, you very kindly made a frankly,' the lip twitch turns into a full-on smirk, 'fucking *massive* donation to a conservation charity earlier. Really nice of you. Your whole bank account, too! I thought it was a bit out of character, but what do I know?'

Chaz neatly ducks out of arm's reach as Miles lets out a bellow of rage. 'Are you *joking*,' Miles screams.

Chaz just scampers over to the stairs. 'Denial is the first stage,' he calls back. 'You'll reach acceptance soon.'

Miles's fists are clenched at his side as I get to my feet too and back away, jostling with Lily; both of us are trying to get in between each other and Miles, who looks like he might punch someone. But no one's in reach, and there are three of us, and he's really not cut out for a physical fight.

'If you leave Felborough alone,' I say, as Lily grips my hand, her strength filling me, 'we'll leave you alone. Deal?'

Miles presses his lips together, his mouth almost disappearing under the force. He's racking his brains for a loophole. But we all stare back as he stands in front of us, his hair wild from running his hand through it.

Eventually, at long last, he nods once. The tall, imposing man – all his charisma and power – has transformed like a lens slipped in front of our eyes, revealing a weak, pitiable person. I almost feel sorry for him. To be this entitled, to believe so desperately that everything was better in the olden days. I want nothing more than to leave Miles behind and never think of him again.

'Excellent,' Chaz says, waving as he presses the door release. 'Pleasure doing business with you.'

As we walk across the terrace to return to the real world, Lily squeezes my hand.

Chapter Thirty-Nine

'Now what?' Lily says. By unspoken agreement, she dropped Chaz off first. He gave me a rib-cracking hug and said, 'Have fun, kids.' I think he genuinely enjoyed the evening.

'Um.' I fiddle with my seatbelt. The thought of going home is suddenly horrible. Val might be there with my dad being all cheery. I'll have to tell him what happened at some point, but not yet. I can't talk to any more people today.

Lily stares at me for a long moment. Then she says, 'Back to mine?'

I nod, struck as always by her generosity. 'Please.'

She drives us home. I stand in the hallway, accepting Eva's greeting, struggling to take off my shoes. Being here, after everything that happened, is almost too much to take in. Lily hangs her jacket on the hook and holds out her hand for mine.

I pass it, charmed by this act of domesticity. Her hand brushes against mine and a jolt of anticipation shocks down to the soles of my feet. I step closer, not letting go of the jacket, using it to draw us closer together.

'Lily,' I whisper. 'Can you ever forgive me? After what I've put you through—' I don't know how to ask, but I think I need to. 'Do you really want me here?'

She twists her mouth, her gaze resting on my lips. 'I just thought . . . What you said about your dad.' She stops, heaving a breath. 'You've met my parents. They're annoying. But they're my parents. As in,' she shoots me a quick look, 'they parent me. And if I was in trouble they'd be there for me to fall back on. They're a safety net, emotionally and financially. And I'm lucky to have that, even if the net does, like, criticise my appearance and pressure me about grandchildren.'

We share a smile. It seems ridiculous now, after everything that's happened.

'But if I didn't have that,' she continues, 'I don't know what I'd be like. Maybe I'd have done the same as you.'

'Lily,' I say, laughing despite the warmth spreading in my chest at her words. 'Don't pretend.'

'Maybe not the orchid,' she admits. 'But I might have tried to rob a bank and immediately got arrested or something. It's hard to know. Because I can never truly understand what it's like not having that security. So I'm not saying I agree with what you did,' she adds. She looks up to meet my gaze, her eyes very clear. 'But who am I to judge you for doing it?'

'Lily,' I say again softly.

She nods. Then her lip twitches. 'And thank fuck you

failed,' she adds, 'because I'd have had a really hard time forgiving that. Even for you, I don't think I'd have managed it.'

Even for me.

'That's fair,' I nod, as if my pulse isn't thrumming like a hummingbird's.

'Plus, you told HG the whole thing was your fault.' She raises an eyebrow. 'If that isn't an old-fashioned, heroic, throwing-yourself-on-your-sword move, I don't know what is.'

I have to laugh once more. She's unbelievable. 'Lily,' I murmur, and her throat moves as she swallows.

She's standing too close now to hold off any longer.

My cheeks heat as I look into her sweet face, her expression open as she looks back. I need to sort things out, get my life together. But, quite frankly, the rest of the world can wait. My toes curl into the softness of the rug in anticipation and I reach, slowly, to cup Lily's face, my thumb grazing her cheekbone. Her breath catches.

I want to give her time to move away, to change her mind. But this time, when I lean in to kiss her, she gets there first, one of her hands covering mine on her cheek, the other slipping round to the curve of my lower back, pulling me in closer too. She still tastes like sunlight, somehow. Her tongue darts against mine, meeting it, spiking a kaleidoscope of sensation right through me.

At our feet, Eva paws at my leg and then whines. We break apart, both laughing.

'You are the loveliest person in the world,' I mumble against her lips. 'I've never met anyone like you.'

She pulls me closer and we stumble across the narrow hallway. I push her up against the wall and she gasps as I tuck her hands behind her and hold them there with one hand, using the other to bury my fingers in her hair and tug, very gently, to give me better access to her neck. When my lips meet her skin, she sighs in a sound that's better than anything I could have imagined.

'Make that sound for me again and I'll die happy,' I whisper, tracing a line up her neck with my tongue.

'God,' she breathes, aching her back. 'Phil. You can't just say stuff like—'

Eva barks, then, when we ignore her, barks again and paws at the back of my knees. 'Oh my God,' I exclaim, reluctantly breaking away and glaring down at her. '*What*?'

'She's saying get a room,' Lily says, her eyes smoky grey. She slips a hand under my T-shirt and strokes a fiery line up my ribcage, just brushing the underside of my breast.

'Fuck,' I sigh, involuntarily. 'Well, I'd hate to embarrass her further.'

Still kissing, still entwined, Lily drags me upstairs. In her bedroom, we pause for a breath as I slowly shut the door behind us so Eva doesn't follow us in. It clicks audibly closed, my heart jolting with it.

Lily's wearing a simple white T-shirt and cargo trousers, the kind with far too many pockets. I love them: the way they just hint at the curve of her hip, her thigh. I can't decide if I want to rip them off her or undo every pocket and zip slowly until she's begging me to hurry.

I take a step closer, and she does the same. I'm breathing hard.

'Are you nervous?' she whispers.

I close my eyes. That same question I asked her at the gala. At the time, I said no. But the stakes were lower then.

'Yeah,' I admit, my voice husky. I clear my throat. 'I can't believe this is happening.'

'It is,' she says, her voice soft but firm. She reaches her hand to tuck lightly against my waist, over my shirt. My skin is fizzing, vibrating at her touch.

I can't take this any more.

We both take a step at the same time and we're suddenly, finally, kissing, embracing hard, pulling each other together. My fingers bury deep in her hair, an exquisite intimacy I could never, ever get used to. As an experiment, I tug gently like before and she makes that sound again, the one that makes me feel like I'm going to pass out.

Her hands are scrabbling at my waistband, pulling my black T-shirt up and over my head. I slide hers off as well, revealing a dreamy swathe of skin, interrupted by a simple dark red bralette with thin straps I'm desperate to run my fingers under. I trace the outline with my thumb, the triangle of the fabric, before I bend to lower my mouth to lick at the place where her nipple has hardened to a peak. She gasps, fingers pulling at my hair as I move to the other side before I slowly, reverently peel back the bralette to reveal her, to give me more access. I swirl my tongue in a circle and think briefly that my whole life has been leading to this feeling, one hand caressing the smoothness of her stomach, the other feeling its way down her long limbs, the taut strength of her muscles.

'Phil, oh my God, I can't—' she's saying. I hum against her skin, letting my teeth graze just the tiniest bit.

She gasps. Then, nudging me away for a split second, she takes a couple of steps back and pulls me with her, almost lifting at the same time so we both land on the bed, her on her back, me astride her.

'I could get used to this.' I shake my head as I drink in the sight of her below me. She's too beautiful to comprehend. 'You wouldn't believe how often I've imagined you in this exact position.'

'Me too,' she says, half-laughing. 'But it was more like—' She leans up to roll us over, despite my protests.

'Just wait,' she says as she slides off the bed for a moment to undo my jeans. Slowly, too slowly, she peels them off, her fingertips tracing lines down my skin, leaving a trail of goosebumps.

When the fabric has pooled on the floor, kicked away into a corner, she splays a hand across my thighs, thumbs reaching down, making me gasp, 'Are you trying to kill me?'

'In a way,' she says dreamily, her turn to lean above me now as I prop myself on my elbows. 'Can I?' she asks, tucking her fingertips under the waistband on my underwear and starting to pull them down.

'God, yes,' I say. 'But first—' I sit up, undo her trousers too, no time to mess around with all those stupid pockets now; I slide them down before pulling her onto my lap. I'm sitting on the edge of the bed, Lily straddling me. My hands range across her back, tucking around the sides of her waist to pull her closer with one hand as the other slides inside her underwear, caressing the lines of her, inching towards the damp heat of her centre. She bites at my lip, her tongue licking at mine, and every second is better than the last, more intense, my heart pounding in my chest so hard I'm sure she can feel it. I need more.

With superhuman strength I didn't know I had, I lift and turn to drop her carefully on the bed so she's lying at the edge, her feet on the floor.

'Please,' I say, as she starts to sit up. 'Will you let me?'

'I was going to—' she says, breathing heavily as I kneel between her legs. I drop a kiss on the inside of her knee, then the other side and draw her underwear down.

'Can I?' I ask, as I drop another kiss higher up, then trace a line with my tongue, higher and higher. 'I have to taste you.'

She lets out a strangled laugh-moan, dropping her head back onto the bed and raising her hands to cover her face. 'Oh my God.'

'Is that a yes?' I ask, pausing as I let out a warm breath, not quite touching her but close enough, so close. The moment hangs in the air, a delicious drop of stillness. Then—

'Yes,' she whispers. 'Please.'

I need no more encouragement. My tongue parts her as I finally live another fantasy. Her fingers tangle in my hair, long enough now for her to get a grip on it in both hands as she presses me closer, my tongue swirling and dipping. She moans and I feel it in my tightened nipples, in the lightning spark at my centre. Her thigh hooked over my shoulder, pulling me close.

I want to stay in this moment forever.

Until the moment a little while later – not long enough – when I feel her clenching around me, sighing my name, my hands on her stomach and breasts as she gasps. This is the moment I want to live in.

Or possibly the one a little later still when she brings me to a shuddering halt around her fingers, her hair falling softly over my face as she presses her body into mine, her thigh curled across me, every part of us touching as closely as we can.

I can't choose. I want all of them. I want her beside me, above me, inside me. She's under my skin and I can't imagine she'll ever leave. I'm sunk. I'm dead.

'You've killed me,' I say, presently. 'I can't believe this is how it ends.'

'With a bang and also a whimper?' she says, her voice muffled as she speaks into my neck. We pulled the duvet half over us, afterwards, when we were getting chilly, creating a warm cocoon. The daylight has faded but we've not yet turned on a light, watching the room fade to a greyish dusk. I trace a pattern across the side of her breast, dipping down to the curve of her waist, her hip. Her skin is warm and satiny under my touch. She shivers theatrically.

'Sorry, am I tickling?' I ask.

She shakes her head. 'No. Just . . . nice. You're nice.'

371

I consider saying *You're making me blush,* or something similar, but I don't need to. I'm pretty sure Lily can read my mind. Judging by her responses just now, I'm fairly confident I've got a direct line to hers too.

'Oh, by the way,' Lily says, a few minutes later after I've done a bit more exploring. 'I've been meaning to tell you something.'

She places a hand over mine to stop it moving and I freeze, dread gripping me, which instantly dissipates as Lily starts to laugh.

'You know you suspected Anthony of stealing the orchid?'

I bury my head in the duvet and groan. So embarrassing. 'Please never tell him.'

'OK, but don't you want to know why he was there that night?'

I turn onto one side. I do actually. And I want to know why Lily looks so gleeful. 'Go on.'

'Because . . .' she pauses for effect. 'He and Diego were on a *date*. By the lake.'

'No way.'

'Yeah!' She laughs again, the sound sparkling deep in my chest. 'Benny texted me earlier. They were going to sneak into the glasshouses later on to see the orchid.'

'Oh my God.' I start laughing too. 'And I thought you were so original, suggesting we meet there the night of the gala.'

Lily shakes her head. 'Turns out it's a romantic hotspot.'

I snuggle closer to her. Those glasshouses. I've never felt so fond of them. We lie there for a moment.

'Phil,' Lily says, as though trying it out.

'Lily,' I agree.

'Do you think you'll keep volunteering at Fells?'

I hum into her hair. 'Do you think I should?'

The thought is delightful, until I remember . . . wait. I need to get a proper job again. Our house is on the market. We have to move out. Everything is changing.

I flop back onto the pillow, turning to look up at the ceiling. 'Oh man,' I say. 'It's been a big old day. Did I mention my dad is selling our house?'

'What?' Lily exclaims.

'Yeah. He told me earlier. Don't worry,' I add, 'I think it's a good thing. Or he thinks it is anyway.' I lean my head back further on the pillow. 'Obviously he didn't think to tell me before. But you know our debts? He remortgaged and then couldn't keep up with the payments. Hence the whole orchid fiasco in the first place. But apparently it's fine,' I continue, aware I'm beginning to gabble, 'it's not a problem because he's found someone to buy it, apart from obviously now we won't have a house. So he'll move into a little flat, like a supported-living situation. He has a new friend who seems non-terrible, which makes a nice change. I'll need to keep an eye, obviously. But it's actually turned out pretty nicely.'

Lily is looking at me as though I'm a very fragile object she doesn't want to make any sudden movements near in case she knocks me over and I shatter. 'What does this mean, Phil?' she asks, placing her palm flat on my chest, her fingers splayed. It's surprisingly grounding.

'It means . . . I guess I'm moving out. Don't worry,' I add quickly, seeing a flash of something in her expression, 'I'm not trying to move in with you.'

She laughs, although she doesn't meet my eye. 'Yep, I would . . . hate that. Definitely. Of course. No doubt. But this is a good thing, right?'

I sigh. It is. I'd be mad to argue. But my dad's issues have hung over me for so long. And now, all of a sudden, he's figured out how to stand on his own two feet; and here I am, staring after him, a little bit lost.

'It's weird,' I say, eventually. 'I kind of don't know what to do when I'm not looking after him.'

'Maybe you can look after yourself for a bit,' she suggests. 'Or, wilder still, maybe you could take a turn being looked after.'

I haven't had a sip of alcohol in days but I feel drunk, my limbs floppy. The orchid is safe. Miles is done. The house where we've lived for so long will be out of our lives, but so will the debt. If I believe it. I don't know if I do. My mind hasn't stopped racing for weeks.

We lie for a moment in silence. I can see Lily mulling it over and I bite my lip to stop myself speaking in case something pathetically, revealingly needy slips out. My toes dig into the mattress, as if trying to put down roots. I'm not exactly being a fun house guest. Lily would be well within her rights to send me away. But there's nowhere I feel safer.

'Do you want a bath?' she asks suddenly, tapping my breastbone very gently.

'A bath?' I stare at her. Apart from anything else, this house is so small and perfectly formed I didn't think there'd be room for a bathtub.

She shrugs. 'You mentioned you never have baths and I find them comforting, sometimes, so I thought it might be nice. Never mind,' she says, as I stare, 'silly idea.'

'No,' I say quickly. I don't know when I last had a bath. Not for years. Maybe not since I was a child. 'I'd love one.'

Her face brightens. 'Great. I'll go and run it.' She disappears and I stay in bed, my hand resting on Eva's back after she sneaks inside, trying to ignore the heart-crushing knowledge of how happy it made Lily to offer this care and for me to accept it.

A while later, Lily calls, 'All ready.'

Walking into the tiny bathroom, I look around in amazement. The walls are a deep, royal blue, beautifully offsetting the white claw-footed bath and antique gold taps. She's filled the tub most of the way to the top and a delicious, fresh green scent fills the air, which is hazy with steam. On the windowsill, on a shelf above the bath and hanging from the back of the door are pots of sprawling, thriving plants. Of course. Because wherever Lily goes, things bloom and grow and live.

Lily twists her hands, seeing my expression. 'They like it in here. Ferns and such. My hot baths are the closest I get to their favourite tropical storms and humidity. I hope you like rosemary and lavender?' she asks, her voice anxious. 'It's my favourite bath salt. But I think I also have a pink one somewhere?'

I shake my head. 'It's perfect.' She's hung a fluffy green towel over the wooden rail beside the bath. The only sounds are the quiet popping of the thin layer of bubbles on the water and the last couple of drips from the tap. It might be the most beautiful, calming sight I've ever seen.

'Oh, nearly forgot,' Lily adds. She hurries out and comes back with a stocky white candle in one hand and a box of matches in the other. 'For the atmosphere,' she says, setting it on the side. 'Now,' she looks around, hands brushing down the T-shirt she quickly pulled on, 'what have I forgotten?'

I laugh at the ridiculous delight of it all. 'Lily, I don't want to make this weird,' I say, reaching a hand to take hers, gently interlacing our fingers, 'but this might be the nicest thing anyone's ever done for me.'

'No,' she says, cheeks flushing, 'please tell me you're not serious. This isn't a big deal.'

But after my weeks of fretting, the stress of being caught, the fire, the confessing, the never-ending planning and worrying – after all that, this bathroom is like a mirage. It's an oasis in the desert. 'It *is* a big deal,' I insist.

Later, Lily brings me a glass of wine and I drink it in the bath, Lily sitting on the edge with her own, until the water cools and the suds have disappeared into nothing. I invite her to join me, but she insists this is *my* bath. She'll get in next time. For now, it's only about me.

She thinks there'll be a next time.

When she realises I'm getting cold, Lily reaches for the towel and comes over, holding it out by the top corners. I stand and turn my back and Lily wraps the towel around me tightly, then hands me the ends as I step out. The actions are so tender that all I can do is stand there, speechless, while she gives my upper arms a quick rub.

'There you go,' she says. 'Are you warm enough?'

Still silent, I turn on the spot and fight a hand free to pull her closer again. She wraps her arms around me, her heat burning away the chill.

Chapter Forty

Four months later

The sky is a pale, glossy blue as I drive the familiar road to Felborough, late-October coolness lacing the air. The oak trees lining the drive spread a red-orange canopy above and I slow the car to take it in. There's no one behind and I'm in no rush.

Those spring days when this all started were magical, everything bursting into life, and the following summer was hazily sultry and slow. But nothing prepared me for the beauty of Felborough in autumn. It's half a year of falling in love, learning each other's foibles and how we change with the seasons, and I'm well and truly smitten.

I park in my usual spot. My new, excitingly personalised lanyard with its Senior Volunteer title and unattractive ID photo bounces against my chest as I stroll towards the gardens. Ethel is on the visitor-centre desk today.

She greets me with a wave. 'Morning, hot stuff. Lovely day.'

'Isn't it just?' I swipe my card against the barrier and it whirs reassuringly as it opens.

It's still early, just a couple of keen visitors at this hour. I wander towards the house, looking out for Lily. I came straight from my flat this morning – *my flat*. The words are still delicious, even several months on.

Lily helped me search and, after a few stressful weeks of flat-hunting, we struck gold. It's very small, even smaller than her place, but it has big windows, lots of light, and space for a double bed. I've furnished it with bookcases and bits from Freecycle, artwork and photos and, of course, plants. Lily brings a new one every few weeks, promising she'll teach me to care for it. So far they're all still thriving, although Lily wouldn't allow anything less, and she's there often to keep an eye. I go to her house too and we hang out with Eva and cook dinner and read and have baths and make plans. I love being with her. I love having my own space. I sometimes have to pinch myself that this is real, that these levels of joy are truly for me.

My dad is happily settled too, a short drive away. I went for dinner last week and instead of me bringing food and heating it up for us both, as I'd been doing until now, he'd made stir fry with tofu. Val taught him. It was delicious, too. I kept laughing with disbelief as I drove home.

The Felborough cafe looks warm and inviting as I pass; not as freshly refurbished now but a bit lived in, which is nicer. A couple of volunteers are setting up tables outside for the hardier guests and I greet them with a wave. Inside, others are arranging pastries and slicing cakes. Maybe Lily and I will go in for lunch later.

I went out last night with some new friends from my teacher training course for a couple of drinks to decompress after our first experience in schools this week. I started at the local college last month, after an enormous amount of persuasion from Lily, Chaz, my dad, the gardeners, everyone really. Ms Lenson offered me a part-time role at Felborough, which was tempting. But when she heard about my possible teacher training she rescinded the offer, saying she couldn't in good conscience give me a reason not to at least try the job I was born to do. It almost made me cry. I applied that evening.

I was worried everyone there would be fresh out of school or uni and it would be me as the pitiful, ageing loser who'd never got their shit together before now. But although there are quite a few recently graduated infants, most of them are nice. There's something a bit self-selecting about people who choose to be teachers.

Better still, there are quite a lot of old fogies who, like me, dare to be older than twenty-five. One, for example, in their mid-thirties, left their unfulfilling wanker job in the City (their words) to try teaching. Another new friend is an actual grandma and is giving teaching a go as her fourth or fifth career. It turns out there's more than one way to live a life. The path is broader and has more branches than you think, and there's no race to the finish.

I'm walking up the steps to the glasshouses when the door opens and Lily runs straight into me. I catch her before we both fall down the steps.

'Oops,' she comments breathlessly, looking up from the step below. 'Hi.'

'Aren't you glad that was me?' I tuck a strand of hair behind her ear. 'I could have been anyone.'

She cut her hair a few months ago, shortly after her promotion to Deputy Head Gardener. It now falls in beautiful, healthy waves to just below her chin. It's curlier than before, as though a weight has been lifted, letting it bounce up. She wears it down more often. It's all I can do to keep myself from burying my fingers in it every time I see her.

We're so close now, though, I don't feel I need to hold back. I lean down and press a kiss to her lips. She responds with alacrity, her hand sliding to my behind.

A cleared throat makes us surface and I turn quickly as HG comes out of the glasshouse, pinning us with what she clearly thinks is a disapproving stare. But the corner of her mouth is turning up slightly.

'For goodness' sake,' she says. 'Control yourselves.'

'Sorry,' I say, smiling sunnily, 'just saying hello.'

'I hope that isn't how you greet all your colleagues,' HG mutters as she marches past.

That woman continues to intimidate and captivate me in equal measure – especially after witnessing in the weeks after the fire how cut-throat she can be to protect her own. The public line is that the orchid was lost to the flames, but

Lily told me that privately the Board knows the truth: it was stolen. As part of HG's project to get Lily her job back, HG argued that if it hadn't been for Hook's overzealous, malfunctioning new security system, they'd have caught the thief. She also revealed Hook's amended legal contract; painted him as grasping and xenophobic, both of which are true; pointed out how quick Hook was to blame Lily, the most promising employee Fells has had in years; and threatened to resign if he didn't step down.

HG's gamble that Fells wanted her more than Hook paid off. He resigned in disgrace, much to the delight of the local press, to be replaced by hot celebrity Finlay Slater – a man significantly better for Fells' international PR.

So that's very satisfying. I think Chaz may also be working on a secret project to further fuck up Hook's life. Just as a hobby. For deniability though, I've asked him not to tell me anything about it.

Lily hops up to join me on my step. Her sleeves are rolled above the elbow, revealing her new fern tattoo healed into the skin of her forearm as though it's always been there. I brush a finger over it, as is my habit. I went with her to get it, of course. I have a new one too: a flowering sweet pea plant, curling around my inner bicep just below my cowboy mermaid. It fits in well.

There's something different about Lily this morning. I can't quite put my finger on it. But she's jigging on the spot and, as I look at her, she takes my face in both hands and presses her forehead to mine.

'Phil,' she says.

'Lily,' I agree. We didn't spend the night last night as I got back late and Lily was out with the gardeners again in yet another pub quiz championship. They never seem to have much success, although they all insist, Lily included, that they're improving every week. But unless they've had their biggest victory ever, that doesn't explain why she's vibrating with excitement.

'Everything OK?' I ask. 'What's going on?'

She withdraws her forehead and smiles, unreadable emotion in her eyes. 'Something's happened. I was coming to find you.'

Turning, she grabs my hand and tugs me up the steps into the glasshouse, restored to former smoke-free glory just a few short weeks after the fire. It's hard to imagine that it happened at all; you'd never know. The greenery is as vivacious as ever.

I follow Lily along the serpentine path, brushing past the overhanging leaves and branches with none of Lily's usual care. I suppress wild questions about what it could be. It can't be bad; she would've said. She wouldn't have smiled or kissed me like that, with promise.

We reach the orchid room at last, that fateful place. It's been open to the public for the last few months, the security relaxed during the day.

The place where the Splendid Paradise Orchid was growing has been left empty since the night of the heist. As with an art gallery where a painting has been stolen but the frame still hangs to mark what should've been, that patch of brown earth has stood empty. A small sign nearby gives the orchid's name and description and a few words about what was lost. It's uncomfortably like a gravestone. I've only been in here once since.

Lily pauses. 'Are you ready?'

I bite my lip. My heart is hammering suddenly. Then, 'Yes,' I say. 'Show me.'

We step through the doorway together.

There, in the centre of the room, is a tiny, hardly noticeable green plant. It's small – shrivelled, almost. It looks like nothing at all. I can barely breathe.

We stop at the low wall to the pond and gaze over the rippling, dark green water. 'It's back,' I whisper. It's really back. After months of nothing, there it is. 'What does this mean?'

Lily is glowing with inner light. 'It means,' she murmurs, holding my arm tightly against her body as though she can hardly believe it, 'germinating worked. HG was successful. And I have it on good authority that an article on the Splendid Paradise Orchid's care was anonymously submitted to several top botanical journals this week.'

'No way,' I breathe.

She smiles, shaking her head. 'It reports the author anonymously sent samples to Felborough for us to cultivate in our glasshouses, as well as to other botanic gardens around the world. The case has been cracked wide open.'

We stand looking across the water at the small, delicate plant. It feels important to mark this moment. The orchid's return. The real meaning of this: conservation, research, sustaining this miraculous flower. I swallow back the lump in my throat.

'The botanical world is going to lose its mind,' I say, when we eventually turn towards the exit.

'As they should,' Lily replies, her voice a delightful mixture of smug and joyful.

We follow the path back towards the gardens. 'Come on,' Lily says, as we pass through the gate, the pumpkin patch on our left in glowing resplendence, ready for a late harvest. 'I'll let you make me a cup of tea in the kitchens before your shift.'

'Oh, thanks,' I say, interlacing my fingers through hers again.

We walk across the sunny lawns, past the hedges turning russet and amber and the late-flowering roses, and up towards the imposing magnificence of Felborough Hall.

Acknowledgements

Buckle up, lads. It's a literal, genuine, ridiculous dream to have a book published and you won't *believe* how many people I need to thank for the privilege.

Firstly, Hannah Todd, dream agent. I'm so lucky to get to work with you. Thank you for believing in me and for being a human ray of sunshine. And to everyone at Madeleine Milburn: again, actual dream team. You are all rockstars.

Jenni Edgecombe, sensational editor: I'm so grateful to have you as an advocate. Thank you for your passion and skill, for enjoying plant puns even more than I do, and for cheerfully accepting the unnecessary references I included for my own entertainment. To all at Mountain Leopard Press, Headline and beyond – especially Beth Wickington, Marta Juncosa, Clémence Gouy, Amy Cox, Caroline Hogg, Jade Craddock – thank you for everything you've done to make this book a reality. Thank you also to Emma Leong, the first publishing person who spotted this book! I quite possibly owe it all to you.

I wanted to briefly acknowledge the gambling addiction experienced by Phil's dad. Addiction isn't a joke or to be blamed on individuals; I hope I've treated it with the respect it deserves. Thank you to those working for the systemic change needed to hold the gambling industry accountable.

Felborough was inspired by numerous places that fall under the broad category of "Wholesome day out in nature, possibly visiting a very old building". In particular, three National Trust places in Norfolk: Sheringham Park (where the idea was born), Blickling, Felbrigg; and several botanic gardens, all of which are glorious and I can't recommend highly enough: Kew (of course), Oxford (where I went whenever I needed a boost), Dublin, and Edinburgh.

Alice, always my first reader: thank you for ploughing through all (!) my messy first drafts and being so generous with your critique and hype. I wouldn't have survived querying without you. Thank you to my other wonderful beta readers: Anna, Zoé, Lisa, Hannah. Peach, thank you for your incredible patience and generosity explaining the so-called 'benefits' system. Betty, thank you for always yelling your compliments. Lex, thank you for the advice and reality checks, and for changing my life by starting our cult. To all the hellions: I'm not going to wait for Lisa's annual trip to tell you how grateful I am for you. I love you dearly. See you in hell.

Abbie and Zoe, thank you for the hysterical voice notes and endless support, and Zoe, for sobbing at every piece of good news. Jess, thank you for inspiring me with your quiet adventurousness and for being so proud of me. Abiola, thank you for always jumping straight to Big Talk. Ciaron, thank you for the glamour hammer inspiration. Lastly, Emilie, the Diana Barry to my Anne Shirley – or the Anne to my Diana? Either way: kindred spirit and soulmate. Thank you for seeing me.

Tilda and Jules, my sisters – thank you for being extensions of me, but much better. I can't believe how wonderful you are. As you know, everything I do is to try and make you proud. Uh oh! Time to cry.

Father John (FJ), thank you for the gardening tips and the orchid's Latin name. Thank you also for the relentless chaos and for being probably the most eccentric, delightful, ridiculous person in existence. Growing up, I thought all dads were like this but truly, they are not.

Jane, thank you for giving us a childhood so reliant on books that your house might as well be built from them. I'm a product of all the stories you gave me. Thank you also for thinking I'm the coolest, cleverest, most beautiful person on earth (sorry to your other two daughters) – what a gift.

The Pacittis, thank you for your kind, unwavering support. I know you'll buy my book and force your friends to as well. Please don't feel you have to read it.

The Davies/Pelham-Burns, thank you for being my extended family. Special thanks to Celia for your market research into whether younger readers will get the Dr Evil reference. You really threw me a frickin' bone here.

Grandie, I miss you. You wouldn't have liked this book at all.

To the real Eva – Norfolk terrier and stinky lady: you are my muse. And thank you Marion for letting us be Eva's second family. I did try to rename the dog in this, but Eva was just too powerful.

Thank you/sorry to anyone I've borrowed real life details from. It's usually unintentional and always done with love.

Marc, thank you for being my partner. For your love and patience and all the meals. Despite what you think, I *could* look after myself without you, but I don't want to. I love you so much.

Thank you to my brilliant writing community online and in person. To everyone who's been so generous with your advice, support, kindness and excited comments: thank you! I wouldn't be where I am without you. To those of you starting out: hang in there! Find your people. Writing doesn't have to be sad and solitary and the sooner you start sharing it, the more fun it will be. And to those who write in secret or sporadically, who've never yet shown anyone their words, who are wondering if you count as a writer even if you don't yet have this or that thing: you do. You are already a writer.

Lastly, in praise of joyful queer books: I wish I'd had more growing up, but it's been incredible seeing the growing number in recent years that are as comforting, funny, joyful and silly as straight books are allowed to be. Long may it continue.

About the Author

Eleanor Vendrell is a writer and researcher interested in the easy topics of love, relationships, identity and the meaning of it all. A lifelong reader of books that make you laugh and sob, she enjoys nothing more than earnest discussions about the importance of joyful fiction and books that include kissing. She lives in Oxford with her partner.

About the Author